Nils

The Wonderful Adventures of Nils
and
The Further Adventures of Nils Holgersson
Combined Unabridged Editions—Two Books in One

by Selma Lagerlöf

translated from the Swedish by
Velma Swanston Howard

illustrations reproduced from the originals by
Astri Heiberg

Penfield
BOOKS

ACKNOWLEDGEMENTS

The Wonderful Adventures of Nils and *The Further Adventures of Nils* were written for use in schools as "supplementary reading," with the special idea of introducing educational and entertaining subjects to children from the ages of nine to eleven. The books were adopted in the public schools of Sweden, but adults have found them books of permanent value.

This combined edition of the two works includes: *The Wonderful Adventures of Nils,* translated by Velma Swanston Howard, first published by Doubleday, Page & Company, Garden City, New York, 1917, and *The Further Adventures of Nils,* translated by Velma Swanston Howard, first published by Grosset & Dunlap, New York, New York.

Associate editors: Joan Liffring-Zug Bourret, Melinda Bradnan, Dorothy Crum, Maureen Patterson, and Deb Schense

Cover design by M.A. Cook Design
Front cover illustration from the 1917 edition hand colored by Diane Heusinkveld

CONTENTS

THE WONDERFUL ADVENTURES OF NILS

THE FURTHER ADVENTURES OF NILS

TRANSLATOR'S INTRODUCTION

Some of the purely geographical matter in the Swedish original of *The Further Adventures of Nils* was eliminated from the English version. The author rendered valuable assistance in cutting certain chapters and abridging others. Also, with the author's approval, cuts were made where the descriptive matter was merely of local interest. But the story itself is intact.

— *V. S. H.*

Translator's Reference

The names Miss Lagerlöf has given to the animals are descriptive:

- Smirre Fox is cunning fox.
- Sirle Squirrel is graceful or nimble squirrel.
- Gripe Otter means grabbing or clutching otter.
- Mons is a pet name applied to cats, like Tommy and Pussy cat.
- Monsie house-cat is equivalent to Tommy house-cat.
- Mårten gåskarl (Morten Goosie-Gander) is a pet name for a tame gander, just as we use Dickie-Bird for a pet bird.
- Fru is the Swedish for Mrs. This title is usually applied to gentlewomen only. The author has used this meaning of "fru."
- A Goa-Nisse is an elf-king, and corresponds to the English Puck or Robin Goodfellow.

Table of Pronunciation

- The final (e) is sounded in Skåne, Sirle, Gripe, etc.
- The (å) in Skåne and Småland is pronounced like (o) in ore.
- (j) is like the English (y). Nuolja, Oviksfjällen, Sjangeli, Jarro, etc., should sound as if they were spelled: Nuolya, Oviksfyellen, syang (one syllable) elee, Yarro, etc.
- (g) when followed by e, i, y, ä, or ö, is also like (y). Example, Göta is pronounced Yöta. When (g) is followed by a, o, u, or å, it is hard, as in go.
- (k) in Norrköping, Linköping, Kivik (pronounced Cheeveek), etc., is like (ch) in cheer. (k) is hard when it precedes a, o, u, or å. Example, Kaksi, Kolmi.
- (ä) is pronounced as in fare. Example, Färs.
- There is no sound in the English language which corresponds to the Swedish ö. It is like the French eu in jeu.
- Gripe is pronounced Greep-e.
- In Sirle, the first syllable has the same sound as sir, in sirup.

I

THE BOY

THE ELF

Once there was a boy. He was—let us say—something like fourteen years old, long and loose jointed and towheaded. He wasn't good for much, that boy. His chief delight was to eat and sleep, and after that—he liked best to make mischief.

It was a Sunday morning and the boy's parents were getting ready to go to church. The boy sat on the edge of the table, in his shirt sleeves, and thought how lucky it was that both Father and Mother were going away, and the coast would be clear for a couple of hours. "Good! Now I can take down Pop's gun and fire off a shot, without anybody's meddling interference," he said to himself.

But it was almost as if Father should have guessed the boy's thoughts, for just as he was on the threshold—ready to start—he stopped short, and turned toward the boy, "Since you won't come to church with Mother and me," he said, "the least you can do, is to read the service at home. Will you promise to do so?" "Yes," said the boy, "that I can do easy enough." And he thought, of course, that he wouldn't read any more than he felt like reading.

The boy thought that never had he seen his mother so persistent. In a second she was over by the shelf near the fireplace, and took down Luther's *Commentary* and laid it on the table in front of the window— opened at the service for the day. She also opened the New Testament and placed it beside the *Commentary*. Finally, she drew up the big armchair, which was bought at the parish auction the year before, and which, as a rule, no one but Father was permitted to occupy.

The boy sat thinking that his mother was giving herself altogether too much trouble with this spread, for he had no intention of reading more than a page or so. But now, for the second time, it was almost as if his father were able to see right through him. He walked up to the boy, and said in a severe tone, "Now, remember, that you are to read carefully! For when we come back, I shall question you thoroughly, and if you have skipped a single page, it will not go well with you."

"The service is fourteen and a half pages long," said his mother, just as if she wanted to heap up the measure of his misfortune. "You'll have to sit down and begin the reading at once if you expect to get through with it."

With that they departed. And as the boy stood in the doorway watching them, he thought that he had been caught in a trap. "There they go congratulating themselves, I suppose, in the belief that they've hit upon something so good that I'll be forced to sit and hang over the sermon the whole time that they are away," thought he.

But his father and mother were certainly not congratulating themselves upon anything of the sort, but, on the contrary, they were very much distressed. They were poor farmers, and their place was not much bigger than a garden plot. When they first moved there, the place couldn't feed more than one pig and a pair of chickens, but they were uncommonly industrious and capable folk—and now they had both cows and geese. Things had turned out very well for them, and they would have gone to church that beautiful morning—satisfied and happy—if they hadn't had their son to think of. Father complained that he was dull and lazy; he had not cared to learn anything at school, and he was such an all-around good-for-nothing that he could barely be made to tend geese. Mother did not deny that this was true, but she was most distressed because he was wild and bad, cruel to animals, and ill-willed toward human beings. "May God soften his hard heart, and give him a better disposition!" said the mother, "or else he will be a misfortune, both to himself and to us."

The boy stood for a long time and pondered whether he should read the service or not. Finally, he came to the conclusion that, this time, it was best to be obedient. He seated himself in the easy chair, and began to read. But when he had been rattling away in an undertone for a little while, this mumbling seemed to have a soothing effect upon him—and he began to nod.

It was the most beautiful weather outside! It was only the twentieth of March, but the boy lived in West Vemminghög Township, down in Southern Skåne, where the spring was already in full swing. It was not as yet green, but it was fresh and budding. There was water in all the trenches, and the colt's-foot on the edge of the ditch was in bloom. All the weeds that grew in among the stones, were brown and shiny. The beech woods in the distance seemed to swell and grow thicker with every second. The skies were high—and a clear blue. The cottage door stood ajar, and the lark's trill could be heard in the room. The hens and geese pattered about in the yard, and the cows, who felt the spring air in their stalls, lowed their approval every now and then.

The boy read and nodded and fought against drowsiness. "No! I don't want to fall asleep," thought he, "for then I'll not get through this thing the whole forenoon."

But—somehow—he fell asleep.

He did not know whether he had slept a short while, or a long while, but he was awakened by hearing a slight noise back of him.

On the window sill, facing the boy, stood a small looking glass, and almost the entire cottage could be seen in this. As the boy raised his head, he happened to look in the glass, and then he saw that the cover to his mother's chest had been opened.

His mother owned a great, heavy, iron-bound oak chest, which she permitted no one but herself to open. Here she treasured all the things she had inherited from her mother, and of these she was especially careful. Here lay a couple of old-time peasant dresses, of old red homespun cloth, with short bodice and plaited skirt, and a pearl-bedecked breast pin. There were starched white linen headdresses, and heavy silver ornaments and chains. Folks don't care to go about dressed like that in these days, and several times his mother had thought of getting rid of the old things, but somehow, she hadn't had the heart to do it.

Now the boy saw distinctly—in the glass—that the chest lid was open. He could not understand how this had happened, for his mother had closed the chest before she went away. She never would have left that precious chest open when he was at home, alone.

He became low-spirited and apprehensive. He was afraid that a thief had sneaked his way into the cottage. He didn't dare to move, but sat still and stared into the looking glass.

While he sat there and waited for the thief to make his appearance, he began to wonder what the dark shadow was which fell across the edge of the chest. He looked and looked—and did not want to believe his eyes. But the thing, which at first seemed shadowy, became more and more clear to him, and soon he saw that it was something real. It was no less a thing than an elf who sat there—astride the edge of the chest!

To be sure, the boy had heard stories about elves, but he had never dreamed that they were such tiny creatures. He was no taller than a hand's breadth—this one, who sat on the edge of the chest. He had an old, wrinkled and beardless face, and was dressed in a black frock coat, knee breeches and a broad-brimmed black hat. He was very trim and smart with his white laces about the throat and wristbands, his buckled shoes, and the bows on his garters. He had taken from the chest an embroidered piece, and sat and looked at the old-fashioned handiwork with such an air of veneration that he did not observe the boy had awakened.

The boy was somewhat surprised to see the elf, but, on the other hand, he was not particularly frightened. It was impossible to be afraid of one who was so little. And since the elf was so absorbed in his own thoughts that he neither saw nor heard, the boy thought that it would be great fun to play a trick on him: to push him over into the chest and shut the lid on him, or something of that kind.

But the boy was not so courageous that he dared to touch the elf with his hands; instead he looked around the room for something to poke him with. He let his gaze wander from the sofa to the leaf-table, from the leaf-table to the fireplace. He looked at the kettles, then at the coffee urn, which stood on a shelf near the fireplace, at the water bucket near the door, and at the spoons and knives and forks and saucers and plates which could be seen through the half-open cupboard door. He looked at his father's gun which hung on the wall beside the portrait of the Danish royal family, and at the geraniums and fuchsias which blossomed in the window. And last, he caught sight of an old butterfly snare that hung on the window frame. He had hardly set eyes on that butterfly snare before he reached over and snatched it and jumped up and swung it alongside the edge of the chest. He was astonished at the luck he had. He hardly knew how he had managed it—but he had actually snared the elf. The poor little chap lay, head downward, in the bottom of a long snare, and could not free himself.

The first moment the boy hadn't the least idea what he should do with his prize. He was careful to swing the snare backward and forward, to prevent the elf from getting a foothold and clambering up.

The elf began to speak, and begged, oh, so pitifully, for his freedom. He had brought them good luck these many years he said, and deserved better treatment. Now, if the boy would set him free, he would give him an old coin, a silver spoon, and a gold penny, as big as the case on his father's silver watch.

The boy didn't think that this was much of an offer, but it so happened that after he had gotten the elf in his power, he was afraid of him. He felt that he had entered into an agreement with something weird and uncanny, something which did not belong to his world, and he was only too glad to get rid of the horrid thing.

For this reason, he agreed at once to the bargain and held the snare still so the elf could crawl out of it. But when the elf was almost out of the snare, the boy happened to think that he ought to have bargained for large estates, and all sorts of good things. He should at least have made this stipulation: that the elf must conjure the sermon into his head. "What a fool I was to let him go!" thought he, and began to shake the snare violently so the elf would tumble down again.

But the instant the boy did this, he received such a stinging box on the ear, that he thought his head would fly in pieces. He was dashed first against one wall, then against the other; he sank to the floor, and lay there, senseless.

When he awoke, he was alone in the cottage. The chest lid was down, and the butterfly snare hung in its usual place by the window. If he had not felt how the right cheek burned from that box on the ear, he would have been tempted to believe the whole thing had been a dream. "At any rate, Father and Mother will be sure to insist that it was nothing else," thought he. "They are not likely to make any allowances for that old sermon, on account of the elf. It's best for me to get at that reading again," thought he.

But as he walked toward the table, he noticed something remarkable. It couldn't be possible that the cottage had grown. But why was he obliged to take so many more steps than usual to get to the table? And what was the matter with the chair? It looked no bigger than it did a while ago, but now he had to step on the rung first, and then clamber up in order to reach the seat. It was the same thing with the table. He could not look over the top without climbing to the arm of the chair.

"What in all the world is this?" said the boy. "I believe the elf has bewitched both the arm chair and the table—and the whole cottage."

The *Commentary* lay on the table and, to all appearances, it was not changed, but there must have been something queer about that too, for he could not manage to read a single word of it without actually standing right in the book itself.

He read a couple of lines, and then he chanced to look up. With that, his glance fell on the looking glass, and then he cried aloud, "Look! There's another one!"

For in the glass he saw plainly a little, little creature who was dressed in a hood and leather breeches.

"Why, that one is dressed exactly like me!" said the boy, and clasped his hands in astonishment. But then he saw that the thing in the mirror did the same thing. Then he began to pull his hair and pinch his arms and swing round, and instantly he did the same thing after him— he, who was seen in the mirror.

The boy ran around the glass several times to see if there wasn't a little man hidden behind it, but he found no one there, and then he began to shake with terror. For now he understood that the elf had bewitched him, and that the creature whose image he saw in the glass was he, himself.

THE WILD GEESE

The boy simply could not make himself believe that he had been transformed into an elf. "It can't be anything but a dream—a queer fancy," thought he. "If I wait a few moments, I'll surely be turned back into a human being again."

He placed himself before the glass and closed his eyes. He opened them again after a couple of minutes, and then expected to find that it had all passed over, but it hadn't. He was—and remained—just as little. In other respects, he was the same as before. The thin, straw-colored hair, the freckles across his nose, the patches on his leather breeches and the darns on his stockings, were all like themselves, with the exception that they had become diminished.

No, it would do no good for him to stand still and wait—of this he was certain. He must try something else, and he thought the wisest thing that he could do was to try to find the elf, and make his peace with him.

And while he sought, he cried and prayed and promised everything he could think of. Nevermore would he break his word to anyone; never again would he be naughty; never, never would he fall asleep again over the sermon. If he only might be a human being once more, he would be such a good and helpful and obedient boy. But no matter how much he promised, it did not help him the least little bit.

Suddenly he remembered that he had heard his mother say that all the tiny folk made their home in the cow sheds, and, at once, he concluded to go there, and see if he couldn't find the elf. It was a lucky thing that the cottage door stood partly open, for he never could have reached the bolt and opened it, but now he slipped through without any difficulty.

When he came out in the hallway, he looked around for his wooden shoes; for in the house, to be sure, he had gone about in his stocking feet. He wondered how he should manage with these big, clumsy wooden shoes, but just then he saw a pair of tiny shoes on the doorstep. When he observed that the elf had been so thoughtful that he had also bewitched the wooden shoes, he was even more troubled. It was evidently the elf's intention that this affliction should last a long time.

On the wooden boardwalk in front of the cottage, hopped a gray sparrow. He had hardly set eyes on the boy before he called out, "Teetee! Teetee! Look at Nils goosy-boy! Look at Thumbietot! Look at Nils Holgersson Thumbietot!"

Instantly, both the geese and the chickens turned and stared at the boy, and then they set up a fearful cackling. "Cock-el-i-coo," crowed the rooster, "good enough for him! Cock-el-i-coo, he has pulled my comb."

"Ka, ka, kada, serves him right!" cried the hens, and with that, they kept up a continuous cackle. The geese got together in a tight group, stuck their heads together and asked: "Who can have done this? Who can have done this?"

But the strangest thing of all was that the boy understood what they said. He was so astonished that he stood there as if rooted to the doorstep and listened. "It must be because I am changed into an elf," said he. "This is probably why I understand bird talk."

He thought it was unbearable that the hens would not stop saying that it served him right. He threw a stone at them and shouted: "Shut up, you pack!"

But it hadn't occurred to him that he was no longer the sort of boy the hens need fear. The whole hen yard made a rush for him, and formed a ring around him, then they all cried at once: "Ka, ka, kada, served you right! Ka, ka, kada, served you right!"

The boy tried to get away, but the chickens ran after him and screamed until he thought he'd lose his hearing. It is more than likely that he never could have gotten away from them if the house cat hadn't come along just then. As soon as the chickens saw the cat, they quieted down and pretended to be thinking of nothing else than just to scratch in the earth for worms.

Immediately the boy ran up to the cat. "You, dear pussy!" said he, "you must know all the corners and hiding places about here? You'll be a good little kitty and tell me where I can find the elf."

The cat did not reply at once. He seated himself, curled his tail into a graceful ring around his paws and stared at the boy. It was a large black cat with one white spot on his chest. His fur lay sleek and soft, and shone in the sunlight. The claws were drawn in and the eyes were a dull gray with just a little narrow dark streak down the center. The cat looked thoroughly good-natured and inoffensive.

"I know well enough where the elf lives," he said in a soft voice, "but that doesn't say that I'm going to tell *you* about it."

"Dear pussy, you must tell me where the elf lives!" said the boy. "Can't you see how he has bewitched me?"

The cat opened his eyes a little, so that the green wickedness began to shine forth. He spun around and purred with satisfaction before he replied. "Shall I perhaps help you because you have so often grabbed me by the tail?" he said at last.

Then the boy was furious and forgot entirely how little and helpless he was now. "Oh! I can pull your tail again, I can," said he, and ran toward the cat.

The next instant the cat was so changed that the boy could scarcely believe it was same animal. Every separate hair on his body stood on end. The back was bent; the legs had become elongated; the claws scraped the ground; the tail had grown thick and short; the ears were laid back; the mouth was frothy, and the eyes were wide open and glistened like sparks of red fire.

The boy didn't want to let himself be scared by a cat, and he took a step forward. Then the cat made one spring and landed right on the boy, knocked him down and stood over him—his forepaws on his chest, and his jaws wide apart over his throat.

The boy felt how the sharp claws sank through his vest and shirt and into his skin, and how the sharp eyeteeth tickled his throat. He shrieked for help, as loudly as he could, but no one came. He thought surely that his last hour had come. Then he felt that the cat drew in his claws and let go the hold on his throat.

"There!" he said, "that will do now. I'll let you go this time for my mistress's sake. I only wanted you to know which one of us two has the power now."

With that the cat walked away—looking as smooth and pious as he did when he first appeared on the scene. The boy was so crestfallen that he didn't say a word, but only hurried to the cow house to look for the elf.

There were not more than three cows, but when the boy came in, there was such a bellowing and such a kick-up that one might easily have believed that there were at least thirty.

"Moo, moo, moo," bellowed Mayrose. "It is well there is such a thing as justice in this world."

"Moo, moo, moo," sang the three of them in unison. He couldn't hear what they said, for each one tried to out bellow the others.

The boy wanted to ask after the elf, but he couldn't make himself heard because the cows were in full uproar. They carried on as they used to do when he let a strange dog in on them. They kicked with their hind legs, shook their necks, stretched their heads, and measured the distance with their horns.

"Come here, you!" said Mayrose, "And you'll get a kick that you won't forget in a hurry!"

"Come here," said Gold Lily, "and you shall dance on my horns!"

"Come here, and you shall taste how it felt when you threw your wooden shoes at me, as you did last summer!" bawled Star.

"Come here, and you shall be repaid for that wasp you let loose in my ear!" growled Gold Lily.

Mayrose was the oldest and the wisest of them, and she was the very maddest. "Come here!" said she, "that I may pay you back for the many times that you have jerked the milk pail away from your mother, and for all the snares you laid for her when she came carrying the milk pails, and for all the tears which she has stood here and wept over you!"

The boy wanted to tell them how he regretted that he had been unkind to them, and that never, never—from now on—should he be anything but good if they would only tell him where the elf was. But the cows didn't listen to him. They made such a racket that he began to fear one of them would succeed in breaking loose, and he thought that the best thing for him was to go quietly away from the cow house.

When he came out, he was thoroughly disheartened. He could understand that no one on the place wanted to help him find the elf, and little good would it do him, probably, if the elf were found.

He crawled up on the broad hedge which fenced in the farm and which was overgrown with briers and lichen. There he sat down to think about how it would go with him, if he never became a human being again. When Father and Mother came home from church, there would be a surprise for them. Yes, a surprise, it would be all over the land, and people would come flocking from East Vemminghög and from Torp and from Skerup. The whole Vemminghög township would come to stare at him. Perhaps Father and Mother would take him with them and show him at the market place in Kivik.

No, that was too horrible to think about. He would rather that no human being should ever see him again.

His unhappiness was simply frightful! No one in all the world was so unhappy as he. He was no longer a human being, but now a freak.

Little by little he began to comprehend what it meant—to be no longer human. He was separated from everything now; he could no longer play with other boys; he could not take charge of the farm after his parents were gone, and certainly no girl would think of marrying *him*.

He sat and looked at his home. It was a little log house, which lay as if it had been crushed down to earth under the high, sloping roof. The outhouses were also small, and the patches of ground were so narrow that a horse could barely turn around on them. But little and poor though the place was, it was much too good for him now. He couldn't ask for any better place than a hole under the stable floor.

It was wondrously beautiful weather! It budded, and it rippled, and it murmured, and it twittered all around him. But he sat there with such a heavy sorrow. He should never be happy any more about anything.

Never had he seen the skies as blue as they were today. Birds of passage came on their travels. They came from foreign lands, and had traveled over the East Sea, by way of Smygahuk, and were now on their way North. They were of many different kinds, but he was only familiar with the wild geese who came flying in two long rows which met at an angle.

Several flocks of wild geese had already flown by. They flew very high, still he could hear how they shrieked: "To the hills! Now we're off to the hills!"

When the wild geese saw the tame geese, who walked about the farm, they sank nearer the earth and called: "Come along! Come along! We're off to the hills!"

The tame geese could not resist the temptation to raise their heads and listen, but they answered very sensibly, "We're pretty well off where we are. We're pretty well off where we are."

It was, as we have said, an uncommonly fine day with an atmosphere that it must have been a real delight to fly in—so light and bracing. With each new flock of wild geese that flew by, the tame geese became more and more unruly. A couple of times they flapped their wings as if they had half a mind to fly along. But then an old mother goose would always say to them: "Now don't be silly. Those creatures will have to suffer both hunger and cold."

There was a young gander whom the wild geese had fired with a passion for adventure. "If another flock comes this way, I'll follow them," said he.

Then there came a new flock, which shrieked like the others, and the young gander answered, "Wait a minute! Wait a minute! I'm coming."

He spread his wings and raised himself into the air, but he was so unaccustomed to flying that he fell to the ground again.

At any rate, the wild geese must have heard his call, for they turned and flew back slowly to see if he was coming.

"Wait, wait!" he cried, and made another attempt to fly.

All this the boy heard from where he lay on the hedge. "It would be a great pity," thought he, "if the big goosy-gander should go away. It would be a big loss to Father and Mother if he was gone when they came home from church."

When he thought of this, once again he entirely forgot that he was little and helpless. He took one leap right down into the goose flock, and threw his arms around the neck of the goosey-gander. "Oh, no! You don't fly away this time, sir!" cried he.

But just about then, the gander was considering how he should go to work to raise himself from the ground. He couldn't stop to shake the boy off, hence he had to go along with him—up in the air.

They bore on toward the heights so rapidly, that the boy fairly gasped. Before he had time to think that he ought to let go his hold around the gander's neck, he was so high up that he would have been killed instantly if he had fallen to the ground.

The only thing that he could do to make himself a little more comfortable, was to try to get upon the gander's back. And there he wriggled himself forthwith, but not without considerable trouble. And it was not an easy matter, either, to hold himself securely on the slippery back between two swaying wings. He had to dig deep into feathers and down with both hands to keep from tumbling to the ground.

THE BIG CHECKED CLOTH

*T*he boy had grown so giddy that it was a long while before he came to himself. The winds howled and beat against him, and the rustle of feathers and swaying of wings sounded like a whole storm. Thirteen geese flew around him, flapping their wings and honking. They danced before his eyes, and they buzzed in his ears. He didn't know whether they flew high or low, or in what direction they were traveling.

After a bit, he regained just enough sense to understand that he ought to find out where the geese were taking him. But this was not so easy, for he didn't know how he should ever muster up courage enough to look down. He was sure he'd faint if he attempted it.

The wild geese were not flying very high because the new traveling companion could not breathe in the very thinnest air. For his sake, they also flew a little slower than usual.

At last the boy just made himself cast one glance down to earth. Then he thought that a great big rug lay spread beneath him, which was made up of an incredible number of large and small checkmarks.

"Where in all the world am I now?" he wondered.

He saw nothing but checkmarks upon checkmarks. Some were broad and ran crosswise, and some were long and narrow—all over, there were angles. Nothing was round, and nothing was crooked.

"What kind of a big, checked cloth is this that I'm looking down on?" said the boy to himself without expecting anyone to answer him.

But instantly, the wild geese who flew about him, called out: "Fields and meadows. Fields and meadows."

Then he understood that the big, checked cloth he was traveling over was the flat land of southern Sweden, and he began to comprehend why it looked so checked and multi-colored. The bright green checks he recognized first; they were rye fields that had been sown in the fall and had kept themselves green under the winter snows. The yellowish-gray checks were stubble-fields—the remains of the oat crop which had grown there the summer before. The brownish ones were old clover meadows, and the black ones were deserted grazing lands or plowed-up fallow pastures. The brown checks with the yellow edges were, undoubtedly, beech-tree forests, for in these you'll find the big trees which grow in the heart of the forest—naked in winter. The little beech trees, which grow along the borders, keep their dry, yellowed leaves way into the spring. There were also dark checks with gray centers. These were the large, built-up estates encircled by the small cottages with their blackening straw roofs and their stone-divided landplots. And then there were checks green in the middle with brown borders; these were the orchards, where the grass carpets were already turning green, although the trees and bushes around them were still in their nude, brown bark.

The boy could not keep from laughing when he saw how checked everything looked.

But when the wild geese heard him laugh, they called out—kind of reprovingly, "Fertile and good land. Fertile and good land."

The boy had already become serious. "To think that you can laugh, you, who have met with the most terrible misfortune that can possibly happen to a human being!" thought he. And for a moment he was pretty serious, but it wasn't long before he was laughing again.

Now that he had grown somewhat accustomed to the ride and the speed, he could think of something besides holding himself on the gander's back. He began to notice how full the air was of birds flying northward. There was a shouting and a calling from flock to flock. "So you came over today?" shrieked some. "Yes," answered the geese. "How do you think the spring's getting on?" "Not a leaf on the trees and ice-cold water in the lakes," came back the answer.

When the geese flew over a place where they saw any tame, half-naked fowl, they shouted: "What's the name of this place? What's the name of this place?" Then the roosters cocked their heads and answered, "Its name's Lillgarde this year—the same as last year, the same as last year."

Most of the cottages were probably named after their owners, which is the custom in Skåne. But instead of saying this is "Per Matsson's," or "Ola Bosson's," the roosters hit upon the kind of names which, to their way of thinking, were more appropriate. Those who lived on small farms, and belonged to poor cottagers, cried, "This place is called Grainscarce." And those who belonged to the poorest hut-dwellers screamed, "The name of this place is Little-to-Eat, Little-to-Eat, Little-to-Eat."

The big, well-cared-for farms got high-sounding names from the roosters—such as Luckymeadow, Eggberga and Moneyville.

But the roosters on the great landed estates were too high and mighty to condescend to anything like jesting. One of them crowed and called out with such gusto that it sounded as if he wanted to be heard clear up to the sun, "This is Herr Dybeck's estate, the same this year as last year, this year as last year."

A little further on strutted one rooster who crowed, "This is Swanholm, surely all the world knows that!"

The boy observed that the geese did not fly straight forward, but zigzagged hither and thither over the whole South country, just as though they were glad to be in Skåne again and wanted to pay their respects to every separate place.

They came to one place where there were a number of big, clumsy-looking buildings with great, tall chimneys, and all around these were a lot of smaller houses. "This is Jordberga Sugar Refinery," cried the roosters. The boy shuddered as he sat there on the goose's back. He ought to have recognized this place, for it was not very far from his home.

Here he had worked the year before as a watch boy, but, to be sure, nothing was exactly like itself when one saw it like that—from up above.

And think! Just think of Osa the goose girl and little Mats, who were his comrades last year! Indeed the boy would have been glad to know if they still were anywhere about here. Fancy what they would have said had they suspected that he was flying over their heads!

Soon Jordberga was lost to sight, and they traveled toward Svedala and Skaber Lake and back again over Görringe Cloister and Häckeberga. The boy saw more of Skåne in this one day than he had ever seen in all the years that he had lived.

Whenever the wild geese happened across any tame geese, they had the best fun! They flew forward very slowly and called down, "We're off to the hills. Are you coming along? Are you coming along?"

But the tame geese answered, "It's still winter in this country. You're out too soon. Fly back! Fly back!"

The wild geese lowered themselves that they might be heard a little better, and called, "Come along! We'll teach you how to fly and swim."

Then the tame geese got mad and wouldn't answer them with a single honk. The wild geese sank themselves still lower—until they almost touched the ground, then, quick as lightning, they raised themselves, just as if they'd been terribly frightened. "Oh, oh, oh!" they exclaimed. "Those things were not geese. They were only sheep, they were only sheep."

The ones on the ground were beside themselves with rage and shrieked, "May you be shot, the whole lot o' you! The whole lot o' you!"

When the boy heard all this teasing, he laughed. Then he remembered how badly things had gone with him, and he cried, but the next second, he was laughing again. Never before had he ridden so fast, and to ride fast and recklessly—that he had always liked. And, of course, he had never dreamed that it could be as fresh and bracing as it was, up in the air, or that there rose from the earth such a fine scent of resin and soil. Nor had he ever dreamed what it could be like to ride so high above the earth. It was just like flying away from sorrow and trouble and annoyances of every kind that could be imagined.

II

AKKA FROM KEBNEKAISE

Evening

The big tame goosey-gander that had followed them up in the air felt very proud of being permitted to travel back and forth over the south country with the wild geese and crack jokes with the tame birds. But in spite of his keen delight, he began to tire as the afternoon wore on. He tried to take deeper breaths and quicker wingstrokes, but even so, he remained several goose-lengths behind the others.

When the wild geese who flew last noticed that the tame one couldn't keep up with them, they began to call to the goose who rode in the center of the angle and led the procession: "Akka from Kebnekaise! Akka from Kebnekaise!"

"What do you want of me?" asked the leader.

"The white one will be left behind; the white one will be left behind."

"Tell him it's easier to fly fast than slow!" called the leader, and raced on as before.

The goosey-gander certainly tried to follow the advice and increased his speed, but then he became so exhausted that he sank way down to the drooping willows that bordered the fields and meadows.

"Akka, Akka, Akka from Kebnekaise!" cried those who flew last and saw what a hard time he was having.

"What do you want now?" asked the leader—and she sounded awfully angry.

"The white one sinks to the earth; the white one sinks to the earth." "Tell him it's easier to fly high than low!" shouted the leader, and she didn't slow up the least little bit, but raced on as before.

The goosey-gander tried also to follow this advice, but when he wanted to raise himself, he became so winded that he almost burst his breast. "Akka, Akka!" again cried those who flew last.

"Can't you let me fly in peace?" asked the leader, and she sounded even madder than before.

"The white one is ready to collapse."

"Tell him that he who has not the strength to fly with the flock, can go back home!" cried the leader. She certainly had no idea of decreasing her speed—but raced on as before.

"Oh! is that the way the wind blows," thought the goosey-gander. He understood at once that the wild geese had never intended to take him along up to Lapland. They had only lured him away from home in sport.

He felt thoroughly exasperated. To think that his strength should fail him now, so he wouldn't be able to show these tramps that even a tame goose was good for something! But the most provoking thing of all was that he had fallen in with Akka from Kebnekaise. Tame goose that he was, he had heard about a leader goose, named Akka, who was more than a hundred years old. She had such a big name that the best wild geese in the world followed her. But no one had such a contempt for tame geese as Akka and her flock, and gladly he would have shown them that he was their equal.

He flew slowly behind the rest while he deliberated whether he should turn back or continue. Finally, the little creature that he carried on his back said: "Dear Morten Goosey-Gander, you know well enough that it is simply impossible for you, who have never flown, to go with the wild geese all the way up to Lapland. Won't you turn back before you kill yourself?"

But the farmer's lad was about the worst thing the goosey-gander knew anything about, and as soon as it had dawned on him that this puny creature actually believed that he couldn't make the trip, he decided to stick it out. "If you say another word about this, I'll drop you into the first ditch we ride over!" said he, and at the same time, his fury gave him so much strength that he began to fly almost as well as any of the others.

It isn't likely that he could have kept this pace up very long, neither was it necessary, for, just then, the sun sank quickly, and at sunset the geese flew down, and before the boy and the goosey-gander knew what had happened, they stood on the shores of Vomb Lake.

"They probably intend that we shall spend the night here," thought the boy, and jumped down from the goose's back.

He stood on a narrow beach by a fair-sized lake. It was ugly to look upon, because it was almost entirely covered with an ice crust that was blackened and uneven and full of cracks and holes—as spring ice generally is.

The ice was already breaking up. It was loose and floating and had a broad belt of dark, shiny water all around it, but there was still enough of it left to spread chill and winter terror over the place.

On the other side of the lake, there appeared to be an open and light country, but where the geese had alighted, there was a thick pine growth. It looked as if the forest of firs and pines had the power to bind the winter to itself. Everywhere else the ground was bare, but beneath the sharp pine branches lay snow that had been melting and freezing, melting and freezing, until it was as hard as ice.

The boy thought he had struck an Arctic wilderness, and he was so miserable that he wanted to scream. He was hungry too. He hadn't eaten a bite the whole day. But where should he find any food? Nothing edible grew on either ground or tree in the month of March.

Yes, where was he to find food, and who would give him shelter, and who would fix his bed, and who would protect him from the wild beasts?

For now the sun was away and frost came from the lake; darkness sank down from heaven, and terror stole forward on the twilight's trail, and in the forest it began to patter and rustle.

Now the good humor which the boy had felt when he was up in the air, was gone, and in his misery, he looked around for his traveling companions. He had no one but them to cling to now.

Then he saw that the goosey-gander was having even a worse time of it than he. He was lying prostrate on the spot where he had alighted, and it looked as if he were ready to die. His neck lay flat against the ground, his eyes were closed, and his breathing sounded like a feeble hissing.

"Dear Morten Goosey-Gander," said the boy, "try to get a swallow of water! It isn't two steps to the lake."

But the goosey-gander didn't stir.

The boy had certainly been cruel to all animals, and to the goosey-gander in times gone by, but now he felt that the goosey-gander was the only comfort he had left, and he was dreadfully afraid of losing him.

At once the boy began to push and drag him to get him into the water, but the goosey-gander was big and heavy, and it was mighty hard work for the boy, but at last he succeeded.

The goosey-gander got in head first. For an instant, he lay motionless in the slime, but soon he poked up his head, shook the water from his eyes and sniffed. Then he swam, proudly, between reeds and seaweed.

The wild geese were in the lake before him. They had not looked around for either the goosey-gander or for his rider, but had made straight for the water. They had bathed and primped, and now they lay and gulped half-rotten pond weed and water clover.

The white goosey-gander had the good fortune to spy a perch. He grabbed it quickly, swam ashore with it, and laid it down in front of the boy. "Here's a thank you for helping me into the water," said he.

It was the first time the boy had heard a friendly word that day. He was so happy that he wanted to throw his arms around the goosey-gander's neck, but he refrained, and he was also thankful for the gift. At first he must have thought that it would be impossible to eat raw fish, and then he had a notion to try it.

He felt to see if he still had his sheath knife with him, and, sure enough, there it hung on the back button of his trousers, although it was so diminished that it was hardly as long as a match. Well, at any rate, it served to scale and cleanse fish, and it wasn't long before the perch was eaten.

When the boy had satisfied his hunger, he felt a little ashamed because he had been able to eat a raw thing. "It's evident that I'm not a human being any longer, but a real elf," thought he.

While the boy ate, the goosey-gander stood silently beside him, but when the boy had swallowed the last bite, he said in a low voice: "It's a fact that we have run across stuck-up goose folk who despise all tame birds."

"Yes, I've observed that," said the boy.

"What a triumph it would be for me if I could follow them clear up to Lapland, and show them that even a tame goose can do things!"

"Y-e-e-s," said the boy, and drawled it out because he didn't believe the goosey-gander could ever do it, yet he didn't wish to contradict him. "But I don't think I can get along all alone on such a journey," said the goosey-gander. "I'd like to ask if you couldn't come along and help me?"

The boy, of course, hadn't expected anything but to return to his home as soon as possible, and he was so surprised that he hardly knew what he should reply. "I thought that we were enemies, you and I," said he. But this the goosey-gander seemed to have forgotten entirely. He only remembered that the boy had but just saved his life. "I suppose I really ought to go home to Father and Mother," said the boy.

"Oh! I'll get you back to them sometime in the fall," said the goosey-gander. "I shall not leave you until I put you down on your own doorstep."

The boy thought it might be just as well for him if he escaped showing himself before his parents for a while. He was not disinclined to favor the scheme, and was just on the point of saying that he agreed to it when they heard a loud rumbling behind them. It was the wild geese who had come up from the lake—all at one time—and stood shaking the water from their backs. After that they arranged themselves in a long row—with the leader goose in the center—and came toward them.

As the white goosey-gander sized up the wild geese, he felt ill at ease. He had expected that they should be more like tame geese, and that he should feel a closer kinship with them. They were much smaller than he, and none of them was white. They were all gray with a sprinkling of brown. He was almost afraid of their eyes, which were yellow, and shone as if a fire had been kindled back of them. The goosey-gander had always been taught that it was most fitting to move slowly and with a rolling motion, but these creatures did not walk—they half-ran. He grew most alarmed, however, when he looked at their feet. These were large, and the soles were torn and ragged-looking. It was evident that the wild geese never questioned what they tramped upon. They took no by-paths. They were very neat and well cared for in other respects, but one could see by their feet that they were poor wilderness folk.

The goosey-gander only had time to whisper to the boy, "Speak up quickly for yourself, but don't tell them who you are!" before the geese were upon them.

When the wild geese had stopped in front of them, they curtsied with their necks many times, and the goosey-gander did likewise many more times. As soon as the ceremonies were over, the leader goose said, "Now I presume we shall hear what kind of creatures you are."

"There isn't much to tell about me," said the goosey-gander. "I was born in Skanor last spring. In the fall I was sold to Holger Nilsson of West Vemminghög, and there I have lived ever since."

"You don't seem to have any pedigree to boast of," said the leader goose. "What is it, then, that makes you so high-minded that you wish to associate with wild geese?"

"It may be because I want to show you wild geese that we tame ones may also be good for something," said the goosey-gander.

"Yes, it would be well if you could show us that," said the leader goose. "We have already observed how much you know about flying, but you are more skilled, perhaps, in other sports. Possibly you are strong in a swimming match?"

"No, I can't boast that I am," said the goosey-gander. It seemed to him that the leader goose had already made up her mind to send him home, so he didn't much care how he answered. "I never swam any farther than across a marl ditch," he continued.

"Then I presume you're a crack sprinter," said the goose. "I have never seen a tame goose run, nor have I ever done it myself," said the goosey-gander, and he made things appear much worse than they really were.

The big white one was sure now that the leader goose would say that under no circumstances could they take him along. He was very much astonished when she said, "You answer questions courageously, and he who has courage can become a good traveling companion, even if he is ignorant in the beginning. What do you say to stopping with us for a couple of days, until we can see what you are good for?"

"That suits me!" said the goosey-gander—and he was thoroughly happy.

Thereupon the leader goose pointed with her bill and said, "But who is that you have with you? I've never seen anything like him before."

"That's my comrade," said the goosey-gander. "He's been a goose-tender all his life. He'll be useful all right to take with us on the trip."

"Yes, he may be all right for a tame goose," answered the wild one. "What do you call him?"

"He has several names," said the goosey-gander—hesitatingly, not knowing what he should hit upon in a hurry for he didn't want to reveal the fact that the boy had a human name. "Oh! his name is Thumbietot," he said at last.

"Does he belong to the elf family?" asked the leader goose.

"At what time do you wild geese usually retire?" said the goosey-gander quickly—trying to evade that last question. "My eyes close of their own accord about this time."

One could easily see that the goose who talked with the gander was very old. Her entire feather outfit was ice-gray, without any dark streaks. The head was larger, the legs coarser, and the feet more worn than any of the others. The feathers were stiff, the shoulders knotty, the neck thin. All this was due to age. It was only upon the eyes that time had had no effect. They shone brighter—as if they were younger—than any of the others!

She turned, very haughtily, toward the goosey-gander. "Understand, Mr. Tame Goose that I am Akka from Kebnekaise! And that the goose who flies nearest me, to the right, is Iksi from Vassijaure, and the one to the left, is Kaksi from Nuolja! Understand, also, that the second right-hand goose is Kolmi from Sarjektjakko, and the second, left, is Neljä from Svappavaara, and behind them fly Viisi from Oviksfjällen and Kuusi from Sjangeli! And know that these, as well as the six goslings who fly last—three to the right and three to the left—are all high mountain geese of the finest breed! You must not take us for land-lubbers who strike up a chance acquaintance with any and every-one! And you must not think that we permit anyone to share our quarters, that will not tell us who his ancestors were."

When Akka, the leader goose, talked in this way, the boy stepped briskly forward. It had distressed him that the goosey-gander, who had spoken up so glibly for himself, should give such evasive answers when it concerned him. "I don't care to make a secret of who I am," said he. "My name is Nils Holgersson. I'm a farmer's son, and until today, I have been a human being, but this morning..." He got no further. As soon as he had said that he was human the leader goose staggered three steps backward, and the rest of them even farther back. They all extended their necks and hissed angrily at him.

"I have suspected this ever since I first saw you here on these shores," said Akka, "and now you can clear out of here at once. We tolerate no human beings among us."

"It isn't possible," said the goosey-gander, meditatively, "that you wild geese can be afraid of anyone who is so tiny! By tomorrow, of course, he'll turn back home. You can surely let him stay with us overnight. None of us can afford to let such a poor little creature wander off by himself in the night—among weasels and foxes!"

The wild goose came nearer, but it was evident that it was hard for her to master her fear. "I have been taught to fear everything in human shape—be it big or little," said she, "but if you will answer for this one, and swear that he will not harm us, he can stay with us tonight. But I don't believe our night quarters are suitable either for him or you, for we intend to roost on the broken ice out here."

She thought, of course, that the goosey-gander would be doubtful when he heard this, but he never let on. "She is pretty wise who knows how to choose such a safe bed," said he.

"You will be answerable for his return to his own tomorrow."

"Then I, too, will have to leave you," said the goosey-gander. "I have sworn that I would not forsake him."

"You are free to fly whither you will," said the leader goose.

With this, she raised her wings and flew out over the ice and one after another the wild geese followed her.

The boy was very sad to think that his trip to Lapland would not come off, and, in the bargain, he was afraid of the chilly night quarters. "It will be worse and worse," said he. "In the first place, we'll freeze to death on the ice."

But the gander was in a good humor. "There's no danger," said he. "Only make haste, I beg of you, and gather together as much grass and litter as you can well carry."

When the boy had his arms full of dried grass, the goosey-gander grabbed him by the shirt band, lifted him, and flew out on the ice, where the wild geese were already fast asleep with their bills tucked under their wings.

"Now spread out the grass on the ice, so there will be something to stand on to keep me from freezing fast. You help me and I'll help you," said the goosey-gander.

This the boy did, and when he had finished, the goosey-gander picked him up, once again, by the shirt-band, and tucked him under his wing. "I think you'll lie snug and warm there," said the goosey-gander as he covered him with his wing. The boy was so imbedded in down that he couldn't answer, and he was nice and comfy. Oh, but he was tired! And in less than two winks he was fast asleep.

NIGHT

*I*t is a fact that ice is always treacherous and not to be trusted. In the middle of the night, the loosened ice-cake on Vomb Lake moved about until one corner of it touched the shore. Now it happened that Mr. Smirre Fox, who lived at this time in Övid Cloister Park, on the east side of the lake, caught a glimpse of that one corner, while he was out on his night chase. Smirre had seen the wild geese early in the evening and hadn't dared to hope that he might get at one of them, but now he walked right out on the ice.

When Smirre was very near to the geese, his claws scraped the ice, and the geese awoke, flapped their wings and prepared for flight. But Smirre was too quick for them. He darted forward as though he'd been shot, grabbed a goose by the wing and ran toward land again.

But this night the wild geese were not alone on the ice, for they had a human being among them—little as he was. The boy had awakened when the goosey-gander spread his wings. He had tumbled down on the ice and was sitting there, dazed. He hadn't grasped the whys and wherefores of all this confusion until he caught sight of a little long-legged dog who ran over the ice with a goose in his mouth.

In a minute the boy was after that dog to try to take the goose away from him. He must have heard the goosey-gander call to him: "Have a care, Thumbietot! Have a care!" But the boy thought that such a little runt of a dog was nothing to be afraid of and he rushed ahead.

The wild goose that Smirre Fox tugged after him, heard the clatter as the boy's wooden shoes beat against the ice, and she could hardly believe her ears. "Does that infant think he can take me away from the fox?" she wondered. And in spite of her misery, she began to cackle merrily, deep down in her windpipe. It was almost as if she had laughed.

"The first thing he knows, he'll fall through a crack in the ice," she thought.

But dark as the night was, the boy saw distinctly all the cracks and holes there were, and took daring leaps over them. This was because he had the elf's good eyesight now and could see in the dark. He saw both lake and shore just as clearly as if it had been daylight.

Smirre Fox left the ice where it touched the shore, and just as he was working his way up to the land edge, the boy shouted to him: "Drop that goose, you sneak!" Smirre didn't know who was calling to him and wasted no time in looking around, but he increased his pace.

The fox made straight for the forest and the boy followed him with never a thought of the danger he was running. On the contrary, he thought all the while about the contemptuous way in which he had been received by the wild geese that evening, and he made up his mind to let them see that a human being was something higher than all else created.

He shouted, again and again, to that dog, to make him drop his game. "What kind of a dog are you, who can steal a whole goose and not feel ashamed of yourself? Drop her at once or you'll see what a beating you'll get. Drop her, I say, or I'll tell your master how you behave!"

When Smirre Fox saw that he had been mistaken for a scary dog, he was so amused that he came near dropping the goose. Smirre was a great plunderer who wasn't satisfied with only hunting rats and pigeons in the fields, but he also ventured into the farm yards to steal chickens and geese. He knew that he was feared throughout the district, and anything as idiotic as this he had not heard since he was a baby.

The boy ran so fast that the thick beech trees appeared to be running past him backward, but he caught up with Smirre. Finally, he was so close to him that he got a hold on his tail. "Now I'll take the goose from you anyway," cried he, and held on as hard as ever he could, but he hadn't strength enough to stop Smirre. The fox dragged him along until the dry foliage whirled around him.

But now it began to dawn on Smirre how harmless the thing was that pursued him. He stopped short, put the goose on the ground, and stood on her with his forepaws so she couldn't fly away. He was just about to bite off her neck, but then he couldn't resist the desire to tease the boy a little. "Hurry off and complain to the master, for now I'm going to bite the goose to death!" he said.

Certainly the one who was surprised—when he saw what a pointed nose, and what a hoarse and angry voice that dog which he was pursuing had—was the boy! But now he was so enraged because the fox had made fun of him, that he never thought of being frightened. He took a firmer hold on the tail, braced himself against a beech trunk, and just as the fox opened his jaws over the goose's throat, he pulled as hard as he could. Smirre was so astonished that he let himself be pulled backward a couple of steps, and the wild goose got away. She fluttered upward feebly and heavily. One wing was so badly wounded that she could barely use it. In addition to this, she could not see in the night darkness of the forest but was as helpless as the blind. Therefore she could in no way help the boy, so she groped her way through the branches and flew down to the lake again.

Then Smirre made a dash for the boy. "If I don't get the one, I shall certainly have the other," he said, and you could tell by his voice how mad he was.

"Oh, don't you believe it!" said the boy, who was in the best of spirits because he had saved the goose. He held himself fast by the fox-tail, and swung with it—to one side—when the fox tried to catch him. There was such a dance in that forest that the dry beech leaves fairly flew! Smirre swung round and round, but the tail swung too while the boy kept a tight grip on it so the fox couldn't grab him. The boy was so gay after his success that he only laughed and made fun of the fox.

But Smirre was persevering—as old hunters generally are—and the boy began to fear that he should be captured in the end. Then he caught sight of a little young beech tree that had shot up as slender as a rod, that it might soon reach the free air above the canopy of branches which the old beeches spread over it. Quick as a flash, he let go of the fox-tail and climbed the beech tree. Smirre Fox was so excited that he continued to dance around after his tail for a long time.

"Don't bother with the dance any longer!" said the boy.

But Smirre couldn't endure the humiliation of his failure to get the better of such a little tot, so he lay down under the tree, that he might keep a close watch on him.

The boy didn't have any too good a time of it where he sat astride a frail branch. The young beech did not, as yet, reach the high-branch canopy, so the boy couldn't get over to another tree, and he didn't dare to come down again. He was so cold and numb that he almost lost his hold around the branch. He was dreadfully sleepy, but he didn't dare fall asleep for fear of tumbling down. My! but it was dismal to sit in that way the whole night through in the forest! He never before understood the real meaning of "night." It was just as if the whole world had become petrified and never could come to life again.

Then as it began to dawn, the boy was glad that everything began to look like itself once more, although the chill was even sharper than it had been during the night. Finally, when the sun got up, it wasn't yellow but red. The boy thought it looked as though it were angry and he wondered what it was angry about. Perhaps it was because the night had made it so cold and gloomy on earth while the sun was away.

The sunbeams came down in great clusters, to see what the night had been up to. It could be seen how everything blushed—as if they all had guilty consciences. The clouds up in the skies, the satiny beech limbs, the little intertwined branches of the forest canopy, the hoarfrost that covered the foliage on the ground—everything grew flushed and red. More and more sunbeams came bursting through space, and soon the night's terrors were driven away, and such a marvelous lot of living things came forward. The black woodpecker, with the red neck, began to hammer with its bill on the branch. The squirrel glided from his nest with a nut, and sat down on a branch and began to shell it. The starling came flying with a worm, and the bulfinch sang in the treetop.

Then the boy understood that the sun had said to all these tiny creatures: "Wake up now, and come out of your nests! I'm here! Now you need be afraid of nothing."

The wild goose call was heard from the lake as they were preparing for flight, and soon all fourteen geese came flying through the forest. The boy tried to call to them, but they flew so high that his voice couldn't reach them. They probably believed the fox had eaten him up, and they didn't trouble themselves to look for him.

The boy came near to crying with regret, but the sun stood up there—orange-colored and happy—and put courage into the whole world. "It isn't worthwhile, Nils Holgersson, for you to be troubled about anything, as long as I'm here," said the sun.

GOOSE-PLAY

Monday, March twenty-first

Everything remained unchanged in the forest—about as long as it takes a goose to eat her breakfast. But just as the morning was verging on forenoon, a goose came flying, all by herself, under the thick tree canopy. She groped her way, hesitatingly, between the stems and branches, and flew very slowly. As soon as Smirre Fox saw her, he left his place under the beech tree, and sneaked up toward her. The wild goose didn't avoid the fox, but flew very close to him. Smirre made a high jump for her but he missed her, and the goose went on her way down to the lake.

It was not long before another goose came flying. She took the same route as the first one, and flew still lower and slower. She, too, flew close to Smirre Fox, and he made such a high spring for her that his ears brushed her feet. But she, too, got away from him unhurt, and went her way toward the lake, silent as a shadow.

A little while passed and then there came another wild goose. She flew still slower and lower, and it seemed even more difficult for her to find her way between the beech branches. Smirre made a powerful spring! He was within a hair's breadth of catching her, but that goose also managed to save herself.

Just after she had disappeared, came a fourth. She flew so slowly, and so badly, that Smirre Fox thought he could catch her without much effort, but he was afraid of failure now, and concluded to let her fly past unmolested. She took the same direction the others had taken, and just as she had come right above Smirre, she sank down so far that he was tempted to jump for her. He jumped so high that he touched her with his tail, but she flung herself quickly to one side and saved her life.

Before Smirre got through panting, three more geese came flying in a row. They flew just like the rest, and Smirre made high springs for them all, but he did not succeed in catching any of them.

After that came five geese, but these flew better than the others. And although it seemed as if they wanted to lure Smirre to jump, he withstood the temptation. After quite a long time came one single goose. It was the thirteenth. This one was so old that she was gray all over, without a dark speck anywhere on her body. She didn't appear to use one wing very well, but flew so wretchedly and crookedly that she almost touched the ground. Smirre not only made a high leap for her, but he pursued her, running and jumping all the way down to the lake. But not even this time did he get anything for his trouble.

When the fourteenth goose came along, it looked very pretty because it was white, and, as its great wings swayed, it glistened like a light, in the dark forest. When Smirre Fox saw this one, he mustered all his resources and jumped halfway up to the tree canopy, but the white one flew by unhurt like the rest.

Now it was quiet for a moment under the beeches. It looked as if the whole wild goose flock had traveled past. Suddenly Smirre remembered his prisoner and raised his eyes toward the young beech tree. Just as he might have expected, the boy had disappeared. But Smirre didn't have much time to think about him, for now the first goose came back again from the lake and flew slowly under the canopy.

In spite of all his ill luck, Smirre was glad that she came back, and darted about her with a high leap. But he had been in too much of a hurry and hadn't taken time to calculate the distance, and landed at one side of the goose. Then there came still another goose, then a third, a fourth, a fifth, and so on, until the angle closed in with the old ice-gray one, and the big white one. They all flew low and slow. Just as they swayed in the vicinity of Smirre Fox, they sank down—kind of inviting-like—for him to take them. Smirre ran after them and made leaps a couple of fathoms high, but he couldn't manage to get hold of a single one of them.

It was the most awful day that Smirre Fox had ever experienced. The wild geese kept on traveling over his head. They came and went, came and went. Great splendid geese, who had eaten themselves fat on the German heaths and grain fields, swayed all day through the woods, and so close to him that he touched them many times, yet he was not permitted to appease his hunger with a single one of them.

The winter was hardly gone yet, and Smirre recalled nights and days when he had been forced to tramp around in idleness with not so much as a hare to hunt, when the rats hid themselves under the frozen earth, and when the chickens were all shut up. But all the winter's hunger had not been as hard to endure as this day's miscalculations.

Smirre was no young fox. He had had the dogs after him many a time, and had heard the bullets whizz around his ears. He had lain in hiding down in the lair while the dachshunds crept into the crevices and all but found him. But all the anguish that Smirre Fox had been forced to suffer under this hot chase was not to be compared with what he suffered every time he missed one of the wild geese.

In the morning, when the play began, Smirre Fox had looked so stunning that the geese were amazed when they saw him. Smirre loved display. His coat was a brilliant red, his breast white, his nose black, and his tail was as bushy as a plume. But when the evening of this day had come, Smirre's coat hung in loose folds. He was bathed in sweat; his eyes were without luster; his tongue hung far out from his gaping jaws, and froth oozed from his mouth.

In the afternoon, Smirre was so exhausted that he grew delirious. He saw nothing before his eyes but flying geese. He made leaps for sun spots which he saw on the ground, and for a poor little butterfly that had come out of his chrysalis too soon.

The wild geese flew and flew, unceasingly. All day long they continued to torment Smirre. They were not moved to pity because Smirre was done up, fevered, and out of his head. They continued without a letup, although they understood that he hardly saw them and that he jumped after their shadows.

When Smirre Fox sank down on a pile of dry leaves, weak and powerless and almost ready to give up the ghost, they stopped teasing him.

"Now you know, Mr. Fox, what happens to the one who dares to come near Akka of Kebnekaise!" they shouted in his ear, and with that they left him in peace.

III

THE WONDERFUL JOURNEY OF NILS

ON THE FARM

Thursday, March twenty-fourth

J ust at that time a thing happened in Skåne which created a good deal of discussion and even got into the newspapers, but which many believed to be a fable because they had not been able to explain it.

It was about like this: A lady squirrel had been captured in the hazelbrush that grew on the shores of Vomb Lake, and was carried to a farmhouse close by. All the folks on the farm—both young and old— were delighted with the pretty creature with the bushy tail, the wise inquisitive eyes, and the natty little feet. They intended to amuse themselves all summer by watching its nimble movements, its ingenious way of shelling nuts, and its droll play. They immediately ordered an old squirrel cage with a little green house and a wire cylinder wheel. The little house, which had both doors and windows, the lady squirrel was to use as a dining room and bedroom. For this reason they placed therein a bed of leaves, a bowl of milk and some nuts. The cylinder wheel, on the other hand, she was to use as a playhouse, where she could run and climb and swing around.

The people believed that they had arranged things very comfortably for the lady squirrel, and they were astonished because she didn't seem to be contented, but instead she sat there, downcast and moody, in a corner of her room. Every now and again, she would let out a shrill, agonized cry. She did not touch the food, and not once did she swing around on the wheel. "It's probably because she's frightened," said the farmer folk. "Tomorrow, when she feels more at home, she will both eat and play."

Meanwhile, the womenfolk were making preparations for a feast, and just on that day when the lady squirrel had been captured, they were busy with an elaborate bake. They had had bad luck with something: either the dough wouldn't rise, or else they had been dilatory, for they were obliged to work long after dark.

Naturally there was a great deal of excitement and bustle in the kitchen, and probably no one there took time to think about the squirrel, or to wonder how she was getting on. But there was an old grandma in the house who was too aged to take a hand in the baking; this she herself understood, but just the same she did not relish the idea of being left out of the game. She felt rather downhearted, and for this reason she did not go to bed but seated herself by the sitting room window and looked out.

They had opened the kitchen door on account of the heat, and through it a clear ray of light streamed out on the yard, and it became so well lit out there that the old woman could see all the cracks and holes of the plastering on the wall opposite. She saw the squirrel cage which hung just where the light fell clearest. And she noticed how the squirrel ran from her room to the wheel, and from the wheel to her room, all night long, without stopping an instant. She thought it was a strange sort of unrest that had come over the animal, but she believed, of course, that the strong light kept her awake.

Between the cow house and the stable there was a broad, handsome carriage gate; this too came within the light radius. As the night wore on, the old grandma saw a tiny creature, no bigger than a hand's breadth, cautiously steal his way through the gate. He was dressed in leather breeches and wooden shoes like any other working man. The old grandma knew at once that it was the elf, and she was not the least bit frightened. She had always heard that the elf kept himself somewhere about the place, although she had never seen him before, and an elf, to be sure, brought good luck wherever he appeared.

As soon as the elf came into the stone-paved yard, he ran right up to the squirrel cage. And since it hung so high that he could not reach it, he went over to the storehouse after a rod, placed it against the cage, and swung himself up—in the same way that a sailor climbs a rope.

When he had reached the cage, he shook the door of the little green house as if he wanted to open it, but the old grandma didn't move, for she knew that the children had put a padlock on the door, as they feared that the boys on the neighboring farms would try to steal the squirrel. The old woman saw that when the boy could not get the door open, the lady squirrel came out to the wider wheel. There they held a long conference together. And when the boy had listened to all that the imprisoned animal had to say to him, he slid down the rod to the ground, and ran out through the carriage gate.

The old woman didn't expect to see anything more of the elf that night. Nevertheless, she remained at the window. After a few moments had gone by, he returned. He was in such a hurry that it seemed to her as though his feet hardly touched the ground, and he rushed right up the squirrel cage. The old woman, with her far-sighted eyes, saw him distinctly, and she also saw that he carried something in his hands, but what it was she couldn't imagine. The thing he carried in his left hand he laid down on the pavement, but that which he held in his right hand he took with him to the cage. He kicked so hard with his wooden shoes on the little window that the glass was broken. He poked in the thing which he held in his hand to the lady squirrel. Then he slid down again, and took up that which he had laid upon the ground, and climbed up to the cage with that also. The next instant he ran off again with such haste that the old woman could hardly follow him with her eyes.

But now it was the old grandma who could no longer sit still in the cottage, but who, very slowly, went out to the back yard and stationed herself in the shadow of the pump to await the elf's return. And there was one other who had also seen him and had become curious. This was the house cat. He crept along slyly and stopped close to the wall, just two steps away from the stream of light. They both stood and waited, long and patiently, on that chilly March night, and the old woman was just beginning to think about going in again, when she heard a clatter on the pavement, and saw that the little mite of an elf came trotting along once more, carrying a burden in each hand, as he had done before. That which he bore squealed and squirmed. And now a light dawned on the old grandma. She understood that the elf had hurried down to the hazel grove and brought back the lady squirrel's babies, and that he was carrying them to her so they shouldn't starve to death.

The old grandma stood very still, and it did not look as if the elf had noticed her. He was just going to lay one of the babies on the ground so that he could swing himself up to the cage with the other one—when he saw the house cat's green eyes glisten close beside him. He stood there, bewildered, with a young one in each hand.

He turned around and looked in all directions, then he became aware of the old grandma's presence. Then he did not hesitate long, but walked forward, stretched his arms as high as he could reach, for her to take one of the baby squirrels.

The old grandma did not wish to prove herself unworthy of the confidence, so she bent down and took the baby squirrel, and stood there and held it until the boy had swung himself up to the cage with the other one. Then he came back for the one he had entrusted to her care.

The next morning, when the farm folk had gathered together for breakfast, it was impossible for the old woman to refrain from telling them of what she had seen the night before. They all laughed at her, of course, and said that she had been only dreaming. There were no baby squirrels this early in the year.

But she was sure of her ground. She begged them to take a look into the squirrel cage, and this they did. And there lay on the bed of leaves, four tiny half-naked, half-blind baby squirrels, who were at least a couple of days old.

When the farmer himself saw the young ones, he said, "Be it as it may with this, but one thing is certain, we on this farm have behaved in such a manner that we are shamed before both animals and human beings." And, thereupon, he took the mother squirrel and all her young ones from the cage, and laid them in the old grandma's lap. "Go thou out to the hazel grove with them," said he, "and let them have their freedom back again!"

It was this event that was so much talked about, and which even got into the newspapers, but which the majority would not credit because they were not able to explain how anything like that could have happened.

VITTSKÖVLE

Saturday, March twenty-sixth

Two days later, another strange thing happened. A flock of wild geese came flying one morning, and lit on a meadow down in eastern Skåne not very far from Vittskövle manor. In the flock were thirteen wild geese, of the usual gray variety, and one white goosey-gander, who carried on his back a tiny lad dressed in yellow leather breeches, green vest, and a white woolen-toboggan hood.

They were now very near the eastern sea. On the meadow where the geese had alighted the soil was sandy, as it usually is on the seacoast. It looked as if there had been flying sand which had to be held down, for in several directions large, planted pine woods could be seen.

When the wild geese had been feeding a while, several children came along, and walked on the edge of the meadow. The goose who was on guard at once raised herself into the air with noisy wing strokes, so the whole flock should hear that there was danger on foot. All the wild geese flew upward, but the white one trotted along the ground unconcerned. When he saw the others fly he raised his head and called after them, "You needn't fly away from them, they are only a couple of children!"

The little creature who had been riding on his back, sat down upon a knoll on the outskirts of the wood and picked a pine cone in pieces that he might get at the seeds. The children were so close to him that he did not dare to run across the meadow to the white one. He concealed himself under a big, dry thistle leaf, and at the same time gave a warning cry. But the white one had evidently made up his mind not to let himself be scared. He walked along on the ground all the while, and not once did he look to see in what direction they were going.

Meanwhile, they turned from the path, walked across the field, getting nearer and nearer to the goosey-gander. When he finally did look up, they were right upon him. He was so dumfounded, and became so confused, he forgot that he could fly, and tried to get out of their reach by running. But the children followed, chasing him into a ditch, and there they caught him. The larger of the two stuck him under his arm and carried him off.

When the boy, who lay under the thistle leaf, saw this, he sprang up as if he wanted to take the goosey-gander away from them, then he must have remembered how little and powerless he was, for he threw himself on the knoll and beat upon the ground with his clenched fists.

The goosey-gander cried with all his might for help, "Thumbietot, come and help me! Oh, Thumbietot, come and help me!" The boy began to laugh in the midst of his distress. "Oh, yes! I'm just the right one to help anybody, I am!" said he.

Anyway he got up and followed the goosey-gander. "I can't help him," said he, "but I shall at least find out where they are taking him."

The children had a good start, but the boy had no difficulty in keeping them within sight until they came to a hollow where a brook gushed forth. But here he was obliged to run alongside of it for some little time, before he could find a place narrow enough for him to jump over.

When he came up from the hollow the children had disappeared. He could see their footprints on a narrow path which led to the woods, and these he continued to follow.

Soon he came to a crossroad. Here the children must have separated, for there were footprints in two directions. The boy looked now as if all hope had fled. Then he saw a little white down on a heather knoll, and he understood that the goosey-gander had dropped this by the wayside to let him know in which direction he had been carried, and therefore he continued his search. He followed the children through the entire wood. The goosey-gander he did not see, but wherever he was likely to miss his way, lay a little white down to put him right.

The boy continued faithfully to follow the bits of down. They led him out of the wood, across a couple of meadows, up on a road, and finally through the entrance of a broad *allée*. At the end of the *allée* there were gables and towers of red tiling, decorated with bright borders and other ornamentations that glittered and shone. When the boy saw that this was some great manor, he thought he knew what had become of the goosey-gander. "No doubt the children have carried the goosey-gander to the manor and sold him there. By this time he's probably butchered," he said to himself. But he did not seem to be satisfied with anything less than proof positive, and with renewed courage he ran forward. He met no one in the *allée* and that was well, for such as he are generally afraid of being seen by human beings.

The mansion which he came to was a splendid, old-time structure with four great wings which inclosed a courtyard. On the east wing, there was a high arch leading into the courtyard. This far the boy ran without hesitation, but when he got there he stopped. He dared not venture farther, but stood still and pondered what he should do now.

There he stood, with his finger on his nose, thinking, when he heard footsteps behind him, and as he turned around he saw a whole company march up the *alleé*. In haste he stole behind a water barrel which stood near the arch, and hid himself.

Those who came up were some twenty young men from a high school out on a pedestrian tour. They were accompanied by one of the instructors. When they had come as far as the arch, the teacher requested them to wait there a moment, while he went in and asked if they might see the old castle of Vittskövle.

The newcomers were warm and tired, as if they had been on a long tramp. One of them was so thirsty that he went over to the water barrel and stooped down to drink. He had a tin box, such as botanists use, hanging about his neck. He evidently thought that this was in his way, for he threw it down on the ground. With this, the lid flew open, and one could see that there were a few spring flowers in it.

The botanist's box dropped just in front of the boy, and he must have thought that here was his opportunity to get into the castle and find out what had become of the goosey-gander. He smuggled himself quickly into the box and concealed himself as well as he could under the anemones and coltsfoot.

He was hardly hidden before the young man picked the box up, hung it around his neck, and slammed down the cover.

Then the teacher came back and said that they had been given permission to enter the castle. At first he conducted them no farther than the courtyard. There he stopped and began to talk to them about this ancient structure.

He called their attention to the first human beings who had inhabited this country, and who had been obliged to live in mountain-grottoes and earth caves, in the dens of wild beasts, and in the brushwood, and that a very long period had elapsed before they learned to build themselves huts from the trunks of trees. And afterward how long they had been forced to labor and struggle before they had advanced from the log cabin, with its single room, to the building of a castle with a hundred rooms like Vittskövle!

It was about three hundred and fifty years ago that the rich and powerful built such castles for themselves, he said. It was very evident that Vittskövle had been erected at a time when wars and robbers made it unsafe in Skåne. All around the castle was a deep trench filled with water, and across this there had been a bridge in bygone days that could be hoisted up. Over the gate arch there is, even to this day, a watchtower, and all along the sides of the castle ran sentry galleries, and in the corners stood towers with walls a meter thick. Yet the castle had not been erected in the most savage war times, for Jens Brahe, who built it, had also studied to make of it a beautiful and decorative ornament. If they could see the big, solid stone structure at Glimminge, which had been built only a generation earlier, they would readily see that Jens Holgersen Ulfstand, the builder, hadn't figured upon anything else— only to build big and strong and secure, without bestowing a thought upon making it beautiful and comfortable. If they visited such castles as Marsvinsholm, Snogeholm and Ovid's Cloister—which were erected a hundred years or so later—they would find that the times had become less warlike. The gentlemen who built these places had not furnished them with fortifications, but had only taken pains to provide themselves with great, splendid dwelling houses.

The teacher talked at length in detail, and the boy who lay shut up in the box was pretty impatient. But he must have lain very still, for the owner of the box hadn't the least suspicion that he was carrying him along.

Finally the company went into the castle. But if the boy had hoped for a chance to crawl out of that box, he was deceived, for the student carried it upon him all the while, and the boy was obliged to accompany him through all the rooms. It was a tedious tramp. The teacher stopped every other minute to explain and instruct.

In one room he found an old fireplace, and before this he stopped to talk about the different kinds of fireplaces that had been used in the course of time. The first indoors fireplace had been a big, flat stone on the floor of the hut, with an opening in the roof which let in both wind and rain. The next had been a big stone hearth with no opening in the roof. This must have made the hut very warm, but it also filled it with soot and smoke. When Vittskövle was built, the people had advanced far enough to open the fireplace, which at that time had a wide chimney for the smoke, but it also took most of the warmth up in the air with it.

If that boy had ever in his life been cross and impatient, he was given a good lesson in patience that day. It must have been a whole hour now that he had lain perfectly still.

In the next room they came to, the teacher stopped before an old-time bed with its high canopy and rich curtains. Immediately he began to talk about the beds and bed places of olden days.

The teacher didn't hurry himself, but then he did not know, of course, that a poor little creature lay shut up in a botanist's box, and only waited for him to get through. When they came to a room with gilded leather hangings, he talked to them about how the people had dressed their walls and ceilings ever since the beginning of time. And when he came to an old family portrait, he told them all about the different changes in dress. And in the banquet halls he described ancient customs of celebrating weddings and funerals.

Thereupon, the teacher talked a little about the excellent men and women who had lived in the castle, about the old Brahes, and the old Barnekows, of Christian Barnekow, who had given his horse to the king to help him escape, of Margareta Ascheberg who had been married to Kjell Barnekow and who, when a widow, had managed the estates and the whole district for fifty-three years, of banker Hageman, a farmer's son from Vittskövle, who had grown so rich that he had bought the entire estate, about the Stjernsvärds, who had given the people of Skåne better plows, which enabled them to discard the ridiculous old wooden plows that three oxen were hardly able to drag. During all this, the boy lay still. If he had ever been mischievous and shut the cellar door on his father or mother, he understood now how they had felt, for it was hours and hours before that teacher got through.

At last the teacher went out into the courtyard again. And there he discoursed upon the tireless labor of mankind to procure for themselves tools and weapons, clothes and houses and ornaments. He said that such an old castle as Vittskövle was a milepost on time's highway. Here one could see how far the people had advanced three hundred and fifty years ago, and one could judge for oneself whether things had gone forward or backward since their time.

But this dissertation the boy escaped hearing, for the student who carried him was thirsty again, and stole into the kitchen to ask for a drink of water. When the boy was carried into the kitchen, he should have tried to look around for the goosey-gander. He had begun to move, and as he did this, he happened to press too hard against the lid and it flew open. As botanists' box-lids are always flying open, the student thought no more about the matter but pressed it down again. Then the cook asked him if he had a snake in the box.

"No, I have only a few plants," the student replied. "It was certainly something that moved there," insisted the cook. The student threw back the lid to show her that she was mistaken, "See for yourself if—"

But he got no further, for now the boy dared not stay in the box any longer, but with one bound he stood on the floor, and out he rushed. The maids hardly had time to see what it was that ran, but they hurried after it, nevertheless.

The teacher still stood and talked when he was interrupted by shrill cries. "Catch him, catch him!" shrieked those who had come from the kitchen, and all the young men raced after the boy, who glided away faster than a rat. They tried to intercept him at the gate, but it was not so easy to get a hold on such a little creature, so, luckily, he got out in the open.

The boy did not dare to run down toward the open *allée*, but turned in another direction. He rushed through the garden into the back yard. All the while the people raced after him, shrieking and laughing. The poor little thing ran as hard as ever he could to get out of their way, but still it looked as though the people would catch up with him.

As he rushed past a laborer's cottage, he heard a goose cackle, and saw a white down lying on the doorstep. There, at last, was the goosey-gander! He had been on the wrong track before. He thought no more of housemaids and men who were hounding him, but climbed up the steps and into the hallway. Farther he couldn't come, for the door was locked. He heard how the goosey-gander cried and moaned inside, but he couldn't get the door open. The hunters who were pursuing him came nearer and nearer, and, in the room, the goosey-gander cried more and more pitifully. In this direst of needs the boy finally plucked up courage and pounded on the door with all his might.

A child opened it, and the boy looked into the room. In the middle of the floor sat a woman who held the goosey-gander tight—to clip his quill-feathers. It was her children who had found him, and she didn't want to do him any harm. It was her intention to let him in among her own geese, had she only succeeded in clipping his wings so he couldn't fly away. But a worse fate could hardly have happened to the goosey-gander, and he shrieked and moaned with all his might.

And a lucky thing it was that the woman hadn't started the clipping sooner. Now only two quills had fallen under the shears when the door was opened—and the boy stood on the doorsill. But a creature like that the woman had never seen before. She couldn't believe anything else but that it was Goa-Nisse himself, and in her terror she dropped the shears, clasped her hands and forgot to hold on to the goosey-gander.

As soon as he felt himself freed, he ran toward the door. He didn't give himself time to stop, but, as he ran past him, he grabbed the boy by the neck-band and carried him along with him. On the stoop he spread his wings and flew up in the air; at the same time he made a graceful sweep with his neck and seated the boy on his smooth, downy back.

And off the they flew while all Vittskövle stood and stared after them.

IN ÖVID CLOISTER PARK

All that day, when the wild geese played with the fox, the boy lay and slept in a deserted squirrel nest. When he awoke, along toward evening, he felt very uneasy. "Well, now I shall soon be sent home again! Then I'll have to exhibit myself before Father and Mother," thought he. But when he looked up and saw the wild geese, who lay and bathed in Vomb Lake—not one of them said a word about his going. "They probably think the white one is too tired to travel home with me tonight," thought the boy.

The next morning the geese were awake at daybreak, long before sunrise. Now the boy felt sure that he'd have to go home, but, curiously enough, both he and the white goosey-gander were permitted to follow the wild ones on their morning tour. The boy couldn't comprehend the reason for the delay, but he figured it out in this way, that the wild geese did not care to send the goosey-gander on such a long journey until they had both eaten their fill. Come what might, he was only glad for every moment that should pass before he must face his parents.

The wild geese traveled over Övid's Cloister estate which was situated in a beautiful park east of the lake, and looked very imposing with its great castle: its well-planned court surrounded by low walls and pavilions; its fine old-time garden with covered arbors, streams and fountains; its wonderful trees, trimmed bushes, and its evenly mown lawns with their beds of beautiful spring flowers.

When the wild geese rode over the estate in the early morning hour there was no human being about. When they had carefully assured themselves of this, they lowered themselves toward the dog kennel, and shouted, "What kind of a little hut is this? What kind of a little hut is this?"

Instantly the dog came out of his kennel—furiously angry—and barked at the air.

"Do you call this a hut, you tramps! Can't you see that this is a great stone castle? Can't you see what fine terraces, and what a lot of pretty walls and windows and great doors it has, bow, wow, wow, wow? Don't you see the grounds, can't you see the garden, can't you see the conservatories, can't you see the marble statues? You call this a hut, do you? Do huts have parks with beech groves and hazel bushes and trailing vines and oak trees and firs and hunting grounds filled with game, wow, wow, wow? Do you call this a hut? Have you seen huts with so many outhouses around them that they look like a whole village? You must know of a lot of huts that have their own church and their own parsonage, and that rule over the district and the peasant homes and the neighboring farms and barracks, wow, wow, wow? Do you call this a hut? To this hut belong the richest possessions in Skåne, you beggars! You can't see a bit of land, from where you hang in the clouds, that does not obey commands from this hut, wow, wow, wow!"

All this the dog managed to cry out in one breath, and the wild geese flew back and forth over the estate, and listened to him until he was winded. But then they cried, "What are you so mad about? We didn't ask about the castle; we only wanted to know about your kennel, stupid!"

When the boy heard this joke, he laughed, then a thought stole in on him which at once made him serious. "Think how many of these amusing things you would hear, if you could go with the wild geese through the whole country, all the way up to Lapland!" said he to himself. "And just now, when you are in such a bad fix, a trip like that would be the best thing you could hit upon."

The wild geese traveled to one of the wide fields, east of the estate, to eat grass roots, and they kept this up for hours. In the meantime, the boy wandered in the great park which bordered the field. He hunted up a beech-nut grove and began to look up at the bushes, to see if a nut from last fall still hung there. But again and again the thought of the trip came over him, as he walked in the park. He pictured to himself what a fine time he would have if he went with the wild geese. To freeze and starve, that he believed he should have to do often enough, but as a recompense, he would escape both work and study.

As he walked there, the old gray leader goose came up to him and asked if he had found anything eatable. No that he hadn't, he replied, and then she tried to help him. She couldn't find any nuts either, but she discovered a couple of dried blossoms that hung on a brier bush. These the boy ate with relish. But he wondered what Mother would say, if she knew that he had lived on raw fish and old winter-dried blossoms.

When the wild geese had finally eaten themselves full, they bore off toward the lake again, where they amused themselves with games until almost dinner time.

The wild geese challenged the white goosey-gander to take part in all kinds of sports. They had swimming races, running races, and flying races with him. The big tame one did his level best to hold his own, but the clever wild geese beat him every time. All the while, the boy sat on the goosey-gander's back and encouraged him, and had as much fun as the rest. They laughed and screamed and cackled, and it was remarkable that the people on the estate didn't hear them.

When the wild geese were tired of play, they flew out on the ice and rested for a couple of hours. The afternoon they spent in pretty much the same way as the forenoon. First a couple of hours feeding, then bathing and play in the water near the ice-edge until sunset, when they immediately arranged themselves for sleep.

"This is just the life that suits me," thought the boy when he crept in under the gander's wing. "But tomorrow, I suppose I'll be sent home."

Before he fell asleep, he lay and thought that if he might go along with the wild geese, he would escape all scoldings because he was lazy. Then he could cut loose every day, and his only worry would be to get something to eat. But he needed so little nowadays, and there would always be a way to get that.

So he pictured the whole scene to himself, what he should see, and all the adventures that he would be in on. Yes, it would be something different from the wear and tear at home. "If I could only go with the wild geese on their travels, I shouldn't grieve because I'd been trans-formed," thought the boy.

He wasn't afraid of anything—except being sent home, but not even on Wednesday did the geese say anything to him about going. That day passed in the same way as Tuesday, and the boy grew more and more contented with the outdoor life. He thought that he had the lovely Övid Cloister park—which was as large as a forest—all to himself, and he wasn't anxious to go back to the stuffy cabin and the little patch of ground there at home.

On Wednesday he believed that the wild geese thought of keeping him with them, but on Thursday he lost hope again.

Thursday began just like the other days; the geese fed on the broad meadows, and the boy hunted for food in the park. After a while Akka came to him, and asked if he had found anything to eat. No, he had not, and then she looked up a dry caraway herb, that had kept all its tiny seeds intact.

When the boy had eaten, Akka said that she thought he ran around in the park altogether too recklessly. She wondered if he knew how many enemies he had to guard against—he, who was so little. No, he didn't know anything at all about that. Then Akka began to enumerate them for him.

Whenever he walked in the park, she said, that he must look for for the fox and the marten; when he came to the shores of the lake, he must think of the otters; as he sat on the stone wall, he must not forget the weasels, who could creep through the smallest holes, and if he wished to lie down and sleep on a pile of leaves, he must first find out if the adders were not sleeping their winter sleep in the same pile. As soon as he came out in the open fields, he should keep an eye out for hawks and buzzards, for eagles and falcons that soared in the air. In the bramble bush he could be captured by the sparrow-hawk; magpies and crows were found everywhere and in these he mustn't place any too much confidence. As soon as it was dusk, he must keep his ears open and listen for the big owls, who flew along with such soundless wing-strokes that they could come right up to him before he was aware of their presence.

When the boy heard that there were so many who were after his life, he thought that it would be simply impossible for him to escape. He was not particularly afraid to die, but he didn't like the idea of being eaten up, so he asked Akka what he should do to protect himself from the carnivorous animals.

Akka answered at once that the boy should try to get on good terms with all the small animals in the woods and fields: with the squirrel-folk, and the hare family, with bullfinches and titmice and woodpeckers and larks. If he made friends with them, they could warn him against dangers, find hiding places for him, and protect him.

But, later in the day, when the boy tried to profit by this counsel, and turned to Sirle Squirrel to ask for his protection, it was evident that he did not care to help him. "You surely can't expect anything from me, or the rest of the small animals!" said Sirle. "Don't you think we know that you are Nils the goose boy, who tore down the swallow's nest last year, crushed the starling's eggs, threw baby crows in the marl ditch, caught thrushes in snares, and put squirrels in cages? You just help yourself as well as you can, and you may be thankful that we do not form a league against you, and drive you back to your own kind!"

This was just the sort of answer the boy would not have let go unpunished, in the days when he was Nils the goose boy. But now he was only fearful lest the wild geese, too, had found out how wicked he could be. He had been so anxious for fear he wouldn't be permitted to stay with the wild geese, that he hadn't dared to get into the least little mischief since he joined their company. It was true that he didn't have the power to do much harm now, but, little as he was, he could have destroyed many birds' nests, and crushed many eggs, if he'd been a mind to. Now he had been good. He hadn't pulled a feather from a goose-wing, or given anyone a rude answer, and every morning when he called upon Akka he had always removed his cap and bowed.

All day Thursday he thought it was surely on account of his wickedness that the wild geese did not care to take him along up to Lapland. And in the evening, when he heard that Sirle Squirrel's wife had been stolen, and her children were starving to death, he made up his mind to help them. And we have already been told how well he succeeded.

When the boy came into the park on Friday, he heard the bullfinches sing in every bush, of how Sirle Squirrel's wife had been carried away from her children by cruel robbers, and how Nils, the goose boy, had risked his life among human beings, and taken the little squirrel children to her.

"And who is so honored in Övid Cloister park now, as Thumbietot!" sang the bullfinch, "he, whom all feared when he was Nils the goose boy? Sirle Squirrel will give him nuts; the poor hares are going to play with him; the small wild animals will carry him on their backs, and fly away with him when Smirre Fox approaches. The titmice are going to warn him against the hawk, and the finches and larks will sing of his valour."

The boy was absolutely certain that both Akka and the wild geese had heard all this. But still Friday passed and not one word did they say about his remaining with them.

Until Saturday the wild geese fed in the fields around Ovid, undisturbed by Smirre Fox.

But on Saturday morning, when they came out in the meadows, he lay in wait for them, and chased them from one field to another and they were not allowed to eat in peace. When Akka understood that he didn't intend to leave them in peace, she came to a decision quickly, raised herself into the air and flew with her flock several miles away, over Färs' plains and Linderödsosen's hills. They did not stop before they had arrived in the district of Vittskövle.

But at Vittskövle the goosey-gander was stolen, and how it happened has already been related. If the boy hadn't used all his powers to help him, he would never again have been found.

On Saturday evening, as the boy came back to Vomb Lake with the goosey-gander, he thought that he had done a good day's work, and he speculated a good deal on what Akka and the wild geese would say to him. The wild geese were not at all sparing in their praises, but they did not say the word he was longing to hear.

Then Sunday came again. A whole week had gone by since the boy had been bewitched, and he was still just as little.

But he didn't appear to be giving himself any extra worry on account of this thing. On Sunday afternoon he sat huddled together in a big, fluffy, osier-bush, down by the lake, and blew on a reed-pipe. All around him there sat as many finches and bullfinches and starlings as the bush could well hold—who sang songs which he tried to teach himself to play. But the boy was not at home in this art. He blew so false that the feathers raised themselves on the little music masters, and they shrieked and fluttered in their despair. The boy laughed so heartily at their excitement that he dropped his pipe.

He began once again, and that went just as badly. Then all the little birds wailed, "Today you play worse than usual, Thumbietot. You don't take one true note! Where are your thoughts, Thumbietot?"

"They are elsewhere," said the boy—and this was true. He sat there and pondered how long he would be allowed to remain with the wild geese, or if he should be sent home perhaps today.

Finally the boy threw down his pipe and jumped from the bush. He had seen Akka, and all the wild geese, coming toward him in a long row. They walked so uncommonly slow and dignified-like that the boy immediately understood that now he should learn what they intended to do with him.

When they stopped at last, Akka said, "You may well have reason to wonder at me, Thumbietot, who have not said thanks to you for saving me from Smirre Fox. But I am one of those who would rather give thanks by deeds than words. I have sent word to the elf that bewitched you. At first he didn't want to hear anything about curing you, but I have sent message upon message to him, and told him how well you have conducted yourself among us. He greets you, and says, that as soon as you turn back home, you shall be human again."

But think of it! Just as happy as the boy had been when the wild geese began to speak, just that miserable was he when they had finished. He didn't say a word, but turned away and wept.

"What in all the world is this?" said Akka. "It looks as though you had expected more of me than I have offered you."

But the boy was thinking of the carefree days and the banter, and of adventure and freedom and travel, high above the earth, that he should miss, and he actually bawled with grief. "I don't want to be human," said he. "I want to go with you to Lapland."

"I'll tell you something," said Akka. "That elf is very touchy, and I'm afraid that if you do not accept his offer now, it will be difficult for you to coax him another time."

It was a strange thing about that boy—as long as he had lived, he had never cared for anyone. He had not cared for his father or mother, not for the school teacher, not for his schoolmates, nor for the boys in the neighborhood. All that they had wished to have him do—whether it had been work or play—he had only thought tiresome. Therefore there was no one whom he missed or longed for.

The only ones that he had come anywhere near agreeing with, were Osa, the goose girl, and little Mats—a couple of children who had tended geese in the fields, like himself. But he didn't care particularly for them either. No, far from it! "I don't want to be human," bawled the boy. "I want to go with you to Lapland. That's why I've been good for a whole week!"

"I don't want to forbid you to come along with us as far as you like," said Akka, "but think first if you wouldn't rather go home again. A day may come when you will regret this."

"No," said the boy, "that's nothing to regret. I have never been as well off as here with you."

"Well then, let it be as you wish," said Akka.

"Thanks!" said the boy, and he felt so happy that he had to cry for very joy—just as he had cried before from sorrow.

IV

GLIMMINGE CASTLE

BLACK RATS
AND GRAY RATS

*I*n southeastern Skåne, not far from the sea, there is an old castle called Glimminge. It is a big and substantial stone house, and can be seen over the plain for miles around. It is not more than four stories high, but it is so ponderous that an ordinary farmhouse, which stands on the same estate, looks like a little children's playhouse in comparison.

The big stone house has such thick ceilings and partitions that there is scarcely room in its interior for anything but the thick walls. The stairs are narrow, the entrances small, and the rooms few. That the walls might retain their strength, there are only the fewest number of windows in the upper stories, and none at all are found in the lower ones. In the old war times, the people were just as glad that they could shut themselves up in a strong and massive house like this, as one is nowadays to be able to creep into furs in a snapping cold winter. But when the time of peace came, they did not care to live in the dark and cold stone halls of the old castle any longer. They have long since deserted the big Glimminge castle, and moved into dwelling places where the light and air can penetrate.

At the time when Nils Holgersson wandered around with the wild geese, there were no human beings in the Glimminge castle, but for all that, it was not without inhabitants. Every summer there lived a stork couple in a large nest on the roof. In a nest in the attic lived a pair of gray owls; in the secret passages hung bats; in the kitchen oven lived an old cat, and down in the cellar there were hundreds of old black rats.

Rats are not held in very high esteem by other animals, but the black rats at Glimminge castle were an exception. They were always mentioned with respect, because they had shown great valor in battle with their enemies, and much endurance under the great misfortunes which had befallen their kind. They nominally belonged to a rat-folk who, at one time, had been very numerous and powerful, but who were now dying out. During a long period of time, the black rats owned Skåne and the whole country. They were found in every cellar, in every attic, in larders and cowhouses and barns, in breweries and flour mills, in churches and castles, in every man-constructed building. But now they were banished from all this—and were almost exterminated. Only in one and another old and secluded place could one run across a few of them, and nowhere were they to be found in such large numbers as in Glimminge castle.

When an animal folk die out, it is generally the human kind who are the cause of it, but that was not the case in this instance. The people had certainly struggled with the black rats, but they had not been able to do them any harm worth mentioning. Those who had conquered them were an animal folk of their own kind, who were called gray rats.

These gray rats had not lived in the land since time immemorial, like the black rats, but descended from a couple of poor immigrants who landed in Malmö from a Libyan sloop about a hundred years ago. They were homeless, starved-out wretches who stuck close to the harbor, swam among the piles under the bridges, and ate refuse that was thrown in the water. They never ventured into the city, which was owned by the black rats.

But gradually, as the gray rats increased in number they grew bolder. At first they moved over to some waste places and condemned old houses which the black rats had abandoned. They hunted their food in gutters and dirt heaps, and made the most of all the rubbish that the black rats did not deign to take care of. They were hardy, contented and fearless, and within a few years they had become so powerful that they undertook to drive the black rats out of Malmö. They took from them attics, cellars and storerooms, starved them out or bit them to death for they were not at all afraid of fighting.

When Malmö was captured, they marched forward in small and large companies to conquer the whole country. It is almost impossible to comprehend why the black rats did not muster themselves into a great, united war expedition to exterminate the gray rats, while these were still few in numbers. But the black rats were so certain of their power that they could not believe it possible for them to lose it. They sat still on their estates, and in the meantime the gray rats took from them farm after farm, city after city. They were starved out, forced out, rooted out. In Skåne they had not been able to maintain themselves in a single place except Glimminge castle.

The old castle had such secure walls and such few rat passages led through these, that the black rats had managed to protect themselves, and to prevent the gray rats from crowding in. Night after night, year after year, the struggle had continued between the aggressors and the defenders, but the black rats had kept faithful watch, and had fought with the utmost contempt for death, and, thanks to the fine old house, they had always conquered.

It will have to be acknowledged that as long as the black rats were in power they were as much shunned by all other living creatures as the gray rats are in our day—and for just cause, they had thrown themselves upon poor, lettered prisoners, and tortured them; they had ravished the dead; they had stolen the last turnip from the cellars of the poor, bitten off the feet of sleeping geese, robbed eggs and chicks from the hens, and committed a thousand depredations. But since they had come to grief, all this seemed to have been forgotten, and no one could help but marvel at the last of a race that had held out so long against its enemies.

The gray rats that lived in the courtyard at Glimminge and in the vicinity, kept up a continuous warfare and tried to watch out for every possible chance to capture the castle. One would fancy that they should have allowed the little company of black rats to occupy Glimminge castle in peace, since they themselves had acquired all the rest of the country, but you may be sure this thought never occurred to them. They were wont to say that it was a point of honour with them to conquer the black rats at some time or other. But those who were acquainted with the gray rats must have known that it was because the human kind used Glimminge castle as a grain storehouse that the gray ones could not rest before they had taken possession of the place.

THE STORK

Monday, March twenty-eighth

Early one morning the wild geese who stood and slept on the ice in Vomb Lake were awakened by long calls from the air. "Trirop, Trirop!" it sounded, "Trianut, the crane, sends greetings to Akka, the wild goose, and her flock. Tomorrow will be the day of the great crane dance on Kullaberg."

Akka raised her head and answered at once, "Greetings and thanks! Greetings and thanks!"

With that, the cranes flew farther, and the wild geese heard them for a long while—where they traveled and called out over every field, and every wooded hill, "Trianut sends greetings. Tomorrow will be the day of the great crane dance on Kullaberg."

The wild geese were very happy over this invitation. "You're in luck," they said to the white goosey-gander, "to be permitted to attend the great crane dance on Kullaberg!"

"Is it then so remarkable to see cranes dance?" asked the goosey-gander.

"It is something that you have never even dreamed about!" replied the wild geese.

"Now we must think out what we shall do with Thumbietot tomorrow—so that no harm can come to him, while we run over to Kullaberg," said Akka. "Thumbietot shall not be left alone," said the goosey-gander. "If the cranes won't let him see their dance, then I'll stay with him."

"No human being has ever been permitted to attend the Animals' Congress, at Kullaberg," said Akka, "and I shouldn't dare to take Thumbietot along. But we'll discuss this more at length later in the day. Now we must first and foremost think about getting something to eat."

With that Akka gave the signal to adjourn. On this day she also sought her feeding place a good distance away, on Smirre Fox's account, and she didn't alight until she came to the swampy meadows a little south of Glimminge castle.

All that day the boy sat on the shores of a little pond, and blew on reed-pipes. He was out of sorts because he shouldn't see the crane dance, and he just couldn't say a word, either to the goosey-gander or to any of the others.

It was pretty hard that Akka should still doubt him. When a boy had given up being human, just to travel around with a few wild geese, they surely ought to understand that he had no desire to betray them. Then, too, they ought to understand that when he had renounced so much to follow them, it was their duty to let him see all the wonders they could show him.

"I'll have to speak my mind right out to them," thought he. But hour after hour passed, and still he hadn't come around to it. It may sound remarkable—but the boy had actually acquired a kind of respect for the old leader goose. He felt that it was not easy to pit his will against hers.

On one side of the swampy meadow where the wild geese fed, there was a broad stone hedge. Toward evening when the boy finally raised his head, to speak to Akka, his glance happened to rest on this hedge. He uttered a little cry of surprise, and all the wild geese instantly looked up, and stared in the same direction. At first, both the geese and the boy thought that all the round, gray stones in the hedge had acquired legs, and were starting on a run, but soon they saw that it was a company of rats who ran over it. They moved very rapidly, and ran forward, tightly packed, line upon line, and were so numerous that, for some time, they covered the entire stone hedge.

The boy had been afraid of rats, even when he was a big, strong human being. Then what must his feelings be now, when he was so tiny that two or three of them could overpower him? One shudder after another traveled down his spinal column as he stood and stared at them.

But strangely enough, the wild geese seemed to feel the same aversion toward the rats that he did. They did not speak to them, and when they were gone, they shook themselves as if their feathers had been mud-spattered.

"Such a lot of gray rats abroad!" said Iksi from Vassijaure. "That's not a good omen."

The boy intended to take advantage of this opportunity to say to Akka that he thought she ought to let him go with them to Kullaberg, but he was prevented anew, for all of a sudden a big bird came down in the midst of the geese.

One could believe, when one looked at this bird, that he had borrowed body, neck and head from a little white goose. But in addition to this, he had procured for himself large black wings, long red legs, and a thick bill, which was too large for the little head, and weighed it down until it gave him a sad and worried look.

Akka at once straightened out the folds of her wings, and curtsied many times as she approached the stork. She wasn't especially surprised to see him in Skåne so early in the spring, because she knew that the male storks are in the habit of coming over in good season to take a look at the nest, and see that it hasn't been damaged during the winter, before the female storks go to the trouble of flying over the East Sea. But she wondered very much what it might signify that he sought her out, since storks prefer to associate with members of their own family.

"I can hardly believe that there is anything wrong with your house, Herr Erinenrich," said Akka.

It was apparent now that it is true what they say: a stork can seldom open his bill without complaining. But what made the thing he said sound even more doleful was that it was difficult for him to speak out. He stood for a long time and only clattered with his bill, afterward he spoke in a hoarse and feeble voice. He complained about everything: the nest—which was situated at the very top of the roof-tree at Glimminge castle—had been totally destroyed by winter storms, and no food could he get any more in Skåne. The people of Skåne were appropriating all his possessions. They dug out his marshes and laid waste his swamps. He intended to move away from this country, and never return to it again.

While the stork grumbled, Akka, the wild goose who had neither home nor protection, could not help thinking to herself, "If I had things as comfortable as you have, Herr Ermenrich, I should be above complaining. You have remained a free and wild bird, and still you stand so well with human beings that no one will fire a shot at you, or steal an egg from your nest." But all this she kept to herself. To the stork she only remarked that she couldn't believe he would be willing to move from a house where storks had resided ever since it was built.

Then the stork suddenly asked the geese if they had seen the gray rats who were marching toward Glimminge castle. When Akka replied that she had seen the horrid creatures, he began to tell her about the brave black rats who, for years, had defended the castle. "But this night Glimminge castle will fall into the gray rats' power," sighed the stork.

"And why just this night, Herr Ermenrich?" asked Akka.

"Well, because nearly all the black rats went over to Kullaberg last night," said the stork, "since they had counted on all the rest of the animals also hurrying there. But you see that the gray rats have stayed at home, and now they are mustering to storm the castle tonight, when it will be defended by only a few old creatures who are too feeble to go over to Kullaberg. They'll probably accomplish their purpose. But I have lived here in harmony with the black rats for so many years that it does not please me to live in a place inhabited by their enemies."

Akka understood now that the stork had become so enraged over the gray rats' mode of action that he had sought her out as an excuse to complain about them. But after the manner of storks, he certainly had done nothing to avert the disaster. "Have you sent word to the black rats, Herr Ermenrich?" she asked. "No," replied the stork. That wouldn't be of any use. Before they can get back, the castle will be taken." "You mustn't be so sure of that, Herr Erinenrich," said Akka. "I know an old wild goose, I do, who will gladly prevent outrages of this kind."

When Akka said this, the stork raised his head and stared at her. And it was not surprising, for Akka had neither claws nor bill that were fit for fighting, and, in the bargain, she was a day bird, and as soon as it grew dark she fell helplessly asleep, while the rats did their fighting.

But Akka had evidently made up her mind to help the black rats. She called Iksi from Vassijaure, and ordered him to take the wild geese over to Vomb Lake, and when the geese made excuses, she said authoritatively, "I believe it will be best for us all that you obey me. I must fly over to the big stone house, and if you follow me, the people on the place will be sure to see us, and shoot us down. The only one that I want to take with me on this trip is Thumbietot. He can be of great service to me because he has good eyes, and can keep awake at night."

The boy was in his most contrary mood that day. And when he heard what Akka said, he raised himself to his full height and stepped forward, his hands behind him and his nose in the air, and he intended to say that he, most assuredly, did not wish to take a hand in the fight with gray rats. She might look around for assistance elsewhere.

But the instant the boy was seen, the stork began to move. He had stood before, as storks generally stand, with head bent downward and the bill pressed against the neck. But now a gurgle was heard deep down in his windpipe, as though he would have laughed. Quick as a flash, he lowered the bill, grabbed the boy, and tossed him a couple of meters in the air. This feat he performed seven times, while the boy shrieked and the geese shouted, "What are you trying to do, Herr Ermenrich? That's not a frog. That's a human being, Herr Ermenrich."

Finally the stork put the boy down entirely unhurt. Thereupon he said to Akka, "I'll fly back to Glimminge castle now, Mother Akka. All who live there were very much worried when I left. You may be sure they'll be very glad when I tell them that Akka, the wild goose, and Thumbietot, the human elf, are on their way to rescue them." With that the stork craned his neck, raised his wings, and darted off like an arrow when it leaves a well-drawn bow. Akka understood that he was making fun of her, but she didn't let it bother her. She waited until the boy had found his wooden shoes, which the stork had shaken off, then she put him on her back and followed the stork. On his own account, the boy made no objection, and said not a word about not wanting to go along. He had become so furious with the stork that he actually sat and puffed. That long, red-legged thing believed he was of no account just because he was little, but he would show him what kind of a man Nils Holgersson from West Vemminghög was.

A couple of moments later Akka stood in the storks' nest at Glimminge castle. It was a fine, large nest. It had a wheel for foundation, and over this lay several grassmats, and some twigs. The nest was so old that many shrubs and plants had taken root up there, and when the mother stork sat on her eggs in the round hole in the middle of the nest, she not only had the beautiful outlook over a goodly portion of Skåne to enjoy, but she had also the wild brier blossoms and house leeks to look upon.

Both Akka and the boy saw immediately that something was going on here, which turned up and down—in the most regular order. On the edge of the stork nest sat two gray owls, an old, gray-streaked cat, and a dozen old, decrepit rats with protruding teeth and watery eyes. They were not exactly the sort of animals one usually finds living peaceably together.

Not one of them turned around to look at Akka, or to bid her welcome. They thought of nothing except to sit and stare at some long, gray lines, which came into sight here and there—on the winter-naked meadows.

All the black rats were silent. One could see that they were in deep despair, and probably knew that they could neither defend their own lives—or the castle. The two owls sat and rolled their big eyes, and twisted their great, encircling eyebrows, and talked in hollow, ghost-like voices, about the awful cruelty of the gray rats and that they would have to move away from their nest, because they had heard it said of them that they spared neither eggs nor baby birds. The old gray-streaked cat was positive that the gray rats would bite him to death, since they were coming into the castle in such great numbers, and he scolded the black rats incessantly. "How could you be so idiotic as to let your best fighters go away?" said he. "How could you trust the gray rats? It is absolutely unpardonable!"

The twelve black rats did not say a word. But the stork, despite his misery, could not refrain from teasing the cat. "Don't worry so, Monsie house-cat!" said he. "Can't you see that Mother Akka and Thumbietot have come to save the castle? You can be certain that they'll succeed. Now I must stand up to sleep—and I do so with the utmost calm. Tomorrow, when I awaken, there won't be a single gray rat in Glimminge castle."

The boy winked at Akka, and made a sign—as the stork stood upon the very edge of the nest, with one leg drawn up, to sleep—that he wanted to push him down to the ground, but Akka restrained him. She did not seem to be the least bit angry. Instead, she said in a confident tone of voice: "It would be pretty poor business if one who is as old as I am could not manage to get out of worse difficulties than this. If only Mr. and Mrs. Owl, who can stay awake all night, will fly off with a couple of messages for me, I think that all will go well."

Both owls were willing. Then Akka bade the gentleman owl that he should go and seek the black rats who had gone off, and counsel them to hurry home immediately. The lady owl he sent to Flammea, the steeple owl, who lived in Lund cathedral, with a commission which was so secret that Akka only dared to confide it to her in a whisper.

THE RAT CHARMER

*I*t was getting on toward midnight when the gray rats after a diligent search succeeded in finding an open air-hole in the cellar. This was pretty high upon the wall but the rats got up on one anothers' shoulders, and it wasn't long before the most daring among them sat in the air-hole, ready to force its way into Glimminge castle, outside whose walls so many of their forebears had fallen.

The gray rat sat still for a moment in the hole, and waited for an attack from within. The leader of the defenders was certainly away, but she assumed that the black rats who were still in the castle wouldn't surrender without a struggle. With thumping heart she listened for the slightest sound, but everything remained quiet. Then the leader of the gray rats plucked up courage and jumped down in the coal-black cellar.

One after another of the gray rats followed the leader. They all kept very quiet, and all expected to be ambushed by the black rats. Not until so many of them had crowded into the cellar that the floor couldn't hold any more, did they venture farther.

Although they had never before been inside the building, they had no difficulty in finding their way. They soon found the passages in the walls which the black rats had used to get to the upper floors. Before they began to clamber up these narrow and steep steps, they listened again with great attention. They felt more frightened because the black rats held themselves aloof in this way, than if they had met them in open battle. They could hardly believe their luck when they reached the first story without any mishaps.

Immediately upon their entrance the gray rats caught the scent of the grain, which was stored in great bins on the floor. But it was not as yet time for them to begin to enjoy their conquest. They searched first, with the utmost caution, through the somber, empty rooms. They ran up in the fireplace, which stood on the floor in the old castle kitchen, and they almost tumbled into the well, in the inner room. Not one of the narrow peepholes did they leave uninspected, but they found no black rats. When this floor was wholly in their possession, they began, with the same caution, to acquire the next. Then they had to venture on a bold and dangerous climb through the walls, while, with breathless anxiety, they awaited an assault from the enemy. And although they were tempted by the most delicious odor from the grain bins, they forced themselves most systematically to inspect the old-time warriors' pillar-propped kitchen, their stone table, and fireplace, the deep window niches, and the hole in the floor—which in olden time had been opened to pour down boiling pitch on the intruding enemy.

All this time the black rats were invisible. The gray ones groped their way to the third story, and into the lord of the castle's great banquet hall—which stood there cold and empty, like all the other rooms in the old house. They even groped their way to the upper story, which had but one big, barren room. The only place they did not think of exploring, was the big stork nest on the roof—where, just at this time, the lady owl awakened Akka, and informed her that Flammea, the steeple owl, had granted her request, and had sent her the thing she wished for.

Since the gray rats had so conscientiously inspected the entire castle, they felt at ease. They took it for granted that the black rats had flown, and didn't intend to offer any resistance, and, with light hearts, they ran up into the grain bins.

But the gray rats had hardly swallowed the first wheat grains, before the sound of a little shrill pipe was heard from the yard. The gray rats raised their heads, listened anxiously, ran a few steps as if they intended to leave the bin, then they turned back and began to eat once more.

Again the pipe sounded a sharp and piercing note—and now something wonderful happened. One rat, two rats—yes, a whole lot of rats left the grain, jumped from the bins and hurried down to the cellar by the shortest cut, to get out of the house. Still there were many gray rats left. These thought of all the toil and trouble it had cost them to win Glimminge castle, and they did not want to leave it. But again they caught the tones from the pipe, and had to follow them. With wild excitement they rushed up from the bins, slid down through the narrow holes in the walls, and tumbled over each other in their eagerness to get out.

In the middle of the courtyard stood a tiny creature, who blew upon a pipe. All round him he had a whole circle of rats who listened to him, astonished and fascinated, and every moment brought more. Once he took the pipe from his lips—only for a second—put his thumb to his nose and wiggled his fingers at the gray rats, and then it looked as if they wanted to throw themselves on him and bite him to death, but as soon as he blew on his pipe they were in his power.

When the tiny creature had played all the gray rats out of Glimminge castle, he began to wander slowly from the courtyard out on the highway, and all the gray rats followed him, because the tones from that pipe sounded so sweet to their ears that they could not resist them.

The tiny creature walked before them and charmed them along with him, on the road to Vallby. He led them into all sorts of crooks and turns and bends—on through hedges and down into ditches—and wherever he went they had to follow. He blew continuously on his pipe, which appeared to be made from an animal's horn, although the horn was so small that, in our days, there were no animals from whose foreheads it could have been broken. No one knew, either, who had made it. Flammea, the steeple owl, had found it in a niche, in Lund cathedral. She had shown it to Bataki, the raven, and they had both figured out that this was the kind of horn that was used in former times by those who wished to gain power over rats and mice. But the raven was Akka's friend, and it was from him she had learned that Flammea owned a treasure like this.

And it was true that the rats could not resist the pipe. The boy walked before them and played as long as the starlight lasted—and all the while they followed him. He played at daybreak; he played at sunrise, and the whole time the entire procession of gray rats followed him and were enticed farther and farther away from the big grain loft at Glimminge castle.

V
THE GREAT CRANE
DANCE ON KULLABERG

Tuesday, March twenty-ninth

Although there are many magnificent buildings in Skåne, it must be acknowledged that there's not one among them that has such pretty walls as old Kullaberg.

Kullaberg is low and rather long. It is not by any means a big or imposing mountain. On its broad summit you'll find woods and grain fields, and one and another heather heath. Here and there round heather knolls and barren cliffs rise up. It is not especially pretty up there. It looks a good deal like all the other upland places in Skåne.

He who walks along the path which runs across the middle of the mountain, can't help feeling a little disappointed. Then he happens, perhaps, to turn away from the path, and wanders off toward the mountain's sides and looks down over the bluffs, and then, all at once, he will discover so much that is worth seeing, he hardly knows how he'll find time to take in the whole of it. For it happens that Kullaberg does not stand on the land, with plains and valleys around it, like other mountains, but it has plunged into the sea, as far out as it could get. Not even the tiniest strip of land lies below the mountain to protect it against the breakers, but these reach all the way up to the mountain walls, and can polish and mould them to suit themselves. This is why the walls stand there as richly ornamented as the sea and its helpmate, the wind, have been able to effect. You'll find steep ravines that are deeply chiseled in the mountain's sides, and black crags that have become smooth and shiny under the constant lashing of the winds. There are solitary rock columns that spring right up out of the water, and dark grottoes with narrow entrances. There are barren, perpendicular precipices, and soft, leaf-clad inclines. There are small points, and small inlets, and small rolling stones that rattlingly washed up and down with every dashing breaker. There are majestic cliff arches that project over the water. There are sharp stones that are constantly sprayed by a white foam, and others that mirror themselves in unchangeable dark green still water. There are giant troll caverns shaped in the rock, and great crevices that lure the wanderer to venture into the mountain's depths—all the way to Kullman's Hollow.

And over and around all these cliffs and rocks crawl entangled tendrils and weeds. Trees grow there also, but the wind's power is so great that trees have to transform themselves into clinging vines, that they may get a firm hold on the steep precipices. The oaks creep along on the ground, while their foliage hangs over them like a low ceiling, and long-limbed beeches stand in the ravines like great leaf tents.

These remarkable mountain walls, with the blue sea beneath them, and the clear penetrating air above them, is what makes Kullaberg so dear to the people that great crowds of them haunt the place every day as long as the summer lasts. But it is more difficult to tell what it is that makes it so attractive to animals that every year they gather there for a big play meeting. This is a custom that has been observed since time immemorial, and one should have been there when the first sea wave was dashed into foam against the shore, to be able to explain why just Kullaberg was chosen as a rendezvous, in preference to all other places.

When the meeting is to take place, the stags and roebucks and hares and foxes and all the other four-footers make the journey to Kullaberg the night before, so as not to be observed by the human beings. Just before sunrise they all march up to the playground, which is a heather heath on the left side of the road, and not very far from the mountain's most extreme point. The playground is inclosed on all sides by round knolls, which conceal it from any and all who do not happen to come right upon it. And in the month of March it is not at all likely that any pedestrians will stray off up there. All the strangers who usually stroll around on the rocks, and clamber up the mountain's sides the fall storms have driven away these many months past. And the lighthouse keeper out there on the point, the old matron on the mountain farm, and the mountain peasant and his housefolk go their accustomed ways, and do not run about on the desolate heather fields.

When the four-footers have arrived on the playground, they take their places on the round knolls. Each animal family keeps to itself, although it is understood that, on a day like this, universal peace reigns, and no one need fear attack. On this day a little hare might wander over to the foxes' hill, without losing as much as one of his long ears. But still the animals arrange themselves into separate groups. This is an old custom.

After they have all taken their places, they begin to look around for the birds. It is always beautiful weather on this day. The cranes are good weather prophets, and would not call the animals together if they expected rain. Although the air is clear, and nothing obstructs the vision, the four-footers see no birds. This is strange. The sun stands high in the heavens, and the birds should already be on their way.

But what the animals, on the other hand, observe, is one and another little dark cloud that comes slowly forward over the plain. And look! one of these clouds comes gradually along the coast of Öresund, and up toward Kullaberg. When the cloud has come just over the playground it stops, and, simultaneously, the entire cloud begins to ring and chirp, as if it were made of nothing but tone. It rises and sinks, rises and sinks, but all the while it rings and chirps. At last the whole cloud falls down over a knoll—all at once—and the next instant the knoll is entirely covered with gray larks, pretty red-white-gray bullfinches, speckled starlings and greenish yellow titmice.

Soon after that, another cloud comes over the plain. This stops over every bit of land, over peasant cottage and palace, over towns and cities, over farms and railway stations, over fishing hamlets and sugar refineries. Every time it stops, it draws to itself a little whirling column of gray dust grains from the ground. In this way it grows and grows. And at last, when it is all gathered up and heads for Kullaberg it is no longer a cloud but a whole mist, which is so big that it throws a shadow on the ground all the way from Höganäs to Mölle. When it stops over the playground it hides the sun, and for a long while it had to rain gray sparrows on one of the knolls, before those who had been flying in the innermost part of the mist could again catch a glimpse of the daylight.

But still the biggest of these bird clouds is the one which now appears. This has been formed of birds who have traveled from every direction to join it. It is dark bluish gray, and no sun ray can penetrate it. It is full of the ghastliest noises, the most frightful shrieks, the grimmest laughter, and most ill-luck-boding croaking! All on the playground are glad when it finally resolves itself into a storm of fluttering and croaking crows and jackdaws and rooks and ravens.

Thereupon not only clouds are seen in the heavens, but a variety of stripes and figures. Then straight, dotted lines appear in the east and northeast. These are forest birds from the Göinge districts: black grouse and wood grouse who come flying in long lines a couple of meters apart. Swimming birds that live around Måkläppen, just out of Falsterbo, now come floating over Öresund in many extraordinary figures: in triangular and long curves, in sharp hooks and semicircles.

To the great reunion held the year that Nils Holgersson traveled around with the wild geese, came Akka and her flock—later than all the others. And that was not to be wondered at, for Akka had to fly over the whole of Skåne to get to Kullaberg. Beside, as soon as she awoke, she had been obliged to go out and hunt for Thumbietot, who, for many hours, had gone and played to the gray rats, and lured them far away from Glimminge castle. Mr. Owl had returned with the news that the black rats would be at home immediately after sunrise, and there was no longer any danger in letting the steeple owl's pipe be hushed, and to give the gray rats the liberty to go where they pleased.

But it was not Akka who discovered the boy where he walked with his long following, and quickly sank down over him and caught him with the bill and swung into the air with him, but it was Herr Errnenrich, the stork! For Herr Erinenrich had also gone out to look for him, and after he had borne him up to the stork nest, he begged his forgiveness for having treated him with disrespect the evening before.

This pleased the boy immensely, and the stork and he became good friends. Akka, too, showed him that she felt very kindly toward him; she stroked her old head several times against his arms, and commended him because he had helped those who were in trouble.

But this one must say to the boy's credit: that he did not want to accept praise which he had not earned. "No, Mother Akka," he said, "you mustn't think that I lured the gray rats away to help the black ones. I only wanted to show Herr Ermenrich that I was of some consequence."

He had hardly said this before Akka turned to the stork and asked if he thought it was advisable to take Thumbietot along to Kullaberg. "I mean, that we can rely on him as upon ourselves," said she. The stork at once advised, most enthusiastically, that Thumbietot be permitted to come along. "Certainly you shall take Thumbietot along to Kullaberg, Mother Akka," said he. "It is fortunate for us that we can repay him for all that he has endured this night for our sakes. And since it still grieves me to think that I did not conduct myself in a becoming manner toward him the other evening, it is I who will carry him on my back—all the way to the meeting place."

There isn't much that tastes better than to receive praise from those who are themselves wise and capable, and the boy had certainly never felt so happy as he did when the wild goose and the stork talked about him in this way.

Thus the boy made the trip to Kullaberg riding stork-back. Although he knew that this was a great honor, it caused him much anxiety, for Herr Ermenrich was a master flyer, and started off at a very different pace from the wild geese. While Akka flew her straight way with even wing strokes, the stork amused himself by performing a lot of flying tricks. Now he lay still in an immeasurable height, and floated in the air without moving his wings, now he flung himself downward with such sudden haste that it seemed as though he would fall to the ground, helpless as a stone, now he had lots of fun flying all around Akka, in great and small circles, like a whirlwind. The boy had never been on a ride of this sort before, and although he sat there all the while in terror, he had to acknowledge to himself that he had never before known what a good flight meant.

Only a single pause was made during the journey, and that was at Vomb Lake when Akka joined her traveling companions, and called to them that the gray rats had been vanquished. After that, the travelers flew straight to Kullaberg.

There they descended to the knoll reserved for the wild geese, and as the boy let his glance wander from knoll to knoll, he saw on one of them the many-pointed antlers of the stags, and on another, the gray herons' neck-crests. One knoll was red with foxes, one was gray with rats, one was covered with black ravens who shrieked continually, one with larks who simply couldn't keep still, but kept on throwing themselves in the air and singing for very joy.

Just as it has ever been the custom on Kullaberg, it was the crows who began the day's games and frolics with their flying dance. They divided themselves into two flocks, that flew toward each other, met, turned, and began all over again. This dance had many repetitions, and appeared to the spectators who were not familiar with the dance as altogether too monotonous. The crows were very proud of their dance, but all the others were glad when it was over. It appeared to the animals about as gloomy and meaningless as the winter storm's play with the snowflakes. It depressed them to watch it, and they waited eagerly for something that should give them a little pleasure.

They did not have to wait in vain, either, for as soon as the crows had finished, the hares came running. They dashed forward in a long row, without any apparent order. In some of the figures, one single hare came; in others, they ran three and four abreast. They had all raised themselves on two legs, and they rushed forward with such rapidity that their long ears swayed in all directions. As they ran, they spun round, made high leaps and beat their forepaws against their hind paws so that they rattled. Some performed a long succession of somersaults, others doubled themselves up and rolled over like wheels; one stood on one leg and swung round; one walked upon his forepaws. There was no regulation whatever, but there was much that was droll in the hares' play, and the many animals who stood and watched them began to breathe faster. Now it was spring; joy and rapture were advancing. Winter was over; summer was coming. Soon it was only play to live.

When the hares had romped themselves out, it was the great forest birds' turn to perform. Hundreds of wood grouse in shining dark brown array, and with bright red eyebrows, flung themselves up into a great oak that stood in the center of the playground. The one who sat upon the topmost branch fluffed up his feathers, lowered his wings, and lifted his tail so that the white covert feathers were seen. Thereupon he stretched his neck and sent forth a couple of deep notes from his thick throat. "Tjack, tjack, tjack," it sounded. More than this he could not utter. It only gurgled a few times way down in the throat. Then he closed his eyes and whispered, "Sis, sis, sis. Hear how pretty! Sis, sis, sis." At the same time he fell into such an ecstasy that he no longer knew what was going on around him.

While the first wood grouse was sissing, the three nearest under him began to sing, and before they had finished their song, the ten who sat lower down joined in, and thus it continued from branch to branch, until the entire hundred grouse sang and gurgled and sissed. They all fell into the same ecstasy during their song, and this affected the other animals like a contagious transport. Lately the blood had flowed lightly and agreeably; now it began to grow heavy and hot. "Yes, this is surely spring," thought all the animal folk. "Winter chill has vanished. The fires of spring burn over the earth."

When the black grouse saw that the brown grouse were having such success, they could no longer keep quiet. As there was no tree for them to light on, they rushed down on the playground, where the heather stood so high that only their beautifully turned tailfeathers and their thick bills were visible and they began to sing, "Orr, orr, orr."

Just as the black grouse began to compete with the brown grouse, something unprecedented happened. While all the animals thought of nothing but the grouse game, a fox stole slowly over to the wild geese's knoll. He glided very cautiously, and came way up on the knoll before anyone noticed him. Suddenly a goose caught sight of him, and as she could not believe that a fox had sneaked in among the geese for any good purpose, she began to cry, "Have a care, wild geese! Have a care!" The fox struck her across the throat—mostly, perhaps, because he wanted to make her keep quiet—but the wild geese had already heard the cry and they all raised themselves in the air. And when they had flown up, the animals saw Smirre Fox standing on the wild geese's knoll, with a dead goose in his mouth.

But because he had in this way broken the play-day's peace, such a punishment was meted out to Smirre Fox that, for the rest of his days, he must regret he had not been able to control his thirst for revenge, but had attempted to approach Akka and her flock in this manner.

He was immediately surrounded by a crowd of foxes, and doomed in accordance with an old custom, which demands that whosoever disturbs the peace on the great play-day, must go into exile. Not a fox wished to lighten the sentence, since they all knew that the instant they attempted anything of the sort, they would be driven from the playground, and would nevermore be permitted to enter it. Banishment was pronounced upon Smirre without opposition. He was forbidden to remain in Skåne. He was banished from wilde and kindred, from hunting grounds, home, resting places and retreats, which he had hitherto owned, and he must tempt fortune in foreign lands. So that all foxes in Skåne should know that Smirre was outlawed in the district, the oldest of the foxes bit off his right earlap. As soon as this was done, all the young foxes began to yowl from blood-thirst, and threw themselves on Smirre. For him there was no alternative except to take flight, and with all the young foxes in hot pursuit, he rushed away from Kullaberg.

All this happened while black grouse and brown grouse were going on with their games. But these birds lose themselves so completely in their song, that they neither hear nor see. Nor had they permitted themselves to be disturbed.

The forest birds' contest was barely over before the stags from Häckeberga came forward to show their wrestling game. There were several pairs of stags who fought at the same time. They rushed at each other with tremendous force, struck their antlers clashingly together, so that their points were entangled, and tried to force each other backward. The heather heaths were torn up beneath their hoofs; the breath came like smoke from their nostrils; out of their throats strained hideous bellowings, and the froth oozed down on their shoulders.

On the knolls round about there was breathless silence while the skilled stag-wrestlers clinched. In all the animals new emotions were awakened. Each and all felt courageous and strong, enlivened by returning powers, born again with the spring, sprightly, and ready for all kinds of adventures. They felt no enmity toward each other, although, everywhere, wings were lifted, neck feathers raised, and claws sharpened. If the stags from Häckeberga had continued another instant, a wild struggle would have arisen on the knolls, for all had been gripped with a burning desire to show that they too were full of life because the winter's impotence was over and strength surged through their bodies.

But the stags stopped wrestling just at the right moment, and instantly a whisper went from knoll to knoll: "They are coming!"

And then came the gray, dusk-clad birds with plumes in their wings, and red feather ornaments on their necks. The big birds with their tall legs, their slender throats, their small heads, came gliding down the knoll with an abandon that was full of mystery. As they glided forward they swung round—half flying, half dancing. With wings gracefully lifted, they moved with an inconceivable rapidity. There was something marvelous and strange about their dance. It was as though gray shadows had played a game which the eye could scarcely follow. It was as if they had learned it from the mists that hover over desolate morasses. There was witchcraft in it. All those who had never before been on Kullberg understood why the whole meeting took its name from the crane's dance. There was wildness in it, but yet the feeling which it awakened was a delicious longing. No one thought any more about struggling. Instead, both the winged and those who had no wings, all wanted to raise themselves eternally, lift themselves above the clouds, seek that which was hidden beyond them, leave the oppressive body that dragged them down to earth and soar away toward the infinite.

Such longing after the unattainable, after the hidden mysteries back of this life, the animals felt only once a year, and this was on the day when they beheld the great crane dance.

VI

IN RAINY WEATHER

Wednesday, March thirtieth

*I*t was the first rainy day of the trip. As long as the wild geese had remained in the vicinity of Vomb Lake, they had had beautiful weather, but on the day when they set out to travel farther north, it began to rain, and for several hours the boy had to sit on the goose-back, soaking wet, and shivering with the cold.

In the morning when they started, it had been clear and mild. The wild geese had flown high up in the air—evenly, and without haste—with Akka at the head maintaining strict discipline, and the rest in two oblique lines back of her. They had not taken the time to shout any witty sarcasms to the animals on the ground, but, as it was simply impossible for them to keep perfectly silent, they sang out continually—in rhythm with the wing strokes—their usual coaxing call: "Where are you? Here am I. Where are you? Here am I."

They all took part in this persistent calling, and only stopped, now and then, to show the goosey-gander the landmarks they were traveling over. The places on this route included Linderödsosen's dry hills, Ovesholm's manor, Christianstad's church steeple, Bäckaskog's royal castle on the narrow isthmus between Oppmann's lake and Ivös lake, and Ryss mountain's steep precipice.

It had been a monotonous trip, and when the rain clouds made their appearance the boy thought it was a real diversion. In the old days, when he had only seen a rain cloud from below, he had imagined that they were gray and disagreeable, but it was a very different thing to be up amongst them. Now he saw distinctly that the clouds were enormous carts, which drove through the heavens with sky-high loads. Some of them were piled up with huge, gray sacks, some with barrels; some were so large that they could hold a whole lake, and a few were filled with big utensils and bottles which were piled up to an immense height. And when so many of them had driven forward that they filled the whole sky, it appeared as though someone had given a signal, for all at once, water commenced to pour down over the earth, from utensils, barrels, bottles, and sacks.

Just as the first spring showers pattered against the ground, there arose such shouts of joy from all the small birds in groves and pastures, that the whole air rang with them and the boy leaped high where he sat. "Now we'll have rain. Rain gives us spring; spring gives us flowers and green leaves; green leaves and flowers give us worms and insects; worms and insects give us food, and plentiful, and good food is the best thing there is," sang the birds.

The wild geese, too, were glad of the rain which came to awaken the growing things from their long sleep, and to drive holes in the ice roofs on the lakes. They were not able to keep up that seriousness any longer, but began to send merry calls over the neighborhood.

When they flew over the big potato patches, which are so plentiful in the country around Christianstad—and which still lay bare and black—they screamed, "Wake up and be useful! Here comes something that will awaken you. You have idled long enough now."

When they saw people who hurried to get out of the rain, they reproved them, saying: "What are you in such a hurry about? Can't you see that it's raining rye loaves and cookies?"

It was a big, thick mist that moved northward briskly, and followed close upon the geese. They seemed to think that they dragged the mist along with them, and, just now, when they saw great orchards beneath them, they called out proudly: "Here we come with anemones; here we come with roses; here we come with apple blossoms and cherry buds; here we come with peas and beans and turnips and cabbages. He who wills can take them. He who wills can take them."

Thus it had sounded while the first shower fell, and when all were still glad of the rain. But when it continued to fall the whole afternoon, the wild geese grew impatient, and cried to the thirsty forests around Ivös Lake, "Haven't you got enough yet? Haven't you got enough yet?"

The heavens were growing grayer and grayer and the sun hid itself so well that one couldn't imagine where it was. The rain fell faster and faster, and beat harder and harder against the wings, as it tried to find its way between the oily outside feathers, into their skins. The earth was hidden by fogs. Lakes, mountains, and woods floated together in an indistinct maze, and the landmarks could not be distinguished. The flight became slower and slower; the joyful cries were hushed, and the boy felt the cold more and more keenly.

But still he had kept up his courage as long as he had ridden through the air. And in the afternoon, when they had lighted under little stunted pine, in the middle of a large morass, where all was wet, and all was cold, where some knolls were covered with snow, and others stood up naked in a puddle of half-melted ice water, even then he had not felt discouraged, but ran about in fine spirits, and hunted for cranberries and frozen whortle berries. But then came evening, and darkness sank down on them so close that not even such eyes as the boy's could see through it, and all the wilderness became so strangely grim and awful. The boy lay tucked in under the goosey-gander's wing, but could not sleep because he was cold and wet. He heard such a lot of rustling and rattling and stealthy steps and menacing voices, that he was terror-stricken and didn't know where he should go. He must go somewhere, where there was light and heat, if he wasn't going to be entirely scared to death.

"If I should venture where there are human beings, just for this night," thought the boy, "I could sit by a fire for a moment, and get a little food. I could go back to the wild geese before sunrise."

He crept from under the wing and slid down to the ground. He did not awaken either the goosey-gander or any of the other geese, but stole, silently and unobserved, through the morass.

He didn't know exactly where on earth he was: if he was in Skåne, in Srnåland, or in Blekinge. But just before he had gotten down in the morass, he had caught a glimpse of a large village, and thither he directed his steps. It wasn't long, either, before he discovered a road, and soon he was on the village street, which was long, and had planted trees on both sides, and was bordered with garden after garden.

The boy had come to one of the big cathedral towns, which are so common on the uplands, but can hardly be seen at all down in the plain.

The houses were of wood, and very prettily constructed. Most of them had gables and fronts, edged with carved moldings and glass doors, with here and there a colored pane, opening on a veranda. The walls were painted in light oil colors; the doors and window frames shone in blues and greens, and even in reds. While the boy walked about and viewed the houses, he could hear, all the way out to the road, how the people who sat in the warm cottages chattered and laughed. The words he could not distinguish, but he thought it was just lovely to hear human voices. "I wonder what they would say if I knocked and begged to be let in," thought he.

This was, of course, what he had intended to do all along, but now that he saw the lighted windows, his fear of the darkness was gone. Instead, he felt again that shyness which always came over him now when he was near human beings. "I'll take a look around the town for a while longer," thought he, "before I ask anyone to take me in."

On one house there was a balcony. And just as the boy walked by, the doors were thrown open, and a yellow light streamed through the fine, sheer curtains. Then a pretty young woman came out on the balcony and leaned over the railing. "It's raining now. We shall soon have spring," said she. When the boy saw her he felt a strange anxiety. It was as though he wanted to weep. For the first time he was a bit uneasy because he had shut himself out from the human kind.

Shortly after that he walked by a shop. Outside the shop stood a red corn-drill. He stopped and looked at it, and finally crawled up to the driver's place, and seated himself. When he had got there, he smacked with his lips and pretended that he sat and drove. He thought what fun it would be to be permitted to drive such a pretty machine over a grainfield. For a moment he forgot what he was like now, then he remembered it, and jumped down quickly from the machine. Then a greater unrest came over him. After all, human beings were very wonderful and clever.

He walked by the post office, and then he thought of all the newspapers which came every day, with news from all the four corners of the earth. He saw the apothecary's shop and the doctor's home, and he thought about the power of human beings, which was so great that they were able to battle with sickness and death. He came to the church. Then he thought how human beings had built it, that they might hear about another world than the one in which they lived, of God and the resurrection and eternal life. And the longer he walked there, the better he liked human beings.

It is so with children that they never think any farther ahead than the length of their noses. That which lies nearest them, they want promptly, without caring what it may cost them. Nils Holgersson had not understood what he was losing when he chose to remain an elf, but now he began to be dreadfully afraid that, perhaps, he should never again get back his right form.

How in all the world should he go to work in order to become human? This he wanted, oh! so much, to know.

He crawled up on a doorstep, and seated himself in the pouring rain and meditated. He sat there one whole hour—two whole hours, and he thought so hard that his forehead lay in furrows, but he was none the wiser. It seemed as though the thoughts only rolled round and round in his head. The longer he sat there, the more impossible it seemed to him to find any solution.

"This thing is certainly much too difficult for one who has learned as little as I have," he thought at last. "It will probably wind up by my having to go back among human beings after all. I must ask the minister and the doctor and the schoolmaster and others who are learned, and may know a cure for such things."

This he concluded that he would do at once, and shook himself—for he was as wet as a dog that has been in a water pool.

Just about then he saw that a big owl came flying along, and alighted on one of the trees that bordered the village street. The next instant a lady owl, who sat under the cornice of the house, began to call out, "Kivitt, Kivitt! Are you at home again, Mr. Gray Owl? What kind of a time did you have abroad?"

"Thank you, Lady Brown Owl. I had a very comfortable time," said the gray owl. "Has anything out of the ordinary happened here at home during my absence?"

"Not here in Blekinge, Mr. Gray Owl, but in Skåne a marvelous thing has happened! A boy has been transformed by an elf into a goblin no bigger than a squirrel, and since he has gone to Lapland with a tame goose."

"That's a remarkable bit of news, a remarkable bit of news. Can he never be human again, Lady Brown Owl? Can he never be human again?"

"That's a secret, Mr. Gray Owl, but you shall hear it just the same. The elf has said that if the boy watches over the goosey-gander, so that he comes home safe and sound, and...."

"What more Lady Brown Owl? What more? What more?"

"Fly with me up to the church tower, Mr. Gray Owl, and you shall hear the whole story! I fear there may be someone down here in the street."

With that, the owls flew their way, but the boy flung his cap in the air, and shouted, "If I only watch over the goosey-gander, so that he gets back safe and sound, then I shall become a human being again, Hurrah! Hurrah! Then I shall become a human being again!"

He shouted "hurrah" until it was strange that they did not hear him in the houses, but they didn't, and he hurried back to the wild geese, out in the wet morass, as fast as his legs could carry him.

VII

THE STAIRWAY
WITH THE THREE STEPS

Thursday, March thirty-first

The following day the wild geese intended to travel northward through Allbo district, in Småland. They sent Iksi and Kaksi to spy out the land. But when they returned, they said that all the water was frozen, and all the land was snow-covered.

"We may as well remain where we are," said the wild geese. "We cannot travel over a country where there is neither water nor food." "If we remain where we are, we may have to wait here until the next moon," said Akka. "It is better to go eastward, through Blekinge, and see if we can't get to Småland by way of Möre, which lies near the coast, and has an early spring."

Thus the boy came to ride over Blekinge the next day. Now, that it was light again, he was in a merry mood once more, and could not comprehend what had come over him the night before. He certainly didn't want to give up the journey and the outdoor life now.

There lay a thick fog over Blekinge. The boy couldn't see how it looked out there. "I wonder if it is a good, or a poor country that I'm riding over," thought he, and tried to search his memory for the things which he had heard about the country at school. But at the same time he knew well enough that this was useless, as he had never been in the habit of studying his lessons.

At once the boy saw the whole school before him. The children sat by the little desks and raised their hands; the teacher sat in the lectern and looked displeased, and he himself stood before the map and should answer some question about Blekinge, but he hadn't a word to say. The schoolmaster's face grew darker and darker for every second that passed, and the boy thought the teacher was more particular that they should know their geography, than anything else. Now he came down from the lectern, took the pointer from the boy, and sent him back to his seat. "This won't end well," the boy thought then.

But the schoolmaster had gone over to a window, and had stood there for a moment and then he had whistled to himself once. Then he had gone up into the lectern and said that he would tell them something about Blekinge. And that which he then talked about had been so amusing that the boy had listened. When he only stopped and thought for a moment, he remembered every word:

"Småland is a tall house with spruce trees on the roof," said the teacher, "and leading up to it is a broad stairway with three big steps, and this stairway is called Blekinge. It is a stairway that is well-constructed. It stretches forty-two miles along the frontage of Småland house, and anyone who wishes to go all the way down to the East Sea, by way of the stairs, has twenty-four miles to wander.

"A good long time must have elapsed since the stairway was built. Both days and years have gone by since the steps were hewn from gray stones and laid down—evenly and smoothly—for a convenient track between Småland and the East Sea.

"Since the stairway is so old, one can, of course, understand that it doesn't look just the same now, as it did when it was new. I don't know how much they troubled themselves about such matters at that time, but big as it was, no broom could have kept it clean. After a couple of years, moss and lichen began to grow on it. In the autumn dry leaves and dry grass blew down over it, and in the spring it was piled up with falling stones and gravel. And as all these things were left there to mold, they finally gathered so much soil on the steps that not only herbs and grass, but even bushes and trees could take root there.

"But, at the same time, a great disparity has arisen between the three steps. The topmost step, which lies nearest Småland, is mostly covered with poor soil and small stones, and no trees except birches and birdcherry and spruce—which can stand the cold on the heights, and are satisfied with little—can thrive up there. One understands best how poor and dry it is there, when one sees how small the field plots are, that are plowed up from the forest lands, and how many little cabins the people build for themselves, and how far it is between the churches. But on the middle step there is better soil, and it does not lie bound down under such severe cold, either. This one can see at a glance, since the trees are both higher and of finer quality. There you'll find maple and oak and linden and weeping birch and hazel trees growing, but no cone-trees to speak of. And it is still more noticeable because of the amount of cultivated land that you will find there, and also because the people have built themselves great and beautiful houses. On the middle step, there are many churches, with large towns around them, and in every way it makes a better and finer appearance than the top step.

"But the very lowest step is the best of all. It is covered with good rich soil, and, where it lies and bathes in the sea, it hasn't the slightest feeling of the Småland chill. Beeches and chestnut and walnut trees thrive down here, and they grow so big that they tower above the church roofs. Here lie also the largest grain fields, but the people have not only timber and farming to live upon, but they are also occupied with fishing and trading and seafaring. For this reason you will find the most costly residences and the prettiest churches here, and the parishes have developed into villages and cities.

"But this is not all that is said of the three steps. For one must realize that when it rains on the roof of the big Småland house, or when the snow melts up there, the water has to go somewhere, and then, naturally, a lot of it is spilled over the big stairway. In the beginning it probably oozed over the whole stairway, big as it was, then cracks appeared in it, and, gradually, the water has accustomed itself to flow alongside of it, in well-dug grooves. And water is water, whatever one does with it. It never has any rest. In one place it cuts and files away, and in another it adds to. Those grooves it has dug into vales, and the walls of the vales it has decked with soil, and bushes and trees and vines have clung to them ever since—so thick, and in such profusion that they almost hide the stream of water that winds its way down there in the deep. But when the streams come to the landings between the steps, they throw themselves headlong over them; this is why the water comes with such a seething rush that it gathers strength with which to move mill-wheels and machinery—these, too, have sprung up by every waterfall.

"But this does not tell all that is said of the land with the three steps. It must also be told that up in the big house in Småland there lived once upon a time a giant, who had grown very old. And it fatigued him in extreme age to be forced to walk down that long stairway in order to catch salmon from the sea. To him it seemed much more suitable that the salmon should come up to him, where he lived.

"Therefore, he went up on the roof of his great house, and there he stood and threw stones down into the East Sea. He threw them with such force that they flew over the whole of Blekinge and dropped into the sea. And when the stones came down, the salmon got so scared that they came up from the sea and fled toward the Blekinge streams, ran through the rapids, flung themselves with high leaps over the waterfalls, and stopped.

"How true this is, one can see by the number of islands and points that lie along the coast of Blekinge, and which are nothing in the world but the big stones that the giant threw.

"One can also tell because the salmon always go up in the Blekinge streams and work their way up through rapids and still water, all the way to Småland.

"That giant is worthy of great thanks and much honor from the Blekinge people, for salmon in the streams, and stone-cutting on the island —that means work which gives food to many of them even to this day."

VIII

BY RONNEBY RIVER

Friday, April first

Neither the wild geese nor Smirre Fox had believed that they should ever run across each other after they had left Skåne. But now it turned out that the wild geese happened to take the route over Blekinge and thither Smirre Fox had also gone.

So far he had kept himself in the northern parts of the province, and since he had not as yet seen any manor parks, or hunting grounds filled with game and dainty young deer, he was more disgruntled than he could say.

One afternoon, when Smirre tramped around in the desolate forest district of Mellanbygden, not far from Ronneby River, he saw a flock of wild geese fly through the air. Instantly he observed that one of the geese was white and then he knew, of course, with whom he had to deal.

Smirre began immediately to hunt the geese—just as much for the pleasure of getting a good square meal as for the desire to be avenged for all the humiliation that they had heaped upon him. He saw that they flew eastward until they came to Ronneby River. Then they changed their course, and followed the river toward the south. He understood that they intended to seek a sleeping place along the riverbank, and he thought that he should be able to get hold of a pair of them without much trouble. But when Smirre finally discovered the place where the wild geese had taken refuge, he observed they had chosen such a well-protected spot, that he couldn't get near them.

Ronneby River isn't any big or important body of water, nevertheless, it is just as much talked of, for the sake of its pretty shores. At several points it forces its way forward between steep mountain walls that stand upright out of the water, and are entirely overgrown with honeysuckle and bird cherry, mountain ash and osier, and there isn't much that can be more delightful than to row out on the little dark river on a pleasant summer day, and look upward on all the soft green that fastens itself to the rugged mountainsides.

But now, when the wild geese and Smirre came to the river, it was cold and blustery spring-winter. All the trees were nude, and there was probably no one who thought the least little bit about whether the shore was ugly or pretty. The wild geese thanked their good fortune that they had found a sand-strip large enough for them to stand upon, on a steep mountain wall. In front of them rushed the river, which was strong and violent in the snow-melting time; behind them they had an impassable mountain rock wall, and overhanging branches screened them. They couldn't have it better.

The geese were asleep instantly, but the boy couldn't get a wink of sleep. As soon as the sun had disappeared he was seized with a fear of the darkness, and a wilderness terror, and he longed for human beings. Where he lay—tucked in under the goose wing—he could see nothing, and only hear a little, and he thought if any harm came to the goosey-gander, he couldn't save him.

Noises and rustlings were heard from all directions, and he grew so uneasy that he had to creep from under the wing and seat himself on the ground, beside the goose.

Long-sighted Smirre stood on the mountain's summit and looked down upon the wild geese. "You may as well give this pursuit up first as last," he said to himself. "You can't climb such a steep mountain; you can't swim in such a wild torrent, and there isn't the tiniest strip of land below the mountain which leads to the sleeping place. Those geese are too wise for you. Don't ever bother yourself again to hunt them!"

But Smirre, like all foxes, had found it hard to give up an under-taking already begun, and so he lay down on the extremest point of the mountain edge, and did not take his eyes off the wild geese. While he lay and watched them, he thought of all the harm they had done him. Yes, it was their fault that he had been driven from Skåne, and had been obliged to move to poverty-stricken Blekinge. He worked himself up to such a pitch, as he lay there, that he wished they were dead, even if he himself should not have the satisfaction of eating them.

When Smirre's resentment had reached this height, he heard rasp-ing in a large pine that grew close to him, and saw a squirrel come down from the tree, hotly pursued by a marten. Neither of them noticed Smirre, and he sat quietly and watched the chase, which went from tree to tree. He looked at the squirrel, who moved among the branches as lightly as though he'd been able to fly. He looked at the marten, who was not as skilled at climbing as the squirrel, but who still ran up and along the branches just as securely as if they had been even paths in the forest. "If I could only climb half as well as either of them," thought the fox, "those things down there wouldn't sleep in peace very long!"

As soon as the squirrel had been captured, and the chase was at an end, Smirre walked over to the marten, but stopped two steps away from him, to signify that he did not wish to cheat him of his prey. He greeted the marten in a very friendly manner, and wished him good luck with his catch. Smirre chose his words well—as foxes always do. The marten, on the contrary, who, with his long and slender body, his fine head, his soft skin, and his light brown neck-piece, looked like a little marvel of beauty but in reality was nothing but a crude forest dweller, hardly answered him. "It surprises me," said Smirre, "that such a fine hunter as you should be satisfied with chasing squirrels when there is much better game within reach." Here he paused, but when the marten only grinned impudently at him, he continued, "Can it be possible that you haven't seen the wild geese that stand under the mountain wall? Or are you not a good enough climber to get down to them?"

This time he had no need to wait for an answer. The marten rushed up to him with back bent, and every separate hair on end. "Have you seen wild geese?" he hissed. "Where are they? Tell me instantly, or I'll bite your neck off!" "No! you must remember that I'm twice your size so be a little polite. I ask nothing better than to show you the wild geese."

The next instant the marten was on his way down the steep, and while Smirre sat and watched how he swung his snake-like body from branch to branch, he thought: "That pretty tree-hunter has the wickedest heart in all the forest. I believe that the wild geese will have me to thank for a bloody awakening."

But just as Smirre was waiting to hear the geese's death-rattle, he saw the marten tumble from branch to branch and plop into the river so the water splashed high. Soon thereafter, wings beat loudly and strongly and all the geese went up in a hurried flight.

Smirre intended to hurry after the geese, but he was so curious to know how they had been saved, that he sat there until the marten came clambering up. That poor thing was soaked in mud, and stopped every now and then to rub his head with his forepaws. "Now wasn't that just what I thought—that you were a booby, and would go and tumble into the river?" said Smirre, contemptuously.

"I haven't acted boobyishly. You don't need to scold me," said the marten. "I sat—all ready—on one of the lowest branches and thought how I should manage to tear a whole lot of geese to pieces, when a little creature, no bigger than a squirrel, jumped up and threw a stone at my head with such force, that I fell into the water and before I had time to pick myself up—"

The marten didn't have to say any more. He had no audience. Smirre was already a long way off in pursuit of the wild geese.

In the meantime Akka had flown southward in search of a new sleeping place. There was still a little daylight, and, beside, the half-moon stood high in the heavens, so that she could see a little. Luckily, she was well-acquainted in these parts, because it had happened more than once that she had been wind-driven to Blekinge when she traveled over the East Sea in the spring.

She followed the river as long as she saw it winding through the moon-lit landscape like a black, shining snake. In this way she came way down to Djupafors—where the river first hides itself in an underground channel—and then clear and transparent, as though it were made of glass, rushes down in a narrow cleft, and breaks into bits against its bottom in glittering drops and flying foam. Below the white falls lay a few stones, between which the water rushed away in a wild torrent cataract. Here Mother Akka alighted. This was another good sleeping place—especially this late in the evening, when no human beings moved about. At sunset the geese would hardly have been able to camp there, for Djupafors does not lie in any wilderness. On one side of the falls is a paper factory. On the other, which is steep and tree-grown, is Djupadal's park, where people are always strolling on the steep and slippery paths to enjoy the wild stream's rushing movement down in the ravine.

It was about the same here as at the former place; none of the travelers thought the least little bit that they had come to a pretty and

well-known place. They thought rather that it was ghastly and dangerous to stand and sleep on slippery, wet stones, in the middle of a rumbling waterfall. But they had to be content, if only they were protected
from carnivorous animals.

The geese fell asleep instantly, while the boy could find no rest in
sleep, but sat beside them that he might watch over the goosey-gander.

After a while, Smirre came running along the river shore. He spied
the geese immediately where they stood out in the foaming whirlpools,
and understood that he couldn't get at them here, either. Still he couldn't
make up his mind to abandon them, but seated himself on the shore
and looked at them. He felt very much humbled, and thought that his
entire reputation as a hunter was at stake.

All of a sudden he saw an otter come creeping up from the falls
with a fish in his mouth. Smirre approached him but stopped within two
steps of him, to show him that he didn't wish to take his game from him.

"You're a remarkable one, who can content yourself with catching
a fish, while the stones are covered with geese!" said Smirre. He was so
eager, that he hadn't taken the time to arrange his words as carefully as
he was wont to do. The otter didn't turn his head once in the direction
of the river. He was a vagabond—like all otters—and had fished many
times by Vomb Lake, and probably knew Smirre Fox. "I know very well
how you act when you want to coax away a salmon trout, Smirre," said he.

"Oh! is it you, Gripe?" said Smirre, and was delighted, for he knew
that this particular otter was a quick and accomplished swimmer. "I
don't wonder that you do not care to look at the wild geese, since you
can't manage to get out to them." But the otter who had swimming
webs between his toes and a stiff tail—which was as good as an oar—
and a skin that was waterproof, didn't wish to have it said of him that
there was a waterfall that he wasn't able to manage. He turned toward
the stream, and as soon as he caught sight of the wild geese, he threw
the fish away, and rushed down the steep shore and into the river.

If it had been a little later in the spring so that the nightingales in
Djupafors had been at home, they would have sung for many a day, of
Gripe's struggle with the rapid. For the otter was thrust back by the
waves many times, and carried down river, but he fought his way
steadily up again. He swam forward in still water; he crawled over

stones, and gradually came nearer the wild geese. It was a perilous trip, which might well have earned the right to be sung by the nightingales.

Smirre followed the otter's course with his eyes as well as he could. At last he saw that the otter was in the act of climbing up to the wild geese, but just then it shrieked shrill and wild. The otter tumbled backward into the water, and dashed away as if he had been a blind kitten. An instant later, there was a great crackling of geese's wings. They raised themselves and flew away to find another sleeping place.

The otter soon came on land. He said nothing, but commenced to lick one of his forepaws. When Smirre sneered at him because he hadn't succeeded, he broke out, "It was not the fault of my swimming art, Smirre. I had raced all the way over to the geese, and was about to climb up to them, when a tiny creature came running, and jabbed me in the foot with some sharp iron. It hurt so, I lost my footing, and then the current took me."

He didn't have to say any more. Smirre was already far away on his way to the wild geese.

Once again Akka and her flock had to take a night fly. Fortunately, the moon had not gone down, and with the aid of its light, she succeeded in finding another of those sleeping places which she knew in that neighborhood. Again she followed the shining river toward the south. Over Djupadal's manor, and over Ronneby's dark roofs and white waterfalls she swayed forward without alighting. But a little south of the city and not far from the sea lies Ronneby health spring, with its bath house and spring house, with its big hotel and summer cottages for the spring's guests. All these stand empty and desolate in winter—which the birds know perfectly well, and many are the bird-companies who seek shelter on the deserted buildings' balustrades and balconies during hard storm times.

Here the wild geese lit on a balcony, and, as usual, they fell asleep at once. The boy, on the contrary, could not sleep because he hadn't cared to creep in under the goosey-gander's wing.

The balcony faced south, so the boy had an outlook over the sea. And since he could not sleep, he sat there and saw how pretty it looked when sea and land meet, here in Blekinge.

You see that sea and land can meet in many different ways. In many places the land comes down toward the sea with fiat, tufted meadows, and the sea meets the land with flying sand, which piles up in mounds and drifts. It appears as though they both disliked each other so much that they only wished to show the poorest they possessed. But it can also happen that when the land comes toward the sea, it raises a wall of hills in front of it—as though the sea were something dangerous. When the land does this, the sea comes up to it with fiery wrath, and beats and roars and lashes against the rocks, and looks as if it would tear the land hill to pieces.

But in Blekinge it is altogether different when sea and land meet. There the land breaks itself up into points and islands and islets, and the sea divides itself into fjords and bays and sounds, and it is, perhaps, this which makes it look as if they must meet in happiness and harmony.

Think now first and foremost of the sea! Far out it lies desolate and empty and big, and has nothing else to do but to roll its gray billows. When it comes toward the land, it happens across the first obstacle. This it immediately overpowers, tears away everything green, and makes it as gray as itself. Then it meets still another obstacle. With this it does the same thing. And still another. Yes, the same thing happens to this also. It is stripped and plundered, as if it had fallen into robbers' hands. Then the obstacles come nearer and nearer together, and then the sea must understand that the land sends toward it her littlest children, in order to move it to pity. It also becomes more friendly the farther in it comes, rolls its waves less high, moderates its storms, lets the green things stay in cracks and crevices, separates itself into small sounds and inlets, and becomes at last so harmless in the land, that little boats dare venture out on it. It certainly cannot recognize itself—so mild and friendly has it grown.

And then think of the hillside! It lies uniform, and looks the same almost everywhere. It consists of flat grain fields, with one and another birch grove between them, or else of long stretches of forest ranges. It appears as if it had thought about nothing but grain and turnips and potatoes and spruce and pine. Then comes a sea fjord that cuts far into it. It doesn't mind that, but borders it with birch and alder, just as if it was an ordinary freshwater lake. Then still another wave comes driving in. Nor does the hillside bother itself about cringing to this, but it, too, gets the same covering as the first one. Then the fjords begin to broaden and separate, they break up fields and woods and then the hillside cannot help but notice them. "I believe it is the sea itself that is coming," says the hillside, and then it begins to adorn itself. It wreathes itself with blossoms, travels up and down in hills and throws islands into the sea. It no longer cares about pines and spruces, but casts them off like old everyday clothes, and parades later with big oaks and lindens and chestnuts, and with blossoming leafy bowers, and becomes as gorgeous as a manor park. And when it meets the sea, it is so changed that it doesn't know itself. All this one cannot see very well until summertime, but at any rate, the boy observed how mild and friendly nature was, and he began to feel calmer than he had been before that night. Then, suddenly, he heard a sharp and ugly yowl from the bath-house park, and when he stood up he saw, in the white moonlight, a fox standing on the pavement under the balcony. For Smirre had followed the wild geese once more. But when he found the place where they were quartered, he had understood that it was impossible to get at them in any way, then he had not been able to keep from yowling with chagrin.

When the fox yowled in this manner, old Akka, the leader goose, was awakened. Although she could see nothing, she thought she recognized the voice. "Is it you who are out tonight, Smirre?" said she. "Yes," said Smirre, "it is I, and I want to ask what you geese think of the night that I have given you?"

"Do you mean to say that it is you who have sent the marten and the otter against us?" asked Akka. "A good turn shouldn't be denied," said Smirre. "You once played the goose game with me. Now I have begun to play the fox game with you, and I'm not inclined to let up on it so long as a single one of you still lives even if I have to follow you the world over!"

"You, Smirre, ought at least to think whether it is right for you, who are weaponed both teeth and claws, to hound us in this way, we, who are without defense," said Akka.

Smirre thought that Akka sounded scared, and he said quickly, "If you, Akka, will take that Thumbietot, who has so often opposed me, and throw him down to me, I'll promise to make peace with you. Then I'll never pursue you or any of yours."

"I'm not going to give you Thumbietot," said Akka. "From the youngest of us to the oldest, we would willingly give our lives for his sake!"

"Since you're so fond of him," said Smirre, "I'll promise you that he shall be the first among you that I will wreak vengeance upon."

Akka said no more, and after Smirre sent up a few more yowls, all was still. The boy lay all the while awake. Now it was Akka's words to the fox that prevented him from sleeping. Never had he dreamed he should hear anything so great as that anyone was willing to risk life for his sake. From that moment, it could no longer be said of Nils Holgersson that he did not care for anyone.

IX
KARLSKRONA

Saturday, April third

It was a moonlight evening in Karlskrona—calm and beautiful. But earlier in the day, there had been rain and wind, and the people must have thought that the bad weather still continued, for hardly one of them had ventured out on the streets.

While the city lay there so desolate, Akka, the wild goose, and her flock, came flying toward it over Vemmön and Pantarholmen. They were out in the late evening to seek a sleeping place on the islands. They couldn't remain inland because they were disturbed by Smirre Fox wherever they alighted.

When the boy rode along high up in the air, and looked at the sea and the islands which spread themselves before him, he thought that everything appeared so strange and spook-like. The heavens were no longer blue, but encased him like a globe of green glass. The sea was milk white, and as far as he could see rolled small white waves tipped with silver ripples. In the midst of all this white, lay numerous little islets, absolutely coal black. Whether they were big or little, whether they were as even as meadows, or full of cliffs they looked just as black. Even dwelling houses and churches and windmills, which at other times are white or red, were outlined in black against the green sky. The boy thought it was as if the earth had transformed, and he had come to another world.

He thought that just for this one night he wanted to be brave, and not afraid—when he saw something that really frightened him. It was a high cliff island, which was covered with big, angular blocks, and between the blocks shone specks of bright shining gold. He couldn't keep from thinking of Maglestone, by Trolle-Ljungby, which the trolls sometimes raised upon high pillars, and he wondered if this was something like that.

But with the stones and the gold it might have gone fairly well, if such a lot of horrid things had not been lying all around the island. It looked like whales and sharks and other big sea monsters. But the boy understood that it was the sea trolls, who had gathered around the island and intended to crawl up on it, to fight with the land trolls who lived there. And those on the land were probably afraid, for he saw how a big giant stood on the highest point of the island and raised his arms—as if in despair over all the misfortune that should come to him and his island.

The boy was not a little terrified when he noticed that Akka began to descend right over that particular island! "No, for pity's sake! We must not light there," said he.

But the geese continued to descend, and soon the boy was astonished that he could have seen things so awry. In the first place, the big stone blocks were nothing but houses. The whole island was a city, and the shining gold specks were street lamps and lighted window panes. The giant, who stood highest up on the island, and raised his arms, was a church with two cross-towers; all the sea trolls and monsters, which he thought he had seen, were boats and ships of every description, that lay anchored all around the island. On the side which lay toward the land were mostly rowboats and sailboats and small coast steamers, but on the side that faced the sea lay armor-clad battleships, some were broad, with very thick, slanting smokestacks, others were long and narrow, and so constructed that they could glide through water like fishes.

Now what city might this be? That, the boy could figure out because he saw all the battleships. All his life he had loved ships, although he had had nothing to do with any, except the galleys which he had sailed in the road ditches. He knew very well that this city—where so many battleships lay—couldn't be any place but Karlskrona.

The boy's grandfather had been an old marine, and as long as he had lived, he had talked of Karlskrona every day, of the great warship dock, and of all the other things to be seen in that city. The boy felt perfectly at home, and he was glad that he should see all this of which he had heard so much.

But he only had a glimpse of the towers and fortifications which barred the entrance to the harbor, and the many buildings, and the shipyard—before Akka came down on one of the flat church towers.

This was a pretty safe place for those who wanted to get away from a fox, and the boy began to wonder if he couldn't venture to crawl in under the goosey-gander's wing for this one night. Yes, that he might safely do. It would do him good to get a little sleep. He should try to see a little more of the dock and the ships after it had grown light.

The boy himself thought it was strange that he could keep still and wait until the next morning to see the ships. He certainly had not slept five minutes before he slipped out from under the wing and slid down the lightning rod and the water spout all the way down to the ground. Soon he stood on a big square which spread itself in front of the church.

It was covered with round stones, and was just as difficult for him to travel over, as it is for big people to walk on a tufted meadow. Those who are accustomed to live in the open—or way out in the country— always feel uneasy when they come into a city, where the houses stand straight and forbidding, and the streets are open, so that everyone can see who goes there. And it happened in the same way with the boy. When he stood on the big Karlskrona square, and looked at the German church, and town hall, and the cathedral from which he had just descended, he couldn't do anything but wish that he was back on the tower again with the geese.

It was a lucky thing that the square was entirely deserted. There wasn't a human being about—unless he counted a statue that stood on a high pedestal. The boy gazed long at the statue, which represented a big, brawny man in a three-cornered hat, long waistcoat, knee breeches and coarse shoes, and wondered what kind of a one he was. He held a long stick in his hand, and he looked as if he would know how to make use of it, too—for he had an awfully severe countenance, with a big, hooked nose and an ugly mouth.

"What is that long-lipped thing doing here?" said the boy at last. He had never felt so small and insignificant as he did that night. He tried to jolly himself up a bit by saying something audacious. Then he thought no more about the statue, but betook himself to a wide street which led down to the sea.

But the boy hadn't gone far before he heard that someone was following him. Someone was walking behind him, who stamped on the stone pavement with heavy footsteps, and pounded on the ground with a hard stick. It sounded as if the bronze man up in the square had gone out for a promenade.

The boy listened after the steps while he ran down the street, and he became more and more convinced that it was the bronze man. The ground trembled, and the houses shook. It couldn't be anyone but him, who walked so heavily, and the boy grew panic-stricken when he thought of what he had just said to him. He did not dare to turn his head to find out if it really was he.

"Perhaps he is only out walking for recreation," thought the boy. "Surely he can't be offended with me for the words I spoke. They were not at all badly meant."

Instead of going straight on, and trying to get down to the dock, the boy turned into a side street which led east. First and foremost, he wanted to get away from the one who tramped after him.

But the next instant he heard that the bronze man had switched off to the same street, and then the boy was so scared that he didn't know what he would do with himself. And how hard it was to find any hiding places in a city where all the gates were closed! Then he saw on his right an old frame church, which lay a short distance away from the street in the center of a large grove. Not an instant did he pause to consider, but rushed on toward the church. "If I can only get there, then I'll surely be shielded from all harm," thought he.

As he ran forward, he suddenly caught sight of a man who stood on a gravel path and beckoned to him. "There is certainly someone who will help me!" thought the boy; he became intensely happy, and hurried off in that direction. He was actually so frightened that the heart of him fairly thumped in his breast.

But when he came up to the man who stood on the edge of the gravel path, upon a low pedestal, he was absolutely thunderstruck. "Surely, it can't have been that one who beckoned to me!" thought he, for he saw that the entire man was made of wood.

He stood there and stared at him. He was a thick-set man on short legs, with a broad, ruddy countenance, shiny, black hair and full black beard. On his head he wore a wooden hat, on his body, a brown wooden coat, around his waist, a black wooden belt, on his legs he had wide wooden knee breeches and wooden stockings, and on his feet black wooden shoes. He was newly painted and newly varnished, so that he glistened and shone in the moonlight. This undoubtedly had a good deal to do with giving him such a good-natured appearance, that the boy at once placed confidence in him.

In his left hand he held a wooden slate, and there the boy read:

> Most humbly I beg you.
> Though voice I may lack:
> Come drop a penny, do;
> But lift my hat!

Oh ho! the man was only a poor box. The boy felt that he had been done. He had expected that this should be something really remarkable. And now he remembered that grandpa had also spoken of the wooden man, and said that all the children in Karlskrona were so fond of him. And that must have been true, for he too, found it hard to part with the wooden man. He had something so old-timey about him that one could well take him to be many hundred years old, and at the same time, he looked so strong and bold, and animated—just as one might imagine that folks looked in olden times.

The boy had so much fun looking at the wooden man that he entirely forgot the one from whom he was fleeing. But now he heard him. He turned from the street and came into the churchyard. He followed him here too! Where should the boy go?

Just then he saw the wooden man bend down to him and stretch forth his big, broad hand. It was impossible to believe anything but good of him, and with one jump, the boy stood in his hand. The wooden man lifted him to his hat—and stuck him under it.

The boy was just hidden, and the wooden man had just gotten his arm in its right place again, when the bronze man stopped in front of him and banged the stick on the ground, so that the wooden man shook on his pedestal. Thereupon the bronze man said in a strong and resonant voice: "Who might this one be?"

The wooden man's arm went up and creaked in the old woodwork. He touched his hat brim and replied, "Rosenbom, by Your Majesty's leave. Once upon a time boatswain on the man-of-war, *Dristigheten*, after completed service, sexton at the Admiral's church—and, lately, carved in wood and exhibited in the churchyard as a poor-box."

The boy gave a start when he heard that the wooden man said "Your Majesty." For now, when he thought about it, he knew that the statue on the square represented the one who had founded the city. It was probably no less a one than Charles the Eleventh himself, whom he had encountered.

"He gives a good account of himself," said the bronze man. "Can he also tell me if he has seen a little brat who runs around in the city tonight? He's an impudent rascal, if I get hold of him, I'll teach him manners!" With that, he again pounded on the ground with his stick.

"By Your Majesty's leave, I have seen him," said the wooden man, and the boy was so scared that he commenced to shake where he sat under the hat and looked at the bronze man through a crack in the wood. But he calmed down when the wooden man continued:

"Your Majesty is on the wrong track. That youngster certainly intended to run into the shipyard, and conceal himself there."

"Does he say so, Rosenbom? Well then, don't stand still on the pedestal any longer but come with me and help me find him. Four eyes are better than two, Rosenbom."

But the wooden man answered in a doleful voice: "I would most humbly beg to be permitted to stay where I am. I look well and sleek because of the paint, but I'm old and moldy, and cannot stand moving about."

The bronze man was not one of those who liked to be contradicted. "What sort of notions are these? Come along, Rosenbom!" Then he raised his stick and gave the other one a resounding whack on the shoulder. "Does Rosenbom not see that he holds together?"

With that they broke off and walked forward on the streets of Karlskrona—large and mighty—until they came to a high gate, which led to the shipyard. Just outside and on guard walked one of the navy's jacktars, but the bronze man strutted past him and kicked the gate open without the jacktar's pretending to notice it.

As soon as they had gotten into the shipyard, they saw a wide, expansive harbor separated by pile bridges. In the different harbor basins, lay the warships, which looked bigger, and more awe-inspiring than when the boy had seen them from up above. "Then it wasn't so crazy after all, to imagine that they were sea trolls," thought he.

"Where does Rosenbom think it most advisable for us to begin the search?" said the bronze man.

"Such a one as he could most easily conceal himself in the hall of models," replied the wooden man.

On a narrow landstrip which stretched to the right from the gate, all along the harbor, lay ancient structures. The bronze man walked over to a building with low walls, small windows, and a conspicuous roof. He pounded on the door with his stick until it burst open, and tramped up a pair of worn-out steps. Soon they came into a large hall, which was filled with tackled and full-rigged little ships. The boy understood without being told that these were models for the ships which had been built for the Swedish Navy. There were ships of many different varieties. There were old men-of-war, whose sides bristled with cannon, and which had high structures fore and aft, and their masts weighed down with a network of sails and ropes. There were small island boats with rowing benches along the sides; there were undecked cannon sloops and richly gilded frigates, which were models of the ones the kings had used. Finally, there were also the heavy, broad armor-plated ships with towers and cannon on deck—such as are in use nowadays—and narrow, shining torpedo boats which resembled long, slender fishes.

When the boy was carried around among all this, he was awed. "Fancy that such big, splendid ships have been built here in Sweden!" he thought to himself.

He had plenty of time to see all that was to be seen in there, for when the bronze man saw the models, he forgot everything else. He examined them all, from the first to the last, and asked about them. And Rosenbom, the boatswain on the *Dristigheten*, told as much as he knew of the ships' builders, and of those who had manned them, and of the fates they had met. He told them about Chapman and Puke and Trolle, of Hoagland and Svensksund—all the way along until 1809—after that he had not been there. Both he and the bronze man had the most to say about the fine old wooden ships. The new battleships they didn't exactly appear to understand.

"I can hear that Rosenbom doesn't know anything about these new-fangled things," said the bronze man. "Therefore, let us go and look at something else, for this amuses me, Rosenbom."

By this time he had entirely given up his search for the boy, who felt calm and secure where he sat in the wooden hat. Thereupon both men wandered through the big establishment: sail-making shops, anchor smithy, machine and carpenter shops. They saw the mast sheers and the docks; the large magazines, the arsenal, the rope-bridge and the big discarded dock, which had been blasted in the rock. They went out upon the pile-bridges, where the naval vessels lay moored, stepped on board and examined them like two old sea-dogs, wondered, disapproved, approved and became indignant.

The boy sat in safety under the wooden hat, and heard all about how they had laboured and struggled in this place, to equip the navies which had gone out from here. He heard how life and blood had been risked; how the last penny had been sacrificed to build the warships; how skilled men had strained all their powers, in order to perfect these ships which had been their fatherland's safeguard. A couple of times the tears came to the boy's eyes, as he heard all this.

And the very last, they went into an open court, where the galley models of old men-of-war were grouped, and a more remarkable sight the boy had never beheld, for these models had inconceivably powerful and terror-striking faces. They were big, fearless and savage: filled with the same proud spirit that had fitted out the great ships. They were from another time than his. He thought that he shrivelled up before them.

But when they came in here, the bronze man said to the wooden man: "Take off thy hat, Rosenbom, for those that stand here! They have all fought for the fatherland." And Rosenbom—like the bronze man— had forgotten why they had begun this tramp. Without thinking, he lifted the wooden hat from his head and shouted:

"I take off my hat to the one who chose the harbor and founded the shipyard and re-created the navy, to the monarch who has awakened all this into life!"

"Thanks, Rosenbom! That was well spoken. Rosenbom is a fine man. But what is this, Rosenbom?"

For there stood Nils Holgersson, right on top of Rosenbom's bald pate. He wasn't afraid any longer, but raised his white toboggan hood, and shouted, "Hurrah for you, Longlip!"

The bronze man struck the ground hard with his stick, but the boy never learned what he had intended to do for now the sun ran up, and, at the same time, both the bronze man and the wooden man vanished— as if they had been made of mists. While he still stood and stared after them, the wild geese flew up from the church tower and swayed back and forth over the city. Instantly they caught sight of Nils Holgersson, and then the big white one darted down from the sky and fetched him.

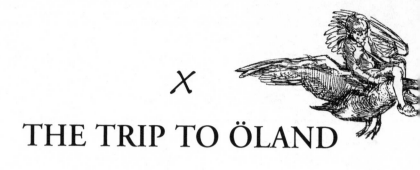

X

THE TRIP TO ÖLAND

Sunday, April third

*T*he wild geese went out on a wooded island to feed. There they happened to run across a few gray geese, who were surprised to see them since they knew very well that their kinsmen, the wild geese, usually travel over the interior of the country.

They were curious and inquisitive, and wouldn't be satisfied with less than that the wild geese should tell them all about the persecution which they had to endure from Smirre Fox. When they had finished, a gray goose, who appeared to be as old and as wise as Akka herself, said: "It was a great misfortune for you that Smirre Fox was declared an outlaw in his own land. He'll be sure to keep his word, and follow you all the way up to Lapland. If I were in your place, I shouldn't travel north over Småland, but would take the outside route over Öland instead, so that he'll be thrown off the track entirely. To really mislead him, you must remain for a couple of days on Öland's southern point. There you'll find lots of food and lots of company. I don't believe you'll regret it, if you go over there."

It was certainly very sensible advice, and the wild geese concluded to follow it. As soon as they had eaten all they could hold, they started on the trip to Öland. None of them had ever been there before, but the gray goose had given them excellent directions. They only had to travel directly south until they came to a large bird track, which extended all along the Blekinge coast. All the birds who had winter residences by the West Sea, and who now intended to travel to Finland and Russia, flew forward there—and, in passing, they were always in the habit of stopping at Öland to rest. The wild geese would have no trouble in finding guides.

That day it was perfectly still and warm—like a summer's day—the best weather in the world for a sea trip. The only grave thing about it was that it was not quite clear, for the sky was gray and veiled. Here and there were enormous mist-clouds which hung way down to the sea's outer edge and obstructed the view.

When the travelers had gotten away from the wooded island, the sea spread itself so smooth and mirror-like that the boy, as he looked down, thought the water had disappeared. There was no longer any earth under him. He had nothing but mist and sky around him. He grew very dizzy, and held himself tight on the goose-back, more frightened than when he sat there for the first time. It seemed as though he couldn't possibly hold on; he must fall in some direction.

It was even worse when they reached the big bird-track, of which the gray goose had spoken. Actually, there came flock after flock flying in exactly the same direction. They seemed to follow a fixed route. There were ducks and gray geese, surf scoters and guillemots, loons and pintail ducks and mergansers and grebes and oyster-catchers and sea grouse. But now, when the boy leaned forward, and looked in the direction where the sea ought to lie, he saw the whole bird procession reflected in the water. But he was so dizzy that he didn't understand how this had come about: he thought that the whole bird procession flew with their bellies upside down. Still he didn't wonder at this so much, for he did not himself know which was up, and which was down.

The birds were tired out and impatient to get on. None of them shrieked or said a funny thing, and this made everything seem peculiarly unreal.

"Think, if we have traveled away from the earth!" he said to himself. "Think, if we are on our way up to heaven!"

He saw nothing but mists and birds around him, and began to look upon it as reasonable that they were traveling heavenward. He was glad, and wondered what he should see up there. The dizziness passed all at once. He was so exceedingly happy at the thought that he was on his way to heaven and was leaving this earth.

Just about then he heard a couple of loud shots, and saw two white smoke columns ascend.

There was a sudden awakening, and an unrest among the birds. "Hunters! Hunters!" they cried. "Fly high! Fly away!"

Then the boy saw, finally, that they were traveling all the while over the sea coast, and that they certainly were not in heaven. In a long row lay small boats filled with hunters, who fired shot upon shot. The nearest bird flocks hadn't noticed them in time. They had flown too low. Several dark bodies sank down toward the sea, and for everyone that fell, there arose cries of anguish from the living.

It was strange for one who had but lately believed himself in heaven, to wake up suddenly to such fear and lamentation. Akka shot toward the heights as fast as she could, and the flock followed with the greatest possible speed. The wild geese got safely out of the way, but the boy couldn't get over his amazement. "To think that anyone could wish to shoot upon such as Akka and Yksi and Kaksi and the goosey-gander and the others! Human beings had no conception of what they did."

So it bore on again, in the still air, and everything was as quiet as heretofore, with the exception that some of the tired birds called out every now and then: "Are we not there soon? Are you sure we're on the right track?" Hereupon, those who flew in the center answered: "We are flying straight to Öland, straight to Öland."

The gray geese were tired out, and the loons flew around them. "Don't be in such a rush!" cried the ducks. "You'll eat up all the food before we get there." "Oh! there'll be enough for both you and us," answered the loons.

Before they had gotten so far that they saw Öland, there came a light wind against them. It brought with it something that resembled immense clouds of white smoke—just as if there was a big fire somewhere.

When the birds saw the first white spiral haze, they became uneasy and increased their speed. But that which resembled smoke blew thicker and thicker, and at last it enveloped them altogether. They smelled no smoke, and the smoke was not dark and dry, but white and damp. Suddenly the boy understood that it was nothing but a mist.

When the mist became so thick that one couldn't see a goose-length ahead, the birds began to carry on like real lunatics. All these, who before had traveled forward in such perfect order, began to play in the mist. They flew hither and thither, to entice one another astray. "Be careful!" they cried. "You're only traveling around and around. Turn back, for pity's sake! You'll never get to Öland in this way."

They all knew perfectly well where the island was, but they did their best to lead each other astray. "Look at those wagtails!" rang out in the mist. "They are going back toward the North Sea!" "Have a care, wild geese!" shrieked someone from another direction. "If you continue like this, you'll get clear up to Rügen."

There was, of course, no danger that the birds who were accustomed to travel here would permit themselves to be lured in a wrong direction. But the ones who had a hard time of it were the wild geese. The jesters observed that they were uncertain as to the way, and did all they could to confuse them.

"Where do you intend to go, good people?" called a swan. He came right up to Akka, and looked sympathetic and serious.

"We shall travel to Öland, but we have never been there before," said Akka. She thought that this was a bird to be trusted.

"It's too bad," said the swan. "They have lured you in the wrong direction. You're on the road to Blekinge. Now come with me, and I'll put you right!"

And so he flew off with them, and when he had taken them so far away from the track that they heard no calls, he disappeared in the mist.

They flew around for a while at random. They had barely succeeded in finding the birds again, when a duck approached them. "It's best that you lie down on the water until the mist clears," said the duck. "It is evident that you are not accustomed to look out for yourselves on journeys."

Those rogues succeeded in making Akka's head swim. As near as the boy could make out, the wild geese flew round and round for a long time.

"Be careful! Can't you see that you are flying up and down?" shouted a loon as he rushed by. The boy positively clutched the gooseygander around the neck. This was something which he had feared for a long time.

No one can tell when they would have arrived, if they hadn't heard a rolling and muffled sound in the distance.

Then Akka craned her neck, snapped hard with her wings, and rushed on at full speed. Now she had something to go by. The gray goose had told her not to light on Öland's southern point, because there was a cannon there, which the people used to shoot the mist with. Now she knew the way, and now no one in the world should lead her astray again.

XI

ÖLAND'S SOUTHERN POINT

April third to sixth

On the most southerly part of Öland lies a royal demesne, which is called Ottenby. It is a rather large estate which extends from shore to shore, straight across the island, and it is remarkable because it has always been a haunt for large bird companies. In the seventeenth century, when the kings used to go over to Öland to hunt, the entire estate was nothing but a deer park. In the eighteenth century there was a stud there, where blooded race horses were bred, and a sheep farm, where several hundred sheep were maintained. In our days you'll find neither blooded horses nor sheep at Ottenby. In place of them, live great herds of young horses, which are to be used by the cavalry.

In all the land there is certainly no place that could be a better abode for animals. Along the extreme eastern shore lies the old sheep meadow, which is a mile and a half long, and the largest meadow in all Öland, where animals can graze and play and run about, as free as if they were in a wilderness. And there you will find the celebrated Ottenby grove with the hundred-year-old oaks, which give shade from the sun, and shelter from the severe Öland winds. And we must not forget the long Ottenby wall, which stretches from shore to shore, and separates Ottenby from the rest of the island, so that the animals may know how far the old royal demesne extends, and be careful about getting in on other ground, where they are not so well-protected.

You'll find plenty of tame animals at Ottenby, but that isn't all. One could almost believe that the wild ones also felt that on an old crown property both the wild and the tame ones can count upon shelter and protection—since they venture there in such great numbers.

Beside, there are still a few stags of the old descent left, and burrow ducks and partridges love to live there, and it offers a resting place, in the spring and late summer, for thousands of migratory birds. Above all it is the swampy eastern shore below the sheep meadow, where the migratory birds alight to rest and feed.

When the wild geese and Nils Holgersson had finally found their way to Öland, they came down, like all the rest, on the shore near the sheep meadow. The mist lay thick over the island, just as it had over the sea. But still the boy was amazed at all the birds which he discerned, only on the little narrow stretch of shore which he could see.

It was a low sand shore with stones and pools, and a lot of cast-up seaweed. If the boy had been permitted to choose, it isn't likely that he would have thought of alighting there, but the bird probably thought of this as a veritable paradise. Ducks and geese walked about and fed on the meadow; nearer the water ran snipe and other coast birds. The loons lay in the sea and fished, but the life and movement was upon the long seaweed banks along the coast. There the birds stood side by side close together and picked grubworms—which must have been found there in limitless quantities for it was very evident that there was never any complaint over a lack of food.

The great majority were going to travel farther, and had only alighted to take a short rest, and as soon as the leader of a flock thought that his comrades had recovered themselves sufficiently he said, "If you are ready now, we may as well move on."

"No, wait, wait! We haven't had anything like enough," said the followers.

"You surely don't believe that I intend to let you eat so much that you will not be able to move?" said the leader, and flapped his wings and started off. Along the outermost seaweed banks lay a flock of swans. They didn't bother about going on land, but rested themselves by lying and rocking on the water. Now and then they dived down with their necks and brought up food from the sea bottom. When they had gotten hold of anything very good, they indulged in loud shouts that sounded like trumpet calls.

When the boy heard that there were swans on the shoals, he hurried out to the seaweed banks. He had never before seen wild swans at close range. He had luck on his side, so that he got close to them.

The boy was not the only one who had heard the swans. The wild geese and the gray geese and the loons swam out between the banks, laid themselves in a ring around the swans and stared at them. The swans ruffled their feathers, raised their wings like sails, and lifted their necks high in the air. Occasionally one and another of them swam up to a goose, or a great loon, or a diving duck, and said a few words. And then it appeared as though the one addressed hardly dared raise his bill to reply.

But then there was a little loon—a tiny mischievous baggage—who couldn't stand all this ceremony. He dived suddenly, and disappeared under the water's edge. Soon after that, one of the swans let out a scream, and swam off so quickly that the water foamed. Then he stopped and began to look majestic once more. But soon, another one shrieked in the same way as the first one, and then a third.

The little loon wasn't able to stay under water any longer, but appeared on the water's edge, little and black and venomous. The swans rushed toward him, but when they saw what a poor little thing it was, they turned abruptly—as if they considered themselves too good to quarrel with him. Then the little loon dived again, and pinched their feet. It certainly must have hurt, and the worst of it was, that they could not maintain their dignity. At once they took a decided stand. They began to beat the air with their wings so that it thundered, came forward a bit—as though they were running on the water—finally, got wind under their wings, and raised themselves.

When the swans were gone they were greatly missed, and those who had lately been amused by the little loon's antics scolded him for his thoughtlessness.

The boy walked toward land again. There he stationed himself to see how the pool snipe played. They resembled small storks, like these, they had little bodies, long legs and necks, and light, swaying movements; only they were not gray, but brown. They stood in a long row on the shore where it was washed by waves. As soon as a wave rolled in, the whole row ran backward; as soon as it receded, they followed it. And they kept this up for hours.

The showiest of all the birds were the burrow ducks. They were undoubtedly related to the ordinary ducks, for, like these, they too had a thick-set body, broad bill, and webbed feet, but they were much more elaborately gotten up. The feather dress, itself, was white, around their necks they wore a broad gold band; the wing mirror shone in green, red, and black, and the wing edges were black, and the head was dark green and shimmered like satin.

As soon as any of these appeared on the shore, the others said, "Now, just look at those things! They know how to tog themselves out." "If they were not so conspicuous, they wouldn't have to dig their nests in the earth, but could lay above ground, like anyone else," said a brown mallard duck. "They may try as much as they please, still they'll never get anywhere with such noses," said a gray goose. And this was actually true. The burrow ducks had a big knob on the base of the bill, which spoiled their appearance.

Close to the shore, sea gulls and sea wallows moved forward on the water and fished. "What kind of fish are you catching?" asked a wild goose. "It's a stickleback. It's Öland stickleback. It's the best stickleback in the world," said a gull. "Won't you taste of it?" And he flew up to the goose, with his mouth full of the little fishes, and wanted to give her some. "Ugh! Do you think that I eat such filth?" said the wild goose.

The next morning it was just as cloudy. The wild geese walked about on the meadow and fed, but the boy had gone to the seashore to gather mussels. There were plenty of them, and when he thought that the next day, perhaps, they would be in some place where they couldn't get any food at all, he concluded that he would try to make himself a little bag, which he could fill with mussels. He found an old sedge on the meadow, which was strong and tough, and out of this he began to braid a knapsack. He worked at this for several hours, and he was well-satisfied with it when it was finished.

At dinner time all the wild geese came running and asked him if he had seen anything of the white goosey-gander. "No, he has not been with me," said the boy. "We had him with us all along until just lately," said Akka, "but now we no longer know where he's to be found."

The boy jumped up, and was terribly frightened. He asked if any fox or eagle had put in an appearance, or if any human being had been seen in the neighborhood. But no one had noticed anything dangerous. The goosey-gander had probably lost his way in the mist.

But it was just as great a misfortune for the boy, in whatever way the white one had been lost, and he started off immediately to hunt for him. The mist shielded him, so that he could run wherever he wished without being seen, but it also prevented him from seeing. He ran southward along the shore—all the way down to the lighthouse and the mist cannon on the island's extreme point. It was the same bird confusion everywhere, but no goosey-gander. He ventured over to Ottenby estate, and he searched every one of the old, hollow oaks in Ottenby grove, but he saw no trace of the goosey-gander.

He searched until it began to grow dark. Then he had to turn back again to the eastern shore. He walked with heavy steps, and was fearfully blue. He didn't know what would become of him if he couldn't find the goosey-gander. There was no one whom he could spare less.

But when he wandered over the sheep meadow, what was that big, white thing that came toward him in the mist if it wasn't the goosey-gander? He was all right, and very glad that, at last, he had been able to find his way back to the others. The mist had made him so dizzy, he said, that he had wandered around on the big meadow all day long.

The boy threw his arms around his neck, for very joy, and begged him to take care of himself and not wander away from the others. He promised, positively, that he never would do this again. No, never again.

But the next morning, when the boy went down to the beach and hunted for mussels, the geese came running and asked if he had seen the goosey-gander. No, of course he hadn't. "Well, then the goosey-gander was lost again. He had gone astray in the mist, just as he had done the day before."

The boy ran off in great terror and began to search. He found one place where the Ottenby wall was so tumble-down that he could climb over it. Later, he went about, first on the shore—which gradually widened and became so large that there was room for fields and meadows and farms—then up on the flat highland, which lay in the middle of the island, and where there were no buildings except windmills, and where the turf was so thin that the white cement shone under it.

Meanwhile, he could not find the goosey-gander, and as it drew on toward evening, and the boy must return to the beach, he couldn't believe anything but that his traveling companion was lost. He was so depressed he did not know what to do with himself.

He had just climbed over the wall again when he heard a stone crash down close beside him. As he turned to see what it was, he thought that he could distinguish something that moved on a stone pile which lay close to the wall. He stole nearer, and saw the goosey-gander come trudging wearily over the stone pile, with several long fibers in his mouth. The goosey-gander didn't see the boy, and the boy did not call to him, but thought it advisable to find out first why the goosey-gander time and again disappeared in this manner.

And he soon learned the reason for it. Up in the stone-pile lay a young gray goose, who cried with joy when the goosey-gander came. The boy crept near, so that he heard what they said, then he found out that the gray goose had been wounded in one wing, so that she could not fly, and that her flock had traveled away from her, and left her alone. She had been near death's door with hunger, when the white goosey-gander had heard her call, the other day, and had sought her out. Ever since, he had been carrying food to her. They had both hoped that she would be well before they left the island, but, as yet, she could neither fly nor walk. She was very much worried over this, but he comforted her with the thought that he shouldn't travel for a long time. At last he bade her good night, and promised to come the next day.

The boy let the goosey-gander go, and as soon as he was gone, he stole, in turn, up to the stone heap. He was angry because he had been deceived, and now he wanted to say to that gray goose that the goosey-gander was his property. He was going to take the boy up to Lapland, and there would be no talk of his staying here on her account. But now, when he saw the young gray goose close up, he understood not only why the goosey-gander had gone and carried food to her for two days, but also why he bad not wished to mention that he had helped her. She had the prettiest little head; her featherdress was like soft satin, and the eyes were mild and pleading.

When she saw the boy, she wanted to run away, but the left wing was out of joint and dragged on the ground, so that it interfered with her movements.

"You mustn't be afraid of me," said the boy, and didn't look nearly so angry as he had intended to appear. "I'm Thumbietot, Morten Goosey-Gander's comrade," he continued. Then he stood there, and didn't know what he wanted to say.

Occasionally one finds something among animals which makes one wonder what sort of creatures they really are. One is almost afraid that they may be transformed human beings. It was something like this with the gray goose. As soon as Thumbietot said who he was, she lowered her neck and head very charmingly before him, and said in a voice that was so pretty that he couldn't believe it was a goose who spoke: "I am very glad that you have come here to help. The white goosey-gander has told me that no one is as wise and as good as you."

She said this with such dignity that the boy grew really embarrassed. "This surely can't be any bird," thought he. "It is certainly some bewitched princess."

He was filled with a desire to help her, and ran his hand under the feathers, and felt along the wing bone. The bone was not broken, but there was something wrong with the joint. He got his finger down into the empty cavity. "Be careful, now!" he said, and got a firm grip on the bone pipe and fitted it into the place where it ought to be. He did it very quickly and well, considering it was the first time that he had attempted anything of the sort. But it must have hurt very much, for the poor young goose uttered a single shrill cry, and then sank down among the stones without showing a sign of life.

The boy was terribly frightened. He had only wished to help her, and now she was dead. He made a big jump from the stone pile, and ran away. He thought it was as though he had murdered a human being.

The next morning it was clear and free from mist, and Akka said that now they should continue their travels. All the others were willing to go, but the white goosey-gander made excuses. The boy understood well enough that he didn't care to leave the gray goose. Akka did not listen to him, but started off.

The boy jumped up on the goosey-gander's back, and the white one followed the flock—albeit slowly and unwillingly. The boy was mighty glad that they could fly away from the island. He was conscience-stricken on account of the gray goose, and had not cared to tell the goosey-gander how it had turned out when he had tried to cure her. It would probably be best if Morten Goosey-Gander never found out about this, he thought, though he wondered, at the same time, how the white one had the heart to leave the gray goose.

But suddenly the goosey-gander turned. The thought of the young gray goose had overpowered him. It could go as it would with the Lapland trip: he couldn't go with the others when he knew that she lay alone and ill, and would starve to death.

With a few wing strokes he was over by the stone pile, but then, there lay no young gray goose between the stones. "Dunfin! Dunfin! Where art thou?" called the goosey-gander.

"The fox has probably been here and taken her," thought the boy. But at that moment he heard a pretty voice answer the goosey-gander. "Here am I, goosey-gander, here am I! I have only been taking a morning bath." And up from the water came the little gray goose—fresh and in good trim—and told how Thumbietot had pulled her wing into place, and that she was entirely well, and ready to follow them on the journey.

The drops of water lay like pearl dew on her shimmery satin-like feathers, and Thumbietot thought once again that she was a real little princess.

XII

THE BIG BUTTERFLY

Wednesday, April sixth

Thee geese traveled alongside the coast of the long island, which lay distinctly visible under them. The boy felt happy and light of heart during the trip. He was just as pleased and well-satisfied as he had been glum and depressed the day before, when he roamed around down on the island, and hunted for the goosey-gander.

He saw now that the interior of the island consisted of a barren high plain, with a wreath of fertile land along the coast, and he began to comprehend the meaning of something which he had heard the other evening.

He had just seated himself to rest a bit by one of the many windmills on the highland, when a couple of shepherds came along with the dogs beside them, and a large herd of sheep in their train. The boy had not been afraid because he was well concealed under the windmill stairs. But as it turned out, the shepherds came and seated themselves on the same stairway, and then there was nothing for him to do but to keep perfectly still.

One of the shepherds was young, and looked about as folks do mostly; the other was an old queer one. His body was large and knotty, but the head was small, and the face had sensitive and delicate features. It appeared as though the body and head didn't want to fit together at all.

One moment he sat silent and gazed into the mist, with an unutterably weary expression. Then he began to talk to his companion. Then the other one took out some bread and cheese from his knapsack, to eat his evening meal. He answered scarcely anything, but listened very patiently, just as if he were thinking, "I might as well give you the pleasure of letting you chatter a while."

"Now I shall tell you something, Eric," said the old shepherd. "I have figured out that in former days, when both human beings and animals were much larger then they are now, that the butterflies, too, must have been uncommonly large. And once there was a butterfly that was many miles long, and had wings as wide as seas. Those wings were blue, and shone like silver, and so gorgeous that, when the butterfly was out flying, all the other animals stood still and stared at it. It had this drawback, however, that it was too large. The wings had hard work to carry it. But probably all would have gone very well, if the butterfly had been wise enough to remain on the hillside. But it wasn't, it ventured out over the East Sea. And it hadn't gotten very far before the storm came along and began to tear at its wings. Well, it's easy to understand, Eric, how things would go when the East Sea storm commenced to wrestle with frail butterfly wings. It wasn't long before they were torn away and scattered, and then, of course, the poor butterfly fell into the sea. At first it was tossed backward and forward on the billows, and then it was stranded upon a few cliff foundations outside of Småland. And there it lay—as large and long as it was.

"Now I think, Eric, that if the butterfly had dropped on land, it would soon have rotted and fallen apart. But since it fell into the sea, it was soaked through and through with lime, and became as hard as a stone. You know, of course, that we have found stones on the shore which were nothing but petrified worms. Now I believe that it went the same way with the big butterfly-body. I believe that it turned where it lay into a long, narrow mountain out in the East Sea. Don't you?"

He paused for a reply, and the other one nodded to him. "Go on, so I may hear what you are driving at," said he.

"And mark you, Eric, that this very Öland, upon which you and I live, is nothing else than the old butterfly body. If one only thinks about it, one can observe that the island is a butterfly. Toward the north, the slender forebody and the round head can be seen, and toward the south, one sees the back-body—which first broadens out, and then narrows to a sharp point."

Here he paused once more and looked at his companion rather anxiously to see how he would take this assertion. But the young man kept on eating with the utmost calm, and nodded to him to continue.

"As soon as the butterfly had been changed into a limestone rock, many different kinds of seeds of herbs and trees came traveling with the winds, and wanted to take root on it. It was a long time before anything but sedge could grow there. Then came sheep sorrel, and the rock-rose and thorn-brush. But even today there is not so much growth on Alvaret, that the mountain is well-covered, but it shines through here and there. And no one can think of plowing and sowing up here, where the earth-rust is so thin. But if you will admit that Alvaret and the strongholds around it, are made of the butterfly-body, then you may well have the right to question where that land which lies beneath the strongholds came from."

"Yes, it is just that," said he who was eating. "That I should indeed like to know."

"Well, you must remember that Öland has lain in the sea for a good many years, and in the course of time all the things which tumble around with the waves—seaweed and sand and clams—have gathered around it, and remained lying there. And then, stone and gravel have fallen down from both the eastern and western strongholds. In this way the island has acquired broad shores, where grain and flowers and trees can grow.

"Up here, on the hard butterfly back, only sheep and cows and little horses go about. Only lapwings and plover live here, and there are no buildings except windmills and a few stone huts, where we shepherds crawl in. But down on the coast lie big villages and churches and parishes and fishing hamlets and a whole city."

He looked questioningly at the other one. This one had finished his meal, and was tying the food sack together. "I wonder where you will end with all this," said he.

"It is only this that I want to know," said the shepherd, as he lowered his voice so that he almost whispered the words, and looked into the mist with his small eyes, which appeared to be worn out from spying after all that which does not exist. "Only this I want to know: if the peasants who live on the built-up farms beneath the strongholds, or the fishermen who take the small herring from the sea, or the merchants in Borgholm, or the bathing guests who come here every summer, or the tourists who wander around in Borgholm's old castle ruin, or the sportsmen who come here in the fall to hunt partridges, or the painters who sit here on Alvaret and paint the sheep and windmills—I should like to know if any of them understand that this island has been a butterfly which flew about with great shimmery wings."

"Ah!" said the young shepherd, suddenly. "It should have occurred to some of them, as they sat on the edge of the stronghold of an evening, and heard the nightingales trill in the groves below them, and looked over Kalmar Sound, that this island could not have come into existence in the same way as the others."

"I want to ask," said the old one, "if no one has had the desire to give wings to the windmills—so large that they could reach to heaven, so large that they could lift the whole island out of the sea and let it fly like a butterfly among butterflies."

"It may be possible that there is something in what you say," said the young one, "for on summer nights, when the heavens widen and open over the island, I have sometimes thought that it was as if it wanted to raise itself from the sea, and fly away."

But when the old one had finally gotten the young one to talk, he didn't listen to him very much. "I would like to know," the old one said in a low tone, "if anyone can explain why one feels such a longing up here on Alvaret. I have felt it every day of my life, and I think it preys upon each and every one who must go about here. I want to know if no one else has understood that all this wistfulness is caused by the fact that the whole island is a butterfly that longs for its wings."

XIII

LITTLE KARL'S ISLAND

THE STORM

Friday, April eighth

The wild geese had spent the night on Öland's northern point, and were now on their way to the continent. A strong south wind blew over Kalmar Sound, and they had been thrown northward. Still they worked their way toward land with good speed. But when they were nearing the first islands a powerful rumbling was heard, as if a lot of strong-winged birds had come flying, and the water under them, all at once, became perfectly black. Akka drew in her wings so suddenly that she almost stood still in the air. Thereupon, she lowered herself to light on the edge of the sea. But before the geese had reached the water, the west storm caught up with them. Already, it drove before it fogs, salt scum and small birds; it also snatched with it the wild geese, threw them on end, and cast them toward the sea.

It was a rough storm. The wild geese tried to turn back, time and again, but they couldn't do it and were driven out toward the East Sea. The storm had already blown them past Öland, and the sea lay before them—empty and desolate. There was nothing for them to do, but to keep out of the water.

When Akka observed that they were unable to turn back she thought that it was needless to let the storm drive them over the entire East Sea. Therefore she sank down to the water. Now the sea was raging, and increased in violence with every second. The sea-green billows rolled forward, with seething foam on their crests. Each one surged higher than the other. It was as though they raced with each other, to see which could foam the wildest. But the wild geese were not afraid of the swells. On the contrary, this seemed to afford them much pleasure.

They did not strain themselves with swimming, but lay and let themselves be washed up with the wave-crests, and down in the water dales, and had just as much fun as children in a swing. Their only anxiety was that the flock should be separated. The few land birds who drove by, up in the storm, cried with envy: "There is no danger for you who can swim."

But the wild geese were certainly not out of all danger. In the first place, the rocking made them helplessly sleepy. They wished continually to turn their heads backward, poke their bills under their wings, and go to sleep. Nothing can be more dangerous than to fall asleep in this way, and Akka called out all the while, "Don't go to sleep, wild geese! He that falls asleep will get away from the flock. He that gets away from the flock is lost."

Despite all attempts at resistance one after another fell asleep, and Akka herself came pretty near dozing off, when she suddenly saw something round and dark rise on the top of a wave. "Seals! Seals! Seals!" cried Akka in a high, shrill voice, and raised herself up in the air with resounding wing strokes. It was just at the crucial moment. Before the last wild goose had time to come up from the water, the seals were so close to her that they made a grab for her feet.

Then the wild geese were once more up in the storm which drove them before it out to sea. No rest did it allow either itself or the wild geese, and no land did they see—only desolate sea.

They lit on the water again, as soon as they dared venture. But when they had rocked upon the waves for a while, they became sleepy again. And when they fell asleep, the seals came swimming. If old Akka had not been so wakeful, not one of them would have escaped.

All day the storm raged, and it caused fearful havoc among the crowds of little birds, which at this time of year were migrating. Some were driven from their course to foreign lands, where they died of starvation; others became so exhausted that they sank down in the sea and were drowned. Many were crushed against the cliff walls, and many became a prey for the seals.

The storm continued all day, and, at last, Akka began to wonder if she and her flock would perish. They were now dead tired, and nowhere did they see any place where they might rest. Toward evening she no longer dared to lie down on the sea, because now it filled up all of a sudden with large ice cakes, which struck against each other, and she feared they should be crushed between these. A couple of times the wild geese tried to stand on the ice-crust, but one time the wild storm swept them into the water; another time, the merciless seals came creeping up on the ice.

At sundown the wild geese were once more up in the air. They flew on—fearful for the night. The darkness seemed to come upon them much too quickly this night—which was so full of dangers.

It was terrible that they, as yet, saw no land. How would it go with them if they were forced to stay out on the sea all night? They would either be crushed between the ice cakes or devoured by seals or separated by the storm.

The heavens were cloud bedecked, the moon hid itself, and the darkness came quickly. At the same time all nature was filled with a horror which caused the most courageous hearts to quail. Distressed bird travelers' cries had sounded over the sea all day long, without anyone having paid the slightest attention to them, but now, when one no longer saw who it was that uttered them, they seemed mournful and terrifying. Down on the sea, the ice drifts crashed against each other with a loud rumbling noise. The seals tuned up their wild hunting songs. It was as though heaven and earth were about to clash.

THE SHEEP

The boy sat for a moment and looked down into the sea. Suddenly he thought that it began to roar louder than ever. He looked up. Right in front of him—only a couple of metres away—stood a rugged and bare mountain-wall. At its base the waves dashed into a foaming spray. The wild geese flew straight toward the cliff, and the boy did not see how they could avoid being dashed to pieces against it. Hardly had he wondered that Akka hadn't seen the danger in time, when they were over by the mountain. Then he also noticed that in front of them was the half-round entrance to a grotto. Into this the geese steered, and the next moment they were safe.

The first thing the wild geese thought of—before they gave themselves time to rejoice over their safety—was to see if all their comrades were also harbored. Yes, there were Akka, Iksi, Kolmi, Nelja, Viisi, Knusi, all the six goslings, the goosey-gander, Dunfin and Thumbietot, but Kaksi from Nuolja, the first left-hand goose, was missing—and no one knew anything about her fate.

When the wild geese discovered that no one but Kaksi had been separated from the flock, they took the matter lightly. Kaksi was old and wise. She knew all their byways and their habits, and she, of course, would know how to find her way back to them.

Then the wild geese began to look around in the cave. Enough daylight came in through the opening, so that they could see the grotto was both deep and wide. They were delighted to think they had found such a fine night barbour, when one of them caught sight of some shining, green dots, which glittered in a dark corner. "These are eyes!" cried Akka. "There are big animals in here." They rushed toward the opening, but Thumbietot called to them: "There is nothing to run away from! It's only a few sheep who are lying alongside the grotto wall." When the wild geese had accustomed themselves to the dim daylight in the grotto, they saw the sheep very distinctly. The grown-up ones might be about as many as there were geese, but beside these there were a few little lambs. An old ram with long, twisted horns appeared to be the most lordly one of the flock. The wild geese went up to him with much bowing and scraping. "We'll met in the wilderness!" they greeted, but the big ram lay still, and did not speak a word of welcome.

Then the wild geese thought that the sheep were displeased because they had taken shelter in their grotto. "It is perhaps not permissible that we have come in here?" said Akka. "But we cannot help it, for we are wind-driven. We have wandered about in the storm all day, and it would be very good to be allowed to stop here tonight." After that a long time passed before any of the sheep answered with words, but, on the other hand, it could be heard distinctly that a pair of them heaved deep sighs. Akka knew, to be sure, that sheep are always shy and peculiar, but these seemed to have no idea how they should conduct themselves. Finally an old ewe, who had a long and pathetic face and a doleful voice, said: "There isn't one among us that refuses to let you stay, but this is a house of mourning, and we cannot receive guests as we did in former days." "You needn't worry about anything of that sort," said

Akka. "If you knew what we have endured this day, you would surely understand that we are satisfied if we only get a safe spot to sleep."

When Akka said this, the old ewe raised herself. "I believe that it would be better for you to fly about in the worst storm than to stop here. But, at least, you shall not go from here before we have had the privilege of offering you the best hospitality which the house affords."

She conducted them to a hollow in the ground, which was filled with water. Beside it lay a pile of bait and husks and chaff, and she bade them make the most of these. "We have had a severe snow winter this year, on the island," said she. "The peasants who own us came out to us with hay and oat straw, so we shouldn't starve to death. And this trash is all there is left of the good cheer."

The geese rushed to the food instantly. They thought that they had fared well, and were in their best humor. They must have observed, of course, that the sheep were anxious, but they knew how easily scared sheep generally are, and didn't believe there was any actual danger on foot. As soon as they had eaten, they intended to stand up to sleep as usual. But then the big ram got up, and walked over to them. The geese thought that they had never seen a sheep with such big and coarse horns. In other respects, also, he was noticeable. He had a high, rolling forehead, intelligent eyes, and a good bearing—as though he were a proud and courageous animal.

"I cannot assume the responsibility of letting you geese remain, without telling you that it is unsafe here," said he. "We cannot receive night guests just now." At last Akka began to comprehend that this was serious. "We shall go away, since you really wish it," said she. "But won't you tell us first, what it is that troubles you? We know nothing about it. We do not even know where we are." "This is Little Karl's Island!" said the ram. "It lies outside of Gottland, and only sheep and sea birds live here." "Perhaps you are wild sheep?" said Akka. "We're not far removed from it," replied the ram. "We have nothing to do with human beings. It's an old agreement between us and some peasants on a farm in Gottland, that they shall supply us with fodder in case we have snow winter, and as a recompense they are permitted to take away those of us who become superfluous. The island is small, so it cannot feed very many of us. But otherwise we take care of ourselves all the year round, and we do not live in houses with doors and locks, but we reside in grottoes like these."

"Do you stay out here in the winter as well?" asked Akka, surprised. "We do," answered the ram. "We have good fodder up here on the mountain, all the year around." "I think it sounds as if you might have it better than other sheep," said Akka. "But what is the misfortune that has befallen you?" "It was bitter cold last winter. The sea froze, and then three foxes came over here on the ice, and here they have been ever since. Otherwise, there are no dangerous animals here on the island." "Oh, ho! do foxes dare to attack such as you?" "Oh, no! not during the day, then I can protect myself and mine," said the ram, shaking his horns. "But they sneak upon us at night when we sleep in the grottoes. We try to keep awake, but one must sleep some of the time, and then they come upon us. They have already killed every sheep in the other grottoes, and there were herds that were just as large as mine."

"It isn't pleasant to tell that we are so helpless," said the old ewe. "We cannot help ourselves any better than if we were tame sheep." "Do you think that they will come here tonight?" asked Akka. There is nothing else in store for us," answered the old ewe. "They were here last night, and stole a lamb from us. They'll be sure to come again, as long as there are any of us alive. This is what they have done in the other places." "But if they are allowed to keep this up, you'll become entirely exterminated," said Akka. "Oh! it won't be long before it is all over with the sheep on Little Karl's Island," said the ewe.

Akka stood there hesitatingly. It was not pleasant, by any means, to venture out in the storm again and it wasn't good to remain in a house where such guests were expected. When she had pondered a while, she turned to Thumbietot. "I wonder if you will help us, as you have done so many times before," said she. Yes, that he would like to do, he replied. "It is a pity for you not to get any sleep!" said the wild goose, "but I wonder if you are able to keep awake until the foxes come, and then to awaken us, so we may fly away." The boy was so very glad of this—for anything was better than to go out in the storm again—so he promised to keep awake.

The boy went down to the grotto opening, crawled in behind a stone, that he might be shielded from the storm, and sat down to watch.

When the boy had been sitting a while, the storm seemed to abate. The sky grew clear, and the moonlight began to play on the waves. The boy stepped to the opening to look out. The grotto was rather high up on the mountain. A narrow path led to it. It was probably here that he must await the foxes.

As yet he saw no foxes, but, on the other hand, there was something which, for the moment, terrified him much more. On the land strip below the mountain stood some giants, or other stone trolls—or perhaps they were actual human beings. At first he thought that he was dreaming, but now he was positive that he had not fallen asleep. He saw the big men so distinctly that it couldn't be an illusion. Some of them stood on the land strip, and others right on the mountain just as if they intended to climb it. Some had big, thick heads; others had no heads at all. Some were one-armed, and some had humps both before and behind. He had never seen anything so extraordinary.

The boy stood and worked himself into a state of panic because of those trolls, so that he almost forgot to keep his eye peeled for the foxes. But now he heard a claw scrape against a stone. He saw three foxes coming up the steep, and as soon as he knew that he had something real to deal with, he was calm again, and not the least bit scared. It struck him that it was a pity to awaken only the geese, and to leave the sheep to their fate. He thought he would like to arrange things, some other way.

He ran quickly to the other end of the grotto, shook the big ram's horns until he awoke, and, at the same time, swung himself upon his back. "Get up, sheep, and we'll try to frighten the foxes a bit!" said the boy.

He had tried to be as quiet as possible, but the foxes must have heard some noise, for when they came up to the mouth of the grotto they stopped and deliberated. "It was certainly someone in there that moved." said one. "I wonder if they are awake." "Oh, go ahead, you!" said another. "At all events, they can't do anything to us."

When they came farther in, in the grotto, they stopped and sniffed. "Who shall we take tonight?" whispered the one who went first. "Tonight we will take the big ram," said the last. "After that, we'll have easy work with the rest."

The boy sat on the old ram's back and saw how they sneaked along. "Now butt straight forward!" whispered the boy. The ram butted, and the first fox was thrust—top over tail—back to the opening. "Now butt to the left!" said the boy, and turned the big ram's head in that direction. The ram measured a terrific assault that caught the second fox in the side. He rolled around several times before he got to his feet again and made his escape. The boy had wished that the third one, too, might have gotten a bump, but this one had already gone.

"Now I think that they've had enough for tonight," said the boy. "I think so too," said the big ram. "Now lie down on my back, and creep into the wool! You deserve to have it warm and comfortable, after all the wind and storm that you have been out in."

HELL'S HOLE

*T*he next day the big ram went around with the boy on his back, and showed him the island. It consisted of a single massive mountain. It was like a large house with perpendicular walls and a flat roof. First the ram walked up on the mountain roof and showed the boy the good grazing lands there, and he had to admit that the island seemed to be especially created for sheep. There wasn't much else than sheep sorrel and such little spicy growths as sheep are fond of that grew on the mountain.

But indeed there was something beside sheep fodder to look at, for one who had gotten well up on the steep. To begin with, the largest part of the sea—which now lay blue and sunlit, and rolled forward in glittering swells—was visible. Only upon one and another point, did the foam spray up. To the east lay Gottland, with even and long-stretched coast, and to the southwest lay Great Karl's Island, which was built on the same plan as the little island. When the ram walked to the very edge of the mountain roof, so the boy could look down the mountain walls, he noticed that they were simply filled with birds' nests, and in the blue sea beneath him, lay surf scoters and eider ducks and kittiwakes and guillemots and razor bills—so pretty and peaceful—busying themselves with fishing for small herring.

"This is really a favored land," said the boy. "You live in a pretty place, you sheep." "Oh, yes! it's pretty enough here," said the big ram. It was as if he wished to add something, but he did not, only sighed. "If you go about here alone you must look out for the crevices which run all around the mountain," he continued after a little. And this was a good warning, for there were deep and broad crevices in several places. The largest of them was called Hell's Hole. That crevice was many fathoms deep and nearly one fathom wide. "If anyone fell down there, it would certainly be the last of him," said the big ram. The boy thought it sounded as if he had a special meaning in what he said.

Then he conducted the boy down to the narrow strip of shore. Now he could see those giants which had frightened him the night before, at close range. They were nothing but tall rock-pillars. The big ram called them "cliffs." The boy couldn't see enough of them. He thought that if there had ever been any trolls who had turned into stone they ought to look just like that.

Although it was pretty down on the shore, the boy liked it still better on the mountain height. It was ghastly down here, for everywhere they came across dead sheep. It was here that the foxes had held their orgies. He saw skeletons whose flesh had been eaten, and bodies that were half-eaten, and others which they had scarcely tasted, but had been allowed to lie untouched. It was heart-rending to see how the wild beasts had thrown themselves upon the sheep just for sport—just to hunt them and tear them to death.

The big ram did not pause in front of the dead, but walked by them in silence. But the boy, meanwhile, could not help seeing all the horror.

Then the big ram went up on the mountain height again, but when he was there he stopped and said: "If someone who is capable and wise could see all the misery which prevails here, he surely would not be able to rest until these foxes had been punished." "The foxes must live, too," said the boy. "Yes," said the big ram. "Those who do not tear in pieces more animals than they need for their sustenance, they may as well live. But these are felons." "The peasants who own the island ought to come here and help you," insisted the boy. "They have rowed over a number of times," replied the ram, "but the foxes always hid themselves in the grottoes and crevices, so they could not get near them, to shoot them." "You surely cannot mean, father, that a poor little creature like me should be able to get at them, when neither you nor the peasants have succeeded in getting the better of them." "He that is little and spry can put many things to rights," said the big ram.

They talked no more about this, and the boy went over and seated himself among the wild geese who fed on the highland. Although he had not cared to show his feelings before the ram, he was very sad on the sheep's account, and he would have been glad to help them. "I can at least talk with Akka and Morten Goosey-Gander about the matter," thought he. "Perhaps they can help me with a good suggestion."

A little later the white goosey-gander took the boy on his back and went over the mountain plain, and in the direction of Hell's Hole at that.

He wandered carefree on the open mountain roof—apparently unconscious of how large and white he was. He didn't seek protection behind tufts, or any other protuberances, but went straight ahead. It was strange that he was not more careful, for it was apparent that he had fared badly in yesterday's storm. He limped on his right leg, and the left wing hung and dragged as if it might be broken.

He acted as if there were no danger, pecked at a grass-blade here and another there, and did not look about him in any direction. The boy lay stretched out full length on the goose-back, and looked up toward the blue sky. He was so accustomed to riding now, that he could both stand and lie down on the goose-back.

When the goosey-gander and the boy were so carefree, they did not observe, of course, that the three foxes had come up on the mountain plain.

And the foxes, who knew that it was well-nigh impossible to take the life of a goose on an open plain, thought at first that they wouldn't chase after the goosey-gander. But as they had nothing else to do, they finally sneaked down on one of the long passes, and tried to steal up to him. They went about it so cautiously that the goosey-gander couldn't see a shadow of them.

They were not far off when the goosey-gander made an attempt to raise himself into the air. He spread his wings, but he did not succeed in lifting himself. When the foxes seemed to grasp the fact that he couldn't fly, they hurried forward with greater eagerness than before. They no longer concealed themselves in the cleft, but came up on the highland. They hurried as fast as they could, behind tufts and hollows, and came nearer and nearer the goosey-gander—without his seeming to notice that he was being hunted. At last the foxes were so near that they could make the final leap. Simultaneously, all three threw themselves, with one long jump at the goosey-gander.

But still at the last moment he must have noticed something, for he ran out of the way, so the foxes missed him. This, at any rate, didn't mean very much, for the goosey-gander only had a couple of meters headway, and, in the bargain, he limped. Anyway, the poor thing ran ahead as fast as he could.

The boy sat upon the goose-back—backward—and shrieked and called to the foxes. "You have eaten yourselves too fat on mutton, foxes. You can't catch up with a goose even." He teased them so that they became crazed with rage and thought only of rushing forward.

The white one ran right straight to the big cleft. When he was there, he made one stroke with his wings, and got over. Just then the foxes were almost upon him.

The goosey-gander hurried on with the same haste as before, even after he had gotten across Hell's Hole. But he had hardly been running two meters before the boy patted him on the neck, and said: "Now you can stop, goosey-gander."

At that instant they heard a number of wild howls behind them, and a scraping of claws, and heavy falls. But of the foxes they saw nothing more.

The next morning the lighthouse keeper on Great Karl's Island found a bit of bark poked under the entrance door, and on it had been cut in slanting, angular letters: "The foxes on the little island have fallen down into Hell's Hole. Take care of them!"

And this the lighthouse keeper did, too.

XIV

TWO CITIES

THE CITY AT THE BOTTOM
OF THE SEA

Saturday, April ninth

*I*t was a calm and clear night. The wild geese did not trouble themselves to seek shelter in any of the grottoes, but stood and slept up
on the mountain top, and the boy had lain down in the short, dry grass
beside the geese.

It was bright moonlight that night, so bright that it was difficult
for the boy to go to sleep. He lay there and thought about just how long
he had been away from home, and he figured out that it was three weeks
since he had started on the trip. At the same time he remembered that
this was Easter eve.

"It is tonight that all the witches come home from Blakulla,"
thought he, and laughed to himself. For he was just a little afraid of both
the sea nymph and the elf, but he didn't believe in witches the least
little bit.

If there had been any witches out that night, he should have seen
them, to be sure. It was so light in the heavens that not the tiniest black
speck could move in the air without his seeing it.

While the boy lay there with his nose in the air and thought about
this, his eye rested on something lovely! The moon's disk was whole and
round, and rather high, and over it a big bird came flying. He did not
fly past the moon, but he moved just as though he might have flown out
from it. The bird looked black against the light background, and the
wings extended from one rim of the disc to the other. He flew on,
evenly, in the same direction, and the boy thought that he was painted

on the moon's disc. The body was small, the neck long and slender, the legs hung down, long and thin. It couldn't be anything but a stork.

A couple of seconds later Herr Ermenrich, the stork, lit beside the boy. He bent down and poked him with his bill to awaken him.

Instantly the boy sat up. "I'm not asleep, Herr Ermenrich," he said. "How does it happen that you are out in the middle of the night, and how is everything at Glimminge castle? Do you want to speak with Mother Akka?"

"It's too light to sleep tonight," answered Herr Ermenrich. "Therefore I concluded to travel over here to Karl's Island and hunt you up, friend Thumbietot. I learned from the seamew that you were spending the night here. I have not as yet moved over to Glimminge castle but am still living at Pommern."

The boy was simply overjoyed to think that Herr Ermenrich had sought him out. They chatted about all sorts of things, like old friends. At last the stork asked the boy if he wouldn't like to go out riding for a while on this beautiful night.

Oh, yes! that the boy wanted to do, if the stork would manage it so that he got back to the wild geese before sunrise. This he promised, so off they went.

Again Herr Ermenrich flew straight toward the moon. They rose and rose; the sea sank deep down, but the flight went so light and easy that it seemed almost as if the boy lay still in the air. When Herr Ermenrich began to descend, the boy thought that the flight had lasted an unreasonably short time.

They landed on a desolate bit of seashore, which was covered with fine, even sand. All along the coast ran a row of flying sand drifts, with lyme grass on their tops. They were not very high, but they prevented the boy from seeing any of the island.

Herr Ermenrich stood on a sand hill, drew up one leg and bent his head backward, so he could stick his bill under the wing. "You can roam around on the shore for a while," he said to Thumbietot, "while I rest myself. But don't go so far away but that you can find your way back to me again!"

To start with, the boy intended to climb a sand hill and see how the land behind it looked. But when he had walked a couple of paces, he stubbed the toe of his wooden shoe against something hard. He stooped down, and saw that a small copper coin lay on the sand, and was so worn with verdigris that it was almost transparent. It was so poor that he didn't even bother to pick it up, but only kicked it out of the way.

But when he straightened himself up once more he was perfectly astounded, for two paces away from him stood a high, dark wall with a big, turreted gate.

The moment before, when the boy bent down, the sea lay there—shimmering and smooth, while now it was hidden by a long wall with towers and battlements. Directly in front of him, where before there had been only a few seaweed banks, the big gate of the wall opened.

The boy probably understood that it was a specter play of some sort, but this was nothing to be afraid of, thought he. It wasn't any dangerous trolls, or any other evil—such as he always dreaded to encounter at night. Both the wall and the gate were so beautifully constructed that he only desired to see what there might be back of them. "I must find out what this can be," thought he, and went in through the gate.

In the deep archway there were guards, dressed in brocaded and puffed suits, with long-handled spears beside them, who sat and threw dice. They thought only of the game, and took no notice of the boy who hurried past them quickly.

Just within the gate he found an open space, paved with large, even stone blocks. All around this were high and magnificent buildings, and between these opened long, narrow streets. On the square—facing the gate—it fairly swarmed with human beings. The men wore long, fur-trimmed capes over satin suits; plume-bedecked hats sat obliquely on their heads; on their chests hung superb chains. They were all so regally gotten up that the whole lot of them might have been kings.

The women went about in high headdresses and long robes with tight-fitting sleeves. They, too, were beautifully dressed, but their splendor was not to be compared with that of the men.

This was exactly like the old storybook which mother took from the chest—only once—and showed to him. The boy simply couldn't believe his eyes.

But that which was even more wonderful to look upon than either the men or the women, was the city itself. Every house was built in such a way that a gable faced the street. And the gables were so highly ornamented, that one could believe they wished to compete with each other as to which one could show the most beautiful decorations.

When one suddenly sees so much that is new, he cannot manage to treasure it all in his memory. But at least the boy could recall that he had seen stairway gables on the various landings, which bore images of the Christ and his Apostles, gables, where there were images in niche after niche all along the wall, gables that were inlaid with multicolored bits of glass, and gables that were striped and checked with white and black marble. As the boy admired all this, a sudden sense of haste came over him. "Anything like this my eyes have never seen before. Anything like this, they would never see again," he said to himself. And he began to run in toward the city—up one street, and down another.

The streets were straight and narrow, but not empty and gloomy, as they were in the cities with which he was familiar. There were people everywhere. Old women sat by their open doors and spun without a spinning wheel—only with the help of a shuttle. The merchants' shops were like marketstalls—opening on the street. All the handworkers did their work out of doors. In one place they were boiling crude oil, in another tanning hides, in a third there was a long rope-walk.

If only the boy had had time enough he could have learned how to make all sorts of things. Here he saw how armorers hammered out thin breastplates; how turners tended their irons; how the shoemakers soled soft, red shoes; how the gold-wire drawers twisted gold thread, and how the weavers inserted silver and gold into their weaving.

But the boy did not have the time to stay. He just rushed on, so that he could manage to see as much as possible before it would all vanish again.

The high wall ran all round the city and shut it in, as a hedge shuts in a field. He saw it at the end of every street—gable ornamented and crenelated. On the top of the wall walked warriors in shining armor, and when he had run from one end of the city to the other, he came to still another gate in the wall. Outside of this lay the sea and harbor. The boy saw olden-time ships, with rowing benches straight across, and high structures fore and aft. Some lay and took on cargo, others were just casting anchor. Carriers and merchants hurried around each other. All over, it was life and bustle.

But not even here did he seem to have the time to linger. He rushed into the city again, and now he came up to the big square. There stood the cathedral with its three high towers and deep vaulted arches filled with images. The walls had been so highly decorated by sculptors that there was not a stone without its own special ornamentation. And what a magnificent display of gilded crosses and gold-trimmed altars and priests in golden vestments, shimmered through the open gate! Directly opposite the church there was a house with a notched roof and a single slender, sky-high tower. That was probably the courthouse. And between the courthouse and the cathedral, all around the square, stood the beautiful gabled houses with their multiplicity of adornments.

The boy had run himself both warm and tired. He thought that now he had seen the most remarkable things, and therefore he began to walk more leisurely. The street which he had turned into now was surely the one where the inhabitants purchased their fine clothing. He saw crowds of people standing before the little stalls where the merchants spread brocades, stiff satins, heavy gold cloth, shimmery velvet, delicate veiling, and laces as sheer as a spider's web.

Before, when the boy ran so fast, no one had paid any attention to him. The people must have thought that it was only a little gray rat that darted by them. But now, when he walked down the street, very slowly, one of the salesmen caught sight of him, and began to beckon to him.

At first the boy was uneasy and wanted to hurry out of the way, but the salesman only beckoned and smiled, and spread out on the counter a lovely piece of satin damask as if he wanted to tempt him.

The boy shook his head. "I will never be so rich that I can buy even a meter of that cloth," thought he.

But now they had caught sight of him in every stall, all along the street. Wherever he looked stood a salesman who beckoned to him. They left their costly wares, and thought only of him. He saw how they hurried into the most hidden corner of the stall to fetch the best that they had to sell, and how their hands trembled with eagerness and haste as they laid it upon the counter.

When the boy continued to go on, one of the merchants jumped over the counter, caught hold of him, and spread before him silver cloth and woven tapestries, which shone with brilliant colours.

The boy couldn't do anything but laugh at him. The salesman certainly must understand that a poor little creature like him couldn't buy such things. He stood still and held out his two empty hands, so they would understand that he had nothing and let him go in peace. But the merchant raised a finger and nodded and pushed the whole pile of beautiful things over to him.

"Can he mean that he will sell all this for a gold piece?" wondered the boy.

The merchant brought out a tiny worn and poor coin—the smallest that one could see—and showed it to him. And he was so eager to sell that he increased his pile with a pair of large, heavy, silver goblets.

Then the boy began to dig down in pockets. He knew, of course, that he didn't possess a single coin, but he couldn't help feeling for it.

All the other merchants stood still and tried to see how the sale would come off, and when they observed that the boy began to search in his pockets, they flung themselves over the counters, filled their hands full of gold and silver ornaments, and offered them to him. And they showed him that what they asked in payment was just one little penny.

But the boy turned both vest and breeches pockets inside out, so they should see that he owned nothing. Then tears filled the eyes of all these regal merchants, who were so much richer than he. At last he was moved because they looked so distressed, and he pondered if he could not in some way help them. And then he happened to think of the rusty coin, which he had but lately seen on the strand.

He started to run down the street, and luck was with him so that he came to the self-same gate which he had happened upon first. He dashed through it, and commenced to search for the little green copper penny which lay on the strand a while ago. He found it too, very promptly, but when he had picked it up, and wanted to run back to the city with it—he saw only the sea before him. No city wall, no gate, no sentinels, no streets, no houses could now be seen—only the sea.

The boy couldn't help that the tears came to his eyes. He had believed in the beginning, that which he saw was nothing but hallucination, but this he had already forgotten. He only thought about how pretty everything was. He felt a genuine, deep sorrow because the city had vanished.

That moment Herr Ermenrich awoke, and came up to him. But he didn't hear him, and the stork had to poke the boy with his bill to attract attention to himself. "I believe that you stand here and sleep just as I do," said Herr Ermenrich.

"Oh, Herr Ermenrich," said the boy, "what was that city which stood here just now?"

"Have you seen a city?" said the stork. "You have slept and dreamed, as I say."

"No! I have not dreamed," said Thumbietot, and he told the stork all that he had experienced.

Then Herr Ermenrich said: "For my part Thumbietot, I believe that you fell asleep here on the strand and dreamed all this. But I will not conceal from you that Bataki, the raven, who is the most learned of all birds, once told me that in former times there was a city on this shore, called Vineta. It was so rich and so fortunate, that no city has ever been more glorious, but its inhabitants, unluckily, gave themselves up to arrogance and love of display. As a punishment for this, says Bataki, the city of Vineta was overtaken by a flood, and sank into the sea. But these inhabitants cannot die, neither is their city destroyed. And one night in every hundred years, it rises in all its splendor up from the sea, and remains on the surface just one hour."

"Yes, it must be so," said Thumbietot, "for this I have seen."

"But when the hour is up, it sinks again into the sea, if, during that time, no merchant in Vineta has sold anything to a single living creature. If you, Thumbietot, only had had an ever so tiny coin, to pay the merchants, Vineta might have remained up here on the shore, and its people could have lived and died like other human beings."

"Herr Ermenrich," said the boy, "now I understand why you came and fetched me in the middle of the night. It was because you believed that I should be able to save the old city. I am so sorry it didn't turn out as you wished, Herr Ermenrich."

He covered his face with his hands and wept. It wasn't easy to say which one looked the more disconsolate—the boy, or Herr Ermenrich.

THE LIVING CITY

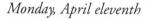

On the afternoon of Easter Monday, the wild geese and Thumbietot were on the wing. They traveled over Gottland.

The large island lay smooth and even beneath them. The ground was checked just as it was in Skåne and there were many churches and farms. But there was this difference, however, that there were more leafy meadows between the fields here, and then the farms were not built up with small houses. And there were no large manors with ancient tower-ornamented castles.

The wild geese had taken the route over Gottland on account of Thumbietot. He had been altogether unlike himself for two days, and hadn't spoken a cheerful word. This was because he had thought of nothing but that city which had appeared to him in such a strange way. He had never seen anything so magnificent and royal, and he could not be reconciled with himself for having failed to save it. Usually he was not chicken-hearted, but now he actually grieved for the beautiful buildings and the stately people.

Both Akka and the goosey-gander tried to convince Thumbietot that he had been the victim of a dream, or an hallucination, but the boy wouldn't listen to anything of that sort. He was so positive that he had really seen what he had seen, that no one could move him from this conviction. He went about so disconsolate that his traveling companions became uneasy for him.

Just as the boy was the most depressed, old Kaksi came back to the flock. She had been blown toward Gottland, and had been compelled to travel over the whole island before she learned through some crows that her comrades were on Little Karl's Island. When Kaksi found out what was wrong with Thumbietot, she said impulsively:

"If Thumbietot is grieving over an old city, we'll soon be able to comfort him. Just come along and I'll take you to a place that I saw yesterday! You will not need to be distressed very long."

Thereupon the geese had taken farewell of the sheep, and were on their way to the place which Kaksi wished to show Thumbietot. As blue as he was, he couldn't keep from looking at the land over which he travelled, as usual.

He thought it looked as though the whole island had in the beginning been just such a high, steep cliff as Karl's Island—though much bigger of course. But afterward, it had in some way been flattened out. Someone had taken a big rolling-pin and rolled over it, as if it had been a lump of dough.

Not that the island had become altogether flat and even, like a bread cake, for it wasn't like that. While they had traveled along the coast, he had seen white lime walls with grottoes and crags, in several directions, but in most of the places they were leveled and sank inconspicuously down toward the sea.

In Gottland they had a pleasant and peaceful holiday afternoon. It turned out to be mild spring weather; the trees had large buds; spring blossoms dressed the ground in the leafy meadows; the poplars' long, thin pendants swayed, and in the little gardens, which one finds around every cottage, the gooseberry bushes were green.

The warmth and the spring budding had tempted the people out into the gardens and roads, and wherever a number of them were together they were playing. It was not the children alone who played, but the grown-ups also. They were throwing stones at a given point, and they threw balls in the air with such exact aim that they almost touched the wild geese. It looked cheerful and pleasant to see big folks at play, and the boy certainly would have enjoyed it if he had been able to forget his grief because he had failed to save the city.

Anyway, he had to admit that this was a lovely trip. There was so much singing and sound in the air. Little children played ring games, and sang as they played. The Salvation Army was out. He saw a lot of people dressed in black and red sitting upon a wooded hill, playing guitars and brass instruments. On one road came a great crowd of people. They were Good Templars who had been on a pleasure trip. He recognized them by the big banners with the gold inscriptions which waved above them. They sang song after song as long as he could hear them.

After that the boy could never think of Gottland without thinking of the games and songs at the same time.

He had been sitting and looking down for a long while, but now he happened to raise his eyes. No one can describe his amazement. Before he was aware of it, the wild geese had left the interior of the island and gone westward—toward the seacoast. Now the wide, blue sea lay before him. However, it was not the sea that was remarkable, but a city which appeared on the seashore.

The boy came from the east, and the sun had just begun to go down in the west. When he came nearer the city, its walls and towers and high, gabled houses and churches stood there, perfectly black, against the light evening sky. He couldn't see therefore what it really looked like, and for a couple of moments he believed that this city was just as beautiful as the one he had seen on Easter night.

When he got right up to it, he saw that it was both like and unlike that city from the bottom of the sea. There was the same contrast between them, as there is between a man whom one sees arrayed in purple and jewels one day, and on another day one sees him dressed in rags.

Yes, this city had probably, once upon a time, been like the one which he sat and thought about. This one, also, was enclosed by a wall with towers and gates. But the towers in this city, which had been allowed to remain on land, were roofless, hollow and empty. The gates were without doors; sentinels and warriors had disappeared. All the glittering splendor was gone. There was nothing left but the naked, gray stone skeleton.

When the boy came farther into the city, he saw that the larger part of it was made up of small, low houses, but here and there were still a few high gabled houses and a few cathedrals, which were from the olden time. The walls of the gabled houses were whitewashed, and entirely without ornamentation, but because the boy had so lately seen the buried city, he seemed to understand how they had been decorated: some with statues, and others with black and white marble. And it was the same with the old cathedrals; the majority of them were roofless with bare interiors. The window openings were empty, the floors were grass-grown, and ivy clambered along the walls. But now he knew how they had looked at one time; that they had been covered with images and paintings, that the chancel had had trimmed altars and gilded crosses, and that there priests had moved about, arrayed in gold vestments.

The boy saw also the narrow streets, which were almost deserted on holiday afternoons. He knew, he did, what a stream of stately people had once upon a time sauntered about on them. He knew that they had been like large workshops—filled with all sorts of workmen.

But that which Nils Holgersson did not see was, that the city—even today—was both beautiful and remarkable. He saw neither the cheery cottages on the side streets, with their black walls, and white bows and red pelargoniums behind the shining windowpanes, nor the many pretty gardens and avenues, nor the beauty in the weed-clad ruins. His eyes were so filled with the preceding glory that he could not see anything good in the present.

The wild geese flew back and forth over the city a couple of times, so that Thumbietot might see everything. Finally they sank down on the grass-grown floor of a cathedral ruin to spend the night.

When they had arranged themselves for sleep, Thumbietot was still awake and looked up through the open arches to the pale pink evening sky. When he had been sitting there a while, he thought he didn't want to grieve any more because he couldn't save the buried city. Not that he didn't want to, now that he had seen this one. If that city, which he had seen, had not sunk into the sea again, then it would perhaps become as dilapidated as this one in a little while. Perhaps it could not have withstood time and decay, but would have stood there with roofless churches and bare houses and desolate, empty streets—just like this one. Then it was better that it should remain in all its glory down in the deep.

"It was best that it happened as it happened," thought he. "If I had the power to save the city, I don't believe that I should care to do it." Then he no longer grieved over that matter.

And there are probably many among the young who think in the same way. But when people are old, and have become accustomed to being satisfied with little, then they are more happy over the Visby that exists, than over a magnificent Vineta at the bottom of the sea.

XV

THE LEGEND OF SMÅLAND

Tuesday, April twelfth

The wild geese had made a good trip over the sea, and had lighted in Tjust Township, in northern Småland. That township didn't seem able to make up its mind whether it wanted to be land or sea. Fjords ran in everywhere, and cut the land into islands and peninsulas and points and capes. The sea was so forceful that the only things which could hold themselves above it were hills and mountains. All the lowlands were hidden away under the water exterior.

It was evening when the wild geese came in from the sea, and the land with the little hills lay prettily between the shimmering fjords. Here and there, on the islands, the boy saw cabins and cottages, and the farther inland he came, the bigger and better became the dwelling houses. Finally, they grew into large, white manors. Along the shores there was generally a border of trees, and within this lay field plots, and on the tops of the little hills there were trees again. He could not help but think of Blekinge. Here again was a place where land and sea met, in such a pretty and peaceful sort of way, just as if they tried to show each other the best and loveliest which they possessed.

The wild geese alighted upon a limestone island a good way in on Goose fjord. With the first glance at the shore they observed that spring had made rapid strides while they had been away on the islands. The fine, big trees were not as yet leaf-clad, but the ground under them was brocaded with white anemones, gagea, and blue anemones.

When the wild geese saw the flower carpet they feared that they had lingered too long in the southern part of the country. Akka said instantly that there was no time in which to hunt up any of the stopping places in Småland. By the next morning they must travel northward, over Östergötland.

The boy should then see nothing of Småland, and this grieved him. He had heard more about Småland than he had about any other province, and he had longed to see it with his own eyes.

The summer before, when he had served as goose boy with a farmer in the neighborhood of Jordberga, he had met a pair of Småland children, almost every day, who also tended geese. These children had irritated him terribly with their Småland.

It wasn't fair to say that Osa, the goose girl, had annoyed him. She was much too wise for that. But the one who could be aggravating with a vengeance, was her brother, little Mats.

"Have you heard, Nils Goose boy, how it went when Småland and Skåne were created?" he would ask, and if Nils Holgersson said no, he began immediately to relate the old joke legend.

"Well, it was at that time when our Lord was creating the world. While he was doing his best work, Saint Peter came walking by. He stopped and looked on, and then he asked if it was hard to do. 'Well, it isn't exactly easy,' said our Lord. Saint Peter stood there a little longer, and when he noticed how easy it was to lay out one landscape after another, he too wanted to try his hand at it. 'Perhaps you need to rest yourself a little,' said Saint Peter, 'I could attend to the work in the meantime for you.' But this our Lord did not wish. 'I do not know if you are so much at home in this art that I can trust you to take hold where I leave off,' he answered. Then Saint Peter was angry, and said that he believed he could create just as fine countries as our Lord himself.

"It happened that our Lord was just then creating Småland. It wasn't even half-ready but it looked as though it would be an indescribably pretty and fertile land. It was difficult for our Lord to say no to Saint Peter, and aside from this, he thought very likely that a thing so well begun no one could spoil. Therefore he said: 'If you like, we will prove which one of us two understands this sort of work the better. You, who are only a novice, shall go on with this which I have begun, and I will create a new land.' To this Saint Peter agreed at once, and so they went to work—each one in his place.

"Our Lord moved southward a bit, and there he undertook to create Skåne. It wasn't long before he was through with it, and soon he asked if Saint Peter had finished, and would come and look at his work.

'I had mine ready long ago,' said Saint Peter, and from the sound of his voice it could be heard how pleased he was with what he had accomplished.

"When Saint Peter saw Skåne, he had to acknowledge that there was nothing but good to be said of that land. It was a fertile land and easy to cultivate, with wide plains wherever one looked, and hardly a sign of hills. It was evident that our Lord had really contemplated making it such that people should feel at home there. 'Yes, this is a good country,' said Saint Peter, 'but I think that mine is better.' 'Then we'll take a look at it,' said our Lord.

"The land was already finished in the north and east when Saint Peter began the work, but the southern and western parts, and the whole interior, he had created all by himself. Now when our Lord came up there, where Saint Peter had been at work, he was so horrified that he stopped short and exclaimed: 'What on earth have you been doing with this land, Saint Peter?'

"Saint Peter, too, stood and looked around—perfectly astonished. He had had the idea that nothing could be so good for a land as a great deal of warmth. Therefore he had gathered together an enormous mass of stones and mountains, and erected a highland, and this he had done so that it should be near the sun, and receive much help from the sun's heat. Over the stone heaps he had spread a thin layer of soil, and then he had thought that everything was well-arranged.

"But while he was down in Skåne, a couple of heavy showers had come up, and more was not needed to show what his work amounted to. When our Lord came to inspect the land, all the soil had been washed away, and the naked mountain foundation shone forth all over. Where it was about the best, lay clay and heavy gravel over the rocks, but it looked so poor that it was easy to understand that hardly anything except spruce and juniper and moss and heather could grow there. But what there was plenty of was water. It had filled up all the clefts in the mountain, and lakes and rivers and brooks; these one saw everywhere, to say nothing of swamps and morasses, which spread over large tracts. And the most exasperating thing of all was, that while some tracts had too much water, it was so scarce in others, that whole fields lay like dry moors, where sand and earth whirled up in clouds with the least little breeze.

"'What can have been your meaning in creating such a land as this?' said our Lord. Saint Peter made excuses, and declared he had wished to build up a land so high that it should have plenty of warmth from the sun. 'But then you will also get much of the night chill,' said our Lord, 'for that too comes from heaven. I am very much afraid the little that can grow here will freeze.' This, to be sure, Saint Peter hadn't thought about.

"'Yes, here it will be a poor and frost-bound land,' said our Lord, 'it can't be helped.'"

When little Mats had gotten this far in his story, Osa, the goose girl, protested, "I cannot bear, little Mats, to hear you say that it is so miserable in Småland," said she. "You forget entirely how much good soil there is there. Only think of Möre district by Kalmar Sound! I wonder where you'll find a richer grain region. There are fields upon fields, just like here in Skåne. The soil is so good that I cannot imagine anything that couldn't grow there."

"I can't help that," said little Mats. "I'm only relating what others have said before."

"And I have heard many say that there is not a more beautiful coast land than Tjust. Think of the bays and islets, and the manors, and the groves!" said Osa. "Yes, that's true enough," little Mats admitted. "And don't you remember," continued Osa, "the school teacher said that such a lively and picturesque district as that bit of Småland which lies south of Lake Vettern is not to be found in all Sweden? Think of the beautiful sea and the yellow coast-mountains, and of Grenna and Jönköping, with its match factory, and think of Huskvarna, and all the big establishments there!" "Yes, that's true enough," said little Mats once again. "And think of Visingsö, little Mats, with the ruins and the oak forests and the legends! Think of the valley through which Emån flows, with all the villages and flour mills and sawmills, and the carpenter shops!" "Yes, that is true enough," said little Mats, and looked troubled.

All of a sudden he had looked up. "Now we are pretty stupid," said he. "All this, of course, lies in our Lord's Småland, in that part of the land which was already finished when Saint Peter undertook the job. It's only natural that it should be pretty and fine there. But in Saint Peter's Småland it looks as it says in the legend. And it wasn't surprising that our Lord was distressed when he saw it," continued little Mats, as he took up the thread of his story again. "Saint Peter didn't lose his courage, at all events, but tried to comfort our Lord. 'Don't be so grieved over this!' said he. 'Only wait until I have created people who can till the swamps and break up fields from the stone hills.'

"That was the end of our Lord's patience—and he said, 'No! you can go down to Skåne and make the Skåninge, but the Smålander I will create myself.' And so our Lord created the Smålander, and made him quick-witted and contented and happy and thrifty and enterprising and capable to get his livelihood in his poor country."

Then little Mats was silent, and if Nils Holgersson had also kept still, all would have gone well, but he couldn't possibly refrain from asking how Saint Peter had succeeded in creating the Skåninge.

"Well, what do you think yourself?" said little Mats, and looked so scornful that Nils Holgersson threw himself upon him, to thrash him. But Mats was only a little tot, and Osa, the goose girl, who was a year older than he, ran forward instantly to help him. Good-natured though she was, she sprang like a lion as soon as anyone touched her brother. And Nils Holgersson did not care to fight a girl, but turned his back, and didn't look at those Småland children for the rest of the day.

XVI

THE CROWS

THE EARTHEN CROCK

*I*n the southwest corner of Småland lies a township called Sonnerbo. It is a rather smooth and even country. And one who sees it in winter, when it is covered with snow, cannot imagine that there is anything under the snow but garden plots, rye fields and clover meadows as is generally the case in flat countries. But, in the beginning of April when the snow finally melts away in Sonnerbo, it is apparent that that which lies hidden under it is only dry, sandy heaths, bare rocks, and big marshy swamps. There are fields here and there, to be sure, but they are so small that they are scarcely worth mentioning, and one also finds a few little red or gray farm houses hidden away in some beech coppice—almost as if they were afraid to show themselves.

Where Sonnerbo township touches the boundaries of Halland, there is a sandy heath which is so far-reaching that he who stands upon one edge of it cannot look across to the other. Nothing except heather grows on the heath, and it wouldn't be easy either to coax other growths to thrive there. To start with, one would have to uproot the heather, for it is thus with heather: although it has, only a little shrunken root, small shrunken branches, and dry, shrunken leaves it fancies that it's a tree. Therefore it acts just like real trees—spreads itself out in forest fashion over wide areas; holds together faithfully, and causes all foreign growths that wish to crowd in upon its territory to die out.

The only place on the heath where the heather is not all-powerful, is a low, stony ridge which passes over it. There you'll find juniper bushes, mountain ash, and a few large, fine oaks. At the time when Nils Holgersson traveled around with the wild geese, a little cabin stood there, with a bit of cleared ground around it. But the people who had lived there at one time, had, for some reason or other, moved away. The little cabin was empty, and the ground lay unused.

When the tenants left the cabin they closed the damper, fastened the window hooks, and locked the door. But no one had thought of the broken window pane which was only stuffed with a rag. After the showers of a couple of summers, the rag had molded and shrunk, and, finally, a crow had succeeded in poking it out.

The ridge on the heather heath was really not as desolate as one might think, for it was inhabited by a large crow-folk. Naturally, the crows did not live there all the year round. They moved to foreign lands in the winter; in the autumn they traveled from one grain field to another all over Götaland, and picked grain. During the summer, they spread themselves over the farms in Sonnerbo township, and lived upon eggs and berries and birdlings, but every spring, when nesting time came, they came back to the heather heath.

The one who had poked the rag from the window was a crow cock named Garm Whitefeather, but he was never called anything but Fumle or Drumle, or out and out Fumle-Drumle, because he always acted awkwardly and stupidly, and wasn't good for anything except to make fun of. Fumle-Drumle was bigger and stronger than any of the other crows, but that didn't help him in the least; he was and remained—a butt for ridicule. And it didn't profit him, either, that he came from very good stock. If everything had gone smoothly, he should have been leader for the whole flock, because this honor had, from time immemorial, belonged to the oldest Whitefeather. But long before Fumle-Drumle was born, the power had gone from his family, and was now wielded by a cruel wild crow named Wind Rush.

This transference of power was due to the fact that the crows on the crow-ridge desired to change their manner of living. Possibly there are many who think that everything in the shape of a crow lives in the same way, but this is not so. There are entire crow folk who lead honorable lives—that is to say, they only eat grain, worms, caterpillars, and dead animals—and there are others who lead a regular bandit's life, who throw themselves upon baby hares and small birds, and plunder every single bird's nest they set eyes on. The ancient Whitefeathers had been strict and temperate, and as long as they had led the flock, the crows had been compelled to conduct themselves in such a way that other birds could speak no ill of them. But the crows were numerous, and poverty was great among them. They didn't care to go the whole length of living a strictly moral life, so they rebelled against the Whitefeathers, and gave the power to Wind Rush, who was the worst nest plunderer and robber that could be imagined—if his wife, Wind Air, wasn't worse still. Under their government the crows had begun to lead such a life that now they were more feared than pigeon-hawks and leech owls.

Naturally, Fumle-Drumle had nothing to say in the flock. The crows were all of the opinion that he did not in the least take after his forefathers, and that he wouldn't suit as a leader. No one would have mentioned him, if he hadn't constantly committed fresh blunders. A few, who were quite sensible, sometimes said perhaps it was lucky for Fumle-Drumle that he was such a bungling idiot, otherwise Wind Rush and Wind Air would hardly have allowed him—who was of the old chieftain stock—to remain with the flock.

Now, on the other hand, they were rather friendly toward him, and willingly took him along with them on their hunting expeditions. There all could observe how much more skilful and daring they were than he.

None of the crows knew that it was Fumle-Drumle who had pecked the rag out of the window, and had they known of this, they would have been very much astonished. Such a thing as daring to approach a human being's dwelling, they had never believed of him. He kept the thing to himself very carefully, and he had his own good reasons for it. Wind Rush and Wind Air always treated him well in the daytime, and when the others were around, but one very dark night, when the comrades sat on the night branch, he was attacked by a couple of crows and nearly murdered. After that he moved every night, after dark, from his usual sleeping quarters into the empty cabin.

Now one afternoon, when the crows had put their nests in order on crow-ridge, they happened upon a remarkable find. Wind Rush, Fumle-Drumle, and a couple of others had flown down into a big hollow in one corner of the heath. The hollow was nothing but a gravel pit, but the crows could not be satisfied with such a simple explanation; they flew down in it continually, and turned every single sand grain to get at the reason why human beings had dug it. While the crows were puttering around down there, a mass of gravel fell from one side. They rushed up to it, and had the good fortune to find amongst the fallen stones and stubble—a large earthen crock, which was locked with a wooden clasp! Naturally they wanted to know if there was anything in it, and they tried both to peck holes in the crock, and to bend up the clasp, but they had no success. They stood perfectly helpless and examined the crock, when they heard someone say, "Shall I come down and assist you crows?" They glanced up quickly. On the edge of the hollow sat a fox and blinked down at them. He was one of the prettiest foxes—both in color and form—that they had ever seen. The only fault with him was that he had lost an ear.

"If you desire to do us a service," said Wind Rush, "we shall not say nay." At the same time, both he and the others flew up from the hollow. Then the fox jumped down in their place, bit at the jar, and pulled at the lock—but he couldn't open it either.

"Can you make out what there is in it?" said Wind Rush. The fox rolled the jar back and forth, and listened attentively. "It must be silver money," said he.

This was more than the crows had expected. "Do you think it can be silver?" said they, and their eyes were ready to pop out of their heads with greed; for remarkable as it may sound, there is nothing in the world which crows love as much as silver money.

"Hear how it rattles!" said the fox and rolled the crock around once more. "Only I can't understand how we shall get at it." "That will surely be impossible," said the crows. The fox stood and rubbed his head against his left leg, and pondered. Now perhaps he might succeed, with the help of the crows, in becoming master of that little imp who always eluded him. "Oh! I know someone who could open the crock for you," said the fox. "Then tell us! Tell us!" cried the crows, and they were so excited that they tumbled down into the pit. "That I will do, if you'll first promise me that you will agree to my terms," said he.

Then the fox told the crows about Thumbietot, and said that if they could bring him to the heath he would open the crock for them. But in payment for this counsel, he demanded that they should deliver Thumbietot to him, as soon as he had gotten the silver money for them. The crows had no reason to spare Thumbietot, so agreed to the compact at once. It was easy enough to agree to this, but it was harder to find out where Thumbietot and the wild geese were stopping.

Wind Rush himself traveled away with fifty crows, and said that he should soon return. But one day after another passed without the crows on crow-ridge seeing a shadow of him.

KIDNAPPED BY CROWS

Wednesday, April thirteenth

The wild geese were up at daybreak, so they should have time to get themselves a bite of food before starting out on the journey toward Östergötland. The island in Goosefjord, where they had slept, was small and barren, but in the water all around it were growths which they could eat their fill upon. It was worse for the boy, however. He couldn't manage to find anything eatable.

As he stood there hungry and drowsy, and looked around in all directions, his glance fell upon a pair of squirrels, who played upon the wooded point, directly opposite the rock island. He wondered if the squirrels still had any of their winter supplies left, and asked the white goosey-gander to take him over to the point, that he might beg a couple of hazelnuts.

Instantly the white one swam across the sound with him, but as luck would have it the squirrels had so much fun chasing each other from tree to tree, that they didn't bother about listening to the boy. They drew farther into the grove. He hurried after them, and was soon out of the goosey-gander's sight—who stayed behind and waited on the shore.

The boy waded forward between some white anemone-stems—which were so they reached to his chin—when he felt that someone caught hold of him from behind, and tried to lift him up. He turned around and saw that a crow had grabbed him by the shirt band. He tried to break loose, but before this was possible, another crow ran up, gripped him by the stocking, and knocked him over.

If Nils Holgersson had immediately cried for help, the white goosey-gander certainly would have been able to save him, but the boy probably thought that he could protect himself, unaided, against a couple of crows. He kicked and struck out, but the crows didn't let go their hold, and they soon succeeded in raising themselves into the air with him. To make matters worse, they flew so recklessly that his head struck against a branch. He received a hard knock over the head, it grew black before his eyes, and he lost consciousness.

When he opened his eyes once more, he found himself high above the ground. He regained his senses slowly; at first he knew neither where he was, nor what he saw. When he glanced down, he saw that under him was spread a tremendously big woolly carpet, which was woven in greens and reds, and in large irregular patterns. The carpet was very thick and fine, but he thought it was a pity that it had been so badly used. It was actually ragged; long tears ran through it; in some places large pieces were torn away. And the strangest of all was that it appeared to be spread over a mirror floor, for under the holes and tears in the carpet shone bright and glittering glass.

The next thing the boy observed was that the sun unrolled itself in the heavens. Instantly, the mirror glass under the holes and tears in the carpet began to shimmer in red and gold. It looked very gorgeous, and the boy was delighted with the pretty color scheme, although he didn't exactly understand what it was that he saw. But now the crows descended, and he saw at once that the big carpet under him was the earth, which was dressed in green and brown cone trees and naked leaftrees, and that the holes and tears were shining fjords and little lakes.

He remembered that the first time he had traveled up in the air, he had thought that the earth in Skåne looked like a piece of checked cloth. But this country which resembled a torn carpet—what might this be?

He began to ask himself a lot of questions! Why wasn't he sitting on the goosey-gander's back? Why did a great swarm of crows fly around him? And why was he being pulled and knocked hither and thither so that he was about to break in pieces?

Then, all at once, the whole thing dawned on him. He had been kidnapped by a couple of crows. The white goosey-gander was still on the shore, waiting, and today the wild geese were going to travel to Östergötland. He was being carried southwest; this he understood because the sun's disc was behind him. The big forest carpet which lay beneath him was surely Småland.

"What will become of the goosey-gander now, when I cannot look after him?" thought the boy, and began to call to the crows to take him back to the wild geese instantly. He wasn't at all uneasy on his own account. He believed that they were carrying him off simply in a spirit of mischief.

The crows didn't pay the slightest attention to his exhortations, but flew on as fast as they could. After a bit, one of them flapped his wings in a manner which meant, "Look out! Danger!" Soon thereafter they came down in a spruce forest, pushed their way between prickly branches to the ground, and put the boy down under a thick spruce, where he was so well-concealed that not even a falcon could have sighted him.

Fifty crows surrounded him, with bills pointed toward him to guard him. "Now perhaps I may hear, crows, what your purpose is in carrying me off," said he. But he was hardly permitted to finish the sentence before a big crow hissed at him, "Keep still! or I'll bore your eyes out."

It was evident that the crow meant what she said, and there was nothing for the boy to do but obey. So he sat there and stared at the crows, and the crows stared at him. The longer he looked at them, the less he liked them. It was dreadful how dusty and unkempt their feather dresses were—as though they knew neither baths nor oiling. Their toes and claws were grimy with dried-in mud, and the corners of their mouths were covered with food drippings. These were very different birds from the wild geese that he observed. He thought they had a sneaky, watchful, and bold appearance, like cutthroats and vagabonds.

"It is certainly a real robber band that I've fallen in with," thought he.

Just then he heard the wild geese's call above him. "Where are you? Here am I. Where are you? Here am I."

He understood that Akka and the others had gone out to search for him, but before he could answer them the big crow who appeared to be the leader of the band hissed in his ear: "Think of your eyes!" And there was nothing else for him to do but to keep still.

The wild geese may not have known that he was so near them, but had just happened, incidentally, to travel over this forest. He heard their call a couple of times more, then it died away. "Well, now you'll have to get along by yourself, Nils Holgersson," he said to himself. "Now you must prove whether you have learned anything during these weeks in the open."

A moment later the crows gave the signal to break up, and since it was still their intention, apparently, to carry him along in such a way that one held on to his shirt band, and one to a stocking, the boy said: "Is there not one among you so strong that he can carry me on his back? You have already traveled so badly with me that I feel as if I were in pieces. Only let me ride! I'll not jump from the crow's back, that I promise you."

"Oh! you needn't think that we care how you have it," said the leader. But now the largest of the crows—a disheveled and uncouth one, who had a white feather in his wing—came forward and said: "It would certainly be best for all of us, Wind Rush, if Thumbietot got there whole, rather than half, and therefore, I shall carry him on my back." "If you can do it, Fumle-Drumle, I have no objection," said Wind Rush. "But don't lose him!"

With this, much was already gained, and the boy actually felt pleased again. "There is nothing to be gained by losing my grit because I have been kidnapped by the crows," thought he. "I'll surely be able to manage those poor little things."

The crows continued to fly southwest, over Småland. It was a glorious morning—sunny and calm, and the birds down on the earth were singing their best love songs. In a high, dark forest sat the thrush himself with drooping wings and swelling throat, and struck up tune after tune. "How pretty you are! How pretty you are! How pretty you are!" sang he. "No one is so pretty. No one is so pretty. No one is so pretty." As soon as he had finished this song, he began it all over again.

But just then the boy rode over the forest, and when he had heard the song a couple of times, and marked that the thrush knew no other, he put both hands up to his mouth as a speaking trumpet, and called down: "We've heard all this before. We've heard all this before." "Who is it? Who is it? Who is it? Who makes fun of me?" asked the thrush, and tried to catch a glimpse of the one who called. "It is Kidnapped-by-Crows who makes fun of your song," answered the boy. At that, the crow chief turned his head and said, "Be careful of your eyes,

Thumbietot!" But the boy thought, "Oh! I don't care about that. I want to show you that I'm not afraid of you!"

Farther and farther inland they traveled, and there were woods and lakes everywhere. In a birch grove sat the wood dove on a naked branch, and before him stood the lady dove. He blew up his feathers, cocked his head, raised and lowered his body, until the breast feathers rattled against the branch. All the while he cooed, "Thou, thou, thou art the loveliest in all the forest. No one in the forest is so lovely as thou, thou, thou!"

But up in the air the boy rode past, and when he heard Mr. Dove, he couldn't keep still. "Don't you believe him! Don't you believe him!" cried he.

"Who, who, who is it that lies about me?" cooed Mr. Dove, and tried to get a sight of the one who shrieked at him. "It is Caught-by-Crows that lies about you," replied the boy. Again Wind Rush turned his head toward the boy and commanded him to shut up, but Fumle-Drumle, who was carrying him, said, "Let him chatter, then all the little birds will think that we crows have become quick-witted and funny birds." "Oh! they're not such fools, either," said Wind Rush, but he liked the idea just the same, for after that he let the boy call out as much as he liked.

They flew mostly over forests and woodlands, but there were churches and parishes and little cabins in the outskirts of the forest. In one place they saw a pretty old manor. It lay with the forest back of it, and the sea in front of it, had red walls and a turreted roof, great sycamores about the grounds, and big, thick gooseberry bushes in the orchard. On the top of the weathercock sat the starling, and sang so loud that every note was heard by the wife, who sat on an egg in the heart of a pear tree. "We have four pretty little eggs," sang the starling. "We have four pretty little round eggs. We have the whole nest filled with fine eggs."

When the starling sang the song for the thousandth time, the boy rode over the place. He put his hands up to his mouth, as a pipe, and called: "The magpie will get them. The magpie will get them."

"Who is it that wants to frighten me?" asked the starling, and flapped his wings uneasily. "It is Captured-by-Crows that frightens you," said the boy. This time the crow chief didn't attempt to hush him.

Instead, both he and his flock were having so much fun that they cawed with satisfaction.

The farther inland they came, the larger were the lakes, and the more plentiful were islands and points. And on a lake shore stood a drake and kowtowed before the duck. "I'll be true to you all the days of my life. I'll be true to you all the days of my life," said the drake. "It won't last until the summer's end," shrieked the boy. "Who are you?" called the drake. "My name's Stolen-by-Crows," shrieked the boy.

At dinner time the crows lighted in a food grove. They walked about and procured food for themselves, but none of them thought about giving the boy anything. Then Fumle-Drumle came riding up to the chief with a dog-rose branch, with a few dried buds on it. "Here's something for you, Wind Rush," said he. "This is pretty food, and suitable for you." Wind Rush sniffed contemptuously. "Do you think that I want to eat old, dry buds?" said he. "And I who thought that you would be pleased with them!" said Fumle-Drumle, and threw away the dog-rose branch as if in despair. But it fell right in front of the boy, and he wasn't slow about grabbing it and eating until he was satisfied.

When the crows had eaten, they began to chatter. "What are you thinking about, Wind Rush? You are so quiet today," said one of them to the leader. "I'm thinking that in this district there lived, once upon a time, a hen, who was very fond of her mistress, and in order to really please her, she went and laid a nest full of eggs, which she hid under the storehouse floor. The mistress of the house wondered, of course, where the hen was keeping herself such a long time. She searched for her, but did not find her. Can you guess, Longbill, who it was that found her and the eggs?"

"I think I can guess it, Wind Rush, but when you have told about this, I will tell you something like it. Do you remember the big, black cat in Hinneryd's parish house? She was dissatisfied because they always took the newborn kittens from her and drowned them. Just once did she succeed in keeping them concealed, and that was when she had laid them in a haystack, outdoors. She was pretty well pleased with those young kittens, but I believe that I got more pleasure out of them than she did."

Now they became so excited that they all talked at once. "What kind of an accomplishment is that—to steal little kittens?" said one. "I once chased a young hare who was almost full-grown. That meant to follow him from covert to covert." He got no further before another took the words from him. "It may be fun, perhaps, to annoy hens and cats, but I find it still more remarkable that a crow can worry a human being. I once stole a silver spoon...."

But now the boy thought he was too good to sit and listen to such gabble. "Now listen to me, you crows!" said he. "I think you ought to be ashamed of yourselves to talk about all your wickedness. I have lived amongst wild geese for three weeks, and of them I have never heard or seen anything but good. You must have a bad chief, since he permits you to rob and murder in this way. You ought to begin to lead new lives, for I can tell you that human beings have grown so tired of your wickedness they are trying with all their might to root you out. And then there will soon be an end of you."

When Wind Rush and the crows heard this, they were so furious that they intended to throw themselves upon him and tear him in pieces. But Fumle-Drumle laughed and cawed and stood in front of him. "Oh, no, no!" said he, and seemed absolutely terrified.

"What think you that Wind Air will say if you tear Thumbietot in pieces before he has gotten that silver money for us?" "It has to be you, Fumle-Drumle, that's afraid of womenfolk," said Rush. But, at any rate, both he and the others left Thumbietot in peace.

Shortly after that the crows went further. Until now the boy thought that Småland wasn't such a poor country as he had heard. Of course it was woody and full of mountain-ridges, but alongside the islands and lakes lay cultivated grounds, and any real desolation he hadn't come upon. But the farther inland they came, the fewer were the villages and cottages. Toward the last, he thought that he was riding over a veritable wilderness where he saw nothing but swamps and heaths and juniper hills.

The sun had gone down, but it was still perfect daylight when the crows reached the large heather heath. Wind Rush sent a crow on ahead, to say that he had met with success, and when it was known, Wind Air, with several hundred crows from crow-ridge, flew to meet the arrivals. In the midst of the deafening cawing which the crows emitted, Fumle-Drumle said to the boy: "You have been so comical and so jolly during the trip that I am really fond of you. Therefore I want to give you some good advice. As soon as we light, you'll be requested to do a bit of work which may seem very easy to you, but beware of doing it!"

Soon thereafter Fumle-Drumle put Nils Holgersson down in the bottom of a sand-pit. The boy flung himself down, rolled over, and lay there as though he was simply done up with fatigue. Such a lot of crows fluttered about him that the air rustled like a windstorm, but he didn't look up.

"Thumbietot," said Wind Rush, "Get up now! You shall help us with a matter which will be very easy for you."

The boy didn't move, but pretended to be asleep. Then Wind Rush took him by the arm, and dragged him over the sand to an earthen crock of old-time make, that was standing in the pit. "Get up, Thumbietot," said he, "and open this crock!" "Why can't you let me sleep?" said the boy. "I'm too tired to do anything tonight. Wait until tomorrow!"

"Open the crock!" said Wind Rush, shaking him. "How shall a poor little child be able to open such a crock? Why, it's quite as large as I am myself." "Open it!" commanded Wind Rush once more, "or it will be a sorry thing for you." The boy got up, tottered over to the crock, fumbled the clasp, and let his arms fall. "I'm not usually so weak," said he. "If you will only let me sleep until morning, I think that I'll be able to manage with that clasp."

But Wind Rush was impatient, and he rushed forward and pinched the boy in the leg. That sort of treatment the boy didn't care to suffer from a crow. He jerked himself loose quickly, ran a couple of paces backward, drew his knife from the sheath, and held it extended in front of him. "You'd better be careful!" he cried to Wind Rush.

This one too was so enraged that he didn't dodge the danger. He rushed at the boy, just as though he'd been blind, and ran so straight against the knife, that it entered through his eye into the head. The boy drew the knife back quickly, but Wind Rush only struck out with his wings, then he fell down—dead.

"Wind Rush is dead! The stranger has killed our chieftain, Wind Rush!" cried the nearest crows, and then there was a terrible uproar. Some wailed, others cried for vengeance. They all ran or fluttered up to the boy, with Fumle-Drumle in the lead. But he acted badly as usual. He only fluttered and spread his wings over the boy, and prevented the others from coming forward and running their bills into him.

The boy thought that things looked very bad for him now. He couldn't run away from the crows, and there was no place where he could hide. Then he happened to think of the earthen crock. He took a firm hold on the clasp, and pulled it off. Then he hopped into the crock to hide in it. But the crock was a poor hiding place, for it was nearly filled to the brim with little, thin silver coins. The boy couldn't get far enough down, so he stooped and began to throw out the coins.

Until now the crows had fluttered around him in a thick swarm and pecked at him, but when he threw out the coins they immediately forgot their thirst for vengeance, and hurried to gather the money. The boy threw out handfuls of it, and all the crows—yes, even Wind Air herself—picked them up. And everyone who succeeded in picking up a coin ran off to the nest with the utmost speed to conceal it.

When the boy had thrown out all the silver pennies from the crock he glanced up. Not more than a single crow was left in the sandpit. That was Fumle-Drumle, with the white feather in his wing; he who had carried Thumbietot. "You have rendered me a greater service than you yourself understand," said the crow—with a very different voice, and a different intonation than the one he had used heretofore—"and I want to save your life. Sit down on my back, and I'll take you to a hiding place where you can be secure for tonight. Tomorrow, I'll arrange it so that you will get back to the wild geese."

THE CABIN

Thursday, April fourteenth

*T*he following morning when the boy awoke, he lay in a bed. When he saw that he was in a house with four walls around him, and a roof over him, he thought that he was at home. "I wonder if mother will come soon with some coffee," he muttered to himself where he lay half-awake. Then he remembered that he was in a deserted cabin on the crow-ridge, and that Fumle-Drumle with the white feather had borne him there the night before.

The boy was sore all over after the journey he had made the day before, and he thought it was lovely to lie still while he waited for Fumle-Drumle who had promised to come and fetch him.

Curtains of checked cotton hung before the bed, and he drew them aside to look out into the cabin. It dawned upon him instantly that he had never seen the mate to a cabin like this. The walls consisted of nothing but a couple of rows of logs, then the roof began. There was no interior ceiling, so he could look clear up to the roof tree. The cabin was so small that it appeared to have been built rather for such as he than for real people. However, the fireplace and chimney were so large, he thought that he had never seen larger. The entrance door was in a gable wall at the side of the fireplace, and was so narrow that it was more like a wicket than a door. In the other gable wall he saw a low, broad window with many panes. There was scarcely any movable furniture in the cabin. The bench on one side and the table under the window were stationary, also the bed where he lay, and the many-colored cupboard.

The boy could not help wondering who owned the cabin, and why it was deserted. It certainly looked as though the people who had lived there expected to return. The coffee urn and the gruel pot stood on the hearth, and there was some wood in the fireplace; the oven rake and baker's peel stood in a corner; the spinning wheel was raised on a bench; on the shelf over the window lay oakum and flax, a couple of skeins of yarn, a candle, and a bunch of matches.

Yes, it surely looked as if those who had lived there had intended to come back. There were bedclothes on the bed, and on the walls there still hung long strips of cloth, upon which three riders named Kasper, Melchior, and Baltasar were painted. The same horses and riders were pictured many times. They rode around the whole cabin, and continued their ride even up toward the joists.

But in the roof the boy saw something which brought him to his senses in a jiffy. It was a couple of loaves of big breadcakes that hung there upon a spit. They looked old and moldy, but it was bread all the same. He gave them a knock with the oven rake and one piece fell to the floor. He ate and stuffed his bag full. It was incredible how good bread was, anyway.

He looked around the cabin once more, to try and discover if there was anything else which he might find useful to take along. "I may as well take what I need, since no one else cares about it," thought he. But most of the things were too big and heavy. The only things that he could carry might be a few matches perhaps.

He clambered up on the table, and swung with the help of the curtains up to the window shelf. While he stood there and stuffed the matches into his bag, the crow with the white feather came in through the window. "Well here I am at last," said Fumle-Drumle as he lit on the table. "I couldn't get here any sooner because we crows have elected a new chieftain in Wind Rush's place," "Whom have you chosen?" said the boy. "Well, we have chosen one who will not permit robbery and injustice. We have elected Garm Whitefeather, lately called Fumle-Drumle," answered he, drawing himself up until he looked absolutely regal. "That was a good choice," said the boy and congratulated him. "You may well wish me luck," said Garm, then he told the boy about the time they had had with Wind Rush and Wind Air.

During this recital the boy heard a voice outside the window which he thought sounded familiar. "Is he here?" inquired the fox. "Yes, he's hidden in there," answered a crow voice. "Be careful, Thumbietot!" cried Garm. "Wind Air stands without with that fox who wants to eat you." More he didn't have time to say, for Smirre dashed against the window. The old, rotten window frame gave way, and the next second Smirre stood upon the window table. Garm Whitefeather, who didn't have time to fly away, he killed instantly. Thereupon he jumped down to the floor, and looked around for the boy. He tried to hide behind a big oakum spiral, but Smirre had already spied him, and was crouched for the final spring. The cabin was so small, and so low, the boy understood that the fox could reach him without the least difficulty. But just at that moment the boy was not without weapons of defense. He struck a match quickly, touched the curtains, and when they were in flames, he threw them down upon Smirre Fox. When the fire enveloped the fox, he was seized with a mad terror. He thought no more about the boy, but rushed wildly out of the cabin.

But it looked as if the boy had escaped one danger to throw himself into a greater one. From the tuft of oakum which he had flung at Smirre the fire had spread to the bed hangings. He jumped down and tried to smother it, but it blazed too quickly now. The cabin was soon filled with smoke, and Smirre Fox, who had remained just outside the window, began to grasp the state of affairs within. "Well, Thumbietot," he called out, "which do you choose now: to be broiled alive in there, or to come out here to me? Of course, I should prefer to have the pleasure of eating you, but in whichever way death meets you it will be dear to me."

The boy could not think but that the fox was right, for the fire was making rapid headway. The whole bed was now in a blaze, and smoke rose from the floor, and along the painted wall strips the fire crept from rider to rider. The boy jumped up in the fireplace, and tried to open the oven door, when he heard a key which turned around slowly in the lock. It must be human beings coming. And in the dire extremity in which he found himself, he was not afraid, but only glad. He was already on the threshold when the door opened. He saw a couple of children facing him, but how they looked when they saw the cabin in flames, he took no time to find out, but rushed past them into the open.

He didn't dare run far. He knew, of course, that Smirre Fox lay in wait for him, and he understood that he must remain near the children. He turned around to see what sort of folk they were, but he hadn't looked at them a second before he ran up to them and cried, "Oh, good day, Osa goose girl! Oh, good day, little Mats!"

For when the boy saw those children he forgot entirely where he was. Crows and burning cabin and talking animals had vanished from his memory. He was walking on a stubble field in West Vemminghög, tending a goose flock, and beside him, on the field, walked those same Småland children with their geese. As soon as he saw them, he ran up on the stone hedge and shouted, "Oh, good day, Osa goose girl! Oh, good day, little Mats!"

But when the children saw such a little creature coming up to them with outstretched hands, they grabbed hold of each other, took a couple of steps backward, and looked scared to death. When the boy noticed their terror he woke up and remembered who he was. And then it seemed to him that nothing worse could happen to him, than that those children should see how he had been bewitched. Shame and grief—because he was no longer a human being—overpowered him. He turned and fled. He knew not whither.

But a glad meeting awaited the boy when he came down to the heath. For there, in the heather, he spied something white, and toward him came the white goosey-gander, accompanied by Dunfin. When the white one saw the boy running with such speed, he thought that dreadful fiends were pursuing him. He flung him in all haste upon his back and flew off with him.

XVII
THE OLD PEASANT WOMAN

Three tired wanderers were out in the late evening in search of a night harbor. They traveled over a poor and desolate portion of northern Småland. But the sort of resting place which they wanted, they should have been able to find, for they were no weaklings who asked for soft beds or comfortable rooms. "If one of these long mountain ridges had a peak so high and steep that a fox couldn't in any way climb up to it, then we should have a good sleeping place," said one of them. "If a single one of the big swamps was thawed out, and was so marshy and wet that a fox wouldn't dare venture out on it, this, too, would be a right good night harbor," said the second. "If the ice on one of the large lakes we travel past were loose, so that a fox could not come out on it, then we should have found just what we are seeking," said the third.

The worst of it was that when the sun had gone down, two of the travelers became so sleepy that every second they were ready to fall to the ground. The third one, who could keep himself awake, grew more and more uneasy as night approached. "Then it was a misfortune that we came to a land where lakes and swamps are frozen, so that a fox can get around everywhere. In other places the ice has melted away, but now we're well up in the very coldest Småland, where spring has not as yet arrived. I don't know how I shall ever manage to find a good sleeping place! Unless I find some spot that is well protected, Smirre Fox will be upon us before morning."

He gazed in all directions, but he saw no shelter where he could lodge. It was a dark and chilly night, with wind and drizzle. It grew more terrible and disagreeable around him every second.

This may sound strange, perhaps, but the travelers didn't seem to have the least desire to ask for house room on any farm. They had already passed many parishes without knocking at a single door. Little hillside cabins on the outskirts of the forest, which all poor wanderers are glad to run across, they took no notice of either. One might almost be tempted to say they deserved to have a hard time of it, since they did not seek help where it was to be had for the asking.

But finally, when it was so dark that there was scarcely a glimmer of light left under the skies and the two who needed sleep journeyed on in a kind of half-sleep, they happened into a farmyard which was a long way off from all neighbors. And not only did it lie there desolate, but it appeared to be uninhabited as well. No smoke rose from the chimney; no light shone through the windows; no human being moved on the place. When the one among the three who could keep awake, saw the place, he thought: "Now come what may, we must try to get in here. Anything better we are not likely to find."

Soon after that, all three stood in the house yard. Two of them fell asleep the instant they stood still, but the third looked about him eagerly, to find where they could get under cover. It was not a small farm. Beside the dwelling house and stable and smoke house, there were long ranges with granaries and storehouses and cattlesheds. But it all looked awfully poor and dilapidated. The houses had gray, moss-grown, leaning walls, which seemed ready to topple over. In the roofs were yawning holes, and the doors hung aslant on broken hinges. It was apparent that no one had taken the trouble to drive a nail into a wall on this place for a long time.

Meanwhile, he who was awake had figured out which house was the cow shed. He roused his traveling companions from their sleep, and conducted them to the cow shed door. Luckily, this was not fastened with anything but a hook, which he could easily push up with a rod. He heaved a sigh of relief at the thought that they should soon be in safety. But when the cow shed door swung open with a sharp creaking, he heard a cow begin to bellow. "Are you coming at last, mistress?" said she. "I thought that you didn't propose to give me any supper tonight."

The one who was awake stopped in the doorway, absolutely terrified when he discovered that the cow shed was not empty. But he soon saw that there was not more than one cow, and three or four chickens, and then he took courage again. "We are three poor travelers who want to come in somewhere, where no fox can assail us, and no human being capture us," said he. "We wonder if this can be a good place for us." "I cannot believe but what it is," answered the cow. "To be sure the walls are poor, but the fox does not walk through them as yet, and no one lives here except an old peasant woman, who isn't at all likely to make a captive of anyone. But who are you?" she continued, as she twisted in her stall to get a sight of the newcomers. "I am Nils Holgersson from Vernminghög, who has been transformed into an elf," replied the first of the incomers, "and I have with me a tame goose, whom I generally ride, and a gray goose." "Such rare guests have never before been within my four walls," said the cow, "and you shall be welcome, although I would have preferred that it had been my mistress, come to give me my supper."

The boy led the geese into the cow shed, which was rather large, and placed them in an empty manger, where they fell asleep instantly. For himself, he made a little bed of straw and expected that he, too, should go to sleep at once.

But this was impossible, for the poor cow, who hadn't had her supper, wasn't still an instant. She shook her flanks, moved around in the stall, and complained of how hungry she was. The boy couldn't get a wink of sleep, but lay there and lived over all the things that had happened to him during these last days.

He thought of Osa, the goose girl, and little Mats, whom he had encountered so unexpectedly, and he fancied that the little cabin which he had set on fire must have been their old home in Småland. He recalled that he had heard them speak of just such a cabin, and of the heather heath which lay below it. Now they had wandered back there to see their old home again, and when they had reached it it was in flames.

It was indeed a great sorrow which he had brought upon them, and it hurt him very much. If he ever again became a human being, he would try to compensate them for the damage and miscalculation.

Then his thoughts wandered to the crows. And when he thought of Fumle-Drumle who had saved his life, and had met his own death so soon after he had been elected chieftain, he was so distressed that tears filled his eyes. He had had a pretty rough time of it these last few days. But, anyway, it was a rare stroke of luck that the goosey-gander and Dunfin had found him.

The goosey-gander had said that as soon as the wild geese discovered that Thumbietot had disappeared, they had asked all the small animals in the forest about him. They soon learned that a flock of Småland crows had carried him off. But the crows were already out of sight, and whither they had directed their course no one had been able to say. That they might find the boy as soon as possible, Akka had commanded the wild geese to start out—two and two—in different directions, to search for him. But after a two-day hunt, whether or not they had found him, they were to meet in northwestern Småland on a high mountain top, which resembled an abrupt, chopped-off tower, and was called Taberg. After Akka had given them the best directions, and described carefully how they should find Taberg, they had separated.

The white goosey-gander had chosen Dunfin as traveling companion, and they had flown about hither and thither with the greatest anxiety for Thumbietot. During this ramble they had heard a thrush, who sat in a tree top, cry and wail that someone, who called himself Kidnapped-by-Crows, had made fun of him. They had talked with the thrush, and he had shown them in which direction that Kidnapped-by-Crows had traveled. Afterward, they had met a dove cock, a starling, and a drake; they had all wailed about a little culprit who had disturbed their song, and who was named Caught-by-Crows, Captured-by-Crows, and Stolen-by-Crows. In this way, they were enabled to trace Thumbietot all the way to the heather heath in Sonnerbo township.

As soon as the goosey-gander and Dunfin had found Thumbietot, they had started toward the north, in order to reach Taberg. But it had been a long road to travel, and the darkness was upon them before they had sighted the mountain top. "If we only get there by tomorrow, surely all our troubles will be over," thought the boy, and dug down into the straw to have it warmer. All the while the cow fussed and fumed in the stall. Then, all of a sudden, she began to talk to the boy. "Everything is wrong with me," said the cow. "I am neither milked nor tended. I have no night fodder in my manger, and no bed bas been made under me. My mistress came here at dusk, to put things in order for me, but she felt so ill, that she had to go in soon again, and she has not returned."

"It's distressing that I should be so little and powerless," said the boy. "I don't believe that I am able to help you." "You can't make me believe that you are powerless because you are little," said the cow. "All the elves that I've ever heard of, were so strong that they could pull a whole load of hay and strike a cow dead with one fist." The boy couldn't help laughing at the cow. "They were a very different kind of elf from me," said he. "But I'll loosen your halter and open the door for you, so that you can go out and drink in one of the pools on the place, and then I'll try to climb up to the hayloft and throw down some hay in your manger." "Yes, that would be some help," said the cow.

The boy did as he had said, and when the cow stood with a full manger in front of her, he thought that at last he should get some sleep. But he had hardly crept down in the bed before she began, anew, to talk to him.

"You'll be clean put out with me if I ask you for one thing more," said the cow. "Oh, no I won't, if it's only something that I'm able to do," said the boy. "Then I will ask you to go into the cabin, directly opposite, and find out how my mistress is getting along. I fear some misfortune has come to her." "No! I can't do that," said the boy. "I dare not show myself before human beings." "Surely you're not afraid of an old and sick woman," said the cow. "But you do not need to go into the cabin. Just stand outside the door and peep in through the crack!" "Oh! if that is all you ask of me, I'll do it of course," said the boy.

With that he opened the cow shed door and went out into the yard. It was a fearful night! Neither moon nor stars shone; the wind blew a gale, and the rain came down in torrents. And the worst of all was that seven great owls sat in a row on the eaves of the cabin. It was awful just to hear them from where they sat and grumbled at the weather, but it was even worse to think what would happen to him if one of them should set eyes on him. That would be the last of him.

"Pity him who is little!" said the boy as he ventured in the yard. He had a right to say this, for he was blown down twice before he got to the house. Once, the wind swept him into a pool, which was so deep that he came near drowning. But he got there nevertheless.

He clambered up a pair of steps, scrambled over a threshold, and came into the hallway. The cabin door was closed, but down in one corner a large piece had been cut away, so the cat might go in and out. It was no difficulty whatever for the boy to see how things were in the cabin. He had hardly cast a glance in there before he staggered back and turned his head away. An old, gray-haired woman lay stretched out on the floor within. She neither moved nor moaned, and her face shone strangely white. It was as if an invisible moon had thrown a feeble light over it.

The boy remembered that when his grandfather had died, his face had also become so strangely white-like. And he understood that the old woman who lay on the cabin floor must be dead. Death had probably come to her so suddenly that she didn't even have time to lie down on her bed.

As he thought of being alone with the dead in the middle of the dark night, he was terribly afraid. He threw himself headlong down the steps, and rushed back to the cow shed.

When he told the cow what he had seen in the cabin, she stopped eating. "So my mistress is dead," said she. "Then it will soon be over for me as well." "There will always be someone to look out for you," said the boy comfortingly. "Ah! you don't know," said the cow, "that I am already twice as old as a cow usually is before she is laid upon the slaughter bench. But then I do not care to live any longer, since she, in there, can come no more to care for me."

She said nothing more for a while, but the boy observed, no doubt, that she neither slept nor ate. It was not long before she began to speak again. "Is she lying on the bare floor?" she asked. "She is," said the boy. "She had a habit of coming out to the cow shed," she continued, "and talking about everything that troubled her. I understood what she said, although I could not answer her. These last few days she talked of how afraid she was lest there would be no one with her when she died. She was anxious for fear no one should close her eyes and fold her hands across her breast, after she was dead. Perhaps you'll go in and do this?" The boy hesitated. He remembered that when his grandfather had died, mother had been very careful about putting everything to rights. He knew this was something which had to be done. But, on the other hand, he felt that he didn't dare go to the dead, in the ghastly night. He didn't say no, neither did he take a step toward the cow shed door. For a couple of seconds the old cow was silent—just as if she had expected an answer. But when the boy said nothing, she did not repeat her request. Instead, she began to talk with him of her mistress.

There was much to tell, first and foremost, about all the children which she had brought up. They had been in the cow shed every day, and in the summer they had taken the cattle to pasture on the swamp and in the groves so the old cow knew all about them. They had been splendid, all of them, and happy and industrious. A cow knew well enough what her caretakers were good for.

There was also much to be said about the farm. It had not always been as poor as it was now. It was very large although the greater part of it consisted of swamps and stony groves. There was not much room for fields, but there was plenty of good fodder everywhere. At one time there had been a cow for every stall in the cow shed, and the ox shed, which was now empty, had at one time been filled with oxen. And then there was life and gayety, both in cabin and cow house. When the mistress opened the cow shed door she would hum and sing, and all the cows lowed with gladness when they heard her coming.

But the good man had died when the children were so small that they could not be of any assistance, and the mistress had to take charge of the farm, and all the work and responsibility. She had been as strong as a man, and had both plowed and reaped. In the evenings, when she came into the cow shed to milk, sometimes she was so tired that she wept. Then she dashed away her tears and was cheerful again. "It doesn't matter. Good times are coming again for me too, if only my children grow up. Yes, if they only grow up."

But as soon as the children were grown, a strange longing came over them. They didn't want to stay at home, but went away to a strange country. Their mother never got any help from them. A couple of her children were married before they went away, and they had left their children behind, in the old home. And now these children followed the mistress in the cow shed, just as her own had done. They tended the cows, and were fine, good folk. And, in the evenings, when the mistress was so tired that she could fall asleep in the middle of the milking, she would rouse herself again to renewed courage by thinking of them: "Good times are coming for me, too," said she—and shook off sleep—"when once they are grown."

But when these children grew up, they went away to their parents in the strange land. No one came back—no one stayed at home—the old mistress was left alone on the farm.

Probably she had never asked them to remain with her. "Think you, Rödlinna, that I would ask them to stay here with me, when they can go out in the world and have things comfortable?" she would say as she stood in the stall with the old cow. "Here in Småland they have only poverty to look forward to."

But when the last grandchild was gone, it was all up with the mistress. All at once she became bent and gray, and tottered as she walked, as if she no longer had the strength to move about. She stopped working. She did not care to look after the farm, but let everything go to rack and ruin. She didn't repair the houses, and she sold both the cows and the oxen. The only one that she kept was the old cow who now talked with Thumbietot. Her she let live because all the children had tended her.

She could have taken maids and farm hands into her service, who would have helped her with the work, but she couldn't bear to see strangers around her, since her own had deserted her. Perhaps she was better satisfied to let the farm go to ruin, since none of her children were coming back to take it after she was gone. She did not mind that she herself became poor, because she didn't value that which was only hers. But she was troubled lest the children should find out how hard she had it. "If only the children do not hear of this! If only the children do not hear of this!" she sighed as she tottered through the cow house.

The children wrote constantly, and begged her to come out to them, but this she did not wish. She didn't want to see the land that had taken them from her. She was angry with it. "It's foolish of me, perhaps, that I do not like that land which has been so good for them," said she. "But I don't want to see it."

She never thought of anything but the children, and of this—that they must have gone. When summer came, she led the cow out to graze in the big swamp. All day she would sit on the edge of the swamp, her hands in her lap, and on the way home she would say: "You see Rödlinna, if there had been large, rich fields here, in place of these barren swamps, then there would have been no need for them to leave."

She could become furious with the swamp which spread out so big, and did no good. She could sit and talk about how it was the swamp's fault that the children had left her.

This last evening she had been more trembly and feeble than ever before. She could not even do the milking. She had leaned against the manger and talked about two strangers who had been to see her, and had asked if they might buy the swamp. They wanted to drain it, and sow and raise grain on it. This had made her both anxious and glad. "Do you hear, Rödlinna," she had said, "do you hear they said that grain can grow on the swamp? Now I shall write to the children to come home. Now they'll not have to stay away any longer, for now they can get their bread here at home." It was this that she had gone into the cabin to do.

The boy heard no more of what the old cow said. He had opened the cow house door and gone across the yard, and in to the dead whom he had but lately been so afraid of.

It was not so poor in the cabin as he had expected. It was well-supplied with the sort of things one generally finds among those who have relatives in America. In a corner there was an American rocking chair; on the table before the window lay a brocaded plush cover; there was a pretty spread on the bed; on the walls, in carved wood frames, hung the photographs of the children and grandchildren who had gone away; on the bureau stood high vases and a couple of candlesticks, with thick, spiral candles in them.

The boy searched for a matchbox and lighted these candles, not because he needed more light than he already had, but because he thought that this was one way to honor the dead.

Then he went up to her, closed her eyes, folded her hands across her breast, and stroked back the thin gray hair from her face.

He thought no more about being afraid of her. He was so deeply grieved because she had been forced to live out her old age in loneliness and longing. He, at least, would watch over her dead body this night.

He hunted up the psalm book, and seated himself to read a couple of psalms in an undertone. But in the middle of the reading he paused—because he had begun to think about his mother and father.

Think, that parents can long so for their children! This he had never known. Think, that life can be as though it was over for them when the children are away! Think, if those at home longed for him in the same way that this old peasant woman had longed!

This thought made him happy, but he dared not believe in it. He had not been such a one that anybody could long for him, but what he had not been, perhaps he could become.

Round about him he saw the portraits of those who were away. They were big, strong men and women with earnest faces. There were brides in long veils, and gentlemen in fine clothes, and there were children with waved hair and pretty white dresses. And he thought that they all stared blindly into vacancy—and did not want to see.

"Poor you!" said the boy to the portraits. "Your mother is dead. You cannot make reparation now, because you went away from her. But my mother is living!"

Here he paused, and nodded and smiled to himself. "My mother is living," said he. "Both Father and Mother are living."

XVIII

FROM TABERG
TO HUSKVARNA

Friday, April fifteenth

The boy sat awake nearly all night, but toward morning he fell asleep and then he dreamed of his father and mother. He could hardly recognize them. They had both grown gray, and had old and wrinkled faces. He asked how this had come about, and they answered that they had aged so because they had longed for him. He was both touched and astonished, for he had never believed but that they were glad to be rid of him.

When the boy awoke the morning had come, with fine, clear weather. First, he himself ate a bit of bread which he found in the cabin, then he gave morning feed to both geese and cow, and opened the cow house door so that the cow could go over to the nearest farm. When the cow came along all by herself the neighbors would no doubt understand that something was wrong with her mistress. They would hurry over to the desolate farm to see how the old woman was getting along, and then they would find her dead body and bury it.

The boy and the geese had barely raised themselves into the air when they caught a glimpse of a high mountain, with almost perpendicular walls, and an abrupt, broken-off top, and they understood that this must be Taberg. On the summit stood Akka, with Yksi and Kaksi, Kolmi and Nelja, Viisi and Knusi, and all six goslings had waited for them. There was a rejoicing, and a cackling, and a fluttering, and a calling which no one can describe, when they saw that the goosey-gander and Dunfin had succeeded in finding Thumbietot.

The woods grew pretty high up on Taberg's sides, but her highest peak was barren, and from there one could look far out in all directions.

If one gazed toward the east, or south, or west, there was hardly anything to be seen but a poor highland with dark spruce trees, brown morasses, ice-clad lakes, and bluish mountain ridges. The boy couldn't keep from thinking it was true that the one who had created this hadn't taken very great pains with his work, but had thrown it together in a hurry. But if one glanced to the north, it was altogether different. Here it looked as if it had been worked out with the utmost care and affection. In this direction one saw only beautiful mountains, soft valleys, and winding rivers, all the way to the big Lake Vettern, which lay ice-free and transparently clear, and shone as if it weren't filled with water but with blue light.

It was Vettern that made it so pretty to look toward the north, because it looked as though a blue stream had risen up from the lake, and spread itself over land also. Groves and hills and roofs, and the spires of Jönköping City—which shimmered along Vettern's shores—lay enveloped in pale blue which caressed the eye. If there were countries in heaven, they, too, must be blue like this, thought the boy, and imagined that he had gotten a faint idea of how it must look in Paradise.

Later in the day, when the geese continued their journey, they flew up toward the blue valley. They were in holiday humor, shrieked and made such a racket that no one who had ears could help hearing them.

This happened to be the first really fine spring day they had had in this section. Until now, the spring had done its work under rain and bluster, and now, when it had all of a sudden become fine weather, the people were filled with such a longing for summer warmth and green woods that they could hardly perform their tasks. And when wild geese rode by, high above the ground, cheerful and free, there wasn't one who did not drop what he had in hand, and glance at them.

The first ones who saw the wild geese that day were miners on Taberg, who were digging ore at the mouth of the mine. When they heard them cackle, they paused in their drilling for ore, and one of them called to the birds: "Where are you going? Where are you going?" The geese didn't understand what he said, but the boy leaned forward over the goose back, and answered for them: "Where there is neither pick nor hammer." When the miners heard the words, they thought it was their own longing that made the goose cackle sound like human speech.

"Take us along with you! Take us along with you!" they cried. "Not this year," shrieked the boy. "Not this year."

The wild geese followed Taber River down toward Monk Lake, and all the while they made the same racket. Here, on the narrow land strip between Monk and Vettern lakes, lay Jönköping with its great factories. The wild geese rode first over Monksjö paper mills. The noon rest hour was just over, and the big workmen were streaming down to the millgate. When they heard the wild geese, they stopped a moment to listen to them. "Where are you going? Where are you going?" called the workmen. The wild geese understood nothing of what they said, but the boy answered for them: "There, where there are neither machines nor steam boxes." When the workmen heard the answer, they believed it was their own longing that made the goose cackle sound like human speech. "Take us along with you!" "Not this year," answered the boy. "Not this year."

Next, the geese rode over the well-known match factory, which lies on the shores of Vettern—large as a fortress—and lifts its high chimneys toward the sky. Not a soul moved out in the yards, but in a large hall young working-women sat and filled matchboxes. They had opened a window on account of the beautiful weather, and through it came the wild geese's call. The one who sat nearest the window, leaned out with a match-box in her hand, and cried, "Where are you going? Where are you going?" "To that land where there is no need of either light or matches," said the boy. The girl thought that what she had heard, was only goose-cackle, but since she thought she had distinguished a couple of words, she called out in answer: "Take me along with you!" "Not this year," replied the boy. "Not this year."

East of the factories rises Jönköping, on the most glorious spot that any city can occupy. The narrow Vettern has high, steep sand-shores, both on the eastern and western sides, but straight south, the sand-walls are broken down just as if to make room for a large gate, through which one reaches the lake. And in the middle of the gate—with mountains to the left, and mountains to the right, with Monk Lake behind it, and Vettern in front of it—lies Jönköping.

The wild geese traveled forward over the long, narrow city, and behaved themselves here just as they had done in the country. But in the city there was no one who answered them. It was not to be expected that city folks should stop out in the streets, and call to the wild geese.

The trip extended further along Vettern's shores, and after a little they came to Sanna Sanitarium. Some of the patients had gone out on the veranda to enjoy the spring air, and in this way they heard the goose-cackle. "Where are you going?" asked one of them with such a feeble voice that he was scarcely heard. "To that land where there is neither sorrow nor sickness," answered the boy. "Take us along with you!" said the sick ones. "Not this year," answered the boy. "Not this year."

When they had traveled still farther on, they came to Huskvarna. It lay in a valley. The mountains around it were steep and beautifully formed. A river rushed along the heights in long and narrow falls. Big workshops and factories lay below the mountain walls, and scattered over the valley bottom were the workingmen's homes, encircled by little gardens, and in the center of the valley lay the schoolhouse. Just as the wild geese came along, a bell rang, and a crowd of school children marched out in line. They were so numerous that the whole schoolyard was filled with them. "Where are you going? Where are you going?" the children shouted when they heard the wild geese. "Where there are neither books nor lessons to be found," answered the boy. "Take us along!" shrieked the children. "Not this year, but next," cried the boy. "Not this year, but next."

XIX
THE BIG BIRD LAKE

JARRO, THE WILD DUCK

O n the eastern shore of Vettern lies Mount Omberg, east of
Omberg lies Dagmosse, east of Dagmosse lies Lake Takern.
Around the whole of Takern spreads the big, even Östergöta plain.

Takern is a pretty large lake and in olden times it must have been
still larger. But then the people thought it covered entirely too much of
the fertile plain, so they attempted to drain the water from it, that they
might sow and reap on the lake bottom. But they did not succeed in lay-
ing waste the entire lake—which had evidently been their intention—
therefore it still hides a lot of land. Since the draining the lake has
become so shallow that hardly at any point is it more than a couple of
meters deep. The shores have become marshy and muddy, and out in
the lake, little mud islets stick up above the water's surface.

Now, there is one who loves to stand with his feet in the water, if he
can just keep his body and head in the air, and that is the reed. And it cannot find a better place to grow than the long, shallow Takern shores, and
around the little mud islets. It thrives so well that it grows taller than a man's
height, and so thick that it is almost impossible to push a boat through it.
It forms a broad green enclosure around the whole lake, so that it is only
accessible in a few places where the people have taken away the reeds.

But if the reeds shut the people out, they give, in return, shelter
and protection to many other things. In the reeds there are a lot of little
dams and canals with green, still water, where duckweed and pondweed
run to seed, and where gnat eggs and blackfish and worms are hatched
out in uncountable masses. And all along the shores of these little dams
and canals, there are many well-concealed places, where seabirds hatch
their eggs, and bring up their young without being disturbed, either by
enemies or food worries.

An incredible number of birds live in the Takern reeds, and more and more gather there every year, as it becomes known what a splendid abode it is. The first who settled there were the wild ducks, and they still live there by thousands. But they no longer own the entire lake, for they have been obliged to share it with swans, grebes, coots, loons, fen-ducks, and a lot of others.

Takern is certainly the largest and choicest bird lake in the whole country, and the birds may count themselves lucky as long as they own such a retreat. But it is uncertain just how long they will be in control of reeds and mud banks, for human beings cannot forget that the lake extends over a considerable portion of good and fertile soil, and every now and then the proposition to drain it comes up among them. And if these propositions were carried out, the many thousands of water birds would be forced to move from this quarter.

At the time when Nils Holgersson traveled around with the wild geese, there lived at Takern a wild duck named Jarro. He was a young bird, who had only lived one summer, one fall, and a winter, now, it was his first spring. He had just returned from South Africa, and had reached Takern in such good season that the ice was still on the lake.

One evening, when he and the other young wild ducks played at racing backward and forward over the lake, a hunter fired a couple of shots at them and Jarro was wounded in the breast. He thought he should die, but in order that the one who had shot him shouldn't get him into his power, he continued to fly as long as he possibly could. He didn't think whither he was directing his course, but only struggled to get far away. When his strength failed him, so that he could not fly any farther, he was no longer on the lake. He had flown a bit inland, and now he sank down before the entrance to one of the big farms which lie along the shores of Takern.

A moment later a young farm hand happened along. He saw Jarro, and came and lifted him up. But Jarro, who asked for nothing but to be let die in peace, gathered his last powers and nipped the farm hand in the finger, so he should let go of him.

Jarro didn't succeed in freeing himself. The encounter had this good in it at any rate: the farm hand noticed that the bird was alive. He carried him very gently into the cottage, and showed him to the mistress of the house—a young woman with a kindly face. At once she took Jarro from the farm hand, stroked him on the back and wiped away the blood which trickled down through the neck feathers. She looked him over very carefully, and when she saw how pretty he was, with his dark green, shining head, his white neck band, his brownish-red back, and his blue wing mirror, she must have thought that it was a pity for him to die. She promptly put a basket in order, and tucked the bird into it.

All the while Jarro fluttered and struggled to get loose, but when he understood that the people didn't intend to kill him, he settled down in the basket with a sense of pleasure. Now it was evident how exhausted he was from pain and loss of blood. The mistress carried the basket across the floor to place it in the corner by the fireplace, but before she put it down Jarro was already fast asleep.

In a little while Jarro was awakened by someone who nudged him gently. When he opened his eyes he experienced such an awful shock that he almost lost his senses. Now he was lost! for there stood the one who was more dangerous than either human beings or birds of prey. It was no less a thing than Caesar himself—the long-haired dog—who nosed around him inquisitively.

How pitifully scared had he not been last summer, when he was still a little yellow-down duckling, every time it had sounded over the reed stems, "Caesar is coming! Caesar is coming!" When he had seen the brown and white spotted dog with the teeth-filled jowls come wading through the reeds, he had believed that he beheld death itself. He had always hoped that he would never have to live through that moment when he should meet Caesar face to face.

But, to his sorrow, he must have fallen down in the very yard where Caesar lived, for there he stood right over him. "Who are you?" he growled. "How did you get into the house? Don't you belong down among the reed banks?"

It was with great difficulty that he gained the courage to answer. "Don't be angry with me, Caesar, because I came into the house!" said he. "It isn't my fault. I have been wounded by a gunshot. It was the people themselves who laid me in this basket."

"Oho! so it's the folks themselves that have placed you here," said Caesar. "Then it is surely their intention to cure you, although, for my part, I think it would be wiser for them to eat you up, since you are in their power. But, at any rate, you are tabooed in the house. You needn't look so scared. Now, we're not down on Takern."

With that Caesar laid himself to sleep in front of the blazing log fire. As soon as Jarro understood that this terrible danger was past, extreme lassitude came over him, and he fell asleep anew.

The next time Jarro awoke, he saw that a dish with grain and water stood before him. He was still quite ill, but he felt hungry nevertheless, and began to eat. When the mistress saw that he ate, she came up and petted him, and looked pleased. After that, Jarro fell asleep again. For several days he did nothing but eat and sleep.

One morning Jarro felt so well that he stepped from the basket and wandered along the floor. But he hadn't gone very far before he keeled over, and lay there. Then came Caesar, who opened his big jaws and grabbed him. Jarro believed that the dog was going to bite him to death, but Caesar carried him back to the basket without harming him. Because of this, Jarro acquired such a confidence in the dog Caesar that on his next walk in the cottage, he went over to the dog and lay down beside him. Thereafter Caesar and he became good friends, and every day, for several hours, Jarro lay and slept between Caesar's paws.

But an even greater affection than he felt for Caesar, did Jarro feel toward his mistress. Of her he had not the least fear, but rubbed his head against her hand when she came and fed him. Whenever she went out of the cottage he sighed with regret, and when she came back he cried welcome to her in his own language.

Jarro forgot entirely how afraid he had been of both dogs and humans in other days. He thought now that they were gentle and kind, and he loved them. He wished that he were well, so he could fly down to Takern and tell the wild ducks that their enemies were not dangerous, and that they need not fear them.

He had observed that the human beings, as well as Caesar, had calm eyes, which it did one good to look into. The only one in the cottage whose glance he did not care to meet, was Clawina, the house cat. She did him no harm, either, but he couldn't place any confidence in her. Then, too, she quarreled with him constantly, because he loved human beings. "You think they protect you because they are fond of you," said Clawina. "You just wait until you are fat enough! Then they'll wring the neck off you. I know them, I do."

Jarro, like all birds, had a tender and affectionate heart, and he was unutterably distressed when he heard this. He couldn't imagine that his mistress would wish to wring the neck off him, nor could he believe any such thing of her son, the little boy who sat for hours beside his basket, and babbled and chattered. He seemed to think that both of them had the same love for him that he had for them. One day, when Jarro and Caesar lay on the usual spot before the fire, Clawina sat on the hearth and began to tease the wild duck.

"I wonder, Jarro, what you wild ducks will do next year, when Takern is drained and turned into grain fields?" said Clawina. "What's that you say, Clawina?" cried Jarro, and jumped up—scared through and through. "I always forget, Jarro, that you do not understand human speech, like Caesar and myself," answered the cat. "Or else you surely would have heard how the men, who were here in the cottage yesterday, said that all the water was going to be drained from Takern, and that next year the lake bottom would be as dry as a house floor. And now I wonder where you wild ducks will go." When Jarro heard this he was so furious that he hissed like a snake. "You are just as mean as a common coot!" he screamed at Clawina. "You only want to incite me against human beings. I don't believe they want to do anything of the sort. They must know that Takern is the wild ducks' property. Why should they make so many birds homeless and unhappy? You have certainly hit upon all this to scare me. I hope that you may be torn in pieces by Gorgo, the eagle! I hope that my mistress will chop off your whiskers!"

But Jarro couldn't shut Clawina up with this outburst. "So you think I'm lying," said she. "Ask Caesar, then! He was also in the house last night. Caesar never lies."

"Caesar," said Jarro, "you understand human speech much better than Clawina. Say that she hasn't heard aright! Think how it would be if the people drained Takern, and changed the lake bottom into fields! Then there would be no more pond weed or duck food for the grown wild ducks, and no blackfish or worms or gnat eggs for the ducklings. Then the reed banks would disappear—where now the ducklings conceal themselves until they are able to fly. All ducks would be compelled to move away from here and seek another home. But where shall they find a retreat like Takern? Caesar, say that Clawina has not heard aright!"

It was extraordinary to watch Caesar's behavior during this conversation. He had been wide awake the whole time before, but now, when Jarro turned to him, he panted, laid his long nose on his forepaws, and was sound asleep within the wink of an eyelid.

The cat looked down at Caesar with a knowing smile. "I believe that Caesar doesn't care to answer you," she said to Jarro. "It is with him as with all dogs; they will never acknowledge that humans can do any wrong. But you can rely upon my word, at any rate. I shall tell you why they wish to drain the lake just now. As long as you wild ducks still had the power on Takern, they did not wish to drain it, for, at least, they got some good out of you, but now, grebes and coots and other birds who are no good as food, have infested nearly all the reed banks, and the people don't think they need let the lake remain on their account."

Jarro didn't trouble himself to answer Clawina, but raised his head, and shouted in Caesar's ear, "Caesar! You know that on Takern there are still so many ducks left that they fill the air like clouds. Say it isn't true that human beings intend to make all of these homeless!"

Then Caesar sprang up with such a sudden outburst at Clawina that she had to save herself by jumping up on a shelf. "I'll teach you to keep quiet when I want to sleep," bawled Caesar. "Of course I know that there is some talk about draining the lake this year. But there's been talk of this many times before without anything coming of it. And that draining business is a matter in which I take no stock whatever. For how would it go with the game if Takern were laid waste. You're a donkey to gloat over a thing like that. What will you and I have to amuse ourselves with, when there are no more birds on Takern?"

THE DECOY DUCK

Sunday, April seventeenth

A couple of days later Jarro was so well that he could fly all about the house. Then he was petted a good deal by the mistress, and the little boy ran out in the yard and plucked the first grass blades for him which had sprung up. When the mistress caressed him, Jarro thought that, although he was now so strong that he could fly down to Takern at any time, he shouldn't care to be separated from the human beings. He had no objection to remaining with them all his life.

But early one morning the mistress placed a halter, or noose, over Jarro, which prevented him from using his wings, and then she turned him over to the farm hand who had found him in the yard. The farm hand poked him under his arm, and went down to Takern with him.

The ice had melted away while Jarro had been ill. The old, dry fall leaves still stood along the shores and islets, but all the water growths had begun to take root down in the deep, and the green stems had already reached the surface. And now nearly all the migratory birds were at home. The curlews' hooked bills peeped out from the reeds. The grebes glided about with new feather collars around the neck, and the jack snipes were gathering straws for their nests.

The farm hand got into a scow, laid Jarro in the bottom of the boat, and began to pole himself out on the lake. Jarro, who had now accustomed himself to expect only good of human beings, said to Caesar, who was also in the party, that he was very grateful toward the farm hand for taking him out on the lake. But there was no need to keep him so closely guarded, for he did not intend to fly away. To this Caesar made no reply. He was very close-mouthed that morning.

The only thing which struck Jarro as being a bit peculiar was that the farm hand had taken his gun along. He couldn't believe that any of the good folk in the cottage would want to shoot birds. And, beside, Caesar had told him that the people didn't hunt at this time of the year. "It is a prohibited time," he had said, "although this doesn't concern me, of course."

The farm hand went over to one of the little reed-enclosed mud islets. There he stepped from the boat, gathered some old reeds into a pile, and lay down behind it. Jarro was permitted to wander around on the ground, with the halter over his wings, and tethered to the boat, with a long string.

Suddenly Jarro caught sight of some young ducks and drakes, in whose company he had formerly raced backward and forward over the lake. They were a long way off, but Jarro called them to him with a couple of loud shouts. They responded, and a large and beautiful flock approached. Before they got there, Jarro began to tell them about his marvelous rescue, and of the kindness of human beings. Just then, two shots sounded behind him. Three ducks sank down in the reeds—lifeless—and Caesar bounced out and captured them.

Then Jarro understood. The human beings had only saved him that they might use him as a decoy duck. And they had also succeeded. Three ducks had died on his account. He thought he should die of shame. He thought that even his friend Caesar looked contemptuously at him, and when they came home to the cottage, he didn't dare lie down and sleep beside the dog.

The next morning Jarro was again taken out on the shallows. This time, too, he saw some ducks. But when he observed that they flew toward him, he called to them: "Away! Away! Be careful! Fly in another direction! There's a hunter hidden behind the reed pile. I'm only a decoy bird!" And he actually succeeded in preventing them from coming within shooting distance.

Jarro had scarcely had time to taste of a grass blade, so busy was he in keeping watch. He called out his warning as soon as a bird drew nigh. He even warned the grebes, although he detested them because they crowded the ducks out of their best hiding places. But he did not wish that any bird should meet with misfortune on his account. And, thanks to Jarro's vigilance, the farmhand had to go home without firing a single shot.

Despite this fact, Caesar looked less displeased than on the previous day, and when evening came he took Jarro in his mouth, carried him over to the fireplace, and let him sleep between his forepaws.

Nevertheless Jarro was no longer contented in the cottage, but was grievously unhappy. His heart suffered at the thought that humans never had loved him. When the mistress, or the little boy, came forward to caress him, he stuck his bill under his wing and pretended that he slept.

For several days Jarro continued his distressful watch service, and already he was known all over Takern. Then it happened one morning, while he called as usual, "Have a care, birds! Don't come near me! I'm only a decoy duck," then a grebe nest came floating toward the shallows where he was tied. This was nothing especially remarkable. It was a nest from the year before, and since grebe nests are built in such a way that they can move on water like boats, it often happens that they drift out toward the lake. Still Jarro stood there and stared at the nest, because it came so straight toward the islet that it looked as though someone had steered its course over the water.

As the nest came nearer, Jarro saw that a little human being—the tiniest he had ever seen—sat in the nest and rowed it forward with a pair of sticks. And this little human called to him: "Go as near the water as you can, Jarro, and be ready to fly. You shall soon be freed."

A few seconds later the grebe nest lay near land, but the little oarsman did not leave it, but sat huddled up between branches and straw. Jarro too held himself almost immovable. He was actually paralysed with fear lest the rescuer should be discovered.

The next thing which occurred was that a flock of wild geese came along. Then Jarro woke up to business, and warned them with loud shrieks, but in spite of this they flew over the shallows and back several times. They held themselves so high that they were beyond shooting distance, still the farm hand let himself be tempted to fire a couple of shots at them. These shots were hardly fired before the little creature ran up on land, drew a tiny knife from its sheath, and, with a couple of quick strokes, cut loose Jarro's halter. "Now fly away, Jarro, before the man has time to load again!" cried he, while he himself ran down to the grebe nest and poled away from the shore.

The hunter had had his gaze fixed upon the geese, and hadn't observed that Jarro had been freed, but Caesar had followed more carefully that which happened, and just as Jarro raised his wings, he dashed forward and grabbed him by the neck.

Jarro cried pitifully, and the boy who had freed him said quietly to Caesar: "If you are just as honorable as you look, surely you cannot wish to force a good bird to sit here and entice others into trouble."

When Caesar heard these words, he grinned viciously with his upper lip, but the next second he dropped Jarro. "Fly, Jarro!" said he. "You are certainly too good to be a decoy duck. It wasn't for this that I wanted to keep you here, but because it will be lonely in the cottage without you."

THE LOWERING OF THE LAKE

Wednesday, April twentieth

*I*t was indeed very lonely in the cottage without Jarro. The dog and the cat found the time long, when they didn't have him to wrangle over, and the housewife missed the glad quacking which he had indulged in every time she entered the house. But the one who longed most for Jarro, was the little boy, Per Ola. He was but three years old, and the only child, and in all his life he had never had a playmate like Jarro. When he heard that Jarro had gone back to Takern and the wild ducks, he couldn't be satisfied with this, but thought constantly of how he should get him back again.

Per Ola had talked a good deal with Jarro while he lay still in his basket, and he was certain that the duck understood him. He begged his mother to take him down to the lake that he might find Jarro, and persuade him to come back to them. Mother wouldn't listen to this, but the little one didn't give up his plan on that account.

The day after Jarro had disappeared, Per Ola was running about in the yard. He played by himself as usual, but Caesar lay on the stoop, and when mother let the boy out, she said: "Take care of Per Ola, Caesar!"

Now if all had been as usual, Caesar would also have obeyed the command, and the boy would have been so well-guarded that he couldn't have run the least risk. But Caesar was not like himself these days. He knew that the farmers who lived along Takern had held frequent conferences about the lowering of the lake, and that they had almost settled the matter. The ducks must leave, and Caesar should nevermore behold a glorious chase. He was so preoccupied with thoughts of this misfortune, that he did not remember to watch over Per Ola.

And the little one had scarcely been alone in the yard a minute, before he realized that now the right moment had come to go down to Takern and talk with Jarro. He opened a gate, and wandered down toward the lake on the narrow path which ran along the banks. As long as he could be seen from the house, he walked slowly, but afterward he increased his pace. He was very much afraid that Mother, or someone else, should call to him that he couldn't go. He didn't wish to do anything naughty, only to persuade Jarro to come home, but he felt that those at home would not have approved of the undertaking.

When Per Ola came down to the lakeshore, he called Jarro several times. Thereupon he stood for a long time and waited, but no Jarro appeared. He saw several birds that resembled the wild duck, but they flew by without noticing him, and he could understand that none among them was the right one.

When Jarro didn't come to him, the little boy thought that it would be easier to find him if he went out on the lake. There were several good craft lying along the shore, but they were tied. The one that lay loose, and at liberty, was an old leaky scow which was so unfit that no one thought of using it. But Per Ola scrambled up in it without caring that the whole bottom was filled with water. He had not strength enough to use the oars, but instead, he seated himself to swing and rock in the scow. Certainly no grown person would have succeeded in moving a scow out on Takern in that manner, but when the tide is high—and ill-luck to the fore—little children have a marvelous faculty for getting out to sea. Per Ola was soon riding around on Takern, and calling for Jarro.

When the old scow was rocked like this—out to sea—its cracks opened wider and wider, and the water actually streamed into it. Per Ola didn't pay the slightest attention to this. He sat upon the little bench in front and called to every bird he saw, and wondered why Jarro didn't appear.

At last Jarro caught sight of Per Ola. He heard that someone called him by the name which he had borne among human beings, and he understood that the boy had gone out on Takern to search for him. Jarro was unspeakably happy to find that one of the humans really loved him. He shot down toward Per Ola, like an arrow, seated himself beside him, and let him caress him. They were both very happy to see each other again. But suddenly Jarro noticed the condition of the scow. It was half-filled with water, and was almost ready to sink. Jarro tried to tell Per Ola that he, who could neither fly nor swim, must try to get upon land, but Per Ola didn't understand him. Then Jarro did not wait an instant, but hurried away to get help.

Jarro came back in a little while, and carried on his back a tiny thing, who was much smaller than Per Ola himself. If he hadn't been able to talk and move, the boy would have believed that it was a doll. Instantly, the little one ordered Per Ola to pick up a long, slender pole that lay in the bottom of the scow, and try to pole it toward one of the reed islands. Per Ola obeyed him, and he and the tiny creature, together, steered the scow. With a couple of strokes they were on a little reed-encircled island, and now Per Ola was told that he must step on land. And just the very moment that Per Ola set foot on land, the scow was filled with water, and sank to the bottom.

When Per Ola saw this he was sure that Father and Mother would be very angry with him. He would have started in to cry if he hadn't found something else to think about soon, namely, a flock of big, gray birds, who lighted on the island. The little midget took him up to them, and told him their names, and what they said. And this was so funny that Per Ola forgot everything else.

Meanwhile the folks on the farm had discovered that the boy had disappeared, and had started to search for him. They searched the out-houses, looked in the well, and hunted through the cellar. Then they went out into the highways and by-paths, wandered to the neighboring farm to find out if he had strayed over there, and searched for him also down by Takern. But no matter how much they sought they did not find him.

Caesar, the dog, understood very well that the farmer folk were looking for Per Ola, but he did nothing to lead them on the right track, instead, he lay still as though the matter didn't concern him.

Later in the day, Per Ola's footprints were discovered down by the boat landing. And then came the thought that the old, leaky scow was no longer on the strand. Then one began to understand how the whole affair had come about.

The farmer and his helpers immediately took out the boats and went in search of the boy. They rowed around on Takern until late in the evening, without seeing the least shadow of him. They couldn't help believing that the old scow had gone down, and that the little one lay dead on the lake bottom.

In the evening, Per Ola's mother hunted around on the strand. Everyone else was convinced that the boy was drowned, but she could not bring herself to believe this. She searched all the while. She searched between reeds and bulrushes, tramped and tramped on the muddy shore, never thinking of how deep her foot sank, and how wet she had become. She was unspeakably desperate. Her heart ached in her breast. She did not weep, but wrung her hands and called for her child in loud piercing tones.

Round about her she heard swans' and ducks' and curlews' shrieks. She thought that they followed her, and moaned and wailed—they too. "Surely, they, too, must be in trouble, since they moan so," thought she. Then she remembered: these were only birds that she heard complain. They surely had no worries.

It was strange that they did not quiet down after sunset. But she heard all these uncountable bird throngs, which lived along Takern, send forth cry upon cry. Several of them followed her wherever she went; others came rustling past on light wings. All the air was filled with moans and lamentations.

But the anguish which she herself was suffering, opened her heart. She thought that she was not as far removed from all other living creatures as people usually think. She understood much better than ever before, how birds fared. They had their constant worries for home and children, they, as she. There was surely not such a great difference between them and her as she had heretofore believed.

Then she happened to think that it was as good as settled that these thousands of swans and ducks and loons would lose their homes here by Takern. "It will be very hard for them," she thought. "Where shall they bring up their children now?"

She stood still and mused on this. It appeared to be an excellent and agreeable accomplishment to change a lake into fields and meadows, but let it be some other lake than Takern, some other lake, which was not the home of so many thousand creatures. She remembered how on the following day the proposition to lower the lake was to be decided, and she wondered if this was why her little son had been lost—

just today. Was it God's meaning that sorrow should come and open her heart—just today—before it was too late to avert the cruel act?

She walked rapidly up to the house, and began to talk with her husband about this. She spoke of the lake, and of the birds, and said that she believed it was God's judgment on them both. And she soon found that he was of the same opinion.

They already owned a large place, but if the lake draining was carried into effect, such a goodly portion of the lake bottom would fall to their share that their property would be nearly doubled. For this reason they had been more eager for the undertaking than any of the other shore owners. The others had been worried about expenses, and anxious lest the draining should not prove any more successful this time than it was the last. Per Ola's father knew in his heart that it was he who had influenced them to undertake the work. He had exercised all his eloquence, so that he might leave to his son a farm as large again as his father had left to him.

He stood and pondered if God's hand was back of the fact that Takern had taken his son from him on the day before he was to draw up the contract to lay it waste. The wife didn't have to say many words to him, before he answered: "It may be that God does not want us to interfere with His order. I'll talk with the others about this tomorrow, and I think we'll conclude that all may remain as it is."

While the farmer folk were talking this over, Caesar lay before the fire. He raised his head and listened very attentively. When he thought that he was sure of the outcome, he walked up to the mistress, took her by the skirt, and led her to the door. "But Caesar!" said she, and wanted to break loose. "Do you know where Per Ola is?" she exclaimed. Caesar barked joyfully, and threw himself against the door. She opened it, and Caesar dashed down toward Takern. The mistress was so positive he knew where Per Ola was, that she rushed after him. And no sooner had they reached the shore than they heard a child's cry out on the lake.

Per Ola had had the best day of his life, in company with Thumbietot and the birds, but now he had begun to cry because he was hungry and afraid of the darkness. And he was glad when Father and Mother and Caesar came for him.

XX

ULVÅSA-LADY

THE PROPHECY

Friday, April twenty-second

One night when the boy lay and slept on an island in Takern, he was awakened by oar strokes. He had hardly gotten his eyes open before there fell such a dazzling light on them that he began to blink.

At first he couldn't make out what it was that shone so brightly out here on the lake, but he soon saw that a scow with a big burning torch stuck up on a spike, aft, lay near the edge of the reeds. The red flame from the torch was clearly reflected in the night-dark lake, and the brilliant light must have lured the fish, for round about the flame in the deep a mass of dark specks were seen that moved continually, and changed places.

There were two old men in the scow. One sat at the oars, and the other stood on a bench in the stern and held in his hand a short spear which was coarsely barbed. The one who rowed was apparently a poor fisherman. He was small, dried-up and weather-beaten, and wore a thin, threadbare coat. One could see that he was so used to being out in all sorts of weather that he didn't mind the cold. The other was well-dressed and looked like a prosperous and self-complacent farmer.

"Now, stop!" said the farmer, when they were opposite the island where the boy lay. At the same time he plunged the spear into the water. When he drew it out again, a long, fine eel came with it.

"Look at that!" said he as he released the eel from the spear. "That was one who was worth while. Now I think we have so many that we can turn back."

His comrade did not lift the oars, but sat and looked around. "It is lovely out here on the lake tonight," said he. And so it was. It was absolutely still, so that the entire water surface lay in undisturbed rest with the exception of the streak where the boat had gone forward. This lay like a path of gold, and shimmered in the firelight. The sky was clear and dark blue and thickly studded with stars. The shores were hidden by the reed islands except toward the west. There Mount Omberg loomed up high and dark, much more impressive than usual, and cut away a big, three-cornered piece of the vaulted heavens.

The other one turned his head to get the light out of his eyes, and looked about him. "Yes, it is lovely here in Östergylln," said he. "Still the best thing about the province is not its beauty." "Then what is it that's best?" asked the oarsman. "That it has always been a respected and honored province." "That may be true enough." "And then this, that one knows it will always continue to be so." "But how in the world can one know this?" said the one who sat at the oars.

The farmer straightened up where he stood and braced himself with the spear. "There is an old story which has been handed down from father to son in my family, and in it one learns what will happen to Östergötland." "Then you may as well tell it to me," said the oarsman. "We do not tell it to anyone and everyone, but I do not wish to keep it a secret from an old comrade.

"At Ulvåsa, here in Östergötland," he continued (and one could tell by the tone of his voice that he talked of something which he had heard from others, and knew by heart), "many, many years ago, there lived a lady who had the gift of looking into the future, and telling people what was going to happen to them—just as certainly and accurately as though it had already occurred. For this she became widely noted, and it is easy to understand that people would come to her, both from far and near, to find out what they were going to pass through of good or evil.

"One day, when Ulvåsa-Lady sat in her hall and spun, as was customary in former days, a poor peasant came into the room and seated himself on the bench near the door.

"'I wonder what you are sitting and thinking about dear lady,' said the peasant after a little. 'I am sitting and thinking about high and holy things.' answered she. 'Then it is not fitting, perhaps, that I ask you about something which weighs on my heart,' said the peasant.

195

"'It is probably nothing else that weighs on your heart than that you may reap much grain on your field. But I am accustomed to receive communications from the Emperor about how it will go with his crown, and from the Pope, about how it will go with his keys.' 'Such things cannot be easy to answer,' said the peasant. 'I have also heard that no one seems to go from here without being dissatisfied with what he has heard.'

"When the peasant said this, he saw that Ulvåsa-Lady bit her lip, and moved higher up on the bench. 'So this is what you have heard about me,' said she. 'Then you may as well tempt fortune by asking me about the thing you wish to know, and you shall see if I can answer so that you will be satisfied.'

"After this the peasant did not hesitate to state his errand. He said that he had come to ask how it would go with Östergötland in the future. There was nothing which was so dear to him as his native province, and he felt that he should be happy until his dying day if he could get a satisfactory reply to his query.

"'Oh! is that all you wish to know,' said the wise lady, 'then I think that you will be content. For here where I now sit, I can tell you that it will be like this with Östergötland: it will always have something to boast of ahead of other provinces.'

"'Yes, that was a good answer, dear lady,' said the peasant, 'and now I would be entirely at peace if I could only comprehend how such a thing should be possible.'

"'Why should it not be possible?' said Ulvåsa-Lady. 'Don't you know that Östergötland is already renowned? Or think you there is any place in Sweden that can boast of owning, at the same time, two such cloisters as the ones in Alvastra and Vreta, and such a beautiful cathedral as the one in Linköping?'

"'That may be so,' said the peasant. 'But I'm an old man, and I know that people's minds are changeable. I fear that there will come a time when they won't want to give us any glory, either for Alvastra or Vreta or for the cathedral.'

"'Herein you may be right,' said Ulvåsa-Lady, 'but you need not doubt prophecy on that account. I shall now build up a new cloister on Vadstena, and that will become the most celebrated in the North. Thither both the high and the lowly shall make pilgrimages, and all shall sing the praises of the province because it has such a holy place within its confines.'

"The peasant replied that he was right glad to know this. But he also knew, of course, that everything was perishable, and he wondered much what would give distinction to the province, if Vadstena Cloister should once fall into disrepute.

"'You are not easy to satisfy,' said Ulvåsa-Lady, 'but surely I can see so far ahead that I can tell you, before Vadstena Cloister shall have lost its splendor, there will be a castle erected close by, which will be the most magnificent of its period. Kings and dukes will be guests there, and it shall be accounted an honor to the whole province, that it owns such an ornament.'

"'This I am also glad to hear,' said the peasant. 'But I'm an old man, and I know how it generally turns out with this world's glories. And if the castle goes to ruin, I wonder much what there will be that can attract the people's attention to this province.'

"'It's not a little that you want to know,' said Ulvåsa-Lady, 'but, certainly, I can look far enough into the future to see that there will be life and movement in the forests around Finspång. I see how cabins and smithies arise there, and I believe that the whole province shall be renowned because iron will be moulded within its confines.'

"The peasant didn't deny that he was delighted to hear this. 'But if it should go so badly that even Finspång's foundry went down in importance, then it would hardly be possible that any new thing could arise of which Östergötland might boast.'

"'You are not easy to please,' said Ulvåsa-Lady, 'but I can see so far into the future that I mark how, along the lake shores, great manors—large as castles—are built by gentlemen who have carried on wars in foreign lands. I believe that the manors will bring the province just as much honor as anything else that I have mentioned.'

"'But if there comes a time when no one lauds the great manors?' insisted the peasant.

"'You need not be uneasy at all events,' said Ulvåsa-Lady. 'I see how health springs bubble on Medevi meadows, by Vätter's shores. I believe that the wells at Medevi will bring the land as much praise as you can desire.'

"'That is a mighty good thing to know,' said the peasant. 'But if there comes a time when people will seek their health at other springs?'

"'You must not give yourself any anxiety on that account,' answered Ulvåsa-Lady. 'I see how people dig and labor, from Motala to Mem. They dig a canal right through the country, and then Östergötland's praise is again on everyone's lips.'

"But, nevertheless, the peasant looked distraught.

"'I see that the rapids in Motala stream begin to draw wheels,' said Ulvåsa-Lady." And now two bright red spots came to her cheeks, for she began to be impatient: 'I hear hammers resound in Motala, and looms clatter in Norrköping.'

"'Yes, that's good to know,' said the peasant, 'but everything is perishable, and I'm afraid that even this can be forgotten, and go into oblivion.'

"When the peasant was not satisfied even now, there was an end to the lady's patience. 'You say that everything is perishable,' said she, 'but now I shall still name something which will always be like itself, and that is that such arrogant and pig-headed peasants as you will always be found in this province—until the end of time.'

"Hardly had Ulvåsa-Lady said this before the peasant rose—happy and satisfied—and thanked her for a good answer. Now, at last, he was satisfied, he said.

"'Verily, I understand now how you look at it,' then said Ulvåsa-Lady.

"'Well, I look at it in this way, dear lady,' said the peasant, 'that everything which kings and priests and noblemen and merchants build and accomplish, can only endure for a few years. But when you tell me that in Östergötland there will always be peasants who are honor-loving and persevering, then I know also that it will be able to keep its ancient glory. For it is only those who go bent under the eternal labor with the soil, who can hold this land in good repute and honor—from one time to another.'"

XXI

THE HOMESPUN CLOTH

Saturday, April twenty-third

The boy rode forward—way up in the air. He had the great Östergötland plain under him, and sat and counted the many white churches which towered above the small leafy groves around them. It wasn't long before he had counted fifty. After that he became confused and couldn't keep track of the counting.

Nearly all the farms were built up with large, whitewashed two-story houses, which looked so imposing that the boy couldn't help admiring them. "There can't be any peasants in this land," he said to himself, "since I do not see any peasant farms."

Immediately all the wild geese shrieked, "Here the peasants live like gentlemen. Here the peasants live like gentlemen."

On the plains the ice and snow had disappeared, and the spring work had begun. "What kind of long crabs are those that creep over the fields?" asked the boy after a bit. "Plows and oxen. Plows and oxen," answered the wild geese.

The oxen moved so slowly down on the fields, that one could scarcely perceive they were in motion, and the geese shouted to them: "You won't get there before next year. You won't get there before next year." But the oxen were equal to the occasion. They raised their muzzles in the air and bellowed, "We do more good in an hour than such as you do in a whole lifetime."

In a few places the plows were drawn by horses. They went along with much more eagerness and haste than the oxen, but the geese could not keep from teasing these either. Cried the wild geese, "Aren't you ashamed, yourselves, to be doing lazy man's duty?" The horses neighed back at them.

But while horses and oxen were at work in the fields, the stable ram walked about in the barnyard. He was newly clipped and touchy, knocked over the small boys, chased the shepherd dog into his kennel, and then strutted about as though he alone were lord of the whole place. "Rammie, rammie, what have you done with your wool?" asked the wild geese, who rode up in the air. "That I have sent to Drag's woolen mills in Norrköping," replied the ram with a long, drawn-out bleat. "Rammie, rammie, what have you done with your horns?" asked the geese. But any horns the rammie had never possessed, to his sorrow, and one couldn't offer him a greater insult than to ask after them. He ran around a long time, and butted at the air, so furious was he.

On the country road came a man who drove a flock of Skåne pigs that were not more than a few weeks old, and were going to be sold up country. They trotted along bravely, as little as they were, and kept close together—as if they sought protection. "Nuff, nuff, nuff, we came away too soon from Father and Mother. Nuff, nuff, nuff, how will it go with us poor children?" said the little pigs. The wild geese didn't have the heart to tease such poor little creatures. "It will be better for you than you can ever believe," they cried as they flew past them.

The wild geese were never so merry as when they flew over a flat country. Then they did not hurry themselves, but flew from farm to farm, and joked with the tame animals.

As the boy rode over the plain, he happened to think of a legend which he had heard a long time ago. He didn't remember it exactly, but it was something about a petticoat—half of which was made of gold-woven velvet, and half of gray homespun cloth. But the one who owned the petticoat adorned the homespun cloth with such a lot of pearls and precious stones that it looked richer and more gorgeous than the gold cloth.

He remembered this about the homespun cloth, as he looked down on Österötland, because it was made up of a large plain, which lay wedged in between two mountainous forest tracts—one to the north, the other to the south. The two forest heights lay there, a lovely blue, and shimmered in the morning light, as if they were decked with golden veils, and the plain, which simply spread out one winter-naked field after another, was, in and of itself, prettier to look upon than gray homespun.

But the people must have been contented on the plain, because it was generous and kind, and they had tried to decorate it in the best way possible. High up—where the boy rode by—he thought that cities and farms, churches and factories, castles and railway stations were scattered over it, like large and small trinkets. It shone on the roofs, and the window panes glittered like jewels. Yellow country roads, shining railway tracks and blue canals ran along between the districts like embroidered loops. Linköping lay around its cathedral like a pearl setting around a precious stone, and the gardens in the country were like little brooches and buttons. There was not much regulation in the pattern, but it was a display of grandeur which one could never tire of admiring.

The geese had left Öberg district, and traveled toward the east along Göta Canal. This was also getting itself ready for the summer. Workmen laid canal banks, and tarred the huge lock gates. They were working everywhere to receive spring fittingly, even in the cities. There, masons and painters stood on scaffoldings and made fine the exteriors of the houses while maids were cleaning the windows. Down at the harbor, sailboats and steamers were being washed and dressed up.

At Norrköping the wild geese left the plain, and flew up toward Kolmården. For a time they had followed an old, hilly country road, which wound around cliffs, and ran forward under wild mountainwalls—when the boy suddenly let out a shriek. He had been sitting and swinging his foot back and forth, and one of his wooden shoes had slipped off.

"Goosey-gander, goosey-gander, I have dropped my shoe!" cried the boy. The goosey-gander turned about and sank toward the ground, then the boy saw that two children, who were walking along the road, had picked up his shoe. "Goosey-gander, goosey-gander," screamed the boy excitedly, "fly upward again! It is too late. I cannot get my shoe back again."

Down on the road stood Osa, the goose girl, and her brother, little Mats, looking at a tiny wooden shoe that had fallen from the skies.

Osa, the goose girl, stood silent a long while, and pondered over the find. At last she said, slowly and thoughtfully: "Do you remember, little Mats, that when we went past Övid Cloister, we heard that the folks in a farmyard had seen an elf who was dressed in leather breeches, and had wooden shoes on his feet, like any other working man? And do you recollect when we came to Vittskövle, a girl told us that she had seen a Goa-Nisse with wooden shoes, who flew away on the back of a goose? And when we ourselves came home to our cabin, little Mats, we saw a goblin who was dressed in the same way, and who also straddled the back of a goose—and flew away. Maybe it was the same one who rode along on his goose up here in the air and dropped his wooden shoe."

"Yes, it must have been," said little Mats.

They turned the wooden shoe about and examined it carefully—for it isn't every day that one happens across a Goa-Nisse's wooden shoe on the highway.

"Wait, wait, little Mats!" said Osa, the goose girl. "There is something written on one side of it."

"Why, so there is! but they are such tiny letters."

"Let me see! It says—it says: 'Nils Holgersson from W. Vemminghög.' That's the most wonderful thing I've ever heard!" said little Mats.

Nils

The Further Adventures of Nils Holgersson

by
Selma Lagerlöf

translated from the Swedish by
Velma Swanston Howard

illustrations reproduced from the originals by
Astri Heiberg

I
THE STORY OF KARR
AND GRAYSKIN

KARR
Kolmården

About twelve years before Nils Holgersson started on his travels with the wild geese there was a manufacturer at Kolmården who wanted to be rid of one of his dogs. He sent for his gamekeeper and said to him that it was impossible to keep the dog because he could not be broken of the habit of chasing all the sheep and fowl he set eyes on, and he asked the man to take the dog into the forest and shoot him.

The gamekeeper slipped the leash on the dog to lead him to a spot in the forest where all the superannuated dogs from the manor were shot and buried. He was not a cruel man, but he was very glad to shoot that dog, for he knew that sheep and chickens were not the only creatures he hunted. Times without number he had gone into the forest and helped himself to a hare or a grouse-chick.

The dog was a little black and tan setter. His name was Karr, and he was so wise he understood all that was said.

As the gamekeeper was leading him through the thickets, Karr knew only too well what was in store for him. But this no one could have guessed by his behavior, for he neither hung his head nor dragged his tail, but seemed as unconcerned as ever. It was because they were in the forest that the dog was so careful not to appear the least bit anxious.

There were great stretches of woodland on every side of the factory, and this forest was famed both among animals and human beings because for many, many years the owners had been so careful of it that they had begrudged themselves even the trees needed for firewood. Nor had they had the heart to thin or train them. The trees had been allowed to grow as they pleased. Naturally a forest thus protected was a beloved refuge for wild animals, which were to be found there in great numbers. Among themselves they called it Liberty Forest, and regarded it as the best retreat in the whole country.

As the dog was being led through the woods he thought of what a bugaboo he had been to all the small animals and birds that lived there.

"Now, Karr, wouldn't they be happy in their lairs if they only knew what was awaiting you?" he thought, but at the same time he wagged his tail and barked cheerfully, so that no one should think that he was worried or depressed.

"What fun would there have been in living had I not hunted occasionally?" he reasoned. "Let him who will, regret; it's not going to be Karr!"

But the instant the dog said this, a singular change came over him. He stretched his neck as though he had a mind to howl. He no longer trotted alongside the gamekeeper, but walked behind him. It was plain that he had begun to think of something unpleasant.

It was early summer; the elk cows had just given birth to their young, and, the night before, the dog had succeeded in parting from its mother an elk calf not more than five days old, and had driven it down into the marsh. There he had chased it back and forth over the knolls—not with the idea of capturing it, but merely for the sport of seeing how he could scare it. The elk cow knew that the marsh was bottomless so soon after the thaw, and that it could not as yet hold up so large an animal as herself, so she stood on the solid earth for the longest time, watching! But when Karr kept chasing the calf farther and farther away, she rushed out on the marsh, drove the dog off, took the calf with her, and turned back toward firm land. Elk are more skilled than other animals in traversing dangerous, marshy ground, and it seemed as if she would reach solid land in safety, but when she was almost there, a knoll which she had stepped upon sank into the mire, and she went down with it. She tried to rise, but could get no secure foothold, so she sank and sank. Karr stood and looked on, not daring to move. When he saw that the elk could not save herself, he ran away as fast as he could, for he had begun to think of the beating he would get if it were discovered that he had brought a mother elk to grief. He was so terrified that he dared not pause for breath until he reached home.

It was this that the dog recalled, and it troubled him in a way very different from the recollection of all his other misdeeds. This was doubtless because he had not really meant to kill either the elk cow or her calf, but had deprived them of life without wishing to do so.

"But maybe they are alive yet!" thought the dog. "They were not dead when I ran away, perhaps they saved themselves."

He was seized with an irresistible longing to know for a certainty while yet there was time for him to find out. He noticed that the gamekeeper did not have a firm hold on the leash, so he made a sudden spring, broke loose, and dashed through the woods down to the marsh with such speed that he was out of sight before the gamekeeper had time to level his gun. There was nothing for the gamekeeper to do but to rush after him. When he got to the marsh, he found the dog standing upon a knoll, howling with all his might.

The man thought he had better find out the meaning of this, so he dropped his gun and crawled out over the marsh on hands and knees. He had not gone far when he saw an elk cow lying dead in the quagmire. Close beside her lay a little calf. It was still alive, but so much exhausted that it could not move. Karr was standing beside the calf, now bending down and licking it, now howling shrilly for help.

The gamekeeper raised the calf and began to drag it toward land. When the dog understood that the calf would be saved he was wild with joy. He jumped round and round the gamekeeper, licking his hands and barking with delight.

The man carried the baby elk home and shut it up in a calf stall in the cow shed. Then he got help to drag the mother elk from the marsh. Only after this had been done did he remember that he was to shoot Karr. He called the dog to him, and again took him into the forest.

The gamekeeper walked straight on toward the dog's grave, but all the while he seemed to be thinking deeply. Suddenly he turned and walked toward the manor.

Karr had been trotting along quietly, but when the gamekeeper turned and started for home, he became anxious. The man must have discovered that it was he that had caused the death of the elk, and now he was going back to the manor to be thrashed before he was shot!

To be beaten was worse than all else! With that prospect Karr could no longer keep up his spirits, but hung his head. When he came to the manor he did not look up, but pretended that he knew no one there. The master was standing on the stairs leading to the hall when the gamekeeper came forward.

"Where on earth did that dog come from?" he exclaimed. "Surely it can't be Karr? He must be dead this long time!"

Then the man began to tell his master all about the mother elk, while Karr made himself as little as he could, and crouched behind the gamekeeper's legs. Much to his surprise the man had only praise for him. He said it was plain the dog knew that the elk were in distress, and wished to save them.

"You may do as you like, but I can't shoot that dog!" declared the gamekeeper.

Karr raised himself and pricked up his ears. He could hardly believe that he heard aright. Although he did not want to show how anxious he had been, he couldn't help whining a little. Could it be possible that his life was to be spared simply because he had felt uneasy about the elk?

The master thought that Karr had conducted himself well, but as he did not want the dog, he could not decide at once what should be done with him.

"If you will take charge of him and answer for his good behavior in the future, he may as well live," he said, finally.

This the gamekeeper was only too glad to do, and that was how Karr came to move to the gamekeeper's lodge.

GRAYSKIN'S FLIGHT

From the day that Karr went to live with the gamekeeper he abandoned entirely his forbidden chase in the forest. This was due not only to his having been thoroughly frightened, but also to the fact that he did not wish to make the gamekeeper angry at him. Ever since his new master saved his life the dog loved him above everything else. He thought only of following him and watching over him. If he left the house, Karr would run ahead to make sure that the way was clear, and if he sat at home, Karr would lie before the door and keep a close watch on every one who came and went.

When all was quiet at the lodge, when no footsteps heard on the road, and the gamekeeper was working in his garden, Karr would amuse himself playing with the baby elk.

At first the dog had no desire to leave his master even for a moment. Since he accompanied him everywhere, he went with him to the cow shed. When he gave the elk calf its milk, the dog would sit outside the stall and gaze at it. The gamekeeper called the calf Grayskin because he thought it did not merit a prettier name, and Karr agreed with him on that point.

Every time the dog looked at it he thought that he had never seen anything so ugly and misshapen as the baby elk, with its long, shambly legs, which hung down from the body, like loose stilts. The head was large, old, and wrinkled, and it always drooped to one side. The skin lay in tucks and folds, as if the animal had put on a coat that had not been made for him. Always doleful and discontented, curiously enough, he jumped up every time Karr appeared without the stall, as if glad to see him.

The elk calf became less hopeful from day to day, did not grow any, and at last he could not even rise when he saw Karr. Then the dog jumped up into the crib to greet him, and thereupon a light kindled in the eyes of the poor creature—as if a cherished longing were fulfilled.

After that Karr visited the elk calf every day, and spent many hours with him, licking his coat, playing and racing with him, till he taught him a little of everything a forest animal should know.

It was remarkable that, from the time Karr began to visit the elk calf in his stall, the latter seemed more contented, and began to grow. After he was fairly started, he grew so rapidly that in a couple of weeks the stall could no longer hold him, and he had to be moved into a grove.

When he had been in the grove two months his legs were so long that he could step over the fence whenever he wished. Then the lord of the manor gave the gamekeeper permission to put up a higher fence and to allow him more space. Here the elk lived for several years, and grew up into a strong and handsome animal. Karr kept him company as often as he could, but now it was no longer through pity, for a great friendship had sprung up between the two. The elk was always inclined to be melancholy, listless, and indifferent, but Karr knew how to make him playful and happy.

Grayskin had lived for five summers on the gamekeeper's place, when his owner received a letter from a zoological garden abroad asking if the elk might be purchased.

The master was pleased with the proposal, the gamekeeper was distressed, but had not the power to say no, so it was decided that the elk should be sold. Karr soon discovered what was in the air and ran over to the elk to have a chat with him. The dog was very much distressed at the thought of losing his friend, but the elk took the matter calmly, and seemed neither glad nor sorry.

"Do you think of letting them send you away without offering resistance?" asked Karr.

"What good would it do to resist?" asked Grayskin. "I should prefer to remain where I am, naturally, but if I've been sold, I shall have to go, of course."

Karr looked at Grayskin and measured him with his eyes. It was apparent that the elk was not yet full grown. He did not have the broad antlers, high hump, and long mane of the mature elk, but he certainly had strength enough to fight for his freedom.

"One can see that he has been in captivity all his life," thought Karr, but said nothing.

Karr left and did not return to the grove till long past midnight. By that time he knew Grayskin would be awake and eating his breakfast.

"Of course you are doing right, Grayskin, in letting them take you away," remarked Karr, who appeared now to be calm and satisfied. "You will be a prisoner in a large park and will have no responsibilities. It seems a pity that you must leave here without having seen the forest. You know your ancestors have a saying that 'the elk are one with the forest.' But you haven't even been in a forest!"

Grayskin glanced up from the clover which he stood munching.

"Indeed, I should love to see the forest, but how am I to get over the fence?" he said with his usual apathy.

"Oh, that is difficult for one who has such short legs!" said Karr.

The elk glanced slyly at the dog, who jumped the fence many times a day—little as he was.

He walked over to the fence, and with one spring he was on the other side, without knowing how it happened.

Then Karr and Grayskin went into the forest. It was a beautiful moonlight night in late summer, but in among the trees it was dark, and the elk walked along slowly.

"Perhaps we had better turn back," said Karr. "You, who have never before tramped the wild forest, might easily break your legs." Grayskin moved more rapidly and with more courage.

Karr conducted the elk to a part of the forest where the pines grew so thickly that no wind could penetrate them.

"It is here that your kind are in the habit of seeking shelter from cold and storm," said Karr. "Here they stand under the open skies all winter. But you will fare much better where you are going, for you will stand in a shed, with a roof over your head, like an ox."

Grayskin made no comment, but stood quietly and drank in the strong, piny air.

"Have you anything more to show me, or have I now seen the whole forest?" he asked.

Then Karr went with him to a big marsh, and showed him clods and quagmire.

"Over this marsh the elk take flight when they are in peril," said Karr. "I don't know how they manage it, but, large and heavy as they are, they can walk here without sinking. Of course you couldn't hold yourself up on such dangerous ground, but then there is no occasion for you to do so, for you will never be hounded by hunters."

Grayskin made no retort, but with a leap he was out on the marsh, and happy when he felt how the clods rocked under him. He dashed across the marsh, and came back again to Karr, without having stepped into a mud hole.

"Have we seen the whole forest now?" he asked.

"No, not yet," said Karr. He next conducted the elk to the skirt of the forest, where fine oaks, lindens, and aspens grew.

"Here your kind eat leaves and bark, which they consider the choicest of food but you will probably get better fare abroad."

Grayskin was astonished when he saw the enormous leaf-trees spreading like a great canopy above him. He ate both oak leaves and aspen bark.

"These taste deliciously bitter and good!" he remarked. "Better than clover!"

"Then wasn't it well that you should taste them once?" said the dog. Thereupon he took the elk down to a little forest lake. The water was as smooth as a mirror, and reflected the shores, which were veiled in thin, light mists. When Grayskin saw the lake he stood entranced.

"What is this, Karr?" he asked. It was the first time that he had seen a lake.

"It's a large body of water—a lake," said Karr. "Your people swim across it from shore to shore. One could hardly expect you to be familiar with this, but at least you should go in and take a swim!"

Karr, himself, plunged into the water for a swim. Grayskin stayed back on the shore for some little time, but finally followed. He grew breathless with delight as the cool water stole soothingly around his body. He wanted it over his back, too, so he went farther out. Then he felt that the water could hold him up, and began to swim. He swam all around Karr, ducking and snorting, perfectly at home in the water.

When they were on shore again, the dog asked if they had not better go home now.

"It's a long time until morning," observed Grayskin, "so we can tramp around in the forest a little longer."

They went again into the pine wood. Presently they came to an open glade illumined by the moonlight, where grass and flowers shimmered beneath the dew. Some large animals were grazing on this forest meadow, an elk bull, several elk cows and a number of elk calves. When Grayskin caught sight of them he stopped short. He hardly glanced at the cows or the young ones, but stared at the old bull, which had broad antlers with many taglets, a high hump, and a long-haired fur piece hanging down from his throat.

"What kind of an animal is that?" asked Grayskin in wonderment.

"He is called Antler-Crown," said Karr, "and he is your kinsman. One of these days you, too, will have broad antlers, like those, and just such a mane, and if you were to remain in the forest, very likely you, also, would have a herd to lead."

"If he is my kinsman, I must go closer and have a look at him," said Grayskin. "I never dreamed that an animal could be so stately!"

Grayskin walked over to the elk, but almost immediately he came back to Karr, who had remained at the edge of the clearing.

"You were not very well received, were you?" said Karr.

"I told him that this was the first time I had run across any of my kinsmen, and asked if I might walk with them on their meadow. But they drove me back, threatening me with their antlers."

"You did right to retreat," said Karr. "A young elk bull with only a taglet crown must be careful about fighting with old elk. Another would have disgraced his name in the whole forest by retreating without resistance, but such things needn't worry you who are going to move to a foreign land."

Karr had barely finished speaking when Grayskin turned and walked down to the meadow. The old elk came toward him, and instantly they began to fight. Their antlers met and clashed, and Grayskin was driven backward over the whole meadow. Apparently he did not know how to make use of his strength, but when he came to the edge of the forest, he planted his feet on the ground, pushed hard with his antlers, and began to force Antler-Crown back.

Grayskin fought quietly, while Antler-Crown puffed and snorted. The old elk, in his turn, was now being forced backward over the meadow. Suddenly a loud crash was heard! A taglet in the old elk's antlers had snapped. He tore himself loose, and dashed into the forest.

Karr was still standing at the forest border when Grayskin came along.

"Now that you have seen what there is in the forest," said Karr, "will you come home with me?" "Yes, it's about time," observed the elk.

Both were silent on the way home. Karr sighed several times, as if he was disappointed about something, but Grayskin stepped along—his head in the air—and seemed delighted over the adventure. He walked ahead unhesitatingly until they came to the enclosure. There he paused. He looked in at the narrow pen where he had lived up till now, saw the beaten ground, the stale fodder, the little trough where he had drunk water, and the dark shed in which he had slept.

"The elk are one with the forest!" he cried. Then he threw back his head, so that his neck rested against his back, and rushed wildly into the woods.

HELPLESS, THE WATER SNAKE

*I*n a pine thicket in the heart of Liberty Forest, every year, in the month of August, there appeared a few grayish-white moths of the kind which are called nun moths. They were small and few in number, and scarcely any one noticed them. When they had fluttered about in the depth of the forest a couple of nights, they laid a few thousand eggs on the branches of trees, and shortly afterward dropped lifeless to the ground.

When spring came, little prickly caterpillars crawled out from the eggs and began to eat the pine needles. They had good appetites, but they never seemed to do the trees any serious harm, because they were hotly pursued by birds. It was seldom that more than a few hundred caterpillars escaped the pursuers.

The poor things that lived to be full grown crawled up on the branches, spun white webs around themselves, and sat for a couple of weeks as motionless pupae. During this period, as a rule, more than half of them were abducted. If a hundred nun moths came forth in August, winged and perfect, it was reckoned a good year for them.

This sort of uncertain and obscure existence did the moths lead for many years in Liberty Forest. There were no insect folk in the whole country that were so scarce, and they would have remained quite harmless and powerless had they not, most unexpectedly, received a helper.

This fact has some connection with Grayskin's flight from the gamekeeper's paddock. Grayskin roamed the forest that he might become more familiar with the place. Late in the afternoon he happened to squeeze through some thickets behind a clearing where the soil was muddy and slimy, and in the center of it was a murky pool. This open space was encircled by tall pines almost bare from age and miasmic air. Grayskin was displeased with the place and would have left it at once had he not caught sight of some bright green calla leaves which grew near the pool.

As he bent his head toward the calla stalks, he happened to disturb a big black snake, which lay sleeping under them. Grayskin had heard Karr speak of the poisonous adders that were to be found in the forest. So, when the snake raised its head, shot out its tongue and hissed at him, he thought he had encountered an awfully dangerous reptile. He was terrified and, raising his foot, he struck so hard with his hoof that he crushed the snake's head. Then, away he ran in hot haste!

As soon as Grayskin had gone, another snake, just as long and as black as the first, came up from the pool. It crawled over to the dead one, and licked the poor, crushed-in head.

"Can it be true that you are dead, old Harmless?" hissed the snake. "We two have lived together so many years; we two have been so happy with each other, and have fared so well here in the swamp, that we have lived to be older than all the other water snakes in the forest! This is the worst sorrow that could have befallen me!"

The snake was so broken-hearted that his long body writhed as if it had been wounded. Even the frogs, who lived in constant fear of him, were sorry for him.

"What a wicked creature he must be to murder a poor water snake that cannot defend itself!" hissed the snake. "He certainly deserves a severe punishment. As sure as my name is Helpless and I'm the oldest water snake in the whole forest, I'll be avenged! I shall not rest until that elk lies as dead on the ground as my poor old snake-wife."

When the snake had made this vow he curled up into a hoop and began to ponder. One can hardly imagine anything that would be more difficult for a poor water snake than to wreak vengeance upon a big, strong elk, and old Helpless pondered day and night without finding any solution.

One night, as he lay there with his vengeance thoughts, he heard a slight rustle over his head. He glanced up and saw a few light nun moths playing in among the trees.

He followed them with his eyes a long while, then began to hiss loudly to himself, apparently pleased with the thought that had occurred to him then he fell asleep.

The next morning the water snake went over to see Crawlie, the adder, who lived in a stony and hilly part of Liberty Forest. He told him all about the death of the old water snake, and begged that he who could deal such deadly thrusts would undertake the work of vengeance. But Crawlie was not exactly disposed to go to war with elk.

"If I were to attack an elk," said the adder, "he would instantly kill me. Old Harmless is dead and gone, and we can't bring her back to life, so why should I rush into danger on her account?"

When the water snake got this reply he raised his head a whole foot from the ground, and hissed furiously:

"Vish vash! Vish vash!" he said. "It's a pity that you, who have been blessed with such weapons of defense, should be so cowardly that you don't dare use them!"

When the adder heard this, he too, got angry. "Crawl away, old Helpless!" he hissed. "The poison is in my fangs, but I would rather spare one who is said to be my kinsman."

But the water snake did not move from the spot, and for a long time the snakes lay there hissing abusive epithets at each other.

When Crawlie was so angry that he couldn't hiss, but could only dart his tongue out, the water snake changed the subject, and began to talk in a very different tone.

"I had still another errand, Crawlie," he said, lowering his voice to a mild whisper. "But now I suppose you are so angry that you wouldn't care to help me?"

"If you don't ask anything foolish of me, I shall certainly be at your service."

"In the pine trees down by the swamp live a moth folk that fly around all night."

"I know all about them," remarked Crawlie. "What's up with them now?"

"They are the smallest insect family in the forest," said Helpless, "and the most harmless, since the caterpillars content themselves with gnawing only pine needles."

"Yes, I know," said Crawlie.

"I'm afraid those moths will soon be exterminated," sighed the water snake. "There are so many who pick off the caterpillars in the spring."

Now Crawlie began to understand that the water snake wanted the caterpillars for his own purpose, and he answered pleasantly:

"Do you wish me to say to the owls that they are to leave those pine tree worms in peace?"

"Yes, it would be well if you who have some authority in the forest should do this," said Helpless.

"I might also drop a good word for the pine needle pickers among the thrushes?" volunteered the adder. "I will gladly serve you when you do not demand anything unreasonable."

"Now you have given me a good promise, Crawlie," said Helpless, "and I'm glad that I came to you."

THE NUN MOTHS

O ne morning—several years later—Karr lay asleep on the porch. It was in the early summer, the season of light nights, and it was as bright as day, although the sun was not yet up. Karr was awakened by some one calling his name.

"Is it you, Grayskin?" he asked, for he was accustomed to the elk's nightly visits. Again he heard the call, then he recognized Grayskin's voice, and hastened in the direction of the sound.

Karr heard the elk's footfalls in the distance, as he dashed into the thickest pine wood, and straight through the brush, following a no trodden path. Karr could not catch up with him, and he had great difficulty in even following the trail.

"Karr, Karr!" came the cry, and the voice was certainly Grayskin's, although it had a ring now which the dog had never heard before.

"I'm coming, I'm coming!" the dog responded. "Where are you?"

"Karr, Karr! Don't you see how it falls and falls?" said Grayskin.

Then Karr noticed that the pine needles kept dropping and dropping from the trees, like a steady fall of rain.

"Yes, I see how it falls," he cried, and ran far into the forest in search of the elk.

Grayskin kept running through the thickets, while Karr was about to lose the trail again.

"Karr, Karr!" roared Grayskin, "can't you scent that peculiar odor in the forest?" Karr stopped and sniffed.

He had not thought of it before, but now he remarked that the pines sent forth a much stronger odor than usual.

"Yes, I catch the scent," he said. He did not stop long enough to find out the cause of it, but hurried on after Grayskin.

The elk ran ahead with such speed that the dog could not catch up to him.

"Karr, Karr!" he called, "can't you hear the crunching on the pines?" Now his tone was so plaintive it would have melted a stone.

Karr paused to listen. He heard a faint but distinct "tap, tap," on the trees. It sounded like the ticking of a watch.

"Yes, I hear how it ticks," cried Karr, and ran no farther. He understood that the elk did not want him to follow, but to take notice of something that was happening in the forest.

Karr was standing beneath the drooping branches of a great pine. He looked carefully at it, the needles moved. He went closer and saw a mass of grayish-white caterpillars creeping along the branches, gnawing off the needles. Every branch was covered with them.

The crunch, crunch in the trees came from the working of their busy little jaws. Gnawed-off needles fell to the ground in a continuous shower, and from the poor pines there came such a strong odor that the dog suffered from it.

"What can be the meaning of this?" wondered Karr. "It's too bad about the pretty trees! Soon they'll have no beauty left."

He walked from tree to tree, trying with his poor eyesight to see if all was well with them.

"There's a pine they haven't touched," he thought. But they had taken possession of it, too. "And here's a birch—no, this also! The gamekeeper will not be pleased with this," observed Karr. He ran deeper into the thickets, to learn how far the destruction had spread.

Wherever he went, he heard the same ticking, scented the same odor, saw the same needle rain. There was no need of his pausing to investigate. He understood it all by these signs. The little caterpillars were everywhere. The whole forest was being ravaged by them!

All of a sudden he came to a tract where there was no odor, and where all was still.

"Here's the end of their domain," thought the dog, as he paused and glanced about.

But here it was even worse, for the caterpillars had already done their work, and the trees were without needles. They were like the dead. The only thing that covered them was a network of ragged threads, which the caterpillars had spun to use as roads and bridges.

In there, among the dying trees, Grayskin stood waiting for Karr.

He was not alone. With him were four old elk—the most respected in the forest. Karr knew them: They were Crooked-Back, who was a small elk, but had a larger hump than the others; Antler-Crown, who was the most dignified of the elk; Rough-Mane, with the thick coat, and an old long-legged one, who, up till the autumn before, when he got a bullet in his thigh, had been terribly hot-tempered and quarrelsome.

"What in the world is happening to the forest?" Karr asked when he came up to the elk. They stood with lowered heads, far protruding upper lips, and looked puzzled.

"No one can tell," answered Grayskin. "This insect family used to be the least hurtful of any in the forest, and never before have they done any damage. But these last few years they have been multiplying so fast that now it appears as if the entire forest would be destroyed."

"Yes, it looks bad," Karr agreed, "but I see that the wisest animals in the forest have come together to hold a consultation. Perhaps you have already found some remedy?"

When the dog said this, Crooked-Back solemnly raised his heavy head, pricked up his long ears, and spoke:

"We have summoned you hither, Karr, that we may learn if the humans know of this desolation." "No," said Karr, "no human being ever comes this far into the forest when it's not hunting time. They know nothing of this misfortune."

Then Antler-Crown said: "We who have lived long in the forest do not think that we can fight this insect pest all by ourselves."

"After this there will be no peace in the forest!" put in Rough-Mane.

"But we can't let the whole Liberty Forest go to rack and ruin!" protested Big-and-Strong. "We'll have to consult the humans; there is no alternative."

Karr understood that the elk had difficulty in expressing what they wished to say, and he tried to help them.

"Perhaps you want me to let the people know the conditions here?" he suggested.

All the old elk nodded their heads. "It's most unfortunate that we are obliged to ask help of human beings, but we have no choice."

A moment later Karr was on his way home. As he ran ahead, deeply distressed over all that he had heard and seen, a big black water snake approached him.

"We'll meet in the forest!" hissed the water snake.

"We'll meet again!" snarled Karr and rushed by without stopping.

The snake turned and tried to catch up to him.

"Perhaps that creature also is worried about the forest," thought Karr, and waited.

Immediately the snake began to talk about the great disaster:

"There will be an end of peace and quiet in the forest when human beings are called hither," said the snake.

"I'm afraid there will," the dog agreed, "but the oldest forest dwellers know what they're about!" he added.

"I think I know a better plan," said the snake, "if I can get the reward I wish."

"Are you not the one whom every one around here calls old Helpless?" said the dog, sneeringly.

"I'm an old inhabitant of the forest," said the snake, "and I know how to get rid of such plagues."

"If you clear the forest of that pest, I feel sure you can have anything you ask for," said Karr.

The snake did not respond to this until he had crawled under a tree stump, where he was well protected. Then he said:

"Tell Grayskin that if he will leave Liberty Forest forever, and go far north, where no oak tree grows, I will send sickness and death to all the creeping things that gnaw the pines and spruces!"

"What's that you say?" asked Karr, bristling up. "What harm has Grayskin ever done you?"

"He has slain the one whom I loved best," the snake declared, "and I want to be avenged."

Before the snake had finished speaking, Karr made a dash for him, but the reptile lay safely hidden under the tree stump.

"Stay where you are!" Karr concluded. "We'll manage to drive out the caterpillars without your help."

THE BIG WAR OF THE MOTHS

The following spring, as Karr was dashing through the forest one morning, he heard some one behind him calling: "Karr! Karr!" He turned and saw an old fox standing outside his lair.

"You must tell me if the humans are doing anything for the forest," said the fox. "Yes, you may be sure they are!" said Karr. "They are working as hard as they can."

"They have killed off all my kinsfolk, and they'll be killing me next," protested the fox. "But they shall be pardoned for that if only they save the forest."

That year Karr never ran into the woods without some animal's asking if the humans could save the forest. It was not easy for the dog to answer; the people themselves were not certain that they could conquer the moths. But considering how feared and hated old Kolmården had always been, it was remarkable that every day more than a hundred men went there to work. They cleared away the underbrush.

They felled dead trees, lopped off branches from the live ones so that the caterpillars could not easily crawl from tree to tree; they also dug wide trenches around the ravaged parts and put up lime-washed fences to keep them out of new territory. Then they painted rings of lime around the trunks of trees to prevent the caterpillars leaving those they had already stripped. The idea was to force them to remain where they were until they starved to death.

The people worked with the forest until the spring. They were hopeful, and could wait for the caterpillars to come out from their eggs, feeling certain that they had shut them in so effectively that most of them would die of starvation.

But in the early summer the caterpillars came out, more numerous than ever. They were everywhere! They crawled on the country roads, on fences, on the walls of the cabins. They wandered outside the confines of Liberty Forest to other parts of Kolmården.

"They won't stop till all our forests are destroyed!" sighed the people, who were in great despair, and could not enter the forest without weeping.

Karr was so sick of the sight of all these creeping, gnawing things that he could hardly bear to step outside the door. But one day he felt that he must go and find out how Grayskin was getting on. He took the shortest cut to the elk's haunts, and hurried along his nose close to the earth. When he came to the tree stump where he had met Helpless the year before, the snake was still there, and called to him:

"Have you told Grayskin what I said to you when last we met?" asked the water snake.

Karr only growled and tried to get at him.

"If you haven't told him, by all means do so!" insisted the snake. "You must see that the humans know of no cure for this plague."

"Neither do you!" retorted the dog, and ran on.

Karr found Grayskin, but the elk was so low-spirited that he scarcely greeted the dog. He began at once to talk of the forest.

"I don't know what I wouldn't give if this misery were only at an end!" he said.

"Now I shall tell you that 'tis said you could save the forest." Then Karr delivered the water snake's message.

"If any one but Helpless had promised this, I immediately go into exile," declared the elk. "But how can a poor water snake have the power to work such a miracle?"

"Of course it's only a bluff," said Karr. "Water snakes always like to pretend that they know more than other creatures."

When Karr was ready to go home, Grayskin accompanied him part of the way. Presently Karr heard a thrush, perched on a pine top, cry:

"There goes Grayskin, who has destroyed the forest! There goes Grayskin, who has destroyed the forest!"

Karr thought that he had not heard correctly, but the next moment a hare came darting across the path. When the hare saw them, he stopped, flapped his ears, and screamed:

"Here comes Grayskin, who has destroyed the forest!" Then he ran as fast as he could.

"What do they mean by that?" asked Karr.

"I really don't know," said Grayskin. "I think that the small forest animals are displeased with me because I was the one who proposed that we should ask help of human beings. When the underbrush was cut down, all their lairs and hiding places were destroyed."

They walked on together a while longer, and Karr heard the same cry coming from all directions:

"There goes Grayskin, who has destroyed the forest!"

Grayskin pretended not to hear it, but Karr understood why the elk was so downhearted.

"I say, Grayskin, what does the water snake mean by saying you killed the one he loved best?"

"How can I tell?" said Grayskin. "You know very well that I never kill anything."

Shortly after that they met the four old elk Crooked-Back, Antler-Crown, Rough-Mane, and Big-and-Strong, who were coming along slowly, one after the other.

"We'll meet in the forest!" called Grayskin. "We'll meet in turn!" answered the elk.

"We were just looking for you, Grayskin, to consult with you about the forest."

"The fact is," began Crooked-Back, "we have been informed that a crime has been committed here, and that the whole forest is being destroyed because the criminal has not been punished."

"What kind of a crime was it?"

"Some one killed a harmless creature that he couldn't eat. Such an act is accounted a crime in Liberty Forest."

"Who could have done such a cowardly thing?" wondered Grayskin.

"They say that an elk did it, and we were just going to ask if you knew who it was."

"No," said Grayskin, "I have never heard of an elk killing a harmless creature."

Grayskin parted from the four old elk, and went on with Karr. He was silent and walked with lowered head. They happened to pass Crawlie, the adder, who lay on his shelf of rock.

"There goes Grayskin, who has destroyed the whole forest!" hissed Crawlie, like all the rest.

By that time Grayskin's patience was exhausted. He walked up to the snake, and raised a forefoot.

"Do you think of crushing me as you crushed the old water snake?" hissed Crawlie.

"Did I kill a water snake?" asked Grayskin, astonished.

"The first day you were in the forest you killed the helpless wife of poor old Helpless," said Crawlie.

Grayskin turned quickly from the adder, and continued his walk with Karr. Suddenly he stopped.

"Karr, it was I who committed that crime! I killed a harmless creature, therefore it is on my account that the forest is being destroyed."

"What are you saying?" Karr interrupted.

"You may tell the water snake, Helpless, that Grayskin goes into exile tonight!"

"That I shall never tell him!" protested Karr. "The Far North is a dangerous country for elk."

"Do you think that I wish to remain here, when I have caused a disaster like this?" protested Grayskin.

"Don't be rash! Sleep over it before you do anything!"

"It was you who taught me that the elk are one with the forest," said Grayskin, and so saying he parted from Karr.

The dog went home alone, but this talk with Grayskin troubled him, and the next morning he returned to the forest to seek him, but Grayskin was not to be found, and the dog did not search long for him. He realized that the elk had taken the snake at his word, and had gone into exile.

On his walk home Karr was too unhappy for words! He could not understand why Grayskin should allow that wretch of a water snake to trick him away. He had never heard of such folly! "What power can that old Helpless have?"

As Karr walked along, his mind full of these thoughts, he happened to see the gamekeeper, who stood pointing up at a tree.

"What are you looking at?" asked a man who stood beside him.

"Sickness has come among the caterpillars," observed the gamekeeper. Karr was astonished, but he was even more angered having the power to keep his word. Grayskin would have to stay away a long, long time, for, of course, that water snake would never die.

At the very height of his grief a thought came to Karr which comforted him a little. "Perhaps the water snake won't live so long, after all!" he thought. "Surely he cannot always lie protected under a tree root. As soon as he has cleaned out the caterpillars, I know some one who is going to bite his head off!"

It was true that an illness had made its appearance among the caterpillars. The first summer it did not spread much. It had only just broken out when it was time for the larvae to turn into pupae. From the latter came millions of moths. They flew around in the trees like a blinding snowstorm, and laid countless numbers of eggs. An even greater destruction was prophesied for the following year. The destruction came not only to the forest, but also to the caterpillars. The sickness spread quickly from forest to forest. The sick caterpillars stopped eating, crawled up to the branches of the trees, and died there.

There was great rejoicing among the people when they saw them die, but there was even greater rejoicing among the forest animals. From day to day the dog Karr went about with savage glee, thinking of the hour when he might venture to kill Helpless. But the caterpillars, meanwhile, had spread over miles of pine woods. Not in one summer did the disease reach them all. Many lived to become pupae and moths.

Grayskin sent messages to his friend Karr by the birds of passage, to say that he was alive and faring well. But the birds told Karr confidentially that on several occasions Grayskin had been pursued by poachers, and that only with the greatest difficulty had he escaped. Karr lived in a state of continual grief, yearning, and anxiety. Yet he had to wait two whole summers more before there was an end of the caterpillars! Karr no sooner heard the gamekeeper say that the forest was out of danger than he started on a hunt for Helpless. But when he was in the thick of the forest he made a frightful discovery: He could not hunt any more; he could not run; he could not track his enemy; he could not see at all!

During the long years of waiting, old age had overtaken Karr. He had grown old without having noticed it. He had not the strength even to kill a water snake. He was not able to save his friend Grayskin from his enemy.

RETRIBUTION

One afternoon Akka from Kebnekaise and her flock alighted on the shore of a forest lake.

Spring was backward as it always is in the mountain districts. Ice covered all the lake save a narrow strip next the land. The geese at once plunged into the water to bathe and hunt for food. In the morning Nils Holgersson had dropped one of his wooden shoes, so he went down by the elms and birches that grew along the shore, to look for something to bind around his foot.

The boy walked quite a distance before he found anything that he could use. He glanced about nervously, for he did not fancy being in the forest. "Give me the plains and the lakes!" he thought. "There you can see what you are likely to meet. Now, if this were a grove of little birches, it would be well enough, for then the ground would be almost bare, but how people can like these wild, pathless forests is incomprehensible to me. If I owned this land I would chop down every tree."

At last he caught sight of a piece of birch bark, and just as he was fitting it to his foot he heard a rustle behind him. He turned quickly. A snake darted from the brush straight toward him!

The snake was uncommonly long and thick, but the boy soon saw that it had a white spot on each cheek.

"Why, it's only a water snake," he laughed, "it can't harm me."

But the next instant the snake gave him a powerful blow on the chest that knocked him down. The boy was on his feet in a second and running away, but the snake was after him! The ground was stony and scrubby; the boy could not proceed very fast, and the snake was close at his heels.

Then the boy saw a big rock in front of him, and began to scale it. "I do hope the snake can't follow me here!" he thought, but he had no sooner reached the top of the rock than he saw that the snake was following him.

Quite close to the boy, on a narrow ledge at the top of the rock, lay a round stone as large as a man's head. As the snake came closer, the boy ran behind the stone, and gave it a push. It rolled right down on the snake, drawing it along to the ground, where it landed on its head.

"That stone did its work well!" thought the boy with a sigh of relief, as he saw the snake squirm a little, and then lie perfectly still.

"I don't think I've been in greater peril on the whole journey," he said.

He had hardly recovered from the shock when he heard a rustle above him, and saw a bird circling through the air to light on the ground right beside the snake. The bird was like a crow in size and form, but was dressed in a pretty coat of shiny black feathers.

The boy cautiously retreated into a crevice of the rock. His adventure in being kidnapped by crows was still fresh in his memory, and he did not care to show himself when there was no need of it.

The bird strode back and forth beside the snake's body, and turned it over with his beak. Finally he spread his wings and began to shriek in ear-splitting tones:

"It is certainly Helpless, the water snake, that lies dead here!" Once more he walked the length of the snake, then he stood in a deep study, and scratched his neck with his foot.

"It isn't possible that there can be two such big snakes in the forest," he pondered. "It must surely be Helpless!"

He was just going to thrust his beak into the snake, but suddenly checked himself.

"You mustn't be a numskull, Bataki!" he remarked to himself. "Surely you cannot be thinking of eating the snake until you have called Karr! He wouldn't believe that Helpless was dead unless he could see it with his own eyes."

The boy tried to keep quiet, but the bird was so ludicrously solemn, as he stalked back and forth chattering to himself, that he had to laugh.

The bird heard him, and, with a flap of his wings, he was up on the rock. The boy rose quickly and walked toward him.

"Are you not the one who is called Bataki, the raven? And are you not a friend of Akka from Kebnekaise?" asked the boy.

The bird regarded him intently, then nodded three times.

"Surely, you're not the little chap who flies around with the wild geese, and whom they call Thumbietot?"

"Oh, you're not so far out of the way," said the boy.

"What luck that I should have run across you! Perhaps you can tell me who killed this water snake?"

"The stone which I rolled down on him killed him," replied the boy, and related how the whole thing happened.

"That was cleverly done for one who is as tiny as you are!" said the raven. "I have a friend in these parts who will be glad to know that this snake has been killed, and I should like to render you a service in return."

"Then tell me why you are glad the water snake is dead," responded the boy.

"It's a long story," said the raven, "you wouldn't have the patience to listen to it."

But the boy insisted that he had, and then the raven told him the whole story about Karr and Grayskin and Helpless, the water snake. When he had finished, the boy sat quietly for a moment, looking straight ahead. Then he spoke:

"I seem to like the forest better since hearing this. I wonder if there is anything left of the old Liberty Forest."

"The trees look as if they had passed through a fire. They'll have to be cleared away, and it will take many years before the forest will be what it once was."

"That snake deserved his death!" declared the boy. "But I wonder if it could be possible that he was so wise he could send sickness to the caterpillars?"

"Perhaps he knew that they frequently became sick in that way," intimated Bataki.

"Yes, that may be, but all the same, I must say that he was a very wily snake."

The boy stopped talking because he saw the raven was not listening to him, but sitting with gaze averted. "Hark!" he said. "Karr is in the vicinity. Won't he be happy when he sees that Helpless is dead!"

The boy turned his head in the direction of the sound. "He's talking with the wild geese," he said.

"Oh, you may be sure that he has dragged himself down to the strand to get the latest news about Grayskin!"

Both the boy and the raven jumped to the ground, and hastened down to the shore. All the geese had come out of the lake, and stood talking with an old dog, who was so weak and decrepit that it seemed as if he might drop dead at any moment.

"There's Karr," said Bataki to the boy. "Let him hear first what the wild geese have to say to him; later we shall tell him that the water snake is dead." Presently they heard Akka talking to Karr.

"It happened last year while we were making our usual spring trip," remarked the leader goose. "We started out one morning—Yksi, Kaksi, and I, and we flew over the great boundary forests between Dalecarlia and Hälsingland. Under us we saw only thick pine forests. The snow was still deep among the trees, and the creeks were mostly frozen.

"Suddenly we noticed three poachers down in the forest! They were on skis, had dogs on leash, carried knives in their belts, but had no guns.

"As there was a hard crust on the snow, they did not bother to take the winding forest paths, but skied straight ahead. Apparently they knew very well where they must go to find what they were seeking.

"We flew on, high up in the air, so that the whole forest under us was visible. When we sighted the poachers we wanted to find out where the game was, so we circled up and down, peering through the trees. Then, in a dense thicket, we saw something that looked like big, moss-covered rocks, but couldn't be rocks, for there was no snow on them.

"We shot down, suddenly, and lit in the center of the thicket. The three rocks moved. They were three elk—a bull and two cows resting in the bleak forest.

"When we alighted, the elk bull rose and came toward us. He was the most superb animal we had ever seen. When he saw that it was only some poor wild geese that had awakened him, he lay down again.

"'No, old granddaddy, you mustn't go back to sleep!' I cried. 'Flee as fast as you can! There are poachers in the forest, and they are bound for this very deer fold.'

"'Thank you, goose mother!' said the elk. He seemed to be dropping to sleep while he was speaking. 'But surely you must know that we elk are under the protection of the law at this time of the year. Those poachers are probably out for fox,' he yawned.

"'There are plenty of fox trails in the forest, but the poachers are not looking for them. Believe me, old granddaddy! They know that you are lying here, and are coming to attack you. They have no guns with them only spears and knives—for they dare not fire a shot at this season.'

"The elk bull lay there calmly, but the elk cows felt uneasy.

231

"'It may be as the geese say,' they remarked, beginning to bestir themselves.

"'You just lie down!' said the elk bull. 'There are no poachers coming here, of that you may be certain.'"

"There was nothing more to be done, so we wild geese rose again into the air. But we continued to circle over the place, to see how it would turn out for the elk.

"We had hardly reached our regular flying altitude, when we saw the elk bull come out from the thicket. He sniffed the air a little, then walked straight toward the poachers. As he strode along he stepped upon dry twigs that crackled noisily. A big barren marsh lay just beyond him. Thither he went and took his stand in the middle, where there was nothing to hide him from view.

"There he stood until the poachers emerged from the woods. Then he turned and fled in the opposite direction. The poachers let loose the dogs, and they themselves chased after him at full speed.

"The elk threw back his head and loped as fast as he could. He kicked up snow until it flew like a blizzard about him. Both dogs and men were left far behind. Then the elk stopped, as if to await their approach. When they were within sight he dashed ahead again. We understood that he was purposely tempting the hunters away from the place where the cows were. We thought it brave of him to face danger himself, in order that those who were dear to him might be left in safety. None of us wanted to leave the place until we had seen how all this was to end.

"Thus the chase continued for two hours or more. We wondered that the poachers went to the trouble of pursuing the elk when they were not armed with rifles. They couldn't have thought that they could succeed in tiring out a runner like him!

"Then we noticed that the elk no longer ran so rapidly. He stepped on the snow more carefully, and every time he lifted his feet, blood could be seen in his tracks.

"We understood why the poachers had been so persistent! They had counted on help from the snow. The elk was heavy, and with every step he sank to the bottom of the drift. The hard crust on the snow was scraping his legs. It scraped away the fur, and tore out pieces of flesh, so that he was in torture every time he put his foot down.

"The poachers and the dogs, who were so light that the ice crust could hold their weight, pursued him all the while. He ran on and on—his steps becoming more and more uncertain and faltering. He gasped for breath. Not only did he suffer intense pain, but he was also exhausted from wading through the deep snowdrifts.

"At last he lost all patience. He paused to let poachers and dogs come upon him, and was ready to fight them. As he stood there waiting, he glanced upward. When he saw us wild geese circling above him, he cried out:

"'Stay here, wild geese, until all is over! And the next time you fly over Kolmården, look up Karr, and ask him if he doesn't think that his friend Grayskin has met with a happy end?'"

When Akka had gone so far in her story the old dog rose and walked nearer to her.

"Grayskin led a good life," he said. "He understands me. He knows that I'm a brave dog, and that I shall be glad to hear that he had a happy end. Now tell me how—"

He raised his tail and threw back his head, as if to give himself a bold and proud bearing—then he collapsed.

"Karr! Karr!" called a man's voice from the forest. The old dog rose obediently. "My master is calling me," he said, "and I must not tarry longer. I just saw him load his gun. Now we two are going into the forest for the last time.

"Many thanks, wild goose! I know everything that I need know to die content!"

II

THE WIND WITCH

IN NÄRKE

*I*n bygone days there was something in Närke the like of which was not to be found elsewhere; it was a witch named Ysätter-Kaisa.

The name Kaisa had been given her because she had a good deal to do with wind and storm—and these wind witches are always so called. The surname was added because she was supposed to have come from Ysätter swamp in Asker parish. It seemed as though her real abode must have been at Asker, but she used also to appear at other places. Nowhere in all Närke could one be sure of not meeting her.

She was no dark, mournful witch, but gay and frolicsome, and what she loved most of all was a gale of wind. As soon as there was wind enough, off she would fly to the Närke plain for a good dance. On days when a whirlwind swept the plain, Ysätter-Kaisa had fun! She would stand right in the whirl and spin round, her long hair flying up among the clouds and the long trail of her robe sweeping the ground, like a dust cloud, while the whole plain lay spread out under her, like a ballroom floor.

Of a morning Ysätter-Kaisa would sit up in some tail pine at the top of a precipice, and look across the plain. If it happened to be winter and she saw many teams on the roads she hurriedly blew up a blizzard, piling the drifts so high that people could barely get back to their homes by evening. If it chanced to be summer and good harvest weather, Ysätter-Kaisa would sit quietly until the first hayracks had been loaded, then down she would come with a couple of heavy showers, which put an end to the work for that day.

It was only too true that she seldom thought of anything else than raising mischief. The charcoal burners up in the Kil mountains hardly dared take a cat nap, for as soon as she saw an unwatched kiln, she stole up and blew on it until it began to burn in a great flame. If the metal drivers from Laxå and Svartå were out late of an evening, Ysätter-Kaisa would veil the roads and the country round about in such dark clouds that both men and horses lost their way and drove the heavy trucks down into swamps and morasses.

If, on a summer's day, the dean's wife at Glanshammar had spread the tea table in the garden and along would come a gust of wind that lifted the cloth from the table and turned over cups and saucers, they knew who had raised the mischief. If the mayor of Örebro's hat blew off, so that he had to run across the whole square after it, if the wash on the line blew away and got covered with dirt, or if the smoke poured into the cabins and seemed unable to find its way out through the chimney, it was easy enough to guess who was out making merry!

Although Ysätter-Kaisa was fond of all sorts of tantalizing games, there was nothing really bad about her. One could see that she was hardest on those who were quarrelsome, stingy, or wicked, while honest folk and poor little children she would take under her wing. Old people say of her that, once, when Asker church was burning, Ysätter-Kaisa swept through the air, lit amid fire and smoke on the church roof, and averted the disaster. All the same the Närke folk were often rather tired of Ysätter-Kaisa, but she never tired of playing her tricks on them. As she sat on the edge of a cloud and looked down upon Närke, which rested so peacefully and comfortably beneath her, she must have thought: "The inhabitants would fare much too well if I were not in existence. They would grow sleepy and dull. There must be some one like myself to rouse them and keep them in good spirits."

Then she would laugh wildly and, chattering like a magpie, would rush off, dancing and spinning from one end of the plain to the other. When a Närke man saw her come dragging her dust trail over the plain, he could not help smiling. Provoking and tiresome she certainly was, but she had a merry spirit. It was just as refreshing for the peasants to meet Ysätter-Kaisa as it was for the plain to be lashed by the windstorm.

Nowadays 'tis said that Ysätter-Kaisa is dead and gone, like all other witches, but this one can hardly believe. It is as if someone were to come and tell you that henceforth the air would always be still on the plain, and the wind would never more dance across it with blustering breezes and drenching showers. He who fancies that Ysätter-Kaisa is dead and gone may as well hear what occurred in Närke the year that Nils Holgersson traveled over that part of the country. Then let him tell what he thinks about it.

MARKET EVE

Wednesday, April twenty-seventh

*I*t was the day before the big Cattle Fair at Örebro; it rained in torrents and people thought: "This is exactly as in Ysätter-Kaisa's time! At fairs she used to be more prankish than usual. It was quite in her line to arrange a downpour like this on a market eve."

As the day wore on, the rain increased, and toward evening came regular cloudbursts. The roads were like bottomless swamps. The farmers who had started from home with their cattle early in the morning, that they might arrive at a seasonable hour, fared badly. Cows and oxen were so tired they could hardly move, and many of the poor beasts dropped down in the middle of the road, to show that they were too exhausted to go any farther. All who lived along the roadside had to open their doors to the market bound travelers, and harbor them as best they could. Farm houses, barns, and sheds were soon crowded to their limit.

Meanwhile, those who could struggle along toward the inn did so, but when they arrived they wished they had stopped at some cabin along the road. All the cribs in the barn and all the stalls in the stable were already occupied. There was no other choice than to let horses and cattle stand out in the rain. Their masters could barely manage to get under cover.

The crush and mud and slush in the barn yard were frightful! Some of the animals were standing in puddles and could not even lie down. There were thoughtful masters, of course, who procured straw for their animals to lie on, and spread blankets over them, but there were those, also, who sat in the inn, drinking and gambling, entirely forgetful of the dumb creatures which they should have protected.

The boy and the wild geese had come to a little wooded island in Hjälmar Lake that evening. The island was separated from the mainland by a narrow and shallow stream, and at low tide one could pass over it dry-shod.

It rained just as hard on the island as it did everywhere else. The boy could not sleep for the water that kept dripping down on him. Finally he got up and began to walk. He fancied that he felt the rain less when he moved about.

He had hardly circled the island, when he heard a splashing in the stream. Presently he saw a solitary horse tramping among the trees. Never in all his life had he seen such a wreck of a horse. He was broken-winded and stiff-kneed and so thin that every rib could be seen under the hide. He bore neither harness nor saddle, only an old bridle, from which dangled a half-rotted rope end. Obviously he had had no difficulty in breaking loose.

The horse walked straight toward the spot where the wild geese were sleeping. The boy was afraid that he would step on them.

"Where are you going? Feel your ground!" shouted the boy.

"Oh, there you are!" exclaimed the horse. "I've walked miles to meet you!"

"Have you heard of me?" asked the boy, astonished.

"I've got ears, even if I am old! There are many who talk of you nowadays."

As he spoke, the horse bent his head that he might see better, and the boy noticed that he had a small head, beautiful eyes, and a soft, sensitive nose.

"He must have been a good horse at the start, though he has come to grief in his old age," he thought.

"I wish you would come with me and help me with something," pleaded the horse.

The boy thought it would be embarrassing to accompany a creature who looked so wretched, and excused himself on account of the bad weather.

"You'll be no worse off on my back than you are lying here," said the horse. "*But* perhaps you don't dare to go with an old tramp of a horse like me." "Certainly I dare!" said the boy.

"Then wake the geese, so that we can arrange with them where they shall come for you tomorrow," said the horse.

The boy was soon seated on the animal's back. The old nag trotted along better than he had thought possible. It was a long ride in the rain and darkness before they halted near a large inn, where everything looked terribly uninviting! The wheel tracks were so deep in the road that the boy feared he might drown should he fall down into them. Alongside the fence, which enclosed the yard, some thirty or forty horses and cattle were tied, with no protection against the rain, and in the yard were wagons piled with packing cases, where sheep, calves, hogs, and chickens were shut in.

The horse walked over to the fence and stationed himself. The boy remained seated upon his back, and, with his good night eyes, plainly saw how badly the animals fared.

"How do you happen to be standing out here in the rain?" he asked.

"We're on our way to a fair at Örebro, but we were obliged to put up here on account of the rain. This is an inn, but so many travelers have already arrived that there's no room for us in the barns."

The boy made no reply, but sat quietly looking about him. Not many of the animals were asleep, and on all sides he heard complaints and indignant protests. They had reason enough for grumbling, for the weather was even worse than it had been earlier in the day. A freezing wind had begun to blow, and the rain which came beating down on them was turning to snow. It was easy enough to understand what the horse wanted the boy to help him with.

"Do you see that fine farm yard directly opposite the inn?" remarked the horse.

"Yes, I see it," answered the boy, "and I can't comprehend why they haven't tried to find shelter for all of you in there. They are already full, perhaps?"

"No, there are no strangers in that place," said the horse. "The people who live on that farm are so stingy and selfish that it would be useless for any one to ask them for harbor."

"If that's the case, I suppose you'll have to stand where you are."

"I was born and raised on that farm," said the horse, "I know that there is a large barn and a big cow shed, with many empty stalls and mangers, and I was wondering if you couldn't manage in some way or other to get us in over there."

"I don't think I could venture—" hesitated the boy. But he felt so sorry for the poor beasts that he wanted at least to try.

He ran into the strange barn yard and saw at once that all the outhouses were locked and the keys gone. He stood there, puzzled and helpless, when aid came to him from an unexpected source. A gust of wind came sweeping along with terrific force and flung open a shed door right in front of him.

The boy was not long in getting back to the horse. "It isn't possible to get into the barn or the cow house," he said, "but there's a big, empty hay shed that they have forgotten to bolt. I can lead you into that."

"Thank you!" said the horse. "It will seem good to sleep once more on familiar ground. It's the only happiness I can expect in this life." Meanwhile, at the flourishing farm opposite the inn, the family sat up much later than usual that evening.

The master of the place was a man of thirty-five, tall and dignified, with a handsome but melancholy face. During the day he had been out in the rain and had got wet, like every one else, and at supper he asked his old mother, who was still mistress of the place, to light a fire on the hearth that he might dry his clothes. The mother kindled a feeble blaze—for in that house they were not wasteful with wood—and the master hung his coat on the back of a chair, and placed it before the fire. With one foot on top of the andiron and a hand resting on his knee, he stood gazing into the embers. Thus he stood for two whole hours, making no move other than to cast a log on the fire now and then.

The mistress removed the supper things and turned down his bed for the night before she went to her own room and seated herself. At intervals she came to the door and looked wonderingly at her son.

"It's nothing, Mother. I'm only thinking," he said.

His thoughts were on something that had occurred shortly before: When he passed the inn a horse dealer had asked him if he would not like to purchase a horse, and had shown him an old nag so weather-beaten that he asked the dealer if he took him for a fool, since he wished to palm off such a played out beast on him.

"Oh, no!" said the horse dealer. "I only thought that, inasmuch as the horse once belonged to you, you might wish to give him a comfortable home in his old age; he has need of it."

Then he looked at the horse and recognized it as one which he himself had raised and broken in, but it did not occur to him to purchase such an old and useless creature on that account. No, indeed! He was not one who squandered his money.

All the same, the sight of the horse had awakened many memories and it was the memories that kept him awake.

That horse had been a fine animal. His father had let him tend it from the start. He had broken it in and had loved it above everything else. His father had complained that he used to feed it too well, and often he had been obliged to steal out and smuggle oats to it.

Once, when he ventured to talk with his father about letting him buy a broadcloth suit, or having the cart painted, his father stood as if petrified, and he thought the old man would have a stroke. He tried to make his father understand that, when he had a fine horse to drive, he should look presentable himself.

The father made no reply, but two days later he took the horse to Örebro and sold it.

It was cruel of him. But it was plain that his father had feared that this horse might lead him into vanity and extravagance. And now, so long afterward, he had to admit that his father was right. A horse like that surely would have been a temptation. At first he had grieved terribly over his loss. Many a time he had gone down to Örebro, just to stand on a street corner and see the horse pass by, or to steal into the stable and give him a lump of sugar. He thought: "If I ever get the farm, the first thing I do will be to buy back my horse."

Now his father was gone and he himself had been master for two years, but he had not made a move toward buying the horse. He had not thought of him for ever so long, until tonight.

It was strange that he should have forgotten the beast so entirely!

His father had been a very headstrong, domineering man. When his son was grown and the two had worked together, the father had gained absolute power over him. The boy had come to think that everything his father did was right, and, after he became the master, he only tried to do exactly as his father would have done.

He knew, of course, that folk said his father was stingy, but it was well to keep a tight hold on one's purse and not throw away money needlessly. The goods one has received should not be wasted. It was better to live on a debt-free place and be called stingy, than to carry heavy mortgages, like other farm owners.

He had gone so far in his mind when he was called back by a strange sound. It was as if a shrill, mocking voice were repeating his thoughts: "It's better to keep a firm hold on one's purse and be called stingy, than to be in debt, like other farm owners."

It sounded as if some one was trying to make sport of his wisdom and he was about to lose his temper, when he realized that it was all a mistake. The wind was beginning to rage, and he had been standing there getting so sleepy that he mistook the howling of the wind in the chimney for human speech.

He glanced up at the wall clock, which just then struck eleven.

"It's time that you were in bed," he remarked to himself. Then he remembered that he had not yet gone the rounds of the farm yard, as it was his custom to do every night, to make sure that all doors were closed and all lights extinguished. This was something he had never neglected since he became master. He drew on his coat and went out in the storm.

He found everything as it should be, save that the door to the empty hay shed had been blown open by the wind. He stepped inside for the key, locked the shed door and put the key into his coat pocket. Then he went back to the house, removed his coat, and hung it before the fire. Even now he did not retire, but began pacing the floor. The storm without, with its biting wind and snow-blended rain, was terrible, and his old horse was standing in this storm without so much as a blanket to protect him! He should at least have given his old friend a roof over his head, since he had come such a long distance.

At the inn across the way the boy heard an old wall clock strike eleven times. Just then he was untying the animals to lead them to the shed in the farm yard opposite. It took some time to rouse them and get them into line. When all were ready, they marched in a long procession into the stingy farmer's yard, with the boy as their guide. While the boy had been assembling them, the farmer had gone the rounds of the farm yard and locked the hay shed, so that when the animals came along the door was closed. The boy stood there dismayed. He could not let the creatures stand out there! He must go into the house and find the key.

"Keep them quiet out here while I go in and fetch the key!" he said to the old horse, and off he ran.

On the path right in front of the house he paused to think out how he should get inside. As he stood there he noticed two little wanderers coming down the road, who stopped before the inn.

The boy saw at once that they were two little girls, and ran toward them.

"Come now, Britta Maja!" said one, "you mustn't cry any more. Now we are at the inn. Here they will surely take us in."

The girl had but just said this when the boy called to her:

"No, you mustn't try to get in there. It is simply impossible. But at the farm house opposite there are no guests. Go there instead."

The little girls heard the words distinctly, though they could not see the one who spoke to them. They did not wonder much at that, however, for the night was as black as pitch. The larger of the girls promptly answered:

"We don't care to enter that place, because who live there are stingy and cruel. It is their fault that we two must go out on the highways and beg."

"That may be so," said the boy, "but all the same you should go there. You shall see that it will be well for you."

"We can try, but it is doubtful that they will even let us enter," observed the two little girls as they walked up to the house and knocked.

The master was standing by the fire thinking of the horse when he heard the knocking. He stepped to the door to see what was up, thinking all the while that he would not let himself be tempted into admitting any wayfarer. As he fumbled the lock, a gust of wind came along, wrenched the door from his hand and swung it open. To close it, he had to step out on the porch, and, when he stepped back into the house, the two little girls were standing within.

They were two poor beggar girls, ragged, dirty, and starving—two little tots bent under the burden of their beggar's packs, which were as large as themselves.

"Who are you that go prowling about at this hour of the night?" said the master gruffly.

The two children did not answer immediately, but first removed their packs. Then they walked up to the man and stretched forth their tiny hands in greeting.

"We are Anna and Britta Maja from the Engärd," said the elder, "and we were going to ask for a night's lodging."

He did not take the outstretched hands and was just about to drive out the beggar children, when a fresh recollection faced him. Engärd— was not that a little cabin where a poor widow with five children had lived? The widow had owed his father a few hundred kroner and in order to get back his money he had sold her cabin. After that the widow, with her three eldest children, went to Norrland to seek employment, and the two youngest became a charge on the parish.

As he called this to mind he grew bitter. He knew that his father had been severely censured for squeezing out that money, which by right belonged to him.

"What are you doing nowadays?" he asked in a cross tone. "Didn't the board of charities take charge of you? Why do you roam around and beg?"

"It's not our fault," replied the larger girl. "The people with whom we are living have sent us out to beg."

"Well, your packs are filled," the farmer observed, "so you can't complain. Now you'd better take out some of the food you have with you and eat your fill, for here you'll get no food, as all the women folk are in bed. Later you may lie down in the corner by the hearth, so you won't have to freeze."

He waved his hand, as if to ward them off, and his eyes took on a hard look. He was thankful that he had had a father who had been careful of his property. Otherwise, he might perhaps have been forced in childhood to run about and beg, as these children now did. No sooner had he thought this out to the end than the shrill, mocking voice he had heard once before that evening repeated it, word for word.

He listened, and at once understood that it was nothing, only the wind roaring in the chimney. But the queer thing about it was, when the wind repeated his thoughts, they seemed so strangely stupid and hard and false!

The children meanwhile had stretched themselves, side by side, on the floor. They were not quiet, but lay there muttering.

"Do be still, won't you?" he growled, for he was in such an irritable mood that he could have beaten them.

But the mumbling continued, and again he called for silence.

"When mother went away," piped a clear little voice, "she made me promise that every night I would say my evening prayer. I must do this, and Britta Maja too. As soon as we have said 'God who cares for little children' we'll be quiet."

The master sat quite still while the little ones said their prayers, then he rose and began pacing back and forth, back and forth, wringing his hands all the while, as though he had met with some great sorrow.

"The horse driven out and wrecked, these two children turned into road beggars—both Father's doings! Perhaps Father did not do right after all?" he thought. He sat down again and buried his head in his hands. Suddenly his lips began to quiver and into his eyes came tears, which he hastily wiped away. Fresh tears came, and he was just as prompt to brush these away, but it was useless, for more followed.

When his mother stepped into the room, he swung his chair quickly and turned his back to her. She must have noticed something unusual, for she stood quietly behind him a long while, as if waiting for him to speak. She realized how difficult it always is for men to talk of the things they feel most deeply. She must help him of course.

From her bedroom she had observed all that had taken place in the living room, so that she did not have to ask any questions. She walked very softly over to the two sleeping children, lifted them, and bore them to her own bed. Then she went back to her son.

"Lars," she said, as if she did not see that he was weeping, "you had better let me keep these children."

"What, Mother?" he gasped, trying to smother the sobs.

"I have been suffering for years—ever since Father took the cabin from their mother, and so have you."

"Yes, but—"

"I want to keep them here and make something of them; they are too good to beg."

He could not speak, for now the tears were beyond his control, but he took his old mother's withered hand and patted it.

Then he jumped up, as if something had frightened him.

"What would Father have said of this?"

"Father had his day at ruling," retorted the mother. "Now it is your day. As long as Father lived we had to obey him. Now is the time to show what you are."

Her son was so astonished that he ceased crying.

"But I have just shown what I am!" he returned.

"No, you haven't," protested the mother. "You only try to be like him. Father experienced hard times, which made him fear poverty. He believed that he had to think of himself first. But you have never had any difficulties that should make you hard. You have more than you need, and it would be unnatural of you not to think of others."

When the two little girls entered the house the boy slipped in behind them and secreted himself in a dark corner. He had not been there long before he caught a glimpse of the shed key, which the farmer had thrust into his coat pocket.

"When the master of the house drives the children out, I'll take the key and run," he thought.

But the children were not driven out and the boy crouched in the corner not knowing what he should do next.

The mother talked long with her son, and while she was speaking he stopped weeping. Gradually his features softened; he looked like another person. All the while he was stroking the wasted old hand.

"Now we may as well retire," said the old lady when she saw that he was calm again.

"No," he said, suddenly rising, "I cannot retire yet. There's a stranger without whom I must shelter tonight!"

He said nothing further, but quickly drew on his coat, lit the lantern and went out. There were the same wind and chill without, but as he stepped to the porch he began to sing softly. He wondered if the horse would know him, and if he would be glad to come back to his old stable. As he crossed the house yard he heard a door slam.

"That shed door has blown open again," he thought, and went over to close it.

A moment later he stood by the shed and was just going to shut the door, when he heard a rustling within.

The boy, who had watched his opportunity, had run directly to the shed, where he left the animals, but they were no longer out in the rain. A strong wind had long since thrown open the door and helped them to get a roof over their heads. The patter which the master heard was occasioned by the boy running into the shed.

By the light of the lantern the man could see into the shed. The whole floor was covered with sleeping cattle. There was no human being to be seen; the animals were not bound, but were lying, here and there, in the straw.

He was enraged at the intrusion and began storming and shrieking to rouse the sleepers and drive them out. But the creatures lay still and would not let themselves be disturbed. The only one that rose was an old horse that came slowly toward him.

All of a sudden the man became silent. He recognized the beast by its gait. He raised the lantern, and the horse came over and laid its head on his shoulder. The master parted and stroked it.

"My old horsy, my old horsy!" he said. "What have they done to you? Yes, dear, I'll buy you back. You'll never again have to leave this place. You shall do whatever you like, horsy mine! Those whom you have brought with you may remain here, but you shall come with me to the stable. Now I can give you all the oats you are able to eat, without having to smuggle them. And you're not all used up, either! The most handsome horse on the church knoll—that's what you shall be once more! There, there! There, there!"

III

THE BREAKING UP
OF THE ICE

Thursday, April twenty-eighth

The following day the weather was clear and beautiful. There was a strong west wind; people were glad of that, for it dried up the roads, which had been soaked by the heavy rains of the day before. Early in the morning the two Småland children, Osa, the goose girl, and little Mats, were out on the highway leading from Sörmland to Närke. The road ran alongside the southern shore of Hjälmar Lake and the children were walking along looking at the ice, which covered the greater part of it. The morning sun darted its clear rays upon the ice, which did not look dark and forbidding, like most spring ice, but sparkled temptingly. As far as they could see, the ice was firm and dry. The rain had run down into cracks and hollows, or been absorbed by the ice itself. The children saw only the sound ice.

Osa, the goose girl, and little Mats were on their way north, and they could not help thinking of the steps they would be saved if they could cut straight across the lake instead of going around it. They knew, to be sure, that spring ice is treacherous, but this looked perfectly secure. They could see that it was several inches thick near the shore. They saw a path which they might follow, and the opposite shore appeared to be so near that they ought to be able to get there in an hour.

"Come, let's try!" said little Mats. "If we only look before us, so that we don't go down into some hole, we can do it."

So they went out on the lake. The ice was not very slippery, but rather easy to walk upon. There was more water on it than they expected to see, and here and there were cracks, where the water purled up. One had to watch out for such places, but that was easy to do in broad daylight, with the sun shining.

The children advanced rapidly, and talked only of how sensible they were to have gone out on the ice instead of tramping the slushy road.

When they had been walking a while they came to Vin Island, where an old woman had sighted them from her window. She rushed from her cabin, waved them back, and shouted something which they could not hear. They understood perfectly well that she was warning them not to come any farther, but they thought there was no immediate danger. It would be stupid for them to leave the ice when all was going so well!

Therefore they went on past Vin Island and had a stretch of seven miles of ice ahead of them.

Out there was so much water that the children were obliged to take roundabout ways, but that was sport to them. They vied with each other as to which could find the soundest ice. They were neither tired nor hungry. The whole day was before them, and they laughed at each obstacle they met. Now and then they cast a glance ahead at the farther shore. It still appeared far away, although they had been walking a good hour. They were rather surprised that the lake was so broad.

"The shore seems to be moving farther away from us," little Mats observed.

Out there the children were not protected against the wind, which was becoming stronger and stronger every minute, and was pressing their clothing so close to their bodies that they could hardly go on. The cold wind was the first disagreeable thing they had met with on the journey.

But the amazing part of it was that the wind came sweeping along with a loud roar—as if it brought with it the noise of a large mill or factory, though nothing of the kind was to be found out there on the ice. They had walked to the west of the big island, Valen; now they thought they were nearing the north shore. Suddenly the wind began to blow more and more, while the loud roaring increased so rapidly that they began to feel uneasy.

All at once it occurred to them that the roar was caused by the foaming and rushing of the waves breaking against a shore. Even this seemed improbable, since the lake was still covered with ice.

At all events, they paused and looked about. They noticed far in the west a white bank which stretched clear across the lake. At first they thought it was a snow bank alongside a road. Later they realized it was the foam-capped waves dashing against the ice! They took hold of hands and ran without saying a word. Open sea lay beyond in the west, and suddenly the streak of foam appeared to be moving eastward. They wondered if the ice was going to break all over. What was going to happen? They felt now that they were in great danger.

All at once it seemed as if the ice under their feet rose—rose and sank, as if some one from below were pushing it. Presently they heard a hollow boom, and then there were cracks in the ice all around them. The children could see how they crept along under the ice-covering.

The next moment all was still, then the rising and sinking began again. Thereupon the cracks began to widen into crevices through which the water bubbled up. By and by the crevices became gaps. Soon after that the ice was divided into large floes.

"Osa," said little Mats, "this must be the breaking up of the ice!"

"Why, so it is, little Mats," said Osa, "but as yet we can get to land. Run for your life!"

As a matter of fact, the wind and waves had a good deal of work to do yet to clear the ice from the lake. The hardest part was done when the ice-cake burst into pieces, but all these pieces must be broken and hurled against each other, to be crushed, worn down, and dissolved. There was still a great deal of hard and sound ice left, which formed large, unbroken surfaces.

The greatest danger for the children lay in the fact that they had no general view of the ice. They did not see the places where the gaps were so wide that they could not possibly jump over them, nor did they know where to find any floes that would hold them, so they wandered aimlessly back and forth, going farther out on the lake instead of nearer land. At last, confused and terrified, they stood still and wept.

Then a flock of wild geese in rapid flight came rushing by. They shrieked loudly and sharply, but the strange thing was that above the geese-cackle the little children heard these words:

"You must go to the right, the right, the right!" They began at once to follow the advice, but before long they were again standing irresolute, facing another broad gap.

Again they heard the geese shrieking above them and again, amid the geese-cackle, they distinguished a few words:

"Stand where you are! Stand where you are!"

The children did not say a word to each other, but obeyed and stood still. Soon after that the ice floes floated together, so that they could cross the gap. Then they took hold of hands again and ran. They were afraid not only of the peril, but of the mysterious help that had come to them.

Soon they had to stop again, and immediately the sound of the voice reached them.

"Straight ahead, straight ahead!" it said.

This leading continued for about half an hour; by that time they had reached Ljunger Point, where they left the ice and waded to shore. They were still terribly frightened, even though they were on firm land. They did not stop to look back at the lake where the waves were pitching the ice floes faster and faster—but ran on. When they had gone a short distance along the point, Osa paused suddenly. "Wait here, little Mats," she said, "I have forgotten something."

Osa, the goose girl, went down to the strand again, where she stopped to rummage in her bag. Finally she fished out a little wooden shoe, which she placed on a stone where it could be plainly seen. Then she ran to little Mats without once looking back. But the instant her back was turned, a big white goose shot down from the sky, like a streak of lightning, snatched the wooden shoe, and flew away with it.

IV
THUMBIETOT
AND THE BEARS
THE IRONWORKS

Thursday, April twenty-eighth

When the wild geese and Thumbietot had helped Osa, the goose girl, and little Mats across the ice, they flew into Westmanland, where they alighted in a grain field to feed and rest.

A strong west wind blew almost the entire day on which the wild geese traveled over the mining districts, and as soon as they attempted to direct their course northward they were buffered toward the east. Now, Akka thought that Smirre Fox was at large in the eastern part of the province, therefore she would not fly in that direction, but turned back, time and again, struggling westward with great difficulty. At this rate the wild geese advanced very slowly, and late in the afternoon they were still in the Westmanland mining districts. Toward evening the wind abated suddenly, and the tired travelers hoped that they would have an interval of easy flight before sundown. Then along came a violent gust of wind, which tossed the geese before it, like balls, and the boy, who was sitting comfortably, with no thought of peril, was lifted from the goose's back and hurled into space.

Little and light as he was, he could not fall straight to the ground in such a wind, so at first he was carried along with it, drifting down slowly and spasmodically, as a leaf falls from a tree.

"Why, this isn't so bad!" thought the boy as he fell. "I'm tumbling as easily as if I were only a scrap of paper. Morten Goosey-Gander will doubtless hurry along and pick me up."

The first thing the boy did when he landed was to tear off his cap and wave it, so that the big white gander should see where he was.

"Here am I, where are you? Here am I, where are you?" he called, and was rather surprised that Morten Goosey-Gander was not already at his side.

But the big white gander was not to be seen, nor was the wild goose flock outlined against the sky. It had entirely disappeared.

He thought this rather singular, but he was neither worried nor frightened. Not for a second did it occur to him that folk like Akka and Morten Goosey-Gander would abandon him. The unexpected gust of wind had probably borne them along with it. As soon as they could manage to turn, they would surely come back and fetch him.

But what was this? Where on earth was he anyway? He had been standing gazing toward the sky for some sign of the geese, but now he happened to glance about him. He had not come down on even ground, but had dropped into a deep, wide mountain cave or whatever it might be. It was as large as a church, with almost perpendicular walls on all four sides, and with no roof at all. On the ground were some huge rocks, between which moss and lignon-brush and dwarfed birches grew. Here and there in the wall were projections, from which swung rickety ladders. At one side there was a dark passage, which apparently led far into the mountain.

The boy had not been traveling over the mining districts a whole day for nothing. He comprehended at once that the big cleft had been made by the men who had mined ore in this place.

"I must try and climb back to earth again," he thought, "otherwise I fear that my companions won't find me!"

He was about to go over to the wall when some one seized him from behind, and he heard a gruff voice growl in his ear: "Who are you?"

The boy turned quickly, and, in the confusion of the moment, he thought he was facing a huge rock, covered with brownish moss. Then he noticed that the rock had broad paws to walk with, a head, two eyes, and a growling mouth.

He could not pull himself together to answer, nor did the big beast appear to expect it of him, for it knocked him down, rolled him back and forth with its paws, and nosed him. It seemed just about ready to swallow him, when it changed its mind and called:

"Brumme and Mulle, come here, you cubs, and you shall have something good to eat!"

A pair of frowzy cubs, as uncertain on their feet and as woolly as puppies, came tumbling along.

"What have you got, Mamma Bear? May we see, oh, may we see?" shrieked the cubs excitedly.

"Oh oh! so I've fallen in with bears," thought the boy to himself. "Now Smirre Fox won't have to trouble himself further to chase after me!"

The mother bear pushed the boy along to the cubs. One of them nabbed him quickly and ran off with him, but he did not bite hard. He was playful and wanted to amuse himself awhile with Thumbietot before eating him. The other cub was after the first one to snatch the boy for himself, and as he lumbered along he managed to tumble straight down on the head of the one that carried the boy. So the two cubs rolled over each other, biting, clawing, and snarling.

During the tussle the boy got loose, ran over to the wall, and started to scale it. Then both cubs scurried after him, and, nimbly scaling the cliff, they caught up with him and tossed him down on the moss, like a ball.

"Now I know how a poor little mousie fares when it falls into the cat's claws," thought the boy.

He made several attempts to get away. He ran deep down into the old tunnel and hid behind the rocks and climbed the birches, but the cubs hunted him out, go where he would. The instant they caught him they let him go, so that he could run away again and they should have the fun of recapturing him.

At last the boy got so sick and tired of it all that he threw himself down on the ground.

"Run away," growled the cubs, "or we'll eat you up!" "You'll have to eat me then," said the boy, "for I can't run any more."

Immediately both cubs rushed over to the mother bear and complained:

"Mamma Bear, oh, Mamma Bear, he won't play any more."

"Then you must divide him evenly between you," said Mother Bear.

When the boy heard this he was so scared that he jumped up instantly and began playing again.

As it was bedtime, Mother Bear called to the cubs that they must come now and cuddle up to her and go to sleep. They had been having such a good time that they wished to continue their play next day, so they took the boy between them and laid their paws over him. They did not want him to move without waking them. They went to sleep immediately. The boy thought that after a while he would try to steal away. But never in all his life had he been so tumbled and tossed and hunted and rolled! And he was so tired out that he too fell asleep.

By and by Father Bear came clambering down the mountain wall. The boy was wakened by his tearing away stone and gravel as he swung himself into the old mine. The boy was afraid to move much, but he managed to stretch himself and turn over, so that he could see the big bear. He was a frightfully coarse, huge old beast, with great paws, large, glistening tusks, and wicked little eyes! The boy could not help shuddering as he looked at this old monarch of the forest.

"It smells like a human being around here," said Father Bear the instant he came up to Mother Bear, and his growl was as the rolling of thunder.

"How can you imagine anything so absurd?" said Mother Bear without disturbing herself. "It has been settled for good and all that we are not to harm mankind any more, but if one of them were to put in an appearance here, where the cubs and I have our quarters, there wouldn't be enough left of him for you to catch even a scent of him!"

Father Bear lay down beside Mother Bear. "You ought to know me well enough to understand that I don't allow anything dangerous to come near the cubs. Talk, instead, of what you have been doing. I haven't seen you for a whole week!"

"I've been looking about for a new residence," said Father Bear. "First I went over to Vermland, to learn from our kinsmen at Ekshärad how they fared in that country, but I had my trouble for nothing. There wasn't a bear's den left in the whole forest."

"I believe the humans want the whole earth to themselves," said Mother Bear. "Even if we leave people and cattle in peace and live solely upon lignon and insects and green things, we cannot remain unmolested in the forest! I wonder where we could move to in order to live in peace?"

"We've lived comfortably for many years in this pit," observed Father Bear. "But I can't be content here now since the big noise shop has been built right in our neighborhood. Lately I have been taking a look at the land east of Dal River, over by Garpen Mountain. Old mine pits are plentiful there, too, and other fine retreats. I thought it looked as if one might be fairly well protected against men." The instant Father Bear said this he sat up and began to sniff.

"It's extraordinary that whenever I speak of human beings I catch that queer scent again," he remarked.

"Go and see for yourself if you don't believe me," challenged Mother Bear. "I should just like to know where a human being could manage to hide down here?"

The bear walked all around the cave, and nosed. Finally he went back and lay down without a word.

"What did I tell you?" said Mother Bear. "But of course you think that no one but yourself has any nose or cares!"

"One can't be too careful, with such neighbors as we have," said Father Bear gently. Then he leaped up with a roar. As luck would have it, one of the cubs had moved a paw over to Nils Holgersson's face and the poor little wretch could not breathe, but began to sneeze. It was impossible for Mother Bear to keep Father Bear back any longer. He pushed the young ones to right and left and caught sight of the boy before he had time to sit up.

He would have swallowed him instantly if Mother Bear had not cast herself between them.

"Don't touch him! He belongs to the cubs," she said. "They have had such fun with him the whole evening that they couldn't bear to eat him up, but wanted to save him until morning."

Father Bear pushed Mother Bear aside.

"Don't meddle with what you don't understand!" he roared. "Can't you scent that human odor about him from afar? I shall eat him at once, or he will play us some mean trick."

He opened his jaws again, but meanwhile the boy had had time to think, and, quick as a flash, he dug into his knapsack and brought forth some matches—his sole weapon of defense—struck one on his leather breeches, and stuck the burning match into the bear's open mouth.

Father Bear snorted when he smelled the sulfur, and with that the flame went out. The boy was ready with another match, but, curiously enough, Father Bear did not repeat his attack.

"Can you light many of those little blue roses?" asked Father Bear.

"I can light enough to put an end to the whole forest," replied the boy, for he thought that in this way he might be able to scare Father Bear.

"Perhaps you could also set fire to houses and barns?" said Father Bear. "Oh, that would be no trick for me!" boasted the boy hoping that this would make the bear respect him.

"Good!" exclaimed the bear. "You shall render me a service. Now I'm very glad that I did not eat you!"

Father Bear carefully took the boy between his tusks and climbed up from the pit. He did this with remarkable ease and agility, considering that he was so big and heavy. As soon as he was up, he speedily made for the woods. It was evident that Father Bear was created to squeeze through dense forests. The heavy body pushed through the brushwood as a boat does through the water.

Father Bear ran along till he came to a hill at the skirt of the forest, where he could see the big noise shop. Here he lay down and placed the boy in front of him, holding him securely between his forepaws.

"Now look down at that big noise shop!" he commanded.

The great ironworks, with many tall buildings, stood at the edge of a waterfall. High chimneys sent forth dark clouds of smoke, blasting furnaces were in full blaze, and light shone from all the windows and apertures. Within hammers and rolling mills were going with such force that the air rang with their clatter and boom. All around the workshops proper were immense coal sheds, great slag heaps, warehouses, wood piles, and tool sheds. Just beyond were long rows of workingmen's homes, pretty villas, schoolhouses, assembly halls, and shops. But there, all was quiet and apparently everybody was asleep. The boy did not glance in that direction, but gazed intently at the ironworks. The earth around them was black; the sky above them was like a great fiery dome; the rapids, white with foam, rushed by, while the buildings themselves were sending out light and smoke, fire and sparks. It was the grandest sight the boy had ever seen!

"Surely you don't mean to say you can set fire to a place like that?" remarked the bear doubtingly.

The boy stood wedged between the beast's paws thinking the only thing that might save him would be that the bear should have a high opinion of his capability and power.

"It's all the same to me," he answered with a superior air. "Big or little, I can burn it down."

"Then I'll tell you something," said Father Bear. "My forefathers lived in this region from the time that the forests first sprang up. From them I inherited hunting grounds and pastures, lairs and retreats, and have lived here in peace all my life. In the beginning I wasn't troubled much by the human kind. They dug in the mountains and picked up a little ore down here, by the rapids; they had a forge and a furnace, but the hammers sounded only a few hours during the day, and the furnace was not fired more than two moons at a stretch. It wasn't so bad but that I could stand it, but these last years, since they have built this noise-shop, which keeps up the same racket both day and night, life here has become intolerable. Formerly only a manager and a couple of black-smiths lived here, but now there are so many people that I can never feel safe from them. I thought that I should have to move away, but I have discovered something better!"

The boy wondered what Father Bear had hit upon, but no oppor-tunity was afforded him to ask, as the bear took him between his tusks again and lumbered down the hill. The boy could see nothing, but knew by the increasing noise that they were approaching the rolling mills.

Father Bear was well informed regarding the ironworks. He had prowled around there on many a dark night, had observed what went on within, and had wondered if there would never be any cessation of the work. He had tested the walls with his paws and wished that he were only strong enough to knock down the whole structure with a single blow.

He was not easily distinguishable against the dark ground, and when, in addition, he remained in the shadow of the walls, there was not much danger of his being discovered. Now he walked fearlessly between the workshops and climbed to the top of a slag heap. There he sat up on his haunches, took the boy between his forepaws and held him up.

"Try to look into the house!" he commanded. A strong current of air was forced into a big cylinder which was suspended from the ceiling and filled with molten iron. As this current rushed into the mess of iron with an awful roar, showers of sparks of all colors spurted up in bunches, in sprays, in long clusters! They struck against the wall and came splashing down over the whole big room. Father Bear let the boy watch the gorgeous spectacle until the blowing was over and the flowing and sparkling red steel had been poured into ingot molds.

The boy was completely charmed by the marvelous display and almost forgot that he was imprisoned between a bear's two paws.

Father Bear let him look into the rolling rink. He saw a workman take a short, thick bar of iron at white heat from a furnace opening and place it under a roller. When the iron came out from under the roller, it was flattened and extended. Immediately another workman seized it and placed it beneath a heavier roller, which made it still longer and thinner. Thus it was passed from roller to roller, squeezed and drawn out until, finally, it curled along the floor, like a long red thread.

But while the first bar of iron was being pressed, a second was taken from the furnace and placed under the rollers, and when this was a little along, a third was placed.

Continuously fresh threads came crawling over the floor, like hissing snakes. The boy was dazzled by the iron. But he found it more splendid to watch the workmen who, dexterously and delicately, seized the glowing snakes with their tongs and forced them under the rollers. It seemed like play for them to handle the hissing iron.

"I call that real man's work!" the boy remarked to himself.

The bear then let the boy have a peep at the furnace and the forge, and he became more and more astonished as he saw how the blacksmiths handled iron and fire.

"Those men have no fear of heat and flames," he thought. The workmen were sooty and grimy. He fancied they were some sort of fire folk—that was why they could bend and mold the iron as they wished. He could not believe that they were just ordinary men, since they had such power!

"They keep this up day after day, night after night," said Father Bear, as he dropped wearily down on the ground. "You can understand that one gets rather tired of that kind of thing. I'm mighty glad that at last I can put an end to it!"

"Indeed!" said the boy. "How will you go about it?"

"Oh, I thought that you were going to set fire to the buildings!" said Father Bear. "That would put an end to all this work, and I could remain in my old home."

The boy was all of a shiver.

So it was for this that Father Bear had brought him here!

"If you will set fire to the noise works, I'll promise to spare your life," said Father Bear. "But if you don't do it, I'll make short work of you!"

The huge workshops were built of brick, and the boy was thinking to himself that Father Bear could command as much as he liked, it was impossible to obey him. Presently he saw that it might not be impossible after all. Just beyond them lay a pile of chips and shavings to which he could easily set fire, and beside it was a wood pile that almost reached the coal shed. The coal shed extended over to the workshops, and if that once caught fire, the flames would soon fly over to the roof of the iron foundry. Everything combustible would burn, the walls would fall from the heat, and the machinery would be destroyed.

"Will you or won't you?" demanded Father Bear. The boy knew that he ought to answer promptly that he would not, but he also knew that then the bear's paws would squeeze him to death, therefore he replied:

"I shall have to think it over."

"Very well, do so," assented Father Bear. "Let me say to you that iron is the thing that has given men the advantage over us bears, which is another reason for my wishing to put an end to the work here."

The boy thought he would use the delay to figure out some plan of escape, but he was so worried he could not direct his thoughts where he would, instead he began to think of the great help that iron had been to mankind. They needed iron for everything. There was iron in the plow that broke up the field, in the ax that felled the tree for building houses, in the scythe that mowed the grain, and in the knife, which could be turned to all sorts of uses. There was iron in the horse's bit, in the lock on the door, in the nails that held furniture together, in the sheathing that covered the roof. The rifle which drove away wild beasts was made of iron, also, the pick that had broken up the mine. Iron covered the men-of-war he had seen at Karlskrona; the locomotives steamed through the country on iron rails; the needle that had stitched his coat was of iron; the shears that clipped the sheep and the kettle that cooked the food. Big and little alike, much that was indispensable was made from iron. Father Bear was perfectly right in saying that it was the iron that had given men their mastery over the bears.

"Now will you or won't you?" Father Bear repeated. The boy was startled from his musing. Here he stood thinking of matters that were entirely unnecessary, and had not yet found a way to save himself!

"You mustn't be so impatient," he said. "This is a serious matter for me, and I've got to have time to consider."

"Well, then, consider another moment," said Father Bear. "But let me tell you that it's because of the iron that men have become so much wiser than we bears. For this alone, if for nothing else, I should like to put a stop to the work here."

Again the boy endeavored to think out a plan of escape, but his thoughts wandered, willy nilly. They were taken up with the iron. And gradually he began to comprehend how much thinking and calculating men must have done before they discovered how to produce iron from ore, and he seemed to see sooty blacksmiths of old bending over the forge, pondering how they should properly handle it. Perhaps it was because they had thought so much about the iron that intelligence had been developed in mankind, until finally they became so advanced that they were able to build great works like these. The fact was that men owed more to the iron than they themselves knew.

"Well, what say you? Will you or won't you?" insisted Father Bear.

The boy shrank back. Here he stood thinking needless thoughts, and had no idea as to what he should do to save himself.

"It's not such an easy matter to decide as you think," he answered. "You must give me time for reflection."

"I can wait for you a little longer," said Father Bear. "But after that you'll get no more grace. You must know that it's the fault of the iron that the human kind can live here on the property of the bears. And now you understand why I would be rid of the work."

The boy meant to use the last moment to think out some way to save himself, but, anxious and distraught as he was, his thoughts wandered again. Now he began thinking of all that he had seen when he flew over the mining districts. It was strange that there should be so much life and activity and so much work back there in the wilderness.

"Just think how poor and desolate this place would be had there been no iron here!

"This very foundry gave employment to many, and had gathered around it many homes filled with people, who, in turn, had attracted hither railways and telegraph wires and—"

"Come, come!" growled the bear. "Will you or won't you?"

The boy swept his hand across his forehead. No plan of escape had as yet come to his mind, but this much he knew—he did not wish to do any harm to the iron, which was so useful to rich and poor alike, and which gave bread to so many people in this land.

"I won't!" he said.

Father Bear squeezed him a little harder, but said nothing.

"You'll not get me to destroy the ironworks!" defied the boy. "The iron is so great a blessing that it will never do to harm it."

"Then of course you don't expect to be allowed to live very long?" said the bear.

"No, I don't expect it," returned the boy, looking the bear straight in the eye.

Father Bear gripped him still harder. It hurt so that the boy could not keep the tears back, but he did not cry out or say a word.

"Very well, then," said Father Bear, raising his paw very slowly, hoping that the boy would give in at the last moment.

But just then the boy heard something click very close to them, and saw the muzzle of a rifle two paces away. Both he and Father Bear had been so engrossed in their own affairs they had not observed that a man had stolen right upon them.

"Father Bear! Don't you hear the clicking of a trigger?" cried the boy. "Run, or you'll be shot."

Father Bear grew terribly hurried. However, he allowed himself time enough to pick up the boy and carry him along. As he ran, a couple of shots sounded, and the bullets grazed his ears, but, luckily, he escaped.

The boy thought, as he was dangling from the bear's mouth, that never had he been so stupid as he was tonight. If he had only kept still, the bear would have been shot, and he himself would have been freed. But he had become so accustomed to helping the animals that he did it naturally, and as a matter of course.

When Father Bear had run some distance into the woods, he paused and set the boy down on the ground.

"Thank you, little one!" he said. "I dare say those bullets would have caught me if you hadn't been there. And now I want to do you a service in return. If you should ever meet with another bear, just say to him this—which I shall whisper to you—and he won't touch you."

Father Bear whispered a word or two into the boy's ear and hurried away, for he thought he heard hounds and hunters pursuing him.

The boy stood in the forest, free and unharmed, and could hardly understand how it was possible.

The wild geese had been flying back and forth the whole evening, peering and calling, but they had been unable to find Thumbietot. They searched long after the sun had set, and, finally, when it had grown so dark that they were forced to alight somewhere for the night, they were very downhearted. There was not one among them but thought the boy had been killed by the fall and was lying dead in the forest, where they could not see him.

But the next morning, when the sun peeped over the hills and awakened the wild geese, the boy lay sleeping, as usual, in their midst. When he woke and heard them shrieking and cackling their astonishment, he could not help laughing.

They were so eager to know what had happened to him that they did not care to go to breakfast until he had told them the whole story. The boy soon narrated his entire adventure with the bears, but after that he seemed reluctant to continue.

"How I got back to you perhaps you already know?" he said.

"No, we know nothing. We thought you were killed."

"That's curious!" remarked the boy. "Oh, yes! when Father Bear left me I climbed up into a pine and fell asleep. At daybreak I was awakened by an eagle hovering over me. He picked me up with his talons and carried me away. He didn't hurt me, but flew straight here to you and dropped me down among you."

"Didn't he tell you who he was?" asked the big white gander.

"He was gone before I had time even to thank him. I thought that Mother Akka had sent him after me."

"How extraordinary!" exclaimed the white goosey-gander. "But are you certain that it was an eagle?"

"I had never before seen an eagle," said the boy, "but he was so big and splendid that I can't give him a lovelier name!"

Morten Goosey-Gander turned to the wild geese to hear what they thought of this, but they stood gazing into the air, as though they were thinking of something else.

"We must not forget entirely to eat breakfast today," said Akka, quickly spreading her wings.

THE FLOOD

THE SWANS

May first to fourth

There was a terrible storm raging in the district north of Lake Mälar, which lasted several days. The sky was a dull gray, the wind whistled, and the rain beat. Both people and animals knew the spring could not be ushered in with anything short of this, nevertheless they thought it unbearable.

After it had been raining for a whole day, the snowdrifts in the pine forests began to melt in earnest, and the spring brooks grew lively. All the pools on the farms, the standing water in the ditches, the water that oozed between the tufts in marshes and swamps—all were in motion and tried to find their way to creeks, that they might be borne along to the sea.

The creeks rushed as fast as possible down to the rivers, and the rivers did their utmost to carry the water to Lake Mälar.

All the lakes and rivers in Uppland and the mining district quickly threw off their ice covers on one and the same day, so that the creeks filled with ice floes which rose clear up to their banks.

Swollen as they were, they emptied into Lake Mälar, and it was not long before the lake had taken in as much water as it could well hold. Down by the outlet was a raging torrent. Norrström is a narrow channel, and it could not let out the water quickly enough. Besides, there was a strong easterly wind that lashed against the land, obstructing the stream when it tried to carry the fresh water into the East Sea. Since the rivers kept running to Mälaren with more water than it could dispose of, there was nothing for the big lake to do but overflow its banks.

It rose very slowly, as if reluctant to injure its beautiful shores, but as they were mostly low and gradually sloping, it was not long before the

264

water had flooded several acres of land, and that was enough to create the greatest alarm.

Lake Mälar is unique in its way, being made up of a succession of narrow fjords, bays, and inlets. In no place does it spread into a storm center, but seems to have been created only for pleasure trips, yachting tours, and fishing. Nowhere does it present barren, desolate, wind-swept shores. It looks as if it never thought that its shores could hold anything but country seats, summer villas, manors, and amusement resorts. But, because it usually presents a very agreeable and friendly appearance, there is all the more havoc whenever it happens to drop its smiling expression in the spring, and show that it can be serious.

At that critical time Smirre Fox happened to come sneaking through a birch grove just north of Lake Mälar. As usual, he was thinking of Thumbietot and the wild geese, and wondering how he should ever find them again. He had lost all track of them.

As he stole cautiously along, more discouraged than usual, he caught sight of Agar, the carrier pigeon, who had perched herself on a birch branch.

"My, but I'm in luck to run across you, Agar!" exclaimed Smirre. "Maybe you can tell me where Akka from Kebnekaise and her flock hold forth nowadays?"

"It's quite possible that I know where they are," Agar hinted, "but I'm not likely to tell you!"

"Please yourself!" retorted Smirre. "Nevertheless, you can take a message that I have for them. You probably know the present condition of Lake Mälar? There's a great overflow down there and all the swans who live in Hjälsta Bay are about to see their nests, with all their eggs, destroyed. Daylight, the swan-king, has heard of the midget who travels with the wild geese and knows a remedy for every ill. He has sent me to ask Akka if she will bring Thumbietot down to Hjälsta Bay."

"I dare say I can convey your message," Agar replied, "but I can't understand how the little boy will be able to help the swans."

"Nor do I," said Smirre, "but he can do almost everything it seems."

"It's surprising to me that Daylight should send his messages by a fox," Agar remarked.

"Well, we're not exactly what you'd call good friends," said Smirre smoothly, "but in an emergency like this we must help each other. Perhaps it would be just as well not to tell Akka that you got the message from a fox. Between you and me, she's inclined to be a little suspicious."

The safest refuge for waterfowl in the whole Mälar district is Hjälsta Bay. It has low shores, shallow water and is also covered with reeds.

It is by no means as large as Lake Tåkern, but nevertheless Hjälsta is a good retreat for birds, since it has long been forbidden territory to hunters.

It is the home of a great many swans, and the owner of the old castle near by has prohibited all shooting on the bay, so that they might be unmolested.

As soon as Akka received word that the swans needed her help, she hastened down to Hjälsta Bay.

She arrived with her flock one evening and saw at a glance that there had been a great disaster. The big swans' nests had been torn away, and the strong wind was driving them down the bay. Some had already fallen apart, two or three had capsized, and the eggs lay at the bottom of the lake.

When Akka alighted on the bay, all the swans living there were gathered near the eastern shore, where they were protected from the wind.

Although they had suffered much by the flood, they were too proud to let any one see it.

"It is useless to cry," they said. "There are plenty of root fibers and stems here; we can soon build new nests."

None had thought of asking a stranger to help them, and the swans had no idea that Smirre Fox had sent for the wild geese!

There were several hundred swans resting on the water. They had placed themselves according to rank and station. The young and inexperienced were farthest out, the old and wise nearer the middle of the group, and right in the center sat Daylight, the swan-king and Snow-White, the swan-queen, who were older than any of the others and regarded the rest of the swans as their children.

The geese alighted on the west shore of the bay, but when Akka saw where the swans were, she swam toward them at once. She was very much surprised at their having sent for her, but she regarded it as an honor and did not wish to lose a moment in coming to their aid.

As Akka approached the swans she paused to see if the geese who followed her swam in a straight line, and at even distances apart.

"Now, swim along quickly!" she ordered. "Don't stare at the swans as if you had never before seen anything beautiful, and don't mind what they may say to you!"

This was not the first time that Akka had called on the aristocratic swans. They had always received her in a manner befitting a great traveler like herself.

But still she did not like the idea of swimming in among them. She never felt so gray and insignificant as when she happened upon swans. One or another of them was sure to drop a remark about "common gray feathers" and "poor folk." But it is always best to take no notice of such things.

This time everything passed off uncommonly well. The swans politely made way for the wild geese, who swam forward through a kind of passageway, which formed an avenue bordered by shimmering, white birds.

It was a beautiful sight to watch them as they spread their wings, like sails, to appear well before the strangers. They refrained from making comments, which rather surprised Akka.

Evidently Daylight had noted their misbehavior in the past and had told the swans that they must conduct themselves in a proper manner—so thought the leader goose.

But just as the swans were making an effort to observe the rules of etiquette, they caught sight of the goosey-gander, who swam last in the long goose line. Then there was a murmur of disapproval, even of threats, among the swans, and at once there was an end to their good deportment!

"What's this?" shrieked one. "Do the wild geese intend to dress up in white feathers?"

"They needn't think that will make swans of them," cried another.

They began shrieking—one louder than another—in their strong, resonant voices. It was impossible to explain that a tame goosey-gander had come with the wild geese.

"That must be the goose-king himself coming along," they said tauntingly. "There's no limit to their audacity!"

"That's no goose, it's only a tame duck."

The big white gander remembered Akka's admonition to pay no attention, no matter what he might hear. He kept quiet and swam ahead as fast he could, but it did no good. The swans became more and more impertinent.

"What kind of frog does he carry on his back?" asked one. "They must think we don't see it's a frog because it is dressed like a human."

The swans, who but a moment before had been resting in such perfect order, now swam up and down excitedly. All tried to crowd forward to get a glimpse of the white wild goose.

"That white goosey-gander ought to be ashamed to come here and parade before swans!"

"He's probably as gray as the rest of them. He has only been in a flour barrel at some farm house!"

Akka had just come up to Daylight and was about to ask him what kind of help he wanted of her, when the swan-king noticed the uproar among the swans.

"What do I see? Haven't I taught you to be polite to strangers?" he said with a frown.

Snow-White, the swan-queen, swam out to restore order among her subjects, and again Daylight turned to Akka.

Presently Snow-White came back, appearing greatly agitated.

"Can't you keep them quiet ?" shouted Daylight. "There's a white wild goose over there," answered Snow-White. "Is it not shameful? I don't wonder they are furious!"

"A white wild goose?" scoffed Daylight. "That's too ridiculous! There can't be such a thing. You must be mistaken."

The crowds around Morten Goosey-Gander grew larger and larger. Akka and the other wild geese tried to swim over to him, but were jostled hither and thither and could not get to him.

The old swan-king, who was the strongest among them, swam off quickly, pushed all the others aside, and made his way over to the big white gander. But when he saw that there really was a white goose on the water, he was just as indignant as the rest.

He hissed with rage, flew straight at Morten Goosey-Gander and tore out a few feathers.

"I'll teach you a lesson, wild goose," he shrieked, "so that you'll not come again to the swans, togged out in this way!"

"Fly, Morten Goosey-Gander! Fly, fly!" cried Akka, for she knew that otherwise the swans would pull out every feather the goosey-gander had. "Fly, fly!" screamed Thumbietot, too.

But the goosey-gander was so hedged in by the swans that he had not room enough to spread his wings. All around him the swans stretched their long necks, opened their strong bills, and plucked his feathers.

Morten Goosey-Gander defended himself as best he could, by striking and biting. The wild geese also began to fight the swans.

It was obvious how this would have ended had the geese not received help quite unexpectedly.

A red-tail noticed that they were being roughly treated by the swans. Instantly he cried out the shrill call that little birds use when they need help to drive off a hawk or a falcon.

Three calls had barely sounded when all the little birds in the vicinity came shooting down to Hjälsta Bay, as if on wings of lightning.

These delicate little creatures swooped down upon the swans, screeched in their ears, and obstructed their view with the flutter of their tiny wings. They made them dizzy with their fluttering and drove them to distraction with their cries of "Shame, shame, swans!"

The attack of the small birds lasted but a moment. When they were gone and the swans came to their senses, they saw that the geese had risen and flown over to the other end of the bay.

THE NEW WATCH DOG

*T*here was this at least to be said in the swans' favor: when they saw that the wild geese had escaped, they were too proud to chase them. Moreover, the geese could stand on a clump of reeds with perfect composure, and sleep.

Nils Holgersson was too hungry to sleep.

"It is necessary for me to get something to eat," he said.

At that time, when all kinds of things were floating on the water, it was not difficult for a little boy like Nils Holgersson to find a craft. He did not stop to deliberate, but hopped down on a stump that had drifted in amongst the reeds. Then he picked up a little stick and began to pole toward shore.

Just as he was landing, he heard a splash in the water. He stopped short. First he saw a lady swan asleep in her big nest quite close to him, then he noticed that a fox had taken a few steps into the water and was sneaking up to the swan's nest.

"Hi, hi, hi! Get up, get up!" cried the boy, beating the water with his stick.

The lady swan rose, but not so quickly but that the fox could have pounced upon her had he cared to. However, he refrained and instead hurried straight toward the boy.

Thumbietot saw the fox coming and ran for his life.

Wide stretches of meadow land spread before him. He saw no tree that he could climb, no hole where he might hide; he just had to keep running.

The boy was a good runner, but it stands to reason that he could not race with a fox!

Not far from the bay there were a number of little cabins, with candle lights shining through the windows. Naturally the boy ran in that direction, but he realized that long before he could reach the nearest cabin the fox would catch up to him.

Once the fox was so close that it looked as if the boy would surely be his prey, but Nils quickly sprang aside and turned back toward the bay. By that move the fox lost time, and before he could reach the boy the latter had run up to two men who were on their way home from work.

The men were tired and sleepy; they had noticed neither boy nor fox, although both had been running right in front of them. Nor did the boy ask help of the men; he was content to walk close beside them.

"Surely the fox won't venture to come up to the men," he thought.

But presently the fox came pattering along. He probably counted on the men taking him for a dog, for he went straight up to them.

"Whose dog can that be sneaking around here?" queried one. "He looks as though he were ready to bite."

The other paused and glanced back.

"Go along with you!" he said, and gave the fox a kick that sent it to the opposite side of the road. "What are you doing here?"

After that the fox kept at a safe distance, but followed all the while.

Presently the men reached a cabin and entered it. The boy intended to go in with them, but when he got to the stoop he saw a big, shaggy watch dog rush out from his kennel to greet his master. Suddenly the boy changed his mind and remained out in the open.

"Listen, watch dog!" whispered the boy as soon as the men had shut the door. "I wonder if you would like to help me catch a fox tonight?"

The dog had poor eyesight and had become irritable and cranky from being chained.

"What, I catch a fox?" he barked angrily. "Who are you that makes fun of me? You just come within my reach and I'll teach you not to fool with me!"

"You needn't think that I'm afraid to come near you!" said the boy, running up to the dog.

When the dog saw him he was so astonished that he could not speak.

"I'm the one they call Thumbietot, who travels with the wild geese," said the boy, introducing himself. "Haven't you heard of me?"

"I believe the sparrows have twittered a little about you," the dog returned. "They say that you have done wonderful things for one of your size."

"I've been rather lucky up to the present," admitted the boy. "But now it's all up with me unless you help me! There's a fox at my heels. He's lying in wait for me around the corner."

"Don't you suppose I can smell him?" retorted the dog. "But we'll soon be rid of him!" With that the dog sprang as far as the chain would allow, barking and growling for ever so long. "Now I don't think he will show his face again tonight!" said the dog.

"It will take something besides a free bark to scare that fox!" the boy remarked. "He'll soon be here again, and that is precisely what I wish, for I have set my heart on your catching him."

"Are you poking fun at me now?" asked the dog.

"Only come with me into your kennel, and I'll tell you what to do."

The boy and the watch dog crept into and crouched there, whispering.

By and by the fox stuck his nose out hiding place. When all was quiet he crept along cautiously. He scented the boy all the way to the kennel, but halted at a safe distance and sat down to think of some way to coax him out. Suddenly the watch dog poked his head out and growled at him:

"Go away, or I'll catch you!"

"I'll sit here as long as I please for all of you!" defied the fox.

"Go away!" repeated the dog threateningly, "or there will be no more hunting for you after tonight." But the fox only grinned and did not move an inch.

"I know how far your chain can reach," he said.

"I have warned you twice," said the dog, coming out from his kennel. "Now blame yourself!"

With that the dog sprang at the fox and caught him without the least effort, for he was loose. The boy had unbuckled his collar.

There was a hot struggle, but it was soon over. The dog was the victor. The fox lay on the ground and dared not move.

"Don't stir or I'll kill you!" snarled the dog. Then he took the fox by the scruff of the neck and dragged him to the kennel. There the boy was ready with the chain. He placed the dog collar around the neck of the fox, tightening it so that he was securely chained. During all this the fox had to lie still, for he was afraid to move.

"Now, Smirre Fox, I hope you'll make a good watchdog," laughed the boy when he had finished.

VI

DUNFIN

THE CITY THAT FLOATS
ON THE WATER

Friday, May sixth

No one could be more gentle and kind than the little gray goose Dunfin. All the wild geese loved her, and the tame white goosey-gander would have died for her. When Dunfin asked for anything not even Akka could say no.

As soon as Dunfin came to Lake Mälar the landscape looked familiar to her. Just beyond the lake lay the sea, with many wooded islands, and there, on a little islet, lived her parents and her brothers and sisters. She begged the wild geese to fly to her home before traveling farther north, that she might let her family see that she was still alive. It would be such a joy to them.

Akka frankly declared that she thought Dunfin's parents and brothers and sisters had shown no great love for her when they abandoned her at Öland, but Dunfin would not admit that Akka was in the right. "What else was there to do, when they saw that I could not fly?" she protested. "Surely they couldn't remain at Öland on my account!"

Dunfin began telling the wild geese all about her home in the archipelago, to try to induce them to make the trip. Her family lived on a rock island. Seen from a distance, there appeared to be nothing but stone there, but when one came closer, there were to be found the choicest goose tidbits in clefts and hollows, and one might search long for better nesting places than those that were hidden in the mountain crevices or among the osier bushes. But the best of all was the old fisherman who lived there. Dunfin had heard that in his youth he had been a great shot and had always lain in the offing and hunted birds. But now, in his old age since his wife had died and the children had gone from home, so that he was alone in the hut, he had begun to care for the birds on his island. He never fired a shot at them, nor would he permit others to do so. He walked around amongst the birds' nests, and when the mother birds were sitting he brought them food. Not one was afraid of him. They all loved him.

Dunfin had been in his hut many times, and he had fed her with bread crumbs. Because he was kind to the birds, they flocked to his island in such great numbers that it was becoming overcrowded. If one happened to arrive a little late in the spring, all the nesting places were occupied. That was why Dunfin's family had been obliged to leave her.

Dunfin begged so hard that she finally had her way, although the wild geese felt that they were losing time and really should be going straight north. But a little trip like this to the cliff island would not delay them more than a day.

So they started off one morning, after fortifying themselves with a good breakfast, and flew eastward over Lake Mälar. The boy did not know for certain where they were going, but he noticed that the farther east they flew, the livelier it was on the lake and the more built up were the shores.

Heavily freighted barges and sloops, boats and fishing smacks were on their way east, and these were met and passed by many pretty white steamers. Along the shores ran country roads and railway tracks—all in the same direction. There was some place beyond in the east where all wished to go to in the morning.

On one of the islands the boy saw a big, white castle, and to the east of it the shores were dotted with villas. At the start these lay far apart, then they became closer and closer, and, presently, the whole shore was lined with them. They were of every variety—here a castle, there a cottage, then a low manor house appeared, or a mansion, with many small towers. Some stood in gardens, but most of them were in the wild woods which bordered the shores. Despite their dissimilarity, they had one point of resemblance—they were not plain and somber looking, like other buildings, but were gaudily painted in striking greens and blues, reds and white, like children's playhouses.

As the boy sat on the goose's back and glanced down at the curious shore mansions, Dunfin cried out with delight: "Now I know where I am! Over there lies the City that Floats on the Water."

The boy looked ahead. At first he saw nothing but some light clouds and mists rolling forward over the water, but soon he caught sight of some tall spires, and then one and another house with many rows of windows. They appeared and disappeared—rolling hither and thither—but not a strip of shore did he see! Everything over there appeared to be resting on the water.

Nearer to the city he saw no more pretty playhouses along the shores—only dingy factories. Great heaps of coal and wood were stacked behind tall planks, and alongside black, sooty docks lay bulky freight steamers, but over all was spread a shimmering, transparent mist, which made everything appear so big and strong and wonderful that it was almost beautiful.

The wild geese flew past factories and freight steamers and were nearing the cloud-enveloped spires. Suddenly all the mists sank to the water, save the thin, fleecy ones that circled above their heads, beautifully tinted in blues and pinks. The other clouds rolled over water and land. They entirely obscured the lower portions of the houses, only the upper stories and the roofs and gables were visible. Some of the buildings appeared to be as high as the Tower of Babel. The boy no doubt knew that they were built upon hills and mountains, but these he did not see—only the houses that seemed to float among the white, drifting clouds. In reality the buildings were dark and dingy, for the sun in the east was not shining on them.

The boy knew that he was riding above a large city, for he saw spires and house roofs rising from the clouds in every direction. Sometimes an opening was made in the circling mists, and he looked down into running, tortuous stream, but no land could he see. All this was beautiful to look upon, but he felt quite distraught—as one does when happening upon something one cannot understand.

When he had gone beyond the city, he found that the ground was no longer hidden by clouds, but that shores, streams, and islands were again plainly visible. He turned to see the city better, but could not, for now it looked quite enchanted. The mists had taken on color from the sunshine and were rolling forward in the most brilliant reds, blues, and yellows. The houses were white, as if built of light, and the windows and spires sparkled like fire. All things floated on the water as before.

The geese were traveling straight east. They flew over factories and workshops, then over mansions edging the shores. Steamboats and tugs swarmed on the water, but now they came from the east and were steaming westward toward the city.

The wild geese flew on, but instead of the narrow Mälar fjords and the little islands, broader waters and larger islands spread under them. At last the land was left behind and seen no more.

They flew still farther out, where they found no more large inhabited islands—only numberless little rock islands were scattered on the water. Now the fjords were not crowded by the land. The sea lay before them, vast and limitless.

Here the wild geese alighted on a cliff island, and as soon as their feet touched the ground the boy turned to Dunfin.

"What city did we fly over just now?" he asked. "I don't know what human beings have named it," said Dunfin. "We gray geese call it the 'City that Floats on the Water'."

THE SISTERS

*D*unfin had two sisters, Prettywing and Goldeye. They were strong and intelligent birds, but they did not have such a soft and shiny feather dress as Dunfin, nor did they have her sweet and gentle disposition. From the time they had been little, yellow goslings, their parents and relatives and even the old fisherman had plainly shown them that they thought more of Dunfin than of them. Therefore the sisters had always hated her.

When the wild geese landed on the cliff island, Prettywing and Goldeye were feeding on a bit of grass close to the strand, and immediately caught sight of the strangers.

"See, Sister Goldeye, what fine looking geese have come to our island!" exclaimed Prettywing. "I have rarely seen such graceful birds. Do you notice that they have a white goosey-gander among them? Did you ever set eyes on a handsomer bird? One could almost take him for a swan."

Goldeye agreed with her sister that these were certainly very distinguished strangers that had come to the island, but suddenly she broke off and called: "Sister Prettywing! Oh, Sister Prettywing! Don't you see whom they bring with them?"

Prettywing also caught sight of Dunfin and was so astounded that she stood for a long time with her bill wide open, and only hissed.

"It can't be possible that it is she! How did she manage to get in with people of that class? Why, we left her at Öland to freeze and starve."

"The worst of it is she will tattle to Father and Mother that we flew so close to her that we knocked her wing out of joint," said Goldeye. "You'll see that it will end in our being driven from the island!"

"We have nothing but trouble in store for us, now that that young one has come back!" snapped Prettywing. "Still I think it would be best for us to appear as pleased as possible over her return. She is so stupid that perhaps she didn't even notice that we gave her a push on purpose."

While Prettywing and Goldeye were talking in this strain, the wild geese had been standing on the strand, pluming their feathers after the flight. Now they marched in a long line up the rocky shore to the cleft where Dunfin's parents usually stopped.

Dunfin's parents were good folk. They had lived on the island longer than any one else, and it was their habit to counsel and aid all newcomers. They too had seen the geese approach, but they had not recognized Dunfin in the flock.

"It is strange to see wild geese land on this island," remarked the goose-master. "It is a fine flock—that one can see by their flight."

"But it won't be easy to find pasturage for so many," said the goose-wife, who was gentle and sweet tempered, like Dunfin.

When Akka came marching with her company, Dunfin's parents went out to meet her and welcome her to the island. Dunfin flew from her place at the end of the line and lit between her parents.

"Mother and Father, I'm here at last!" she cried joyously. "Don't you know Dunfin?"

At first the old goose-parents could not quite make out what they saw, but when they recognized Dunfin they were absurdly happy, of course.

While the wild geese and Morten Goosey-Gander and Dunfin were chattering excitedly, trying to tell how she had been rescued, Prettywing and Goldeye came running. They cried "welcome" and pretended to be so happy because Dunfin was at home that she was deeply moved.

The wild geese fared well on the island and decided not to travel farther until the following morning. After a while the sisters asked Dunfin if she would come with them and see the places where they intended to build their nests. She promptly accompanied them, and saw that they had picked out secluded and well protected nesting places.

"Now where will you settle down, Dunfin?" they asked.

"I? Why I don't intend to remain on the island," she said. "I'm going with the wild geese up to Lapland."

"What a pity that you must leave us!" said the sisters.

"I should have been very glad to remain here with Father and Mother and you," said Dunfin, "had I not promised the big, white—"

"What!" shrieked Prettywing. "Are you to have the handsome goosey-gander? Then it is—" But here Goldeye gave her a sharp nudge, and she stopped short.

The two cruel sisters had much to talk about all the afternoon. They were furious because Dunfin had a suitor like the white goosey-gander. They themselves had suitors, but theirs were only common gray geese, and, since they had seen Morten Goosey-Gander, they thought them so homely and low-bred that they did not wish even to look at them.

"This will grieve me to death!" whimpered Goldeye. "If at least it had been you, Sister Prettywing, who had captured him!"

"I would rather see him dead than to go about here the entire summer thinking of Dunfin's capturing a white goosey-gander!" pouted Prettywing.

However, the sisters continued to appear very friendly toward Dunfin, and in the afternoon Goldeye took Dunfin with her, that she might see the one she thought of marrying.

"He's not as attractive as the one you will have," said Goldeye. "But to make up for it, one can be certain that he is what he is."

"What do you mean, Goldeye?" questioned Dunfin. At first Goldeye would not explain what she had meant, but at last she came out with it.

"We have never seen a white goose travel with wild geese," said the sister, "and we wonder if he can be bewitched."

"You are very stupid," retorted Dunfin indignantly. "He is a tame goose, of course."

"He brings with him one who is bewitched," said Goldeye, "and, under the circumstances, he too must be bewitched. Are you not afraid that he may be a black cormorant?" She was a good talker and succeeded in frightening Dunfin thoroughly.

"You don't mean what you are saying," pleaded the little gray goose. "You only wish to frighten me!"

"I wish what is for your good, Dunfin," said Goldeye. "I can't imagine anything worse than for you to fly away with a black cormorant! But now I shall tell you something—try to persuade him to eat some of the roots I have gathered here. If he is bewitched, it will be apparent at once. If he is not, he will remain as he is."

The boy was sitting amongst the wild geese, listening to Akka and the old goose-master, when Dunfin came flying up to him. "Thumbietot, Thumbietot!" she cried. "Morten Goosey-Gander is dying! I have killed him!"

"Let me get up on your back, Dunfin, and take me to him!" Away they flew, and Akka and the other wild geese followed them. When they got to the goosey-gander, he was lying prostrate on the ground. He could not utter a word—only gasped for breath.

"Tickle him under the gorge and slap him on the back!" commanded Akka. The boy did so and presently the big, white gander coughed up a large, white root, which had stuck in his gorge. "Have you been eating of these?" asked Akka, pointing to some roots that lay on the ground.

"Yes," groaned the goosey-gander.

"Then it was well they stuck in your throat," said Akka, "for they are poisonous. Had you swallowed them, you certainly should have died."

"Dunfin bade me eat them," said the goosey-gander.

"My sister gave them to me," protested Dunfin, and she told everything.

"You must beware of those sisters of yours, Dunfin!" warned Akka, "for they wish you no good, depend upon it!"

But Dunfin was so constituted that she could not think evil of any one and, a moment later, when Prettywing asked her to come and meet her intended, she went with her immediately.

"Oh, he isn't as handsome as yours," said the sister, "but he's much more courageous and daring!"

"How do you know he is?" challenged Dunfin. "For some time past there has been weeping and wailing amongst the sea gulls and wild ducks on the island. Every morning at daybreak a strange bird of prey comes and carries off one of them."

"What kind of a bird is it?" asked Dunfin.

"We don't know," replied the sister. "One of his kind has never before been seen on the island, and, strange to say, he has never attacked one of us geese. But now my intended has made up his mind to challenge him tomorrow morning, and drive him away."

"Oh, I hope he'll succeed!" said Dunfin.

"I hardly think he will," returned the sister. "If my goosey-gander was as big and strong as yours, I should have some hope."

"Do you wish me to ask Morten Goosey-Gander to meet the strange bird?" asked Dunfin.

"Indeed, I do!" exclaimed Prettywing excitedly. "You couldn't render me a greater service."

The next morning the goosey-gander was up before the sun. He stationed himself on the highest point of the island and peered in all directions. Presently he saw a big, dark bird coming from the west. His wings were exceedingly large, and it was easy to tell that he was an eagle. The goosey-gander had not expected a more dangerous adversary than an owl, and now he understood that he could not escape this encounter with his life. But it did not occur to him to avoid all struggle with a bird who was many times stronger than himself.

The great bird swooped down on a sea gull and dug his talons into it. Before the eagle could spread his wings, Morten Goosey-Gander rushed up to him.

"Drop that!" he shouted, "and don't come here again or you'll have me to deal with!"

"What kind of a lunatic are you?" said the eagle. "It's lucky for you that I never fight with geese, or you would soon be done for!"

Morten Goosey-Gander thought the eagle considered himself too good to fight with him and flew at him, incensed, biting him on the throat and beating him with his wings. This, naturally, the eagle would not tolerate and he began to fight, but not with his full strength.

The boy lay sleeping in the quarters where Akka and the other wild geese slept, when Dunfin called: "Thumbietot, Thumbietot! Morten Goosey-Gander is being torn to pieces by an eagle."

"Let me get up on your back, Dunfin, and take me to him!" said the boy.

When they arrived on the scene Morten Goosey-Gander was badly torn, and bleeding, but he was still fighting. The boy could not battle with the eagle; all that he could do was to seek more efficient help.

"Hurry, Dunfin, and call Akka and the wild geese!" he cried. The instant he said that, the eagle flew back and stopped fighting.

"Who's speaking of Akka?" he asked. He saw Thumbietot and heard the wild geese honking, so he spread his wings.

"Tell Akka I never expected to run across her or any of her flock out here in the sea!" he said, and soared away in a rapid and graceful flight.

"That is the self-same eagle who once brought me back to the wild geese," the boy remarked, gazing after the bird in astonishment.

The geese had decided to leave the island at dawn, but first they wanted to feed awhile. As they walked about and nibbled, a mountain duck came up to Dunfin.

"I have a message for you from your sisters," said the duck. "They dare not show themselves among the wild geese, but they asked me to remind you not to leave the island without calling on the old fisherman."

"That's so!" exclaimed Dunfin, but she was so frightened now that she would not go alone, and asked the goosey-gander and Thumbietot to accompany her to the hut.

The door was open, so Dunfin entered, but the others remained outside. After a moment they heard Akka give the signal to start, and called Dunfin. A gray goose came out and flew with the wild geese away from the island.

They had traveled quite a distance along the archipelago when the boy began to wonder at the goose who accompanied them. Dunfin always flew lightly and noiselessly, but this one labored with heavy and noisy wing strokes. "We are in the wrong company. It is Prettywing that follows us!"

The boy had barely spoken when the goose uttered such an ugly and angry shriek that all knew who she was. Akka and the others turned to her, but the gray goose did not fly away at once. Instead she bumped against the big goosey-gander, snatched Thumbietot, and flew off with him in her bill.

There was a wild chase over the archipelago. Prettywing flew fast, but the wild geese were close behind her, and there was no chance for her to escape.

Suddenly they saw a puff of smoke rise up from the sea, and heard an explosion. In their excitement they had not noticed that they were directly above a boat in which a lone fisherman was seated.

However, none of the geese was hurt, but just there, above the boat, Prettywing opened her bill and dropped Thumbietot into the sea.

VII

STOCKHOLM

SKANSEN

A few years ago, at Skansen—the great park just outside of Stockholm where they have collected so many wonderful things—there lived a little old man, named Clement Larsson. He was from Halsingland and had come to Skansen with his fiddle to play folk dances and other old melodies. As a performer, he appeared mostly in the evening. During the day it was his business to sit on guard in one of the many pretty peasant cottages which have been moved to Skansen from all parts of the country.

In the beginning Clement thought that he fared better in his old age than he had ever dared dream, but after a time he began to dislike the place terribly, especially while he was on watch duty. It was all very well when visitors came into the cottage to look around, but some days Clement would sit for many hours all alone. Then he felt so homesick that he feared he would have to give up his place. He was very poor and knew that at home he would become a charge on the parish. Therefore he tried to hold out as long as he could, although he felt more unhappy from day to day.

One beautiful evening in the beginning of May Clement had been granted a few hours' leave of absence. He was on his way down the steep hill leading out of Skansen, when he met an island fisherman coming along with his game bag. The fisherman was an active young man who came to Skansen with sea fowl that he had managed to capture alive. Clement had met him before, many times.

The fisherman stopped Clement to ask if the superintendent at Skansen was at home. When Clement had replied, he, in turn, asked what choice thing the fisherman had in his bag. "You can see what I have," the fisherman answered, "if in return you will give me an idea as to what I should ask for it."

He held open the bag and Clement peeped into it once and again, then quickly drew back a step or two. "Good gracious, Ashbjörn!" he exclaimed. "How did you catch that one?"

He remembered that when he was a child his mother used to talk of the tiny folk who lived under the cabin floor. He was not permitted to cry or to be naughty, lest he provoke these small people. After he was grown he believed his mother had made up these stories about the elves to make him behave himself. But it had been no invention of his mother's, it seemed, for there, in Ashbjörn's bag, lay one of the tiny folk.

There was a little of the terror natural to childhood left in Clement, and he felt a shudder run down his spinal column as he peeped into the bag. Ashbjörn saw that he was frightened and began to laugh, but Clement took the matter seriously.

"Tell me, Ashbjörn, where you came across him?" he asked.

"You may be sure that I wasn't lying in wait for him!" said Ashbjörn. "He came to me. I started out early this morning and took my rifle along into the boat. I had just poled away from the shore when I sighted some wild geese coming from the east, shrieking like mad. I sent them a shot, but hit none of them. Instead this creature came tumbling down into the water—so close to the boat that I only had to put my hand out and pick him up."

"I hope you didn't shoot him, Ashbjörn?"

"Oh, no! He is well and sound, but when he came down, he was a little dazed at first, so I took advantage of that fact to wind the ends of two sail threads around his ankles and wrists, so that he couldn't run away. 'Ha! Here's something for Skansen,' I thought instantly."

Clement grew strangely troubled as the fisherman talked. All that he had heard about the tiny folk in his childhood—of their vindictiveness toward enemies and their benevolence toward friends—came back to him. It had never gone well with those who had attempted to hold one of them captive.

"You should have let him go at once, Ashbjörn." said Clement.

"I came precious near being forced to set him free," returned the fisherman. "You may as well know, Clement, that the wild geese followed me all the way home, and they crisscrossed over the island the whole morning, honk honking as if they wanted him back. Not only they, but the entire population—sea gulls, sea swallows, and many others who are not worth a shot of powder, alighted on the island and made an awful racket. When I came out they fluttered about me until I had to turn back. My wife begged me to let him go, but I had made up my mind that he should come here to Skansen, so I placed one of the children's dolls in the window, hid the midget in the bottom of my bag, and started away. The birds must have fancied that it was he who stood in the window, for they permitted me to leave without pursuing me."

"Does it say anything?" asked Clement.

"Yes. At first he tried to call to the birds, but I wouldn't have it and put a gag in his mouth."

"Oh, Ashbjörn!" protested Clement. "How can you treat him so! Don't you see that he is something supernatural?"

"I don't know what he is," said Ashbjörn calmly.

"Let others consider that. I'm satisfied if only I can get a good sum for him. Now tell me, Clement, what you think the doctor at Skansen would give me?"

There was a long pause before Clement replied. He felt very sorry for the poor little chap. He actually imagined that his mother was standing beside him telling him that he must always be kind to the tiny folk.

"I have no idea what the doctor up there would care to give you, Ashbjörn," he said finally. "But if you will leave him with me, I'll pay you twenty kroner for him."

Ashbjörn stared at the fiddler in amazement when he heard him name so large a sum. He thought that Clement believed the midget had some mysterious power and might be of service to him. He was by no means certain that the doctor would think him such a great find or would offer to pay so high a sum for him, so he accepted Clement's proffer.

The fiddler poked his purchase into one of his wide pockets, turned back to Skansen, and went into a moss-covered hut, where there were neither visitors nor guards. He closed the door after him, took out the midget, who was still bound hand and foot and gagged, and laid him down gently on a bench.

"Now listen to what I say!" said Clement. "I know of course that such as you do not like to be seen of men, but prefer to go about and busy yourselves in your own way. Therefore I have decided to give you your liberty—but only on condition that you will remain in this park until I permit you to leave. If you agree to this, nod your head three times." Clement gazed at the midget with confident expectation, but the latter did not move a muscle.

"You shall not fare badly," continued Clement. "I'll see to it that you are fed every day, and you will have so much to do here that the time will not seem long to you. But you mustn't go elsewhere till I give you leave. Now we'll agree as to a signal. So long as I set your food out in a white bowl you are to stay. When I set it out in a blue one you may go."

Clement paused again, expecting the midget to give the sign of approval, but he did not stir.

"Very well," said Clement, "then there's no choice but to show you to the master of this place. Then you'll be put in a glass case, and all the people in the big city of Stockholm will come and stare at you." This scared the midget, and he promptly gave the signal.

"That was right," said Clement as he cut the cord that bound the midget's hands. Then he hurried toward the door.

The boy unloosed the bands around his ankles and tore away the gag before thinking of anything else. When he turned to Clement to thank him, he had gone.

Just outside the door Clement met a handsome, noble-looking gentleman, who was on his way to a place close by from which there was a beautiful outlook. Clement could not recall having seen the stately old man before, but the latter must surely have noticed Clement sometime when he was playing the fiddle, because he stopped and spoke to him.

"Good day, Clement!" he said. "How do you do? You are not ill, are you? I think you have grown a bit thin of late."

There was such an expression of kindliness about the old gentleman that Clement plucked up courage and told him of his homesickness.

"What!" exclaimed the old gentleman. "Are you homesick when you are in Stockholm? It can't be possible!" He looked almost offended. Then he reflected that it was only an ignorant old peasant from Hälsingland that he talked with—and so resumed his friendly attitude.

"Surely you have never heard how the city of Stockholm was founded? If you had, you would comprehend that your anxiety to get away is only a foolish fancy. Come with me to the bench over yonder and I will tell you something about Stockholm."

When the old gentleman was seated on the bench he glanced down at the city, which spread in all its glory below him, and he drew a deep breath, as if he wished to drink in all the beauty of the landscape. Thereupon he turned to the fiddler.

"Look, Clement!" he said, and as he talked he traced with his cane a little map in the sand in front of them. "Here lies Uppland, and here, to the south, a point juts out, which is split up by a number of bays. And here we have Sörmland with another point, which is just as cut up and points straight north. Here, from the west, comes a lake filled with islands: It is Lake Mälar. From the east comes another body of water, which can barely squeeze in between the islands and islets. It is the East Sea. Here, Clement, where Uppland joins Sörmland and Mälaren joins the East Sea, comes a short river, in the center of which lie four little islets that divide the river into several tributaries—one of which is called Norrström but was formerly Stocksund.

"In the beginning these islets were common wooded islands, such as one finds in plenty on Lake Mälar even today, and for ages they were entirely uninhabited. They were well located between two bodies of water and two bodies of land, but this no one remarked. Year after year passed; people settled along Lake Mälar and in the archipelago, but these river islands attracted no settlers. Sometimes it happened that a seafarer put into port at one of them and pitched his tent for the night, but no one remained there long.

"One day a fisherman, who lived on Liding Island, out in Salt Fjord, steered his boat toward Lake Mälar, where he had such good luck with his fishing that he forgot to start for home in time. He got no farther than the four islets, and the best he could do was to land on one and wait until later in the night, when there would be bright moonlight.

"It was late summer and warm. The fisherman hauled his boat on land, lay down beside it, his head resting upon a stone, and fell asleep. When he awoke the moon had been up a long while. It hung right above him and shone with such splendor that it was like broad daylight.

"The man jumped to his feet and was about to push his boat into the water, when he saw a lot of black specks moving out in the stream. A school of seals was heading full speed for the island. When the fisherman saw that they intended to crawl up on land, he bent down for his spear, which he always took with him in the boat. But when he straightened up, he saw no seals. Instead, there stood on the strand the most beautiful young maidens, dressed in green, trailing satin robes, with pearl crowns upon their heads. The fisherman understood that these were mermaids who lived on desolate rock islands far out at sea and had assumed seal disguises in order to come up on land and enjoy the moonlight on the green islets.

"He laid down the spear very cautiously, and when the young maidens came up on the island to play, he stole behind and surveyed them. He had heard that sea-nymphs were so beautiful and fascinating that no one could see them and not be enchanted by their charms, and he had to admit that this was not too much to say of them.

"When he had stood for a while under the shadow of the trees and watched the dance, he went down to the strand, took one of the seal skins lying there, and hid it under a stone. Then he went back to his boat, lay down beside it, and pretended to be asleep.

"Presently he saw the young maidens trip down to the strand to don their seal skins. At first all was play and laughter, which was changed to weeping and wailing when one of the mermaids could not find her seal robe. Her companions ran up and down the strand and helped her search for it, but no trace could they find. While they were seeking they noticed that the sky was growing pale and the day was breaking, so they could tarry no longer, and they all swam away, leaving behind the one whose seal skin was missing. She sat on the strand and wept.

"The fisherman felt sorry for her, of course, but he forced himself to lie still till daybreak. Then he got up, pushed the boat into the water, and stepped into it to make it appear that he saw her by chance after he had lifted the oars.

"'Who are you?' he called out. 'Are you shipwrecked?'

"She ran toward him and asked if he had seen her seal skin. The fisherman looked as if he did not know what she was talking about. She sat down again and wept. Then he determined to take her with him in the boat. 'Come with me to my cottage,' he commanded, 'and my mother will take care of you. You can't stay here on the island, where you have neither food nor shelter!' He talked so convincingly that she was persuaded to step into his boat.

"Both the fisherman and his mother were very kind to the poor mermaid, and she seemed to be happy with them. She grew more contented every day and helped the older woman with her work, and was exactly like any other island lass, only she was much prettier. One day the fisherman asked her if she would be his wife, and she did not object, but at once said yes.

"Preparations were made for the wedding. The mermaid dressed as a bride in her green, trailing robe with the shimmering pearl crown she had worn when the fisherman first saw her. There was neither church nor parson on the island at that time, so the bridal party seated themselves in the boats to row up to the first church they should find.

"The fisherman had the mermaid and his mother in his boat, and he rowed so well that he was far ahead of all the others. When he had come so far that he could see the islet in the river, where he won his bride, he could not help smiling.

"'What are you smiling at?' she asked.

"'Oh, I'm thinking of that night when I hid your seal skin,' answered the fisherman, for he felt so sure of her that he thought there was no longer any need for him to conceal anything.

"'What are you saying?' asked the bride, astonished. 'Surely I have never possessed a seal skin!' It appeared she had forgotten everything.

"'Don't you recollect how you danced with the mermaids?' he asked.

"'I don't know what you mean,' said the bride. 'I think that you must have dreamed a strange dream last night.'

"'If I show you your seal skin, you'll probably believe me!' laughed the fisherman, promptly turning the boat toward the islet. They stepped ashore and he brought the seal skin out from under the stone where he had hidden it.

"But the instant the bride set eyes on the seal skin she grasped it and drew it over her head. It snuggled close to her as if there was life in it and immediately she threw herself into the stream.

"The bridegroom saw her swim away and plunged into the water after her, but he could not catch up to her. When he saw that he could not stop her in any other way, in his despair, he seized his spear and hurled it. He aimed better than he had intended, for the poor mermaid gave a piercing shriek and disappeared in the depths.

"The fisherman stood on the strand waiting for her to appear again. He observed that the water around him began to take on a soft sheen, a beauty that he had never before seen. It shimmered in pink and white, like the color play on the inside of seashells.

"As the glittering water lapped the shores, the fisherman thought that they too were transformed. They began to blossom and waft their perfumes. A soft sheen spread over them and they also took on a beauty which they had never possessed before.

"He understood how all this had come to pass for it is thus with mermaids. One who beholds them must needs find them more beautiful than anyone else for the mermaid's blood being mixed with the water that bathed the shores, her beauty was transferred to both. All who saw them must love them and yearn for them. This was their legacy from the mermaid."

When the stately old gentleman had got thus far in his narrative he turned to Clement and looked at him. Clement nodded reverently but made no comment, as he did not wish to cause a break in the story.

"Now you must bear this in mind, Clement," the old gentleman continued, with a roguish glint in his eyes. "From that time on people emigrated to the islands. At first only fishermen and peasants settled there, but others, too, were attracted to them. One day the king and his earl sailed up the stream. They started at once to talk of these islands, having observed they were so situated that every vessel that sailed toward Lake Mälar had to pass them. The earl suggested that there ought to be a lock put on the channel which could be opened or closed at will, to let in merchant vessels and shut out pirates.

"This idea was carried out," said the old gentleman, as he rose and began to trace in the sand again with his cane. "On the largest of these islands the earl erected a fortress with a strong tower, which was called 'Kärnan.' And around the island a wall was built. Here, at the north and south ends of the wall, they made gates and placed strong towers over them. Across the other islands they built bridges; these were likewise equipped with high towers. Out in the water, round about, they put a wreath of piles with bars that could open and close, so that no vessel could sail past without permission.

"Therefore you see, Clement, the four islands which had lain so long unnoticed were soon strongly fortified. But this was not all, for the shores and the sound tempted people, and before long they came from all quarters to settle there. They built a church, which has since been called 'Storkyrkan.' Here it stands, near the castle. And here, within the walls, were the little huts the pioneers built for themselves. They were primitive, but they served their purpose. More was not needed at that time to make the place pass for a city. And the city was named Stockholm.

"There came a day, Clement, when the earl who had begun the work went to his final rest, and Stockholm was without a master builder. Monks called the Gray Friars came to the country. Stockholm attracted them. They asked permission to erect a monastery there, so the king gave them an island—one of the smaller ones—this one facing Lake Mälar. There they built, and the place was called Gray Friars Island. Other monks came, called the Black Friars. They, too, asked for right to build in Stockholm, near the south gate. On this, the larger of the islands north of the city, a 'Holy Ghost House,' or hospital, was built, while on the smaller one thrifty men put up a mill, and along the little islands close by the monks fished. As you know, there is only one island now, for the canal between the two has filled up, but it is still called Holy Ghost Island.

"And now, Clement, all the little wooded islands were dotted with houses, but still people kept streaming in, for these shores and waters have the power to draw people to them. Hither came pious women of the Order of Saint Clara and asked for ground to build upon. For them there was no choice but to settle on the north shore, at Norrmalm, as it is called. You may be sure that they were not over pleased with this location, for across Norrmalm ran a high ridge, and on that the city had its gallows hill, so that it was a detested spot. Nevertheless the Clara Sisters erected their church and their convent on the strand below the ridge. After they were established there they soon found plenty of followers. Upon the ridge itself were built a hospital and a church, consecrated to Saint Göran, and just below the ridge a church was erected to Saint

Jacob. And even at Södermalm, where the mountain rises perpendicularly from the strand, they began to build. There they raised a church to Saint Mary.

"But you must not think that only cloister folk moved to Stockholm! There were also many others principally German tradesmen and artisans. These were more skilled than the Swedes, and were well received. They settled within the walls of the city where they pulled down the wretched little cabins that stood there and built high, magnificent stone houses. But space was not plentiful within the walls, therefore they had to build the houses close together, with gables facing the narrow by-lanes. So you see, Clement, that Stockholm could attract people!"

At this point in the narrative another gentleman appeared and walked rapidly down the path toward the man who was talking to Clement, but he waved his hand, and the other remained at a distance. The dignified old gentleman still sat on the bench beside the fiddler.

"Now, Clement, you must render me a service," he said. "I have no time to talk more with you, but I will send you a book about Stockholm and you must read it from cover to cover. I have, so to speak, laid the foundations of Stockholm for you. Study the rest out for yourself and learn how the city has thrived and changed. Read how the little, narrow, wall-enclosed city on the islands has spread into this great sea of houses below us. Read how, on the spot where the dark tower Kärnan once stood, the beautiful, light castle below us was erected and how the Gray Friars' church has been turned into the burial place of the Swedish kings, read how islet after islet was built up with factories, how the ridge was lowered and the sound filled in, how the truck gardens at the south and north ends of the city have been converted into beautiful parks or built up quarters, how the King's private deer park has become the people's favorite pleasure resort. You must make yourself at home here, Clement. This city does not belong exclusively to the Stockholmers. It belongs to you and to all Swedes.

"As you read about Stockholm, remember that I have spoken the truth, for the city has the power to draw every one to it. First the King moved here, then the nobles built their palaces here, and then one after another was attracted to the place, so that now, as you see, Stockholm is not a city unto itself or for nearby districts; it has grown into a city for the whole kingdom.

"You know, Clement, that there are judicial courts in every parish throughout the land, but in Stockholm they have jurisdiction for the whole nation. You know that there are judges in every district court in the country, but at Stockholm there is only one court, to which all the others are accountable. You know that there are barracks and troops in every part of the land, but those at Stockholm command the whole army. Everywhere in the country you will find railroads, but the whole great national system is controlled and managed at Stockholm; here you will find the governing boards for the clergy, for teachers, for physicians, for bailiffs and jurors. This is the heart of your country, Clement. All the change you have in your pocket is coined here, and the postage stamps you stick on your letters are made here. There is something here for every Swede. Here no one need feel homesick, for here all Swedes are at home.

"And when you read of all that has been brought here to Stockholm, think too of the latest that the city has attracted to itself: these old-time peasant cottages here at Skansen; the old dances; the old costumes and house-furnishings; the musicians and story-tellers. Everything good of the old times Stockholm has tempted here to Skansen to do it honor, that it may, in turn, stand before the people with renewed glory.

"But, first and last, remember as you read about Stockholm that you are to sit in this place. You must see how the waves sparkle in joyous play and how the shores shimmer with beauty. You will come under the spell of their witchery, Clement."

The handsome old gentleman had raised his voice, so that it rang out strong and commanding, and his eyes shone. Then he rose, and, with a wave of his hand to Clement, walked away. Clement understood that the one who had been talking to him was a great man, and he bowed to him as low as he could. The next day came a royal lackey with a big red book and a letter for Clement, and in the letter it said that the book was from the King. After that the little old man, Clement Larsson, was light-headed for several days, and it was impossible to get a sensible word out of him. When a week had gone by, he went to the superintendent and gave in his notice. He simply had to go home.

"Why must you go home? Can't you learn to be content here?" asked the doctor.

"Oh, I'm contented here," said Clement. "That matter troubles me no longer, but I must go home all the same." Clement was quite perturbed because the King had said that he should learn all about Stockholm and be happy there. But he could not rest until he had told every one at home that the King had said those words to him. He could not renounce the idea of standing on the church knoll at home and telling high and low that the King had been so kind to him, that he had sat beside him on the bench, and had sent him a book, and had taken the time to talk to him—a poor fiddler—for a whole hour, in order to cure him of his homesickness. It was good to relate this to the Laplanders and Dalecarlian peasant girls at Skansen, but what was that compared to being able to tell of it at home?

Even if Clement were to end in the poorhouse, it wouldn't be so hard after this. He was a totally different man from what he had been, and he would be respected and honored in a very different way. This new yearning took possession of Clement. He simply had to go up to the doctor and say that he must go home.

VIII

GORGO, THE EAGLE

IN THE MOUNTAIN GLEN

*F*ar up among the mountains of Lapland there was an old eagle's nest on a ledge which projected from a high cliff. The nest was made of dry twigs of pine and spruce, interlaced one with another until they formed a perfect network. Year by year the nest had been repaired and strengthened. It was about two meters wide, and nearly as high as a Laplander's hut.

The cliff on which the eagle's nest was situated towered above a big glen, which was inhabited in summer by a flock of wild geese, as it was an excellent refuge for them. It was so secluded between cliffs that not many knew of it, even among the Laplanders themselves.

In the heart of this glen there was a small, round lake in which was an abundance of food for the tiny goslings, and on the tufted lake shores which were covered with osier bushes and dwarfed birches the geese found fine nesting places.

In all ages eagles had lived on the mountain, and geese in the glen. Every year the former carried off a few of the latter, but they were very careful not to take so many that the wild geese would be afraid to remain in the glen. The geese, in their turn, found the eagles quite useful. They were robbers, to be sure, but they kept other robbers away.

Two years before Nils Holgersson traveled with the wild geese the old leader goose, Akka from Kebnekaise, was standing at the foot of the mountain slope looking toward the eagle's nest.

The eagles were in the habit of starting on their chase soon after sunrise; during the summers that Akka had lived in the glen she had watched every morning for their departure to find if they stopped in the glen to hunt, or if they flew beyond it to other hunting grounds.

She did not have to wait long before the two eagles left the ledge on the cliff. Stately and terror-striking they soared into the air, directing their course toward the plain, and Akka breathed a sigh of relief.

The old leader goose's days of nesting and rearing of young were over, and during the summer she passed the time going from one goose range to another, giving counsel regarding the brooding and care of the young. Aside from this she kept an eye out not only for eagles but also for mountain fox and owls and all other enemies who were a menace to the wild geese and their young.

About noontime Akka began to watch for the eagles again. This she had done every day during all the summers that she had lived in the glen. She could tell at once by their flight if their hunt had been successful, and in that event she felt relieved for the safety of those who belonged to her. But on this particular day she had not seen the eagles return. "I must be getting old and stupid," she thought, when she had waited a time for them. "The eagles have probably been home this long while."

In the afternoon she looked toward the cliff again, expecting to see the eagles perched on the rocky ledge where they usually took their afternoon rest toward evening, when they took their bath in the dale lake, she tried again to get sight of them, but failed. Again she bemoaned the fact that she was growing old. She was so accustomed to having the eagles on the mountain above her that she could not imagine the possibility of their not having returned.

The following morning Akka was awake in good season to watch for the eagles, but she did not see them. On the other hand, she heard in the morning stillness a cry that sounded both angry and plaintive, and it seemed to come from the eagles' nest. "Can there possibly be anything amiss with the eagles?" she wondered. She spread her wings quickly, and rose so high that she could perfectly well look down into the nest.

There she saw neither of the eagles. There was no one in the nest save a little half-fledged eaglet who was screaming for food.

Akka sank down toward the eagles' nest, slowly and reluctantly. It was a gruesome place to come to! It was plain what kind of robber folk lived there! In the nest and on the cliff ledge lay bleached bones, bloody feathers, pieces of skin, hares' heads, birds' beaks, and the tufted claws of grouse. The eaglet, who was lying in the midst of this, was repulsive to look upon, with his big, gaping bill, his awkward, down-clad body, and his undeveloped wings where the prospective quills stuck out like thorns.

At last Akka conquered her repugnance and alighted on the edge of the nest, at the same time glancing about her anxiously in every direction, for each second she expected to see the old eagles coming back.

"It is well that some one has come at last," cried the baby eagle. "Fetch me some food at once!"

"Well, well, don't be in such haste," said Akka. "Tell me first where your father and mother are."

"That's what I should like to know myself. They went off yesterday morning and left me a lemming to live upon while they were away. You can believe that was eaten long ago. It's a shame for Mother to let me starve in this way!"

Akka began to think that the eagles had really been shot, and she reasoned that if she were to let the eaglet starve she might perhaps be rid of the whole robber tribe for all time. But it went very much against her not to succor a deserted young one so far as she could.

"Why do you sit there and stare?" snapped the eaglet. "Didn't you hear me say I want food?"

Akka spread her wings and sank down to the little lake in the glen. A moment later she returned to the eagles' nest with a salmon trout in her bill.

The eaglet flew into a temper when she dropped the fish in front of him.

"Do you think I can eat such stuff?" he shrieked, pushing it aside, and trying to strike Akka with his bill. "Fetch me a willow grouse or a lemming, do you hear?"

Akka stretched her head forward, and gave the eaglet a sharp nip in the neck. "Let me say to you," remarked the old goose, "that if I'm to procure food for you, you must be satisfied with what I give you. Your father and mother are dead, and from them you can get no help, but if you want to lie here and starve to death while you wait for grouse and lemming, I shall not hinder you."

When Akka had spoken her mind she promptly retired, and did not show her face in the eagles' nest again for some time. But when she did return, the eaglet had eaten the fish, and when she dropped another in front of him he swallowed it at once, although it was plain that he found it very distasteful.

Akka had imposed upon herself a tedious task. The old eagles never appeared again, and she alone had to procure for the eaglet all the food he needed. She gave him fish and frogs and he did not seem to fare badly on this diet, but grew big and strong. He soon forgot his parents, the eagles, and fancied that Akka was his real mother. Akka, in turn, loved him as if he had been her own child. She tried to give him a good bringing up, and to cure him of his wildness and overbearing ways.

After a fortnight Akka observed that the time was approaching for her to molt and put on a new feather dress so as to be ready to fly. For a whole moon she would be unable to carry food to the baby eaglet, and he might starve to death.

So Akka said to him one day: "Gorgo, I can't come to you any more with fish. Everything depends now upon your pluck—which means can you dare to venture into the glen, so that I can continue to procure food for you? You must choose between starvation and flying down to the glen, but that, too, may cost you your life."

Without a second's hesitation the eaglet stepped upon the edge of the nest. Barely taking the trouble to measure the distance to the bottom, he spread his tiny wings and started away. He rolled over and over in space, but nevertheless made enough use of his wings to reach the ground almost unhurt.

Down there in the glen Gorgo passed the summer in company with the little goslings, and was a good comrade for them. Since he regarded himself as a gosling, he tried to live as they lived; when they swam in the lake he followed them until he came near drowning. It was most embarrassing to him that he could not learn to swim, and he went to Akka and complained of his inability.

"Why can't I swim like the others?" he asked. "Your claws grew too hooked, and your toes too large while you were up there on the cliff," Akka replied. "But you'll make a fine bird all the same."

The eaglet's wings soon grew so large that they could carry him, but not until autumn, when the goslings learned to fly, did it dawn upon him that he could use them for flight. There came a proud time for him, for at this sport he was the peer of them all. His companions never stayed up in the air any longer than they had to, but he stayed there nearly the whole day, and practiced the art of flying. So far it had not occurred to him that he was of another species than the geese, but he could not help noting a number of things that surprised him, and he questioned Akka constantly.

"Why do grouse and lemming run and hide when they see my shadow on the cliff?" he queried. "They don't show such fear of the other goslings."

"Your wings grew too big when you were on the cliff," said Akka. "It is that which frightens the little wretches. But don't be unhappy because of that. You'll be a fine bird all the same."

After the eagle had learned to fly, he taught himself to fish, and to catch frogs. But by and by he began to ponder this also.

"How does it happen that I live on fish and frogs?" he asked. "The other goslings don't."

"This is due to the fact that I had no other food to give you when you were on the cliff," said Akka. "But don't let that make you sad. You'll be a fine bird all the same."

When the wild geese began their autumn moving, Gorgo flew along with the flock, regarding himself all the while as one of them. The air was filled with birds who were on their way south, and there was great excitement among them when Akka appeared with an eagle in her train. The wild goose flock was continually surrounded by swarms of the curious who loudly expressed their astonishment. Akka bade them be silent, but it was impossible to stop so many wagging tongues.

"Why do they call me an eagle?" Gorgo asked repeatedly, growing more and more exasperated. "Can't they see that I'm a wild goose? I'm no bird-eater who preys upon his kind. How dare they give me such an ugly name!"

One day they flew above a barn yard where many chickens walked on a dump heap and picked. "An eagle! An eagle!" shrieked the chickens, and started to run for shelter. But Gorgo, who had heard the eagles spoken of as savage criminals, could not control his anger. He snapped his wings together and shot down to the ground, striking his talons into one of the hens. "I'll teach you, I will, that I'm no eaglet" he screamed furiously, and struck with his beak.

That instant he heard Akka call to him from the air, and rose obediently. The wild goose flew toward him and began to reprimand him. "What are you trying to do?" she cried, beating him with her bill. "Was it perhaps your intention to tear that poor hen to pieces?" But when the eagle took his punishment from the wild goose without a protest, there arose from the great bird throng around them a perfect storm of taunts and gibes. The eagle heard this, and turned toward Akka with flaming eyes, as though he would have liked to attack her. But he suddenly changed his mind, and with quick wing strokes bounded into the air, soaring so high that no call could reach him, and he sailed around up there as long as the wild geese saw him.

Two days later he appeared again in the wild goose flock.

"I know who I am," he said to Akka. "Since I am an eagle, I must live as becomes an eagle, but I think that we can be friends all the same. You or any of yours I shall never attack."

But Akka had set her heart on successfully training an eagle into a mild and harmless bird, and she could not tolerate his wanting to do as he chose.

"Do you think that I wish to be the friend of a bird-eater?" she asked. "Live as I have taught you to live, and you may travel with my flock as heretofore."

Both were proud and stubborn, and neither of them would yield. It ended in Akka's forbidding the eagle to show his face in her neighborhood, and her anger toward him was so intense that no one dared speak his name in her presence.

After that Gorgo roamed around the country, alone and shunned, like all great robbers. He was often downhearted, and certainly longed many a time for the days when he thought himself a wild goose, and played with the merry goslings.

Among the animals he had a great reputation for courage. They used to say of him that he feared no one but his foster mother, Akka. And they could also say of him that he never used violence against a wild goose.

IN CAPTIVITY

*G*orgo was only three years old, and had not as yet thought about marrying and procuring a home for himself, when he was captured one day by a hunter, and sold to the Skansen Zoological Garden, where there were already two eagles held captive in a cage built of iron bars and steel wires. The cage stood out in the open, and was so large that a couple of trees had easily been moved into it, and quite a large cairn was piled up in there. Notwithstanding all this, the birds were unhappy. They sat motionless on the same spot nearly all day. Their pretty, dark feather dresses became rough and lusterless, and their eyes were riveted with hopeless longing on the sky without.

During the first week of Gorgo's captivity he was still awake and full of life, but later a heavy torpor came upon him. He perched himself on one spot, like the other eagles, and stared at vacancy. He no longer knew how the days passed. One morning when Gorgo sat in his usual torpor, he heard some one call to him from below. He was so drowsy that he could barely rouse himself enough to lower his glance. "Who is calling me?" he asked.

"Oh, Gorgo! Don't you know me? It's Thumbietot who used to fly around with the wild geese."

"Is Akka also captured?" asked Gorgo in the tone of one who is trying to collect his thoughts after a long sleep.

"No, Akka, the white goosey-gander, and the whole flock are probably safe and sound up in Lapland at this season," said the boy. "It's only I who am a prisoner here."

As the boy was speaking he noticed that Gorgo averted his glance, and began to stare into space again. "Golden eagle!" cried the boy, "I have not forgotten that once you carried me back to the wild geese, and that you saved the white goosey-gander's life! Tell me if I can be of any help to you!"

Gorgo scarcely raised his head. "Don't disturb me, Thumbietot," he yawned. "I'm sitting here dreaming that I am free, and am soaring away up among the clouds. I don't want to be awake."

"You must rouse yourself, and see what goes on around you," the boy admonished, "or you will soon look as wretched as the other eagles."

301

"I wish I were as they are! They are so lost in their dreams that nothing more can trouble them," said the eagle.

When night came, and all three eagles were asleep, there was a light scraping on the steel wires stretched across the top of the cage. The two listless old captives did not allow themselves to be disturbed by the noise, but Gorgo awakened. "Who's there? Who is moving up on the roof?" he asked.

"It's Thumbietot, Gorgo," answered the boy. "I'm sitting here filing away at the steel wires so that you can escape."

The eagle raised his head, and saw in the night light how the boy sat and filed the steel wires at the top of the cage. He felt hopeful for an instant, but soon discouragement got the upper hand. "I'm a big bird, Thumbietot," said Gorgo, "how can you ever manage to file away enough wires for me to come out? You'd better quit that, and leave me in peace."

"Oh, go to sleep, and don't bother about me!" said the boy. "I'll not be through tonight nor tomorrow night, but I shall try to free you in time, for here you'll become a total wreck."

Gorgo fell asleep. When he awoke the next morning he saw at a glance that a number of wires had been filed. That day he felt less drowsy than he had done in the past. He spread his wings, and fluttered from branch to branch to get the stiffness out of his joints.

One morning early, just as the first streak of sunlight made its appearance, Thumbietot awakened the eagle. "Try now, Gorgo!" he whispered.

The eagle looked up. The boy had actually filed off so many wires that now there was a big hole in the wire netting. Gorgo flapped his wings and propelled himself upward. Twice he missed and fell back into the cage, but finally succeeded in getting out. With proud wing strokes he soared into the clouds. Little Thumbietot sat and gazed after him with a mournful expression. He wished that some one would come and give him his freedom too. The boy was domiciled now at Skansen. He had become acquainted with all the animals there, and had made many friends among them. He had to admit that there was so much to see and learn there that it was not difficult for him to pass the time. To be sure his thoughts went forth every day to Morten Goosey-Gander and his other comrades, and he yearned for them. "If only I weren't bound by my promise," he thought, "I'd find some bird to take me to them!"

It may seem strange that Clement Larsson had not restored the boy's liberty, but one must remember how excited the little fiddler had been when he left Skansen. The morning of his departure he had thought of setting out the midget's food in a blue bowl, but, unluckily, he had been unable to find one. All the Skansen folk—Laps, peasant girls, artisans, and gardeners—had come to bid him good-bye, and he had had no time to search for a blue bowl. It was time to start, and at the last moment he had to ask the old Laplander to help him.

"One of the tiny folk happens to be living here at Skansen," said Clement, "and every morning I set out a little food for him. Will you do me the favor of taking these few coppers and purchasing a blue bowl with them? Put a little gruel and milk in it, and tomorrow morning set it out under the steps of Bollnäs cottage."

The old Laplander looked surprised, but there was no time for Clement to explain further, as he had to be off to the railway station. The Laplander went down to the zoological village to purchase the bowl. As he saw no blue one that he thought appropriate, he bought a white one, and this he conscientiously filled and set out every morning. That was why the boy had not been released from his pledge. He knew that Clement had gone away, but he was not allowed to leave. That night the boy longed more than ever for his freedom. This was because summer had come now in earnest. During his travels he had suffered much in cold and stormy weather, and when he first came to Skansen he had thought that perhaps it was just as well that he had been compelled to break the journey. He would have been frozen to death had he gone to Lapland in the month of May. But now it was warm; the earth was green clad, birches and poplars were clothed in their satiny foliage, and the cherry trees—in fact all the fruit trees—were covered with blossoms. The berry bushes had green berries on their stems; the oaks had carefully unfolded their leaves, and peas, cabbages, and beans were growing in the vegetable garden at Skansen.

"Now it must be warm up in Lapland," thought the boy. "I should like to be seated on Morten Goosey-Gander's back on a fine morning like this! It would be great fun to ride around in the warm, still air, and look down at the ground, as it now lies decked with green grass, and embellished with pretty blossoms." He sat musing on this when the eagle suddenly swooped down from the sky, and perched beside the boy, on top of the cage.

"I wanted to try my wings to see if they were still good for anything," said Gorgo. "You didn't suppose that I meant to leave you here in captivity? Get up on my back, and I'll take you to your comrades."

"No, that's impossible!" the boy answered. "I have pledged my word that I would stay here till I am liberated."

"What sort of nonsense are you talking?" protested Gorgo. "In the first place they brought you here against your will, then they forced you to promise that you would remain here. Surely you must understand that such a promise one need not keep?"

"Oh, no, I must keep it," said the boy. "I thank you all the same for your kind intention, but you can't help me."

"Oh, can't I?" said Gorgo. "We'll see about that!" In a twinkling he grasped Nils Holgersson in his big talons, and rose with him toward the skies, disappearing in a northerly direction.

IX

ON OVER GÄSTRIKLAND

THE PRECIOUS GIRDLE

Wednesday, June fifteenth

*T*he eagle kept on flying until he was a long distance north of Stockholm. Then he sank to a wooded hillock where he relaxed his hold on the boy.

The instant Thumbietot was out of Gorgo's clutches he started to run back to the city as fast as he could. The eagle made a long swoop, caught up to the boy, and stopped him with his claw.

"Do you propose to go back to prison?" he demanded.

"That's my affair. I can go where I like, for all of you!" retorted the boy, trying to get away. Thereupon the eagle gripped him with his strong talons, and rose in the air.

Now Gorgo circled over the entire province of Uppland and did not stop again until he came to the great waterfalls at Älvkarleby where he alighted on a rock in the middle of the rushing rapids below the roaring falls. Again he relaxed his hold on the captive.

The boy saw that here there was no chance of escape from the eagle. Above them the white scum wall of the waterfall came tumbling down, and round about the river rushed along in a mighty torrent. Thumbietot was very indignant to think that in this way he had been forced to become a promise breaker. He turned his back to the eagle, and would not speak to him.

Now that the bird had set the boy down in a place from which he could not run away, he told him confidentially that he had been brought up by Akka from Kebnekaise, and that he had quarreled with his foster mother.

"Now, Thumbietot, perhaps you understand why I wish to take you back to the wild geese," he said. "I have heard that you are in great favor with Akka. It was my purpose to ask you to make peace between us."

As soon as the boy comprehended that the eagle had not carried him off in a spirit of contrariness, he felt kindly toward him.

"I should like very much to help you," he returned, "but I am bound by my promise." Thereupon he explained to the eagle how he had fallen into captivity and how Clement Larsson had left Skansen without setting him free.

Nevertheless the eagle would not relinquish his plan.

"Listen to me, Thumbietot," he said. "My wings can carry you wherever you wish to go, and my eyes can search out whatever you wish to find. Tell me how the man looks who exacted this promise from you, and I will find him and take you to him. Then it is for you to do the rest."

Thumbietot approved of the proposition.

"I can see, Gorgo, that you have had a wise bird like Akka for a foster mother," the boy remarked.

He gave a graphic description of Clement Larsson, and added that he had heard at Skansen that the little fiddler was from Hälsingland.

"We'll search for him through the whole of Hälsingland—from Ljungby to Mellansjö, from Great Mountain to Hornland," said the eagle. "Tomorrow before sundown you shall have a talk with the man!"

"I fear you are promising more than you can perform," doubted the boy.

"I should be a mighty poor eagle if I couldn't do that much," said Gorgo.

So when Gorgo and Thumbietot left Älvkarleby they were good friends, and the boy willingly took his mount for a ride on the eagle's back. Thus he had an opportunity to see much of the country.

When clutched in the eagle's talons he had seen nothing. Perhaps it was just as well, for in the forenoon he had traveled over Upsala, Österby's big factories, the Dannemora Mine, and the ancient castle of Örbyhus, and he would have been sadly disappointed at not seeing them had he known of their proximity.

The eagle bore him speedily over Gästrikland. In the southern part of the province there was very little to tempt the eye. But as they flew northward, it began to be interesting.

"This country is clad in a spruce skirt and a gray stone jacket," thought the boy. "But around its waist it wears a girdle which has not its match in value, for it is embroidered with blue lakes and green groves. The great ironworks adorn it like a row of precious stones, and its buckle is a whole city with castles and cathedrals and great clusters of houses."

When the travelers arrived in the northern forest region, Gorgo alighted on top of a mountain. As the boy dismounted, the eagle said:

"There's game in this forest, and I can't forget my late captivity and feel really free until I have gone a hunting. You won't mind my leaving you for a while?"

"No, of course, I won't," the boy assured him.

"You may go where you like so that you are back here by sundown," said the eagle, as he flew off.

The boy sat on a stone gazing across the bare, rocky ground and the great forests round about.

He felt rather lonely. But soon he heard singing in the forest below, and saw something bright moving amongst the trees. Presently he saw a blue and yellow banner, and he knew by the songs and the merry chatter that it was being borne at the head of a procession. On it came, up the winding path; he wondered where it and those who followed it were going. He couldn't believe that anybody would come up to such an ugly, desolate waste as the place where he sat. But the banner was nearing the forest border, and behind it marched many happy people for whom it had led the way. Suddenly there was life and movement all over the mountain plain; after that there was so much for the boy to see that he didn't have a dull moment.

FOREST DAY

On the mountain's broad back, where Gorgo left Thumbietot, there had been a forest fire ten years before. Since that time the charred trees had been felled and removed, and the great fire-swept area had begun to deck itself with green along the edges, where it skirted the healthy forest. However, the larger part of the top was still barren and appallingly desolate. Charred stumps, standing sentinel-like between the rock ledges, bore witness that once there had been a fine forest here, but no fresh shoots sprang from the ground.

One day in the early summer all the children in the parish had assembled in front of the schoolhouse near the fire-swept mountain. Each child carried either a spade or a hoe on its shoulder, and a basket of food in its hand. As soon as all were assembled, they marched in a long procession toward the forest. The banner came first, with the teachers on either side of it, then followed a couple of foresters and a wagon load of pine shrubs and spruce seeds, then the children.

The procession did not pause in any of the birch groves near the settlements, but marched on deep into the forest. As it moved along, the foxes stuck their heads out of the lairs in astonishment, and wondered what kind of backwoods people these were. As they marched past old coal pits where charcoal kilns were fired every autumn, the cross-beaks twisted their hooked bills, and asked one another what kind of coalers these might be who were now thronging the forest.

Finally, the procession reached the big, burnt mountain plain. The rocks had been stripped of the fine twin-flower creepers that once covered them; they had been robbed of the pretty silver moss and the attractive reindeer moss. Around the dark water gathered in clefts and hollows there was now no wood sorrel. The little patches of soil in crevices and between stones were without ferns, without star-flowers, without all the green and red and light and soft and soothing things which usually clothe the forest ground.

It was as if a bright light flashed upon the mountain when all the parish children covered it. Here again was something sweet and delicate, something fresh and rosy, something young and growing. Perhaps these children would bring to the poor abandoned forest a little new life.

When the children had rested and eaten their luncheon, they seized hoes and spades and began to work. The foresters showed them what to do. They set out shrub after shrub on every clear spot of earth they could find.

As they worked, they talked quite knowingly among themselves of how the little shrubs they were planting would bind the soil so that it could not get away, and of how new soil would form under the trees. By and by seeds would drop, and in a few years they would be picking both strawberries and raspberries where now there were only bare rocks. The little shrubs which they were planting would gradually become tall trees. Perhaps big houses and great splendid ships would be built from them!

If the children had not come here and planted while there was still a little soil in the clefts, all the earth would have been carried away by wind and water, and the mountain could never more have been clothed in green.

"It was well that we came," said the children. "We were just in the nick of time!" They felt very were working on the mountain, their at home. By and by they began to the children were getting along. Of course it was only a joke about their planting a forest, but it might be amusing to see what they were trying to do.

So presently both fathers and mothers were on their way to the forest. When they came to the outlying stock farms they met some of their neighbors.

"Are you going to the fire-swept mountain?" they asked.

"There's where we're bound for."

"To have a look at the children?"

"Yes, to see what they're up to."

"It's only play, of course."

"It isn't likely that there will be many forest trees planted by the youngsters. We have brought the coffee pot along so that we can have something warm to drink, since we must stay there all day with only lunch-basket provisions."

So the parents of the children went on up the mountain. At first they thought only of how pretty it looked to see all the rosy-cheeked little children scattered over the gray hills. Later, they observed how the children were working how some were setting out shrubs, while others were digging furrows and sowing seeds. Others again were pulling up heather to prevent its choking the young trees. They saw that the children took the work seriously and were so intent upon what they were doing that they scarcely had time to glance up.

The fathers and mothers stood for a moment and looked on, then they too began to pull up heather just for the fun of it. The children were the instructors, for they were already trained, and had to show their elders what to do.

Thus it happened that all the grown-ups who had come to watch the children took part in the work. Then, of course, it became greater fun than before. By and by the children had even more help. Other implements were needed, so a couple of long-legged boys were sent down to the village for spades and hoes. As they ran past the cabins, the stay-at-homes came out and asked: "What's wrong? Has there been an accident?"

"No, indeed! But the whole parish is up on the fire-swept mountain planting a forest."

"If the whole parish is there, we can't stay at home!" So party after party of peasants went crowding to the top of the burnt mountain. They stood a moment and looked on. The temptation to join the workers was irresistible.

"It's a pleasure to sow one's own acres in the spring, and to think of the grain that will spring up from the earth, but this work is even more alluring," they thought.

Not only slender blades would come from that sowing, but mighty trees with tall trunks and sturdy branches. It meant giving birth not merely to a summer's grain, but to many years' growths. It meant the awakening hum of insects, the song of the thrush, the play of grouse and all kinds of life on the desolate mountain. Moreover, it was like raising a memorial for coming generations. They could have left a bare, treeless height as a heritage. Instead they were to leave a glorious forest.

Coming generations would know their forefathers had been a good and wise folk and they would remember them with reverence and gratitude.

X

A DAY IN HÄLSINGLAND

A LARGE GREEN LEAF

Thursday, June sixteenth

*T*he following day the boy traveled over Hälsingland. It spread beneath him with new, pale green shoots on the pine trees, new birch leaves in the groves, new green grass in the meadows, and sprouting grain in the fields. It was a mountainous country, but directly through it ran a broad, light valley from either side of which branched other valleys—some short and narrow, some broad and long.

"This land resembles a leaf," thought the boy, "for it's as green as a leaf, and the valleys subdivide it in about the same way as the veins of a leaf are foliated."

The branch valleys, like the main one, were filled with lakes, rivers, farms, and villages. They snuggled, light and smiling, between the dark mountains until they were gradually squeezed together by the hills. There they were so narrow that they could not hold more than a little brook.

On the high land between the valleys there were pine forests which had no even ground to grow upon. There were mountains standing all about, and the forest covered the whole, like a woolly hide stretched over a bony body.

It was a picturesque country to look down upon, and the boy saw a good deal of it, because the eagle was trying to find the old fiddler, Clement Larsson, and flew from ravine to ravine looking for him.

A little later in the morning there was life and movement on every farm. The doors of the cattle sheds were thrown wide open and the cows were let out. They were prettily colored, small, supple and sprightly, and so sure-footed that they made the most comic leaps and bounds. After them came the calves and sheep, and it was plainly to be seen that they, too, were in the best of spirits.

It grew livelier every moment in the farm yards. A couple of young girls with knapsacks on their backs walked among the cattle; a boy with a long switch kept the sheep together, and a little dog ran in and out among the cows, barking at the ones that tried to gore him. The farmer hitched a horse to a cart loaded with tubs of butter, boxes of cheese, and all kinds of eatables. The people laughed and chattered.

They and the beasts were alike merry—as if looking forward to a day of real pleasure.

A moment later all were on their way to the forest. One of the girls walked in the lead and coaxed the cattle with pretty, musical calls. The animals followed in a long line. The shepherd boy and the sheep dog ran hither and thither, to see that no creature turned from the right course, and last came the farmer and his hired man. They walked beside the cart to prevent its being upset, for the road they followed was a narrow, stony forest path.

It may have been the custom for all the peasants in Hälsingland to send their cattle into the forests on the same day—or perhaps it only happened so that year; at any rate the boy saw how processions of happy people and cattle wandered out from every valley and every farm and rushed into the lonely forest, filling it with life. From the depths of the dense woods the boy heard the shepherd maidens' songs and the tinkle of the cow bells. Many of the processions had long and difficult roads to travel, and the boy saw how they tramped through marshes, how they had to take roundabout ways to get past windfalls, and how, time and again, the carts bumped against stones and turned over with all their contents. But the people met all the obstacles with jokes and laughter.

In the afternoon they came to a cleared space where cattle sheds and a couple of rude cabins had been built. The cows mooed with delight as they tramped on the luscious green grass in the yards between the cabins, and at once began grazing. The peasants, with merry chatter and banter, carried water and wood and all that had been brought in the carts into the larger cabin. Presently smoke rose from the chimney and then the dairymaids, the shepherd boy, and the men squatted upon a flat rock and ate their supper.

Gorgo, the eagle, was certain that he should find Clement Larsson among those who were off for the forest. Whenever he saw a stock farm procession, he sank down and scrutinized it with his sharp eyes, but hour after hour passed without his finding the one he sought.

After much circling around, toward evening they came to a stony and desolate tract east of the great main valley. There the boy saw another outlying stock farm under him. The people and the cattle had arrived. The men were splitting wood, and the dairymaids were milking the cows.

"Look there!" said Gorgo. "I think we've got him." He sank, and, to his great astonishment, the boy saw that the eagle was right. There indeed stood little Clement Larsson chopping wood.

Gorgo alighted on a pine tree in the thick woods a little away from the house.

"I have fulfilled my obligation," said the eagle, with a proud toss of his head. "Now you must try and have a word with the man. I'll perch here at the top of the thick pine and wait for you."

THE ANIMALS' NEW YEAR'S EVE

*T*he day's work was done at the forest ranches, supper was over, and the peasants sat about and chatted. It was a long time since they had been in the forest of a summer's night, and they seemed reluctant to go to bed and sleep. It was as light as day, and the dairymaids were busy with their needlework. Ever and anon they raised their heads, looked toward the forest and smiled. "Now we are here again!" they said. The town, with its unrest, faded from their minds, and the forest, with its peaceful stillness, enfolded them. When at home they had wondered how they should ever be able to endure the loneliness of the woods, but once there, they felt that they were having their best time.

Many of the young girls and young men from neighboring ranches had come to call upon them, so that there were quite a lot of folk seated on the grass before the cabins, but they did not find it easy to start conversation. The men were going home the next day, so the dairymaids gave them little commissions and bade them take greetings to their friends in the village. This was nearly all that had been said.

Suddenly the eldest of the dairy girls looked up from her work and said laughingly: "There's no need of our sitting here so silent tonight, for we have two storytellers with us. One is Clement Larsson, who sits beside me, and the other is Bernhard from Sunnasjö, who stands back there gazing toward Black's Ridge. I think that we should ask each of them to tell us a story. To the one who entertains us the better I shall give the muffler I am knitting."

This proposal won hearty applause. The two competitors offered lame excuses, naturally, but were quickly persuaded. Clement asked Bernhard to begin, and he did not object. He knew little of Clement Larsson, but assumed that he would come out with some story about ghosts and trolls. As he knew that people liked to listen to such things, he thought it best to choose something of the same sort.

"Some centuries ago," he began, "a dean here in Delsbo township was riding through the dense forest on a New Year's Eve. He was on horseback, dressed in fur coat and cap. On the pommel of his saddle hung a satchel in which he kept the communion service, the prayer-book, and the clerical robe. He had been summoned on a parochial errand to a remote forest settlement, where he had talked with a sick person until late in the evening. Now he was on his way home, but feared that he should not get back to the rectory until after midnight.

"As he had to sit in the saddle when he should have been at home in his bed, he was glad it was not a rough night. The weather was mild, the air still and the skies overcast. Behind the clouds hung a full round moon which gave some light, although it was out of sight. But for that faint light it would have been impossible for him to distinguish paths from fields, for that was a snowless winter, and all things had the same grayish-brown color.

"The horse the dean rode was one he prized very highly. He was strong and sturdy, and quite as wise as a human being. He could find his way home from any place in the township. The dean had observed this on several occasions, and he relied upon it with such a sense of security that he never troubled himself to think where he was going when he rode that horse. So he came along now in the gray night, through the bewildering forest, with the reins dangling and his thoughts far away.

"He was thinking of the sermon he had to preach on the morrow, and of much else besides, and it was a long time before it occurred to him to notice how far along he was on his homeward way. When he did glance up, he saw that the forest was as dense about him as at the beginning, and he was somewhat surprised, for he had ridden so long that he should have come to the inhabited portion of the township.

"Delsbo was about the same then as now. The church and parsonage and all the large farms and villages were at the northern end of the township, while at the southern part there were only forests and mountains. The dean saw that he was still in the unpopulated district and knew that he was in the southern part and must ride to the north to get home. There were no stars, nor was there a moon to guide him, but he was a man who had the four cardinal points in his head. He had the positive feeling that he was traveling southward, or possibly eastward.

"He intended to turn the horse at once, but hesitated. The animal had never strayed, and it did not seem likely that he would do so now. It was more likely that the dean was mistaken. He had been far away in thought and had not looked at the road. So he let the horse continue in the same direction, and again lost himself in his reverie.

"Suddenly a big branch struck him and almost swept him off the horse. Then he realized that he must find out where he was.

"He glanced down and saw that he was riding over a soft marsh, where there was no beaten path. The horse trotted along at a brisk pace and showed no uncertainty. Again the dean was positive that he was going in the wrong direction, and now he did not hesitate to interfere. He seized the reins and turned the horse about, guiding him back to the roadway. No sooner was he there than he turned again and made straight for the woods.

"The dean was certain that he was going wrong, but because the beast was so persistent he thought that probably he was trying to find a better road, and let him go along.

"The horse did very well, although he had no path to follow. If a precipice obstructed his way, he climbed it as nimbly as a goat, and later, when they had to descend, he bunched his hoofs and slid down the rocky inclines.

"'May he only find his way home before church hour!' thought the dean. 'I wonder how the Delsbo folk would take it if I were not at my church on time?'

"He did not have to brood over this long, for soon he came to a place that was familiar to him. It was a little creek where he had fished the summer before. Now he saw it was as he had feared—he was in the depths of the forest, and the horse was plodding along in a south-easterly direction. He seemed determined to carry the dean as far from church and rectory as he could.

"The clergyman dismounted. He could not let the horse carry him into the wilderness. He must go home. And, since the animal persisted in going in the wrong direction, he decided to walk and lead him until they came to more familiar roads. The dean wound the reins around his arm and began to walk. It was not an easy matter to tramp through the forest in a heavy fur coat, but the dean was strong and hardy and had little fear of overexertion.

"The horse, meanwhile, caused him fresh anxiety. He would not follow but planted his hoofs firmly on the ground and balked.

"At last the dean was angry. He had never beaten that horse, nor did he wish to do so now. Instead, he threw down the reins and walked away.

"'We may as well part company here, since you want to go your own way,' he said.

"He had not taken more than two steps before the horse came after him, took a cautious grip on his coat sleeve and stopped him. The dean turned and looked the horse straight in the eyes, as if to search out why he behaved so strangely.

"Afterward the dean could not quite understand how this was possible, but it is certain that, dark as it was, he plainly saw the horse's face and read it like that of a human being. He realized that the animal was in a terrible state of apprehension and fear. He gave his master a look that was both imploring and reproachful.

"'I have served you day after day and done your bidding,' he seemed to say. 'Will you not follow me this one night?'

"The dean was touched by the appeal in the animal's eyes. It was clear that the horse needed his help tonight, in one way or another. Being a man through and through, the dean promptly determined to follow him. Without further delay he sprang into the saddle. 'Go on!' he said. 'I will not desert you since you want me. No one shall say of the dean in Delsbo that he refused to accompany any creature who was in trouble.'

"He let the horse go as he wished and thought only of keeping his seat. It proved to be a hazardous and troublesome journey—uphill most of the way. The forest was so thick that he could not see two feet ahead, but it appeared to him that they were ascending a high mountain. The horse climbed perilous steeps. Had the dean been guiding, he should not have thought of riding over such ground.

"'Surely you don't intend to go up to Black's Ridge, do you?' laughed the dean, who knew that was one of the highest peaks in Hälsingland.

"During the ride he discovered that he and the horse were not the only ones who were out that night. He heard stones roll down and branches crackle, as if animals were breaking their way through the forest. He remembered that wolves were plentiful in that section and wondered if the horse wished to lead him to an encounter with wild beasts.

"They mounted up and up, and the higher they went the more scattered were the trees. At last they rode on almost bare highland, where the dean could look in every direction. He gazed out over immeasurable tracts of land, which went up and down in mountains and valleys covered with somber forests. It was so dark that he had difficulty in seeing any orderly arrangement, but presently he could make out where he was.

"'Why of course it's Black's Ridge that I've come to!' he remarked to himself. 'It can't be any other mountain, for there, in the west, I see Jarv Island, and to the east the sea glitters around Ag Island. Toward the north also I see something shiny. It must be Dellen. In the depths below me I see white smoke from Nian Falls. Yes, I'm up on Black's Ridge. What an adventure!'

"When they were at the summit the horse stopped behind a thick pine, as if to hide. The dean bent forward and pushed aside the branches, that he might have an unobstructed view.

"The mountain's bald pate confronted him. It was not empty and desolate, as he had anticipated. In the middle of the open space was an immense boulder around which many wild beasts had gathered. Apparently they were holding a conclave of some sort.

"Near to the big rock he saw bears, so firmly and heavily built that they seemed like fur-clad blocks of stone. They were lying down and their little eyes blinked impatiently; it was obvious that they had come from their winter sleep to attend court, and that they could hardly keep awake. Behind them, in tight rows, were hundreds of wolves. They were not sleepy, for wolves are more alert in winter than in summer. They sat upon their haunches, like dogs, whipping the ground with their tails and panting—their tongues lolling far out of their jaws. Behind the wolves the lynx skulked, stiff-legged and clumsy, like misshapen cats. They were loath to be among the other beasts, and hissed and spat when one came near them. The row back of the lynx was occupied by the wolverines, with dog faces and bear coats. They were not happy on the ground, and they stamped their pads impatiently, longing to get into the trees. Behind them, covering the entire space to the forest border, leaped the foxes, the weasels, and the martens. These were small and perfectly formed, but they looked even more savage and bloodthirsty than the larger beasts.

"All this the dean plainly saw, for the whole place was illuminated. Upon the huge rock at the center was the wood nymph, who held in her hand a pine torch which burned in a big red flame. The nymph was as tall as the tallest tree in the forest. She wore a spruce-brush mantle and had spruce-cone hair. She stood very still, her face turned toward the forest. She was watching and listening.

"The dean saw everything as plain as plain could be, but his astonishment was so great that he tried to combat it, and would not believe the evidence of his own eyes.

"'Such things cannot possibly happen!' he thought. 'I have ridden much too long in the bleak forest. This is only an optical illusion.'

"Nevertheless he gave the closest attention to the spectacle, and wondered what was about to be done.

"He hadn't long to wait before he caught the sound of a familiar bell, coming from the depths of the forest, and the next moment he heard footfalls and crackling of branches, as when many animals break through the forest.

"A big herd of cattle was climbing the mountain. They came through the forest in the order in which they had marched to the mountain ranches. First came the bell cow followed by the bull, then the other cows and the calves. The sheep, closely herded, followed. After them came the goats, and last were the horses and colts. The sheep dog trotted along beside the sheep, but neither shepherd nor shepherdess attended them.

"The dean thought it heartrending to see the tame animals coming straight toward the wild beasts. He would gladly have blocked their way and called 'Halt!' but he understood that it was not within human power to stop the march of the cattle on this night, therefore he made no move.

"The domestic animals were in a state of torment over that which they had to face. If it happened to be the bell cow's turn, she advanced with drooping head and faltering step. The goats had no desire either to play or to butt. The horses tried to bear up bravely, but their bodies were all of a quiver with fright. The most pathetic of all was the sheep dog. He kept his tail between his legs and crawled on the ground.

"The bell cow led the procession all the way up to the wood nymph, who stood on the boulder at the top of the mountain. The cow walked around the rock and then turned toward the forest without any of the wild beasts touching her. In the same way all the cattle walked unmolested past the wild beasts.

"As the creatures filed past, the dean saw the wood nymph lower her pine torch over one and another of them.

"Every time this occurred the beasts of prey broke into loud, exultant roars—particularly when it was lowered over a cow or some other large creature. The animal that saw the torch turning toward it uttered a piercing shriek, as if it had received a knife thrust in its flesh, while the entire herd to which it belonged bellowed their lamentations.

"Then the dean began to comprehend the meaning of what he saw. Surely he had heard that the animals in Delsbo assembled on Black's Ridge every New Year's Eve, that the wood nymph might mark out which among the tame beasts would that year be prey for the wild beasts. The dean pitied the poor creatures that were at the mercy of savage beasts, when in reality they should have no master but man.

"The leading herd had only just left when another bell tinkled, and the cattle from another farm tramped to the mountain top. These came in the same order as the first and marched past the wood nymph, who stood there, stern and solemn, indicating animal after animal for death.

"Herd upon herd followed, without a break in the line of procession. Some were so small that they included only one cow and a few sheep; others consisted of only a pair of goats. It was apparent that these were from very humble homes, but they too were compelled to pass in review.

"The dean thought of the Delsbo farmers, who had so much love for their beasts. 'Did they but know of it, surely they would not allow a repetition of this!' he thought. 'They would risk their own lives rather than let their cattle wander amongst bears and wolves, to be doomed by the wood nymph!'

"The last herd to appear was the one from the rectory farm. The dean heard the sound of the familiar bell a long way off. The horse, too, must have heard it, for he began to shake in every limb, and was bathed in sweat.

"'So it is your turn now to pass before the wood nymph to receive your sentence,' the dean said to the horse. 'Don't be afraid! Now I know why you brought me here, and I shall not leave you.'

"The fine cattle from the parsonage farm emerged from the forest and marched to the wood nymph and the wild beasts. Last in the line was the horse that had brought his master to Black's Ridge. The dean did not leave the saddle, but let the animal take him to the wood nymph.

"He had neither knife nor gun for his defense, but he had taken out the prayer-book and sat pressing it to his heart as he exposed himself to battle against evil.

"At first it appeared as if none had observed him. The dean's cattle filed past the wood nymph in the same order as the others had done. She did not wave the torch toward any of these, but as soon as the intelligent horse stepped forward, she made a movement to mark him for death.

"Instantly the dean held up the prayer book, and the torch light fell upon the cross on its cover. The wood nymph uttered a loud, shrill cry; the torch dropped from her hand and fell to the ground.

"Immediately the flame was extinguished. In the sudden transition from light to darkness the dean saw nothing, nor did he hear anything. About him reigned the profound stillness of a wilderness in winter.

"Then the dark clouds parted, and through the opening stepped the full round moon to shed its light upon the ground. The dean saw that he and the horse were alone on the summit of Black's Ridge. Not one of the many wild beasts was there. The ground had not been trampled by the herds that had passed over it, but the dean himself sat with his prayer-book before him, while the horse under him stood trembling and foaming.

"By the time the dean reached home he no longer knew whether or not it had been a dream, a vision, or reality—this that he had seen, but he took it as a warning to him to remember the poor creatures who were at the mercy of wild beasts. He preached so powerfully to the Delsbo peasants that in his day all the wolves and bears were exterminated from that section of the country, although they may have returned since his time."

Here Bernhard ended his story. He received praise from all sides and it seemed to be a foregone conclusion that he would get the prize. The majority thought it a pity that Clement had to compete with him. But Clement, undaunted, began: "One day, while I was living at Skansen, just outside of Stockholm, and longing for home—" Then he told about the tiny midget he had ransomed so that he would not have to be confined in a cage, to be stared at by all the people. He told, also, that no sooner had he performed this act of mercy than he was rewarded for it. He talked and talked, and the astonishment of his hearers grew greater and greater, but when he came to the royal lackey and the beautiful book, all the dairy maids dropped their needlework and sat staring at Clement in open-eyed wonder at his marvelous experiences.

As soon as Clement had finished, the eldest of the dairymaids announced that he should have the muffler. "Bernhard related only things that happened to another, but Clement has himself been the hero of a true story, which I consider far more important."

In this all concurred. They regarded Clement with very different eyes after hearing that he had talked with the King, and the little fiddler was afraid to show how proud he felt. But at the very height of his elation some one asked him what had become of the midget.

"I had no time to set out the blue bowl for him myself," said Clement, "so I asked the old Laplander to do it. What has become of him since then I don't know."

No sooner had he spoken than a little pine cone came along and struck him on the nose. It did not drop from a tree, and none of the peasants had thrown it. It was simply impossible to tell whence it had come.

"Aha, Clement!" winked the dairymaid, "it appears as if the tiny folk were listening to us. You should not have left it to another to set out that blue bowl!"

XI

IN MEDELPAD

Friday, June seventeenth

The boy and the eagle were out bright and early the next morning. Gorgo hoped that he would get far up into West Bothnia that day. As luck would have it, he heard the boy remark to himself that in a country like the one through which they were now traveling it must be impossible for people to live.

The land which spread below them was Southern Medelpad. When the eagle heard the boy's remark, he replied:

"Up here they have forests for fields."

The boy thought of the contrast between the light, golden rye fields with their delicate blades that spring up in one summer, and the dark spruce forest with its solid trees which took many years to ripen for harvest.

"One who has to get his livelihood from such a field must have a deal of patience!" he observed.

Nothing more was said until they came to a place where the forest had been cleared, and the ground was covered with stumps and lopped-off branches. As they flew over this ground, the eagle heard the boy mutter to himself that it was a mighty ugly and poverty-stricken place.

"This field was cleared last winter," said the eagle. The boy thought of the harvesters at home, who rode on their reaping machines on fine summer mornings, and in a short time mowed a large field. But the forest field was harvested in winter. The lumber men went out in the wilderness when the snow was deep, and the cold most severe. It was tedious work to fell even one tree, and to hew down a forest such as this they must have been out in the open many weeks.

"They have to be hardy men to mow a field of this kind," he said.

When the eagle had taken two more wing strokes, they sighted a log cabin at the edge of the clearing. It had no windows and only two

323

loose boards for a door. The roof had been covered with bark and twigs, but now it was gaping, and the boy could see that inside the cabin there were only a few big stones to serve as a fireplace, and two board benches. When they were above the cabin the eagle suspected that the boy was wondering who could have lived in such a wretched hut as that.

"The reapers who mowed the forest field lived there," the eagle said.

The boy remembered how the reapers in his home had returned from their day's work, cheerful and happy, and how the best his mother had in the larder was always spread for them; while here, after the arduous work of the day, they must rest on hard benches in a cabin that was worse than an outhouse. And what they had to eat he could not imagine.

"I wonder if there are any harvest festivals for these laborers?" he questioned.

A little farther on they saw below them a wretchedly bad road winding through the forest. It was narrow and zigzag, hilly and stony, and cut up by brooks in many places. As they flew over it the eagle knew that the boy was wondering what was carted over a road like that.

"Over this road the harvest was conveyed to the stack," the eagle said.

The boy recalled what fun they had at home when the harvest wagons drawn by two sturdy horses, carried the grain from the field. The man who drove sat proudly on top of the load; the horses danced and pricked up their ears, while the village children, who were allowed to climb up on the sheaves, sat there laughing and shrieking, half-pleased, half-frightened. But here the great logs were drawn up and down steep hills; here the poor horses must be worked to their limit, and the driver must often be in peril. "I'm afraid there has been very little cheer along this road," the boy observed.

The eagle flew on with powerful wing strokes, and soon they came to a river bank covered with logs, chips, and bark. The eagle perceived that the boy wondered why it looked so littered up down there.

"Here the harvest has been stacked," the eagle told him.

The boy thought of how the grain stacks in his part of the country were piled up close to the farms, as if they were their greatest ornaments, while here the harvest was borne to a desolate river strand, and left there.

"I wonder if any one out in this wilderness counts his stacks, and compares them with his neighbor's?" he said.

A little later they came to Ljungen, a river which glides through a broad valley. Immediately everything was so changed that they might well think they had come to another country. The dark spruce forest had stopped on the inclines above the valley, and the slopes were clad in light-stemmed birches and aspens. The valley was so broad that in many places the river widened into lakes. Along the shores lay a large flourishing town.

As they soared above the valley the eagle realized that the boy was wondering if the fields and meadows here could provide a livelihood for so many people.

"Here live the reapers who mow the forest fields," the eagle said.

The boy was thinking of the lowly cabins and the hedged-in farms down in Skåne when he exclaimed:

"Why, here the peasants live in real manors. It looks as if it might be worth one's while to work in the forest!"

The eagle had intended to travel straight north, but when he had flown out over the river he understood that the boy wondered who handled the timber after it was stacked on the river bank.

The boy recollected how careful they had been at home never to let a grain be wasted, while here were great rafts of logs floating down the river, uncared-for. He could not believe that more than half of the logs ever reached their destination. Many were floating in midstream, and for them all went smoothly; others moved close to the shore, bumping against points of land, and some were left behind in the still waters of the creeks. On the lakes there were so many logs that they covered the entire surface of the water. These appeared to be lodged for an indefinite period. At the bridges they stuck; in the falls they were bunched, then they were pyramided and broken in two; afterward, in the rapids, they were blocked by the stones and massed into great heaps.

"I wonder how long it takes for the logs to get to the mill?" said the boy.

The eagle continued his slow flight down River Ljungen. Over many places he paused in the air on outspread wings, that the boy might see how this kind of harvest work was done.

Presently they came to a place where the loggers were at work. The eagle marked that the boy wondered what they were doing.

"They are the ones who take care of all the belated harvest," the eagle said.

The boy remembered the perfect ease with which his people at home had driven their grain to the mill. Here the men ran alongside the shores with long boat hooks, and with toil and effort urged the logs along. They waded out in the river and were soaked from top to toe. They jumped from stone to stone far out into the rapids, and they tramped on the rolling log heaps as calmly as though they were on flat ground. They were daring and resolute men.

"As I watch this, I'm reminded of the iron molders in the mining districts, who juggle with fire as if it were perfectly harmless," remarked the boy. "These loggers play with water as if they were its masters. They seem to have subjugated it so that it dare not harm them."

Gradually they neared the mouth of the river, and Bothnia Bay was beyond them. Gorgo flew no farther straight ahead, but went northward along the coast. Before they had traveled very far they saw a lumber camp as large as a small city. While the eagle circled back and forth above it, he heard the boy remark that this place looked interesting.

"Here you have the great lumber camp called Svartvik," the eagle said.

The boy thought of the mill at home, which stood peacefully embedded in foliage, and moved its wings very slowly. This mill, where they grind the forest harvest, stood on the water.

The mill pond was crowded with logs. One by one the helpers seized them with their cant hooks, crowded them into the chutes and hurried them along to the whirling saws. What happened the logs inside, the boy could not see, but he heard loud buzzing and roaring, and from the other end of the house small cars ran out, loaded with white planks. The cars ran on shining tracks down to the lumber yard, where the planks were piled in rows, forming streets like blocks of houses in a city. In one place they were building new piles; in another they were pulling down old ones. These were carried aboard two large vessels which lay waiting for cargo. The place was alive with workmen, and in the woods, back of the yard, they had their homes.

"They'll soon manage to saw up all the forests in Medelpad the way they work here," said the boy.

The eagle moved his wings just a little, and carried the boy above another large camp, very much like the first, with the mill, yard, wharf, and the homes of the workmen.

"This is called Kukikenborg," the eagle said.

He flapped his wings slowly, flew past two big lumber camps, and approached a large city. When the eagle heard the boy ask the name of it, he cried: "This is Sundsvall, the manor of the lumber districts."

The boy remembered the cities in Skåne, which looked so old and gray and solemn; while here in the bleak north the city of Sundsvall faced a beautiful bay, and looked young and happy and beaming. There was something odd about the city when one saw it from above, for in the middle stood a cluster of tall stone structures which looked so imposing that their match was hardly to be found in Stockholm. Around the stone buildings there was a large open space, then came a wreath of frame houses which looked pretty and cozy in their little gardens, but they seemed to be conscious of the fact that they were very much poorer than the stone houses, and dared not venture into their neighborhood.

"This must be both a wealthy and powerful city," remarked the boy. "Can it be possible that the poor forest soil is the source of all this?"

The eagle flapped his wings again, and went over to Aln Island, which lies opposite Sundsvall. The boy was greatly surprised to see all the sawmills that decked the shores. On Aln Island they stood, one next another, and on the mainland opposite were mill upon mill, lumber yard upon lumber yard. He counted forty, at least, but believed there were many more.

"How wonderful it all looks from up here!" he marveled. "So much life and activity I have not seen in any place save this on the whole trip. It is a great country that we have! Wherever I go, there is always something new for people to live upon."

XII

A MORNING IN
ÅNGERMANLAND

THE BREAD

Saturday, June eighteenth

Next morning, when the eagle had flown some distance into Ångermanland, he remarked that today he was the one who was hungry, and must find something to eat! He set the boy down in an enormous pine on a high mountain ridge, and away he flew.

The boy found a comfortable seat in a cleft branch from which he could look down over Ångermanland. It was a glorious morning! The sunshine gilded the treetops; a soft breeze played in the pine needles; the sweetest fragrance was wafted through the forest; a beautiful landscape spread before him, and the boy himself was happy and carefree. He felt that no one could be better off.

He had a perfect outlook in every direction. The country west of him was all peaks and table land, and the farther away they were, the higher and wilder they looked. To the east there were also many peaks, but these sank lower and lower toward the sea, where the land became perfectly flat. Everywhere he saw shining rivers and brooks which were having a troublesome journey with rapids and falls so long as they ran between mountains, but spread out clear and broad as they neared the shore of the coast. Bothnia Bay was dotted with islands and notched with points, but farther out was open, blue water, like a summer sky.

When the boy had had enough of the landscape he unloosed his knapsack, took out a morsel of fine white bread, and began to eat.

"I don't think I've ever tasted such good bread," said he. "And how much I have left! There's enough to last me for a couple of days." As he munched he thought of how he had come by the bread.

"It must be because I got it in such a nice way that it tastes so good to me," he said.

The golden eagle had left Medelpad the evening before. He had hardly crossed the border into Ångermanland when the boy caught a glimpse of a fertile valley and a river, which surpassed anything of the kind he had seen before.

As the boy glanced down at the rich valley, he complained of feeling hungry. He had had no food for two whole days, he said, and now he was famished. Gorgo did not wish to have it said that the boy had fared worse in his company than when he traveled with the wild geese, so he slackened his speed.

"Why haven't you spoken of this before?" he asked. "You shall have all the food you want. There's no need of your starving when you have an eagle for a traveling companion."

Just then the eagle sighted a farmer who was sowing a field near the river strand. The man carried the seeds in a basket suspended from his neck, and each time that it was emptied he refilled it from a seed sack which stood at the end of the furrow. The eagle reasoned it out that the sack must be filled with the best food that the boy could wish for, so he darted toward it. But before the bird could get there a terrible clamor arose about him. Sparrows, crows, and swallows came rushing up with wild shrieks, thinking that the eagle meant to swoop down upon some bird.

"Away, away, robber! Away, away, bird-killer!" they cried. They made such a racket that it attracted the farmer, who came running, so that Gorgo had to flee, and the boy got no seed.

The small birds behaved in the most extraordinary manner. Not only did they force the eagle to flee, they pursued him a long distance down the valley, and everywhere the people heard their cries. Women came out and clapped their hands so that it sounded like a volley of musketry, and the men rushed out with rifles.

The same thing was repeated every time the eagle swept toward the ground. The boy abandoned the hope that the eagle could procure any food for him. It had never occurred to him before that Gorgo was so much hated. He almost pitied him.

In a little while they came to a homestead where the housewife had just been baking. She had set a platter of sugared buns in the back yard to cool and was standing beside it, watching, so that the cat and dog should not steal the buns.

The eagle circled down to the yard, but dared not alight right under the eyes of the peasant woman. He flew up and down, irresolute; twice he came down as far as the chimney, then rose again.

The peasant woman noticed the eagle. She raised her head and followed him with her glance.

"How peculiarly he acts!" she remarked. "I believe he wants one of my buns."

She was a beautiful woman, tall and fair, with a cheery, open countenance. Laughing heartily, she took a bun from the platter, and held it above her head.

"If you want it, come and take it!" she challenged.

While the eagle did not understand her language, he knew at once that she was offering him the bun. With lightning speed, he swooped to the bread, snatched it, and flew toward the heights.

When the boy saw the eagle snatch the bread he wept for joy—not because he would escape suffering hunger for a few days, but because he was touched by the peasant woman's sharing her bread with a savage bird of prey.

Where he now sat on the pine branch he could recall at will the tall, fair woman as she stood in the yard and held up the bread.

She must have known that the large bird was a golden eagle—a plunderer, who was usually welcomed with loud shots; doubtless she had also seen the queer changeling he bore on his back. But she had not thought of what they were. As soon as she understood that they were hungry, she shared her good bread with them.

"If I ever become human again," thought the boy, "I shall look up the pretty woman who lives near the great river, and thank her for her kindness to us."

THE FOREST FIRE

While the boy was still at his breakfast he smelled a faint odor of smoke coming from the north. He turned and saw a tiny spiral, white as a mist, rise from a forest ridge—not from the one nearest him, but from the one beyond it. It looked strange to see smoke in the wild forest, but it might be that a mountain stock farm lay over yonder, and the women were boiling their morning coffee. It was remarkable the way that smoke increased and spread! It could not come from a ranch, but perhaps there were charcoal kilns in the forest.

The smoke increased every moment. Now it curled over the whole mountain top. It was not possible that so much smoke could come from a charcoal kiln. There must be a conflagration of some sort, for many birds flew over to the nearest ridge. Hawks, grouse, and other birds, who were so small that it was impossible to recognize them at such a distance, fled from the fire.

The tiny white spiral of smoke grew to a thick white cloud which rolled over the edge of the ridge and sank toward the valley. Sparks and flakes of soot shot up from the clouds, and here and there one could see a red flame in the smoke. A big fire was raging over there, but what was burning? Surely there was no large farm hidden in the forest. Now the smoke came not only from the ridge, but from the valley below it. Great clouds of smoke ascended; the forest itself was burning!

It was difficult for him to grasp the idea that the fresh, green pines could burn. If it really were the forest that was burning, perhaps the fire might spread all the way over to him. It seemed improbable, but he wished the eagle would soon return. It would be best to be away from this. The mere smell of the smoke which he drew in with every breath was a torture. All at once he heard a terrible crackling and sputtering. It came from the ridge nearest him. There, on the highest point, stood a tall pine like the one in which he sat. A moment before it had been a gorgeous red in the morning light; now all the needles flashed, and the pine caught fire. Never before had it looked so beautiful, but this was the last time it could exhibit any beauty, for the pine was the first tree on the ridge to burn. It was impossible to tell how the flames had reached it. Had the fire flown on red wings, or crawled along the ground like a snake? The great pine burned like a birch stem. Now smoke curled up in many places on the ridge. The forest fire was both bird and snake. It could fly in the air over wide stretches, or steal along the ground. The whole ridge was ablaze!

There was a hasty flight of birds that circled up through the smoke like big flakes of soot. They flew across the valley and came to the ridge where the boy sat. A horned owl perched beside him, and on a branch just above him a hen hawk alighted. These would have been dangerous neighbors at any other time, but now they did not even glance in his direction—only stared at the fire. Probably they could not make out what was wrong with the forest. A marten ran up the pine to the tip of a branch, and looked at the burning heights. Close beside the marten sat a squirrel, but they did not appear to notice each other.

Now the fire came rushing down the slope, hissing and roaring like a tornado. One could see the flames dart from tree to tree. Before a branch caught fire it was first enveloped in a thin veil of smoke, then all the needles grew red and it began to crackle and blaze.

In the glen below ran a little brook, bordered by elms and small birches. It appeared as if the flames would halt there. Leafy trees are not so ready to take fire as fir trees. The fire did pause as if before a gate that could stop it. It glowed and crackled and tried to leap across the brook to the pine woods on the other side, but could not reach them. For a short time the fire was thus restrained, then it shot a long flame over to the large, dry pine that stood on the slope, and this was soon ablaze. The fire had crossed the brook! With the roar and rush of the maddest storm and the wildest torrent the forest fire flew over to the ridge.

Then the hawk and the owl rose and the marten dashed down the tree. In a few seconds more the fire would reach the top of the pine, and the boy, too, would have to be moving. It was not easy to slide down the long, straight pine trunk. He took as firm a hold of it as he could, and slid in long stretches between the knotty branches; finally he tumbled headlong to the ground. He had no time to find out if he was hurt—only to hurry away. The fire raced down the pine like a raging tempest; the ground under his feet was hot and smoldering. On either side of him ran a lynx and an adder, and right beside the snake fluttered a mother grouse who was hurrying along with her little downy chicks.

When the refugees descended the mountain to the glen they met people fighting the fire. They had been there for some time, but the boy had been gazing so intently in the direction of the fire that he had not noticed them. In this glen there was a brook, bordered by a row of leaf trees, and back of these trees the people worked. They felled the fir trees nearest the elms, dipped water from the brook and poured it over the ground, washing away heather and myrtle to prevent the fire from stealing up to the birch brush.

The fleeing animals ran in and out among the men's feet, without attracting attention. No one struck at the adder or tried to catch the mother grouse as she ran back and forth with her little peeping birdlings. They did not even bother about Thumbietot. In their hands they held great, charred pine branches which had dropped into the brook, and it appeared as if they intended to challenge the fire with these weapons. There were not many men; it was strange to see them stand there, ready to fight, when all other living creatures were fleeing.

As the fire came roaring and rushing down the slope with its intolerable heat and suffocating smoke, ready to hurl itself over brook and tree wall, the people drew back at first as if unable to withstand it, but they did not flee far before they turned back. The conflagration raged with savage force, sparks poured like a rain of fire over the leaf trees, and long tongues of flame shot hissingly out from the smoke, as if the forest on the other side were sucking them in. But the tree wall was an obstruction behind which the men worked. When the ground began to smolder they brought water in their vessels and dampened it. When a tree became wreathed in smoke they felled it at once, threw it down and put out the flames. Where the fire crept along the heather, they beat it with the wet pine branches and smothered it. The smoke was so dense that it enveloped everything. One could not possibly see how the battle was going, but it was easy enough to understand that it was a hard fight, and that several times the fire came near penetrating farther.

But think! After a while the loud roar of the flames decreased, and the smoke cleared. By that time the leaf trees had lost all their foliage; the ground under them was charred; the faces of the men were blackened by smoke and dripping with sweat, but the forest fire was conquered. Soft white smoke crept along the ground, and from it peeped out a lot of black stumps. This was all there was left of the beautiful forests!

The boy scrambled up on a rock, so that he might see how the fire had been quenched. But now that the forest was saved, his peril began. The owl and the hawk turned their eyes toward him. Just then he heard a familiar voice calling to him. Gorgo, the golden eagle, came sweeping through the forest, and soon the boy was soaring among the clouds rescued from every peril.

XIII

WESTBOTTOM AND LAPLAND

THE FIVE SCOUTS

Once, at Skansen, the boy had sat under the steps of Bollnäs cottage and had overheard Clement Larsson and the old Laplander talk about Norrland. Both agreed that it was the most beautiful part of Sweden. Clement thought that the southern was the best, while the Laplander favored the northern part.

As they argued, it became plain that Clement had never been farther north than Härnösand. The Laplander laughed at him for speaking with such assurance of places that he had never seen.

"I think I shall have to tell you a story, Clement, to give you some idea of Lapland, since you have not seen it," volunteered the Laplander.

"It shall not be said of me that I refuse to listen to a story," retorted Clement, and the old Laplander began:

"It once happened that the birds who lived down in Sweden, south of the great Saméland, thought that they were overcrowded there and suggested moving northward.

"They came together to consider the matter. The young and eager birds wished to start at once, but the older and wiser ones passed a resolution to send scouts to explore the new country.

"'Let each of the five great bird families send out a scout,' said the old and wise birds, 'to learn if there is room for us all up there—food and hiding places.'

"Five intelligent and capable birds were immediately appointed by the five great bird families.

"The forest birds selected a grouse, the field birds a lark, the sea birds a gull, the freshwater birds a loon, and the cliff birds a snow sparrow.

"When the five chosen ones were ready to start, the grouse, who was the largest and most commanding, said:

"'There are great stretches of land ahead. If we travel together, it will be long before we cover all the territory that we must explore. If, on the other hand, we travel singly—each one exploring his special portion of the country—the whole business can be accomplished in a few days.'

"The other scouts thought the suggestion a good one, and agreed to act upon it.

"It was decided that the grouse should explore the midlands. The lark was to travel to the eastward, the sea gull still farther east, where the land bordered on the sea, while the loon should fly over the territory west of the midlands, and the snow sparrow to the extreme west.

"In accordance with this plan, the five birds flew over the whole Northland. Then they turned back and told the assembly of birds what they had discovered.

"The gull, who had traveled along the seacoast, spoke first.

"'The north is a fine country,' he said. 'The sounds are full of fish, and there are points and islands without number. Most of these are uninhabited, and the birds will find plenty of room there. The humans do a little fishing and sailing in the sounds, but not enough to disturb the birds. If the sea birds follow my advice, they will move north immediately.'

"When the gull had finished, the lark, who had explored the land back from the coast, spoke:

"'I don't know what the gull means by his islands and points,' said the lark. 'I have traveled only over great fields and flowery meadows. I have never before seen a country crossed by so many large streams. Their shores are dotted with homesteads, and at the mouth of the rivers are cities, but for the most part the country is very desolate. If the field birds follow my advice, they will move north immediately.'

"After the lark came the grouse, who had flown over the midlands.

"'I know neither what the lark means with his meadows nor the gull with his islands and points,' said he. 'I have seen only pine forests on this whole trip. There are also many rushing streams and great stretches of moss-grown swamp land, but all that is not river or swamp is forest. If the forest birds follow my advice, they will move north immediately.'

"After the grouse came the loon, who had explored the borderland to the west.

"'I don't know what the grouse means by his forests, nor do I know where the eyes of the lark and the gull could have been,' remarked the loon. 'There's hardly any land up there—only big lakes. Between beautiful shores glisten clear, blue mountain lakes, which pour into roaring waterfalls. If the freshwater birds follow my advice, they will move north immediately.'

"The last speaker was the snow sparrow, who had flown along the western boundary.

"'I don't know what the loon means by his lakes, nor do I know what countries the grouse, the lark, and the gull can have seen,' he said. 'I found one vast mountainous region up north. I didn't run across any fields or any pine forests, but peak after peak and highlands. I have seen ice fields and snow and mountain brooks, with water as white as milk. No farmers nor cattle nor homesteads have I seen, but only Laps and reindeer and huts met my eyes. If the cliff birds follow my advice, they will move north immediately.'

"When the five scouts had presented their reports to the assembly, they began to call one another liars, and were ready to fly at each other to prove the truth of their arguments.

"But the old and wise birds who had sent them out, listened to their accounts with joy, and calmed their fighting propensities.

"'You mustn't quarrel among yourselves,' they said. 'We understand from your reports that up north there are large mountain tracts, a big lake region, great forest lands, a wide plain, and a big group of islands. This is more than we have expected more than many a mighty kingdom can boast within its borders.'"

THE MOVING LANDSCAPE

Saturday, June eighteenth

The boy had been reminded of the old Laplander's story because he himself was now traveling over the country of which he had spoken. The eagle told him that the expanse of coast which spread beneath them was Westbottom, and that the blue ridges far to the west were in Lapland.

Only to be once more seated comfortably on Gorgo's back, after all that he had suffered during the forest fire, was a pleasure. Besides, they were having a fine trip. The flight was so easy that at times it seemed as if they were standing still in the air. The eagle beat and beat his wings, without appearing to move from the spot; on the other hand, everything under them seemed in motion. The whole earth and all things on it moved slowly southward. The forests, the fields, the fences, the rivers, the cities, the islands, the sawmills—all were on the march. The boy wondered whither they were bound. Had they grown tired of standing so far north, and wished to move toward the south?

Amid all the objects in motion there was only one that stood still: that was a railway train. It stood directly under them, for it was with the train as with Gorgo—it could not move from the spot. The locomotive sent forth smoke and sparks. The clatter of the wheels could be heard all the way up to the boy, but the train did not seem to move. The forests rushed by; the flag station rushed by; fences and telegraph poles rushed by, but the train stood still. A broad river with a long bridge came toward it, but the river and the bridge glided along under the train with perfect ease. Finally a railway station appeared. The station master stood on the platform with his red flag, and moved slowly toward the train.

When he waved his little flag, the locomotive belched even darker smoke curls than before, and whistled mournfully because it had to stand still. All of a sudden it began to move toward the south, like everything else.

The boy saw all the coach doors open and the passengers step out while both cars and people were moving southward.

He glanced away from the earth and tried to look straight ahead. Staring at the queer railway train had made him dizzy, but after he had gazed for a moment at a little white cloud, he was tired of that and looked down again—thinking all the while that the eagle and himself were quite still and that everything else was traveling on south. Fancy! Suppose the grain field just then running along under him—which must have been newly sown for he had not seen a green blade on it—were to travel all the way down to Skåne where the rye was in full bloom at this season!

Up here the pine forests were different: the trees were bare, the branches short and the needles were almost black. Many trees were bald at the top and looked sickly. If a forest like that were to journey down to Kolmården and see a real forest, how inferior it would feel!

The gardens which he now saw had some pretty bushes, but no fruit trees or lindens or chestnut trees—only mountain ash and birch. There were some vegetable beds, but they were not as yet planted.

"If such an apology for the garden were to come trailing into Sörmland, the province of gardens, wouldn't it think itself a poor wilderness by comparison?"

Imagine an immense plain like the one now gliding beneath him, coming under the very eyes of the poor Småland peasants! They would hurry away begin their meager garden plots and stony fields, to begin plowing and sowing.

There was one thing, however, of which this Northland had more than other lands, and that was light. Night must have set in, for the cranes stood sleeping on the morass, but it was as light as day. The sun had not traveled southward, like every other thing. Instead, it had gone so far north that it shone in the boy's face. To all appearance, it had no setting that night.

If this light and this sun were only shining on West Vemmenhög! It would suit the boy's father and mother to a dot to have a working day that lasted twenty-four hours.

THE DREAM

Sunday, June nineteenth

The boy raised his head and looked around, perfectly bewildered. It was mighty queer! Here he lay sleeping in some place where he had not been before. No, he had never seen this glen nor the mountains round about, and never had he noticed such puny and shrunken birches as those under which he now lay.

Where was the eagle? The boy could see no sign of him. Gorgo must have deserted him. Well, here was another adventure!

The boy lay down again, closed his eyes, and tried to recall the circumstances under which he had dropped to sleep.

He remembered that as long as he was traveling over Westbottom he had fancied that the eagle and he were at a standstill in the air, and that the land under them was moving southward. As the eagle turned northwest, the wind had come from that side, and again he had felt a current of air, so that the land below had stopped moving and he had noticed that the eagle was bearing him onward with terrific speed.

"Now we are flying into Lapland," Gorgo had said, and the boy had bent forward, so that he might see the country of which he had heard so much.

But he had felt rather disappointed at not seeing anything but great tracts of forest land and wide marshes. Forest followed marsh and marsh followed forest. The monotony of the whole finally made him so sleepy that he had nearly dropped to the ground.

He said to the eagle that he could not stay on his back another minute, but must sleep awhile. Gorgo had promptly swooped to the ground, where the boy had dropped down on a moss tuft. Then Gorgo put a talon around him and soared into the air with him again.

"Go to sleep, Thumbietot!" he cried. "The sunshine keeps me awake and I want to continue the journey."

Although the boy hung in this uncomfortable position, he actually dozed and dreamed.

He dreamed that he was on a broad road in southern Sweden, hurrying along as fast as his little legs could carry him. He was not alone, many wayfarers were tramping in the same direction. Close beside him marched grain-filled rye blades, blossoming corn flowers, and yellow daisies. Heavily laden apple trees went puffing along, followed by vine-covered bean stalks, big clusters of white daisies, and masses of berry bushes. Tall beeches and oaks and lindens strolled leisurely in the middle of the road, their branches swaying, and they stepped aside for none. Between the boy's tiny feet darted the little flowers—wild strawberry blossoms, white anemones, clover, and forget-me-nots. At first he thought that only the vegetable family was on the march, but presently he saw that animals and people accompanied them. The insects were buzzing around advancing bushes, the fishes were swimming in moving ditches, the birds were singing in strolling trees. Both tame and wild beasts were racing, and amongst all this people moved along some with spades and scythes, others with axes, and others, again, with fishing nets.

The procession marched with gladness and gaiety, and he did not wonder at that when he saw who was leading it. It was nothing less than the Sun itself that rolled on like a great shining head with hair of many-hued rays and a countenance beaming with merriment and kindliness!

"Forward, march!" it kept calling out. "None need feel anxious whilst I am here. Forward, march!"

"I wonder where the Sun wants to take us to?" remarked the boy. A rye blade that walked beside him heard him, and immediately answered:

"He wants to take us up to Lapland to fight the Ice Witch."

Presently the boy noticed that some of the travelers hesitated, slowed up, and finally stood quite still. He saw that the tall beech tree stopped, and that the roebuck and the wheat blade tarried by the way-side, likewise the blackberry bush, the little yellow buttercup, the chestnut tree, and the grouse.

He glanced about him and tried to reason out why so many stopped. Then he discovered that they were no longer in southern Sweden. The march had been so rapid that they were already in Svealand.

Up there the oak began to move more cautiously. It paused awhile to consider, took a few faltering steps, then came to a standstill.

"Why doesn't the oak come along?" asked the boy.

"It's afraid of the Ice Witch," said a fair young birch that tripped along so boldly and cheerfully that it was a joy to watch it. The crowd hurried on as before. In a short time they were in Norrland, and now it mattered not how much the Sun cried and coaxed—the apple tree stopped, the cherry tree stopped, the rye blade stopped!

The boy turned to them and asked:

"Why don't you come along? Why do you desert the Sun?"

"We dare not! We're afraid of the Ice Witch, who lives in Lapland," they answered.

The boy comprehended that they were far north, as the procession grew thinner and thinner. The rye blade, the barley, the wild strawberry, the blueberry bush, the pea stalk, the currant bush had come along as far as this. The elk and the domestic cow had been walking side by side, but now they stopped. The Sun no doubt would have been almost deserted if new followers had not happened along. Osier bushes and a lot of brushy vegetation joined the procession. Laps and reindeer, mountain owl and mountain fox and willow grouse followed.

Then the boy heard something coming toward them. He saw great rivers and creeks sweeping along with terrible force.

"Why are they in such a hurry?" he asked.

"They are running away from the Ice Witch, who lives up in the mountains."

All of a sudden the boy saw before him a high, dark, turreted wall. Instantly the Sun turned its beaming face toward this wall and flooded it with light. Then it became apparent that it was no wall, but the most glorious mountains, which loomed up one behind another. Their peaks were rose-colored in the sunlight, their slopes azure and gold tinted.

"Onward, onward!" urged the Sun as it climbed the steep cliffs. "There's no danger so long as I am with you."

But half way up, the bold young birch deserted—also the sturdy pine and the persistent spruce, and there, too, the Laplander, the reindeer, and the willow brush deserted. At last, when the Sun reached the top, there was no one but the little tot, Nils Holgersson, who had followed it.

The Sun rolled into a cave, where the walls were bedecked with ice, and Nils Holgersson wanted to follow, but farther than the opening of the cave he dared not venture, for in there he saw something dreadful.

Far back in the cave sat an old witch with an ice body, hair of icicles, and a mantle of snow!

At her feet lay three black wolves, who rose and opened their jaws when the Sun approached. From the mouth of one came a piercing cold, from the second a blustering north wind, and from the third came impenetrable darkness.

"That must be the Ice Witch and her tribe," thought the boy.

He understood that now was the time for him to flee, but he was so curious to see the outcome of the meeting between the Sun and the Ice Witch that he tarried.

The Ice Witch did not move, and only turned her hideous face toward the Sun. The Sun stood still and just beamed and smiled. This continued for a short time. It appeared to the boy that the witch was beginning to sigh and tremble. Her snow mantle fell, and the three ferocious wolves howled less savagely.

Suddenly the Sun cried: "Now my time is up!" and rolled out of the cave. Then the Ice Witch let loose her three wolves. Instantly the North Wind, Cold, and Darkness rushed from the cave and began to chase the Sun.

"Drive him out! Drive him back!" shrieked the Ice Witch. "Chase him so far that he can never come back! Teach him that Lapland is MINE!"

But Nils Holgersson felt so unhappy when he saw that the Sun was to be driven from Lapland that he awakened with a cry. When he recovered his senses, he found himself at the bottom of a ravine. But where was Gorgo? How was he to find out where he himself was? He arose and looked all around him. Then he happened to glance upward and saw a peculiar structure of pine twigs and branches that stood on a cliff ledge.

"That must be one of those eagle nests that Gorgo—" But this was as far as he got. He tore off his cap, waved it in the air, and cheered.

Now he understood where Gorgo had brought him. This was the very glen where the wild geese lived in summer, and just above it was the eagles' cliff. He had arrived!

He would meet Morten Goosey-Gander and Akka and all the other comrades in a few moments. Hurrah!

THE MEETING

All was still in the glen. The sun had not yet stepped above the cliffs, and Nils Holgersson knew that it was too early in the morning for the geese to be awake.

The boy walked along leisurely and searched for his friends. Before he had gone very far, he paused with a smile, for he saw such a pretty sight. A wild goose was sleeping in a neat little nest, and beside her stood her goosey-gander. He too, slept, but it was obvious that he had stationed himself thus near her that he might be on hand in the possible event of danger.

The boy went on without disturbing them and peeped into the willow brush that covered the ground. It was not long before he spied another goose couple. These were strangers, not of his flock, but he was so happy that he began to hum just because he had come across wild geese.

He peeped into another bit of brushwood. There at last he saw two that were familiar.

It was certainly Neljä that was nesting there, and the goosey-gander who stood beside her was surely Kolme. Why, of course!

The boy had a good mind to awaken them, but he let them sleep on, and walked away.

In the next brush he saw Viisi and Kuusi, and not far from them he found Yksi and Kaksi. All four were asleep, and the boy passed by without disturbing them.

As he approached the next brush, he thought he saw something white shimmering among the bushes, and the heart of him thumped with joy.

Yes, it was as he expected. In there sat the dainty Dunfin on an egg-filled nest. Beside her stood her white goosey-gander. Although he slept, it was easy to see how proud he was to watch over his wife up here among the Lapland mountains. The boy did not care to waken the goosey-gander, so he walked on.

He had to seek a long time before he came across any more wild geese. Finally, he saw on a little hillock something that resembled a small, gray moss tuft, and he knew that there was Akka from Kebnekaise. She stood, wide awake, looking about as if she were keeping watch over the whole glen.

"Good morning, Mother Akka!" said the boy. "Please don't waken the other geese yet for awhile; I wish to speak with you in private."

The old leader goose came rushing down the hill and up to the boy.

First she seized hold of him and shook him, then she stroked him with her bill before she shook him again. But she did not say a word, since he asked her not to waken the others.

Thumbietot kissed old Mother Akka on both cheeks, then he told her how he had been carried off to Skansen and held captive there.

"Now I must tell you that Smirre Fox, short of an ear, sat imprisoned in the foxes' cage at Skansen," said the boy. "Although he was very mean to us, I couldn't help feeling sorry for him. There were many other foxes in the cage, and they seemed quite contented there, but Smirre sat all the while looking dejected, longing for liberty.

"I made many good friends at Skansen, and I learned one day from the Lap dog that a man had come to Skansen to buy foxes. He was from some island far out in the ocean. All the foxes had been exterminated there, and the rats were about to get the better of the inhabitants, so they wished the foxes back again.

"As soon as I learned of this, I went to Smirre's cage and said to him:

"'Tomorrow some men are coming here to get a pair of foxes. Don't hide, Smirre, but keep well in the foreground and see to it that you are chosen. Then you'll be free again.'

"He followed my suggestion, and now he is running at large on the island. What say you to this, Mother Akka? If you had been in my place, would you not have done likewise?"

"You have acted in a way that makes me wish I had done that myself," said the leader goose proudly.

"It's a relief to know that you approve," said the boy. "Now there is one thing more I wish to ask you about:

"One day I happened to see Gorgo, the eagle—the one that fought with Morten Goosey-Gander—a prisoner at Skansen. He was in the eagles' cage and looked pitifully forlorn. I was thinking of filing down the wire roof over him and letting him out, but I also thought of his being a dangerous robber and bird eater, and wondered if I should be doing right in letting loose such a plunderer, and if it were not better, perhaps, to let him stay where he was. What say you, Mother Akka? Was it right to think thus?"

"No, it was not right!" retorted Akka. "Say what you will about the eagles, they are proud birds and greater lovers of freedom than all others. It is not right to keep them in captivity.

"Do you know what I would suggest? This: that, as soon as you are well rested, we two make the trip together to the big bird prison, and liberate Gorgo."

"That is just the word I was expecting from you, Mother Akka," returned the boy eagerly.

"There are those who say that you no longer have any love in your heart for the one you reared so tenderly, because he lives as eagles must live. But I know now that it isn't true. I want to see if Morten Goosey-Gander is awake.

"Meanwhile, if you wish to say a 'thank you' to the one who brought me here to you, I think you'll find him up there on the cliff ledge, where once you found a helpless eaglet."

XIV

OSA, THE GOOSE GIRL, AND LITTLE MATS

*T*he year that Nils Holgersson traveled with the wild geese every-body was talking about two little children, a boy and a girl, who tramped through the country. They were from Sunnerbo township, in Småland, and had once lived with their parents and four brothers and sisters in a little cabin on the heath.

While the two children, Osa and Mats, were still small, a poor, homeless woman came to their cabin one night and begged for shelter. Although the place could hardly hold the family, she was taken in and the mother spread a bed for her on the floor. In the night she coughed so hard that the children fancied the house shook. By morning she was too ill to continue her wanderings. The children's father and mother were as kind to her as could be. They gave up their bed to her and slept on the floor, while the father went to the doctor and brought her medicine.

The first few days the sick woman behaved like a savage; she demanded constant attention and never uttered a word of thanks. Later she became more subdued and finally begged to be carried out to the heath and left there to die.

When her hosts would not hear of this, she told them that the last few years she had roamed about with a band of gypsies. She herself was not of gypsy blood, but was the daughter of a well-to-do farmer. She had run away from home and gone with the nomads. She believed that a gypsy woman who was angry at her had brought this sickness upon her. Nor was that all: The gypsy woman had also cursed her, saying that all who took her under their roof or were kind to her should suffer a like fate. She believed this, and therefore begged them to cast her out of the house and never to see her again. She did not want to bring misfortune down upon such good people. But the peasants refused to do her bidding. It was quite possible that they were alarmed, but they were not the kind of folk who could turn out a poor, sick person.

Soon after that she died, and then along came the misfortunes. Before, there had never been anything but happiness in that cabin. Its inmates were poor, yet not so very poor. The father was a maker of weavers' combs, and mother and children helped him with the work. Father made the frames, mother and the older children did the binding, while the smaller ones planed the teeth and cut them out. They worked from morning until night, but the time passed pleasantly, especially when father talked of the days when he traveled about in foreign lands and sold weavers' combs. Father was so jolly that sometimes mother and the children would laugh until their sides ached at his funny quips and jokes.

The weeks following the death of the poor vagabond woman lingered in the minds of the children like a horrible nightmare. They knew not if the time had been long or short, but they remembered that they were always having funerals at home. One after another they lost their brothers and sisters. At last it was very still and sad in the cabin.

The mother kept up some measure of courage, but the father was not a bit like himself. He could no longer work nor jest, but sat from morning till night, his head buried in his hands, and only brooded.

Once—that was after the third burial—the father had broken out into wild talk, which frightened the children. He said that he could not understand why such misfortunes should come upon them. They had done a kindly thing in helping the sick woman. Could it be true, then, that the evil in this world was more powerful than the good?

The mother tried to reason with him, but she was unable to soothe him.

A few days later the eldest sister was stricken. She had always been the father's favorite, so when he realized that she, too, must go, he fled from all the misery. The mother never said anything, but she thought it was best for him to be away, as she feared that he might lose his reason. He had brooded too long over this one idea: that God had allowed a wicked person to bring about so much evil.

After the father went away they became very poor. For a while he sent them money, but afterward things must have gone badly with him, for no more came.

The day of the eldest daughter's burial the mother closed the cabin and left home with the two remaining children, Osa and Mats. She went down to Skåne to work in the beet fields, and found a place at the Jordberga sugar refinery. She was a good worker and had a cheerful and generous nature. Everybody liked her. Many were astonished because she could be so calm after all that she had passed through, but the mother was very strong and patient. When any one spoke to her of her two sturdy children, she only said: "I shall soon lose them also," without a quaver in her voice or a tear in her eye. She had accustomed herself to expect nothing else.

But it did not turn out as she feared. Instead, the sickness came upon herself. She had gone to Skåne in the beginning of summer, before autumn she was gone, and the children were left alone.

While their mother was ill she had often said to the children they must remember that she never regretted having let the sick woman stop with them. It was not hard to die when one had done right, she said, for then one could go with a clear conscience.

Before the mother passed away, she tried to make some provision for her children. She asked the people with whom she lived to let them remain in the room which she had occupied. If the children only had a shelter they would not become a burden to any one. She knew that they could take care of themselves.

Osa and Mats were allowed to keep the room on condition that they would tend the geese, as it was always hard to find children willing to do that work. It turned out as the mother expected: they did maintain themselves. The girl made candy, and the boy carved wooden toys, which they sold at the farm houses. They had a talent for trading and soon began buying eggs and butter from the farmers, which they sold to the workers at the sugar refinery. Osa was the older, and, by the time she was thirteen, she was as responsible as a grown woman. She was quiet and serious, while Mats was lively and talkative. His sister used to say of him that he could out cackle the geese. When the children had been at Jordberga for two years, there was a lecture given one evening at the schoolhouse. Evidently it was meant for grown-ups, but the two Småland children were in the audience. They did not regard themselves as children, and few persons thought of them as such. The lecturer talked about the dread disease called the white plague, which every year carried off so many people in Sweden. He spoke very plainly and the children understood every word.

After the lecture they waited outside the schoolhouse. When the lecturer came out they took hold of hands and walked gravely up to him, asking if they might speak to him.

The stranger must have wondered at the two rosy, baby-faced children standing there talking with an earnestness more in keeping with people three times their age, but he listened graciously to them. They related what had happened in their home, and asked the lecturer if he thought their mother and their sisters and brothers had died of the sickness he had described.

"Very likely," he answered. "It could hardly have been any other disease."

If only the mother and father had known what the children learned that evening, they might have protected themselves. If they had burned the clothing of the vagabond woman, if they had scoured and aired the cabin and had not used the old bedding, all whom the children mourned might have been living yet. The lecturer said he could not say positively, but he believed that none of their dear ones would have been sick had they understood how to guard against the infection.

Osa and Mats waited awhile before putting the next question, for that was the most important of all. It was not true then that the gypsy woman had sent the sickness because they had befriended the one with whom she was angry. It was not something special that had stricken only them. The lecturer assured them that no person had the power to bring sickness upon another in that way.

Thereupon the children thanked him and went to their room. They talked until late that night.

The next day they gave notice that they could not tend geese another year, but must go elsewhere. Where were they going? Why, to try to find their father. They must tell him that their mother and the other children had died of a common ailment and not something special brought upon them by an angry person. They were very glad that they had found out about this. Now it was their duty to tell their father of it, for probably he was still trying to solve the mystery.

Osa and Mats set out for their old home on the heath. When they arrived they were shocked to find the little cabin in flames. They went to the parsonage and there they learned that a railroad workman had seen their father at Malmberget, far up in Lapland. He had been working in a mine and possibly was still there. When the clergyman heard that the children wanted to go in search of their father he brought forth a map and showed them how far it was to Malmberget and tried to dissuade them from making the journey, but the children insisted that they must find their father. He had left home believing something that was not true. They must find him and tell him that it was all a mistake.

They did not want to spend their little savings buying railway tickets, therefore they decided to go all the way on foot, which they never regretted, as it proved to be a remarkably beautiful journey.

Before they were out of Småland, they stopped at a farmhouse to buy food. The housewife was a kind, motherly soul who took an interest in the children. She asked them who they were and where they came from, and they told her their story. "Dear, dear! Dear, dear!" she interpolated time and again when they were speaking. Later she petted the children and stuffed them with all kinds of goodies, for which she would not accept a penny. When they rose to thank her and go, the woman asked them to stop at her brother's farm in the next township. Of course the children were delighted.

"Give him my greetings and tell him what has happened to you," said the peasant woman.

This the children did and were well treated. From every farm after that it was always: "If you happen to go in such and such a direction, stop there or there and tell them what has happened to you."

In every farmhouse to which they were sent there was always a consumptive. So Osa and Mats went through the country unconsciously teaching the people how to combat that dreadful disease.

Long, long ago, when the black plague was ravaging the country, 'twas said that a boy and a girl were seen wandering from house to house. The boy carried a rake, and if he stopped and raked in front of a house, it meant that there many should die, but not all, for the rake has coarse teeth and does not take everything with it. The girl carried a broom, and if she came along and swept before a door, it meant that all who lived within must die, for the broom is an implement that makes a clean sweep.

It seems quite remarkable that in our time two children should wander through the land because of a cruel sickness. But these children did not frighten people with the rake and the broom. They said rather: "We will not content ourselves with merely raking the yard and sweeping the floors, we will use mop and brush, water and soap. We will keep clean inside and outside of the door and we ourselves will be clean in both mind and body. In this way we will conquer the sickness."

One day, while still in Lapland, Akka took the boy to Malmberget, where they discovered little Mats lying unconscious at the mouth of the pit. He and Osa had arrived there a short time before. That morning he had been roaming about, hoping to come across his father. He had ventured too near the shaft and been hurt by flying rocks after the setting off of a blast.

Thumbietot ran to the edge of the shaft and called down to the miners that a little boy was injured.

Immediately a number of laborers came rushing up to little Mats. Two of them carried him to the hut where he and Osa were staying. They did all they could to save him, but it was too late.

Thumbietot felt so sorry for poor Osa. He wanted to help and comfort her, but he knew that if he were to go to her now, he would only frighten her—such as he was!

The night after the burial of little Mats, Osa straightway shut herself in her hut.

She sat alone recalling, one after another, things her brother had said and done. There was so much to think about that she did not go straight to bed, but sat up most of the night. The more she thought of her the more she realized how hard it would be without him. At last she dropped her head on the table and wept.

"What shall I do now that little Mats is gone?" she sobbed.

It was far along toward morning and Osa, spent by the strain of her hard day, finally fell asleep. She dreamed that little Mats softly opened the door and stepped into the room.

"Osa, you must go and find Father," he said.

"How can I when I don't even know where he is?" she replied in her dream.

"Don't worry about that," returned little Mats in his usual, cheery way. "I'll send someone to help you."

Just as Osa, the goose girl, dreamed that little Mats had said this, there was a knock at the door. It was a real knock—not something she heard in the dream, but she was so held by the dream that she could not tell the real from the unreal. As she went on to open the door, she thought:

"This must be the person little Mats promised to send me."

She was right, for it was Thumbietot come to talk to her about her father.

When he saw that she was not afraid of him, he told her in a few words where her father was and how to reach him.

While he was speaking, Osa, the goose girl, gradually regained consciousness; when he had finished she was wide awake.

Then she was so terrified at the thought of talking with an elf that she could not say thank you or anything else, but quickly shut the door.

As she did that she thought she saw an expression of pain flash across the elf's face, but she could not help what she did, for she was beside herself with fright. She crept into bed as quickly as she could and drew the covers over her head.

Although she was afraid of the elf, she had a feeling that he meant well by her. So the next day she made haste to do as he had told her.

WITH THE LAPLANDERS

One afternoon in July it rained frightfully up around Lake Luossajaure. The Laplanders, who live mostly in the open during the summer, had crawled under the tent and were squatting round the fire drinking coffee.

The new settlers on the east shore of the lake worked diligently to have their homes in readiness before the severe Arctic winter set in. They wondered at the Laplanders, who had lived in the far north for centuries without even thinking that better protection was needed against cold and storm than thin tent covering.

The Laplanders, on the other hand, wondered at the new settlers giving themselves so much needless, hard work, when nothing more was necessary to live comfortably than a few reindeer and a tent.

They only had to drive the poles into the ground and spread the covers over them, and their abodes were ready. They did not have to trouble themselves about decorating or furnishing. The principal thing was to scatter some spruce twigs on the floor, spread a few skins, and hang the big kettle, in which they cooked their reindeer meat, on a chain suspended from the top of the tent poles.

While the Laplanders were chatting over their coffee cups, a rowboat coming from the Kiruna side pulled ashore at the Laps' quarters.

A workman and a young girl, between thirteen and fourteen, stepped from the boat. The girl was Osa. The Lap dogs bounded down to them, barking loudly, and a native poked his head out of the tent opening to see what was going on.

He was glad when he saw the workman, for he was a friend of the Laplanders—a kindly and sociable man, who could speak their native tongue. The Lap called to him to crawl under the tent.

354

"You're just in time, Söderberg!" he said. "The coffee pot is on the fire. No one can do any work in this rain, so come in and tell us the news."

The workman went in, and, with much ado and amid a great deal of laughter and joking, places were made for Söderberg and Osa, though the tent was already crowded to the limit with natives. Osa understood none of the conversation. She sat dumb and looked in wonderment at the kettle and coffee pot, at the fire and smoke, at the Lap men and Lap women, at the children and dogs, the walls and floor, the coffee cups and tobacco pipes, the multi-colored costumes and crude implements. All this was new to her.

Suddenly she lowered her glance, conscious that every one in the tent was looking at her. Söderberg must have said something about her, for now both Lap men and Lap women took the short pipes from their mouths and stared at her in open-eyed wonder and awe. The Laplander at her side patted her shoulder and nodded, saying in Swedish, "bra, bra!" (good, good!) A Lap woman filled a cup to the brim with coffee and passed it under difficulties, while a Lap boy, who was about her own age, wriggled and crawled between the squatters over to her.

Osa felt that Söderberg was telling the Laplanders that she had just buried her little brother, Mats. She wished he would find out about her father instead. The elf had said that he lived with the Laps, who camped west of Lake Luossajaure, and she had begged leave to ride up here on a sand truck to seek him, as no regular passenger trains came so far. Both laborers and foremen had assisted her as best they could. An engineer had sent Söderberg across the lake with her, as he spoke Lappish. She had hoped to meet her father as soon as she arrived. Her glance wandered anxiously from face to face, but she saw only natives. Her father was not there.

She noticed that the Laps and the Swede, Söderberg, grew more and more earnest as they talked among themselves. The Laps shook their heads and tapped their foreheads, as if they were speaking of someone that was not quite right in his mind. She became so uneasy that she could no longer endure the suspense and asked Söderberg what the Laplanders knew of her father.

"They say he has gone fishing," said the workman. "They're not sure that he can get back to the camp tonight, but as soon as the weather clears, one of them will go in search of him."

Thereupon he turned to the Laps and went on talking. He did not wish to give Osa an opportunity to question him further about Jon Esserson.

THE NEXT MORNING

Ola Serka himself, who was the most distinguished man among the Laps, had said that he would find Osa's father, but he appeared to be in no haste and sat huddled outside the tent, thinking of Jon Esserson and wondering how best to tell him of his daughter's arrival. It would require diplomacy in order that Jon Esserson might not become alarmed and flee. He was an odd sort of man who was afraid of children. He used to say that the sight of them made him so melancholy that he could not endure it. While Ola Serka deliberated, Osa, the goose girl, and Aslak, the young Lap boy who had stared so hard at her the night before, sat on the ground in front of the tent and chatted.

Aslak had been to school and could speak Swedish. He was telling Osa about the life of the "Saméfolk," assuring her that they fared better than other people.

Osa thought that they lived wretchedly, and told him so.

"You don't know what you are talking about!" said Aslak curtly. "Only stop with us a week and you shall see that we are the happiest people on earth."

"If I were to stop here a whole week, I should be choked by all the smoke in the tent," Osa retorted.

"Don't say that!" protested the boy. "You know nothing of us. Let me tell you something which will make you understand that the longer you stay with us the more contented you will become."

Thereupon Aslak began to tell Osa how a sickness called the black plague once raged throughout the land. He was not certain as to whether it had swept through the real "Saméland," where they now were, but in Jämtland it had raged so brutally that among the Saméfolk, who lived in the forests and mountains there, all had died except a boy of fifteen. Among the Swedes, who lived in the valleys, none was left but a girl, who was also fifteen years old.

The boy and girl separately tramped the desolate country all winter in search of other human beings. Finally, toward spring, the two met. Aslak continued: "The Swedish girl begged the Lap boy to accompany her southward, where she could meet people of her own race. She did not wish to tarry longer in Jämtland, where there were only vacant homesteads.

"'I'll take you wherever you wish to go,' said the boy, 'but not before winter. It's spring now, and my reindeer go westward toward the mountains. You know that we who are of the Saméfolk must go where our reindeer take us.'

"The Swedish girl was the daughter of wealthy parents. She was used to living under a roof, sleeping in a bed, and eating at a table. She had always despised the poor mountaineers and thought that those who lived under the open sky were most unfortunate, but she was afraid to return to her home, where there were none but the dead.

"'At least let me go with you to the mountains,' she said to the boy, 'so that I shan't have to tramp about here all alone and never hear the sound of a human voice.'

"The boy willingly assented, so the girl went with the reindeer to the mountains.

"The herd yearned for the good pastures there, and every day tramped long distances to feed on the moss. There was not time to pitch tents. The children had to lie on the snowy ground and sleep when the reindeer stopped to graze. The girl often sighed and complained of being so tired that she must turn back to the valley. Nevertheless she went along to avoid being left without human companionship.

"When they reached the highlands the boy pitched a tent for the girl on a pretty hill that sloped toward a mountain brook.

"In the evening he lassoed and milked the reindeer, and gave the girl milk to drink. He brought forth dried reindeer meat and reindeer cheese, which his people had stowed away on the heights when they were there the summer before.

"Still the girl grumbled all the while, and was never satisfied. She would eat neither reindeer meat nor reindeer cheese, nor would she drink reindeer milk. She could not accustom herself to squatting in the tent or to lying on the ground with only a reindeer skin and some spruce twigs for a bed.

"The son of the mountains laughed at her woes and continued to treat her kindly.

"After a few days, the girl went up to the boy when he was milking and asked if she might help him. She next undertook to make the fire under the kettle, in which the reindeer meat was to be cooked, then to carry water and to make cheese. So the time passed pleasantly. The weather was mild and food was easily procured. Together they set snares for game, fished for salmon-trout in the rapids and picked cloudberries in the swamp.

"When the summer was gone, they moved farther down the mountains, where pine and leaf forests meet. There they pitched their tent. They had to work hard every day, but fared better, for food was even more plentiful than in the summer because of the game.

"When the snow came and the lakes began to freeze, they drew farther east toward the dense pine forests.

"As soon as the tent was up, the winter's work began. The boy taught the girl to make twine from reindeer sinews, to treat skins, to make shoes and clothing of hides, to make combs and tools of reindeer horn, to travel on skis, and to drive a sledge drawn by reindeer.

"When they had lived through the dark winter and the sun began to shine all day and most of the night, the boy said to the girl that now he would accompany her southward, so that she might meet some of her own race.

"Then the girl looked at him astonished.

"'Why do you want to send me away?' she asked. 'Do you long to be alone with your reindeer?'

"'I thought that you were the one that longed to get away?' said the boy.

"'I have lived the life of the Saméfolk almost a year now,' replied the girl. 'I can't return to my people and live the shut-in life after having wandered freely on mountains and in forests. Don't drive me away, but let me stay here. Your way of living is better than ours.'

"The girl stayed with the boy for the rest of her life, and never again did she long for the valleys. And you, Osa, if you were to stay with us only a month, you could never again part from us."

With these words, Aslak, the Lap boy, finished his story. Just then his father, Ola Serka, took the pipe from his mouth and rose.

Old Ola understood more Swedish than he was willing to have any one know, and he had overheard his son's remarks. While he was listening, it had suddenly flashed on him how he should handle this delicate matter of telling Jon Esserson that his daughter had come in search of him.

Ola Serka went down to Lake Luossajaure and had walked a short distance along the strand, when he happened upon a man who sat on a rock fishing.

The fisherman was gray-haired and bent. His eyes blinked wearily and there was something slack and helpless about him. He looked like a man who had tried to carry a burden too heavy for him, or to solve a problem too difficult for him, who had become broken and despondent over his failure.

"You must have had luck with your fishing, Jon, since you've been at it all night?" said the mountaineer in Lappish, as he approached.

The fisherman gave a start, then glanced up. The bait on his hook was gone and not a fish lay on the strand beside him. He hastened to rebait the hook and throw out the line. In the meantime the mountaineer squatted on the grass beside him.

"There's a matter that I wanted to talk over with you," said Ola. "You know that I had a little daughter who died last winter, and we have always missed her in the tent."

"Yes, I know," said the fisherman abruptly, a cloud passing over his face—as though he disliked being reminded of a dead child.

"It's not worthwhile to spend one's life grieving," said the Laplander.

"I suppose it isn't."

"Now I'm thinking of adopting another child. Don't you think it would be a good idea?"

"That depends on the child, Ola."

"I will tell you what I know of the girl," said Ola. Then he told the fisherman that around midsummer, two strange children—a boy and a girl—had come to the mines to look for their father, but as their father was away, they had stayed to await his return. While there, the boy had been killed by a blast of rock.

Thereupon Ola gave a beautiful description of how brave the little girl had been, and of how she had won the admiration and sympathy of every one.

"Is that the girl you want to take into your tent?" asked the fisherman.

"Yes," returned the Lap. "When we heard her story we were all deeply touched and said among ourselves that so good a sister would also make a good daughter, and we hoped that she would come to us.

The fisherman sat quietly thinking a moment. It was plain that he continued the conversation only to please his friend, the Lap.

"I presume the girl is one of your race?"

"No," said Ola, "she doesn't belong to the Saméfolk."

"Perhaps she's the daughter of some new settler and is accustomed to the life here?"

"No, she's from the far south," replied Ola, as if this was of small importance.

The fisherman grew more interested.

"Then I don't believe that you can take her," he said. "It's doubtful if she could stand living in a tent in winter, since she was not brought up that way."

"She will find kind parents and kind brothers and sisters in the tent," insisted Ola Serka. "It's worse to be alone than to freeze."

The fisherman became more and more zealous to prevent the adoption. It seemed as if he could not bear the thought of a child of Swedish parents being taken in by Laplanders.

"You said just now that she had a father in the mine."

"He's dead," said the Lap abruptly.

"I suppose you have thoroughly investigated this matter, Ola?"

"What's the use of going to all that trouble?" disdained the Lap. "I ought to know! Would the girl and her brother have been obliged to roam about the country if they had a father living? Would two children have been forced to care for themselves if they had a father? The girl herself thinks he's alive, but I say that he must be dead."

The man with the tired eyes turned to Ola. "What is the girl's name, Ola?" he asked. The mountaineer thought awhile, then said: "I can't remember it. I must ask her."

"Ask her! Is she already here?"

"She's down at the camp."

"What, Ola! Have you taken her in before knowing her father's wishes?"

"What do I care for her father! If he isn't dead, he's probably the kind of man who cares nothing for his child. He may be glad to have another take her in hand."

The fisherman threw down his rod and rose with an alertness in his movements that bespoke new life.

"I don't think her father can be like other folk," continued the mountaineer. "I dare say he is a man who is haunted by gloomy forebodings and therefore can not work steadily. What kind of a father would that be for the girl?"

While Ola was talking the fisherman started up the strand.

"Where are you going?" queried the Lap.

"I'm going to have a look at your foster daughter, Ola."

"Good!" said the Lap. "Come along and meet her. I think you'll say that she will be a good daughter to me."

The Swede rushed on so rapidly that the Laplander could hardly keep pace with him.

After a moment Ola said to his companion:

"Now I recall that her name is Osa—this girl I'm adopting."

The other man only kept hurrying along and old Ola Serka was so well pleased that he wanted to laugh aloud.

When they came in sight of the tents, Ola said a few words more.

"She came here to us Saméfolk to find her father and not to become my foster child. But if she doesn't find him, I shall be glad to keep her in my tent." The fisherman hastened all the faster.

"I might have known that he would be alarmed when I threatened to take his daughter into the Laps' quarters," laughed Ola to himself.

When the man from Kiruna, who had brought Osa to the tent, turned back later in the day, he had two people with him in the boat, who sat close together, holding hands—as if they never again wanted to part.

They were Jon Esserson and his daughter. Both were unlike what they had been a few hours earlier.

The father looked less bent and weary and his eyes were clear and good, as if at last he had found the answer to that which had troubled him so long.

Osa, the goose girl, did not glance longingly about, for she had found someone to care for her, and now she could be a child again.

XVI

HOMEWARD BOUND

THE FIRST TRAVELING DAY

Saturday, October first

*T*he boy sat on the goosey-gander's back and rode up amongst the clouds. Some thirty geese, in regular order, flew rapidly southward. There was a rustling of feathers and the many wings beat the air so noisily that one could scarcely hear one's own voice. Akka from Kebnekaise flew in the lead; after her came Yksi and Kaksi, Kolme and Neljä, Viisi and Kuusi, Morten Goosey-Gander and Dunfin. The six goslings that had accompanied the flock the autumn before had now left to look after themselves. Instead, the old geese were taking with them twenty-two goslings that had grown up in the glen that summer. Eleven flew to the right, eleven to the left, and they did their best to fly at even distances, like the big birds. The poor youngsters had never before been on a long trip and at first they had difficulty in keeping up with the rapid flight.

"Akka from Kebnekaise! Akka from Kebnekaise!" they cried in plaintive tones.

"What's the matter?" said the leader goose sharply.

"Our wings are tired of moving, our wings are tired of moving!" wailed the young ones.

"The longer you keep it up, the better it will go," answered the leader goose, without slackening her speed. And she was quite right, for when the goslings had flown two hours longer, they complained no more of being tired. Very soon they began to feel hungry. "Akka, Akka, Akka from Kebnekaise!" wailed the goslings pitifully.

"What's the trouble now?" asked the leader goose. "We're so hungry, we can't fly any more!" whimpered the goslings. "We're so hungry, we can't fly any more!"

"Wild geese must learn to eat air and drink wind," said the leader goose, and kept right on flying. It actually seemed as if the young ones were learning to live on wind and air, for when they had flown a little longer, they said nothing more about being hungry. The goose flock was still in the mountain regions, and the old geese called out the names of all the peaks as they flew past, so that the youngsters might learn them. When they had been calling out a while: "This is Porsotjokko, this is Särjaktjokko, this is Sulitelma," and so on, the goslings became impatient again.

"Akka, Akka, Akka!" they shrieked in heartrending tones.

"What's wrong?" said the leader goose.

"We haven't room in our heads for any more of those awful names!" shrieked the goslings.

"The more you put into your heads the more you can get into them," retorted the leader goose, and continued to call out the names.

The boy sat thinking that it was about time the wild geese betook themselves southward, for so much snow had fallen that the ground was white as far as the eye could see. There was no use denying that it had been rather disagreeable in the glen toward the last. Rain and fog had succeeded each other without any relief, and even if it did clear up once in a while, immediately frost set in. Berries and mushrooms, upon which the boy had subsisted during the summer, were either frozen or decayed. Finally he had been compelled to eat raw fish, which was something he disliked. The days had grown short and the long evenings and late mornings were rather tiresome for one who could not sleep the whole time that the sun was away.

Now, at last, the goslings' wings had grown, so that the geese could start for the south. The boy was so happy that he laughed and sang as he rode on the goose's back. It was not only on account of the darkness and cold that he longed to get away from Lapland; there were other reasons too. The first weeks of his sojourn there the boy had not been the least bit homesick. He thought he had never before seen such a glorious country. The only worry he had had was to keep the mosquitoes from eating him up.

The boy had seen very little of the goosey-gander, because the big, white gander thought only of his Dunfin and was unwilling to leave her for a moment. On the other hand, Thumbietot had stuck to Akka and Gorgo, the eagle, and the three of them had passed many happy hours together. The two birds had taken him with them on long trips. He had stood on snow-capped Mount Kebnekaise, had looked down at the glaciers and visited many high cliffs seldom tramped by human feet. Akka had shown him deep, hidden mountain dales and had let him peep into caves where mother wolves brought up their young. He had also made the acquaintance of the tame reindeer that grazed in herds along the shores of the beautiful Tome Lake, and he had been down to the great falls and brought greetings to the bears that lived thereabouts from their friends and relatives in Westmanland.

Ever since he had seen Osa, the goose girl, he longed for the day when he might go home with Morten Goosey-Gander and be a normal human being once more. He wanted to be himself again, so that Osa would not be afraid to talk to him and would not shut the door in his face. Yes, indeed, he was glad that at last they were speeding southward. He waved his cap and cheered when he saw the first pine forest. In the same manner he greeted the first gray cabin, the first goat, the first cat, and the first chicken. They were continually meeting birds of passage, flying now in greater flocks than in the spring.

"Where are you bound for, wild geese?" called the passing birds.

"We, like yourselves, are going abroad," answered the geese.

"Those goslings of yours aren't ready to fly, screamed the others. "They'll never cross the sea with those puny wings!"

Laplander and reindeer were also leaving the mountains. When the wild geese sighted the reindeer, they circled down and called out: "Thanks for your company this summer!"

"A pleasant journey to you, welcome back!" returned the reindeer.

But when the bears saw the wild geese, they pointed them out to the cubs and growled: "Just look at those geese; they are so afraid of a little cold they don't dare to stay at home in winter."

But the old geese were ready with a retort and cried to their goslings: "Look at those beasts that stay at home and sleep half the year rather than go to the trouble of traveling south!"

Down in the pine forest the young grouse sat huddled together and gazed longingly after the big bird flocks which, amid joy and merriment, proceeded southward. "When will our turn come?" they asked the mother grouse.

"You will have to stay at home with mamma and papa," she said.

XVII

LEGENDS FROM HÄRJEDALEN

Tuesday, October fourth

The boy had had three days' travel in the rain and mist and longed for some sheltered nook, where he might rest awhile. At last the geese alighted to feed and ease their wings a bit. To his great relief the boy saw an observation tower on a hill close by, and dragged himself to it. When he had climbed to the top of the tower he found a party of tourists there, so he quickly crawled into a dark corner and was soon sound asleep.

When the boy awoke, he began to feel uneasy because the tourists lingered so long in the tower telling stories. He thought they would never go. Morten Goosey-Gander could not come for him while they were there and he knew, of course, that the wild geese were in a hurry to continue the journey. In the middle of a story he thought he heard honking and the beating of wings, as if the geese were flying away, but he did not dare to venture over to the balustrade to find out if it was so.

At last, when the tourists were gone, and the boy could crawl from his hiding place, he saw no wild geese, and no Morten Goosey-Gander came to fetch him. He called, "Here am I, where are you?" as loud as he could, but his traveling companions did not appear. He feared that they had met with some mishap and was wondering what he should do to find them, when Bataki, the raven, lit beside him. The boy never dreamed that he should greet Bataki with such a glad welcome.

"Dear Bataki," he burst forth. "How fortunate that you are here! Maybe you know what has become of Morten Goosey-Gander and the wild geese?"

"I've just come with a greeting from them," replied the raven. "Akka saw a hunter prowling about on the mountain and therefore dared not stay to wait for you, but has gone on ahead. Get up on my back and you shall soon be with your friends."

The boy quickly seated himself on the raven's back and Bataki would soon have caught up with the geese had he not been hindered by a fog. It was as if the morning sun had awakened it to life. Little light veils of mist rose suddenly from the lake, from fields, and from the forest. They thickened and spread with marvelous rapidity, and soon the entire ground was hidden from sight by white, rolling mists. Bataki flew along above the fog, but the wild geese must have circled down among the damp clouds, for it was impossible to sight them. The boy and the raven called and shrieked, but got no response.

"Well, this is a stroke of ill luck!" said Bataki finally. "But we know that they are traveling toward the south, and of course I'll find them as soon as the mist clears."

The boy was distressed at the thought of being parted from Morten Goosey-Gander just now, when the geese were on the wing, and the big white one might meet with all sorts of mishaps. After Thumbietot had been sitting worrying for two hours or more, he remarked to himself that, thus far, there had been no mishap, and it was not worth while to lose heart. Just then he heard a rooster crowing down on the ground, and instantly he bent forward on the raven's back and called out: "What's the name of the country I'm traveling over?"

"It's called Härjedalen, Härjedalen," crowed the rooster.

"How does it look down there where you are?" the boy asked.

"Cliffs in the west, woods in the east, broad valleys across the whole country," replied the rooster.

"Thank you," cried the boy. "You give a clear account of it."

When they had traveled a little farther, he heard a crow cawing down in the mist.

"What kind of people live in this country?" shouted the boy.

"Good, thrifty peasants," answered the crow. "Good, thrifty peasants."

"What do they do?" asked the boy. "What do they do?"

"They raise cattle and fell forests," cawed the crow.

"Thanks," replied the boy. "You answer well." A bit farther on he heard a human voice yodeling and singing down in the mist. "Is there any large city in this part of the country?" the boy asked.

"What—what—who is it that calls?" cried the human voice.

"Is there any large city in this region?" the boy repeated.

"I want to know who it is that calls," shouted the human voice.

"I might have known that I could get no information when I asked a human being a civil question," the boy retorted.

It was not long before the mist went away as suddenly as it had come. Then the boy saw a beautiful landscape, with high cliffs as in Jämtland, but there were no large, flourishing settlements on the mountain slopes. The villages lay far apart, and the farms were small. Bataki followed the stream southward till they came within sight of a village. There he alighted in a stubble field and let the boy dismount.

"In the summer grain grew on this ground," said Bataki. "Look around and see if you can't find something eatable."

The boy found a blade of wheat. As he picked out the grains and ate them, Bataki talked to him. "Do you see that mountain towering directly south of us?" he asked.

"Yes, of course, I see it," said the boy.

"It is called Sonfjället," continued the raven, "you can imagine that wolves were plentiful there once upon a time."

"It must have been an ideal place for wolves," said the boy.

"The people who lived here in the valley were frequently attacked by them," remarked the raven.

"Perhaps you remember a good wolf story you could tell me?" said the boy.

"I've been told that a long, long time ago the wolves from Sonfjället are supposed to have waylaid a man who had gone out to peddle his wares," began Bataki. "He was from Hede, a village a few miles down the valley. It was winter time and the wolves made for him as he was driving over the ice on Lake Ljusna. There were about nine or ten, and the man from Hede had a poor old horse, so there was very little hope of his escaping. When the man heard the wolves howl and saw how many there were after him, he lost his head, and it did not occur to him that he ought to dump his casks and jugs out of the sledge, to lighten the load. He only whipped up the horse and made the best speed he could, but he soon observed that the wolves were gaining on him. The shores were desolate and he was fourteen miles from the nearest farm. He thought that his final hour had come, and was paralyzed with fear. While he sat there, terrified, he saw something move in the brush, which had been set in the ice to mark out the road, and when he discovered who it was that walked there, his fear grew more intense.

"Wild beasts were not coming toward him, but a poor old woman, named Finn-Malin, who was in the habit of roaming about on highways and byways. She was a hunchback, and slightly lame, so he recognized her at a distance.

"The old woman was walking straight toward the wolves. The sledge had hidden them from her view, and the man comprehended at once that, if he were drive on without warning her, she would walk right to the jaws of the wild beasts, and while they were rending her, he would have time enough to get away.

"The old woman walked slowly, bent over a cane. It was plain that she was doomed if he did not help her, but even if he were to stop and take her into the sledge, it was by no means certain that she would be safe. More than likely the wolves would catch up with them, and he and she and the horse would all be killed. He wondered if it were not better to sacrifice one life in order that two might be spared—this flashed upon him the minute he saw the old woman. He had also time to think how it would be with him afterward—if perchance he might not regret that he had not succored her, or if people should some day learn of the meeting and that he had not tried to help her. It was a terrible temptation.

"'I would rather not have seen her,' he said to himself.

"Just then the wolves howled savagely. The horse reared, plunged forward, and dashed past the old beggar woman. She, too, had heard the howling of the wolves, and, as the man from Hede drove by, he saw that the old woman knew what awaited her. She stood motionless, her mouth open for a cry, her arms stretched out for help. But she neither cried nor tried to throw herself into the sledge. Something seemed to have turned her to stone. 'It was I,' thought the man. 'I must have looked like a demon as I passed.'

"He tried to feel satisfied, now that he was certain of escape, but at that very moment his heart reproached him. Never before had he done a dastardly thing, and he felt now that his whole life was blasted. 'Let come what may,' he said, and reined in the horse, 'I cannot leave her alone with the wolves!'

"It was with great difficulty that he got the horse to turn, but in the end he managed it and promptly drove back to her. 'Be quick and get into the sledge,' he said gruffly, for he was mad with himself for not leaving the old woman to her fate. 'You might stay at home once in awhile, you old hag!' he growled. 'Now both my horse and I will come to grief on your account.'

"The old woman did not say a word, but the man from Hede was in no mood to spare her. 'The horse has already tramped thirty-five miles today, and the load hasn't lightened any since you got up on it!' he grumbled, 'so that you must understand he'll soon be exhausted.'

"The sledge runners crunched on the ice, but for all that he heard how the wolves panted, and knew that the beasts were almost upon him.

"'It's all up with us!' he said. 'Much good it was, either to you or to me, this attempt to save you, Finn-Malin!'

"Up to this point the old woman had been silent—like one who is accustomed to take abuse—but now she said a few words.

"'I can't understand why you don't throw out your wares and lighten the load. You can come back again tomorrow and gather them up.'

"The man realized that this was sound advice and was surprised that he had not thought of it before. He tossed the reins to the old woman, loosed the ropes that bound the casks, and pitched them out. The wolves were right upon them, but now they stopped to examine that which was thrown on the ice, and the travelers again had the start of them.

"'If this does not help you,' said the old woman, 'you understand, of course, that I will give myself up to the wolves voluntarily, that you may escape.'

"While she was speaking the man was trying to push a heavy brewer's vat from the long sledge. As he tugged at this he paused, as if he could not quite make up his mind to throw it out, but, in reality, his mind was taken up with something altogether different. 'Surely a man and a horse who have no infirmities need not let a feeble old woman be devoured by wolves for their sakes,' he thought. 'There must be some other way of salvation. Why, of course, there is! It's only my stupidity that hinders me from finding the way.'

"Again he started to push the vat, then paused once more and burst out laughing. The old woman was alarmed and wondered if he had gone mad, but the man from Hede was laughing at himself because he had been so stupid all the while. It was the simplest thing in the world to save all three of them. He could not imagine why he had not thought of it before.

"'Listen to what I say to you, Malin?' he said. 'It was splendid of you to be willing to throw yourself to the wolves. But you won't have to do that because I know how we can all three be helped without endangering the life of any. Remember, whatever I may do, you are to sit still and drive down to Linsäll. There you must waken the townspeople and tell them that I'm alone out here on the ice, surrounded by wolves, and ask them to come and help me.'

"The man waited until the wolves were almost upon the sledge. Then he rolled out the big brewer's vat, jumped down, and crawled in under it. It was a huge vat, large enough to hold a whole Christmas brew. The wolves pounced upon it and at the hoops, but the vat was too heavy for them move. They could not get at the man inside.

"He knew that he was safe and laughed at the wolves. After a bit he was serious again. 'For the future, when I get into a tight place, I'll remember this vat, and I shall bear in mind that I need never wrong either myself or others, for there is always a third way out of a difficulty if only one can hit upon it.'"

With this Bataki closed his narrative. The boy noticed that the raven never spoke unless there was some special meaning back of his words, and the longer he listened to him, the more thoughtful he became.

"I wonder why you told me that story?" remarked the boy.

"I just happened to think of it as I stood here, gazing up at Sonfjället," replied the raven.

Now they had traveled farther down Lake Ljusna and in an hour or so they came to Kolsätt, close to the border of Hälsingland. Here the raven alighted near a little hut that had no windows—only a shutter. From the chimney rose sparks and smoke, and from within the sound of heavy hammering was heard.

371

"Whenever I see this smithy," observed the raven, "I'm reminded that, in former times, there were such skilled blacksmiths here in Härjedalen, more especially in this village—that they couldn't be matched in the whole country."

"Perhaps you also remember a story about them?" said the boy. "Yes," returned Bataki, "I remember one about a smith from Härjedalen who once invited two other master blacksmiths—one from Dalecarlia and one from Vermland—to compete with him at nail making. The challenge was accepted and the three blacksmiths met here at Kolsätt. The Dalecarlian began. He forged a dozen nails, so even and smooth and sharp that they couldn't be improved upon. After him came the Vermlander. He, too, forged a dozen nails, which were quite perfect and, moreover, he finished them in half the time that it took the Dalecarlian. When the judges saw this they said to the Härjedal smith that it wouldn't be worth while for him to try, since he could not forge better than the Dalecarlian or faster than the Vermlander.

"'I shan't give up! There must be still another way of excelling,' insisted the Härjedal smith.

"He placed the iron on the anvil without heating it at the forge; he simply hammered it hot and forged nail after nail, without the use of either anvil or bellows. None of the judges had ever seen a blacksmith wield a hammer more masterfully, and the Härjedal smith was proclaimed the best in the land."

With these remarks Bataki subsided, and the boy grew even more thoughtful. "I wonder what your purpose was in telling me that?" he queried.

"The story dropped into my mind when I saw the old smithy again," said Bataki in an offhand manner.

The two travelers rose again into the air and the raven carried the boy southward till they came to Lillhärdal Parish, where he alighted on a leafy mound at the top of a ridge. "I wonder if you know upon what mound you are standing?" said Bataki.

The boy had to confess that he did not know.

"This is a grave," said Bataki. "Beneath this mound lies the first settler in Härjedalen."

"Perhaps you have a story to tell of him too?" said the boy.

"I haven't heard much about him, but I think he was a Norwegian. He had served with a Norwegian king, got into his bad graces, and had to flee the country. Later he went over to the Swedish king, who lived at Upsala, and took service with him. But, after a time, he asked for the hand of the king's sister in marriage, and when the king wouldn't give him such a highborn bride, he eloped with her. By that time he had managed to get himself into such disfavor that it wasn't safe for him to live either in Norway or Sweden, and he did not wish to move to a foreign country. 'But there must still be a course open to me,' he thought. With his servants and treasures, he journeyed through Dalecarlia until he arrived in the desolate forests beyond the outskirts of the province. There he settled, built houses and broke up land. Thus, you see, he was the first man to settle in this part of the country."

As the boy listened to the last story, he looked very serious. "I wonder what your object is in telling me all this?" he repeated.

Bataki twisted and turned and screwed up his eyes, and it was some time before he answered the boy. "Since we are here alone," he said finally, "I shall take this opportunity to question you regarding a certain matter. Have you ever tried to ascertain upon what terms the elf who transformed you was to restore you to a normal human being?"

"The only stipulation I've heard anything about was that I should take the white goosey-gander up to Lapland and bring him back to Skåne, safe and sound."

"I thought as much," said Bataki, "for when last we met, you talked confidently of there being nothing more contemptible than deceiving a friend who trusts one. You'd better ask Akka about the terms. You know, I dare say, that she was at your home and talked with the elf."

"Akka hasn't told me of this," said the boy wonderingly.

"She must have thought that it was best for you not to know just what the elf did say. Naturally she would rather help you than Morten Goosey-Gander."

"It is singular, Bataki, that you always have a way of making me feel unhappy and anxious," said the boy.

"I dare say it might seem so," continued the raven, "but this time I believe that you will be grateful to me for telling you that the elf's words were to this effect: You were to become a normal human being again if you would bring back Morten Goosey-Gander that your mother might lay him on the block and chop his head off."

The boy leaped up. "That's only one of your base fabrications," he cried indignantly.

"You can ask Akka yourself," said Bataki. "I see her coming up there with her whole flock. And don't forget what I have told you today. There is usually a way out of all difficulties, if only one can find it. I shall be interested to see what success you have."

XVIII

VERMLAND AND DALSLAND

Wednesday, October fifth

Today the boy took advantage of the rest hour, when Akka was feeding apart from the other wild geese, to ask her if that which Bataki had related was true, and Akka could not deny it. The boy made the leader goose promise that she would not divulge the secret to Morten Goosey-Gander. The big white gander was so brave and generous that he might do something rash were he to learn of the elf's stipulations.

Later the boy sat on the goose's back, glum and silent, and hung his head. He heard the wild geese call out to the goslings that now they were in Dalarne, they could see Städjan in the North, and that now they were flying over Österdal River to Horrmund Lake and were coming to Vesterdal River. But the boy did not care even to glance at all this.

"I shall probably travel around with wild geese the rest of my life," he remarked to himself, "and I am likely to see more of this land than I wish."

He was quite as indifferent when the wild geese called out to him that now they had arrived in Vermland and that the stream they were following southward was Klarälven.

"I've seen so many rivers already," thought the boy, "why bother to look at one more?" Even had he been more eager for sightseeing, there was not very much to be seen, for northern Vermland is nothing but vast, monotonous forest tracts, through which Klarälven winds narrow and rich in rapids. Here and there one can see a charcoal kiln, a forest clearing, or a few low, chimneyless huts, occupied by Finns. But the forest as a whole is so extensive one might fancy it was far up in Lapland.

A LITTLE HOMESTEAD

Thursday, October sixth

The wild geese followed Klarälven as far as the big iron foundries at Monk Fors. Then they proceeded westward to Fryksdalen. Before they got to Lake Fryken it began to grow dusky, and they lit in a little wet morass on a wooded hill. The morass was certainly a good night quarter for the wild geese, but the boy thought it dismal and rough, and wished for a better sleeping place. While he was still high in the air, he had noticed that below the ridge lay a number of farms, and with great haste he proceeded to seek them out.

They were farther away than he had fancied and several times he was tempted to turn back. Presently the woods became less dense, and he came to a road skirting the edge of the forest. From it branched a pretty birch-bordered lane, which led down to a farm and immediately he hastened toward it.

First the boy entered a farm yard as large as a city marketplace and enclosed by a long row of red houses. As he crossed the yard, he saw another farm where the dwelling house faced a gravel path and a wide lawn. Back of the house there was a garden thick with foliage. The dwelling itself was small and humble, but the garden was edged by a row of exceedingly tall mountain ash trees, so close together that they formed a real wall around it. It appeared to the boy as if he were coming into a great, high vaulted chamber, with the lovely blue sky for a ceiling. The mountain ash were thick with clusters of red berries, the grass plots were still green, of course, but that night there was a full moon, and as the bright moonlight fell upon the grass it looked as white as silver.

No human being was in sight and the boy could wander freely wherever he wished. When he was in the garden he saw something which almost put him in good humor. He had climbed a mountain ash to eat berries, but before he could reach a cluster he caught sight of a barberry bush, which was also full of berries. He slid along the ash branch and clambered up into the barberry bush, but he was no sooner there than he discovered a currant bush, on which still hung long red clusters. Next he saw that the garden was full of gooseberries and rasp-berries and dog rose bushes, that there were cabbages and turnips in the vegetable beds and berries on every bush, seeds on the herbs and grain-filled ears on every blade. And there on the path—no, of course he could not mistake it—was a big red apple that shone in the moonlight.

The boy sat down at the side of the path, with the big red apple in front of him, and began cutting little pieces from it with his sheath knife. "It wouldn't be such a serious matter to be an elf all one's life if it were always as easy to get good food as it is here," he thought.

He sat and mused as he ate, wondering finally if it would not be as well for him to remain here and let the wild geese travel south without him. "I don't know for the life of me how I can ever explain to Morten Goosey-Gander that I cannot go home," thought he. "It would be better if I were to leave him altogether. I could gather provisions enough for the winter, as well as the squirrels do, and if I were to live in a dark corner of the stable or the cow shed, I shouldn't freeze to death."

Just as he was thinking this, he heard a light rustle over his head, and a second later something that resembled a birch stump stood on the ground beside him.

The stump twisted and turned, and two bright dots on top of it glowed like coals of fire. It looked like some enchantment. However, the boy soon remarked that the stump had a hooked beak and big feather wreaths around its glowing eyes. Then he knew that this was no enchantment.

"It is a real pleasure to meet a living creature," remarked the boy. "Perhaps you will be good enough to tell me the name of this place, Mrs. Brown Owl, and what sort of folk live here."

That evening, as on all other evenings, the owl had perched on a rung of the big ladder propped against the roof, from which she had looked down toward the gravel walks and grass plots, watching for rats. Very much to her surprise, not a single grayskin had appeared. She saw instead something that looked like a human being, but much, much smaller, moving about in the garden.

"That's the one who is scaring away the rats!" thought the owl. "What in the world can it be? It's not a squirrel, nor a kitten, nor a weasel," she observed. "I suppose that a bird who has lived on an old place like this as long as I have ought to know about everything in the world, but this is beyond my comprehension," she concluded.

She had been staring at the object that moved on the gravel path until her eyes burned. Finally curiosity got the better of her and she flew down to the ground to have a closer view of the stranger.

When the boy began to speak, the owl bent forward and looked him up and down.

"He has neither claws nor horns," she remarked to herself, "yet who knows but he may have a poisonous fang or some even more dangerous weapon. I must try to find out what he passes for before I venture to touch him."

"The place is called Mårbacka," said the owl, "and gentlefolk lived here once upon a time. But you, yourself, who are you?"

"I think of moving in here," volunteered the boy without answering the owl's question. "Would it be possible, do you think?"

"Oh, yes—but it's not much of a place now compared to what it was once," said the owl. "You can weather it here I dare say. It all depends upon what you expect to live on. Do you intend to take up the rat chase?"

"Oh, by no means!" declared the boy. "There is more fear of the rats eating me than that I shall do them any harm."

"It can't be that he is as harmless as he says," thought the brown owl. "All the same I believe I'll make an attempt—"

She rose into the air, and in a second her claws were fastened in Nils Holgersson's shoulder and she was trying to hack at his eyes. The boy shielded both eyes with one hand and tried to free himself with the other, at the same time calling with all his might for help. He realized that he was in deadly peril and thought that this time, surely, it was all over with him!

Now I must tell you of a strange coincidence: The very year that Nils Holgersson traveled with the wild geese there was a woman who thought of writing a book about Sweden, which would be suitable for children to read in the schools. She had thought of this from Christmas time until the following autumn, but not a line of the book had she written. At last she became so tired of the whole thing that she said to herself: "You are not fitted for such work. Sit down and compose stories and legends, as usual, and let another write this book, which has got to be serious and instructive, and in which there must not be one untruthful word."

It was as good as settled that she would abandon the idea. But she thought, very naturally, it would have been agreeable to write something beautiful about Sweden, and it was hard for her to relinquish her work. Finally, it occurred to her that maybe it was because she lived in a city, with only gray streets and house walls around her, that she could make no headway with the writing. Perhaps if she were to go into the country, where she could see woods and fields, that it might go better.

She was from Vermland, and it was perfectly clear to her that she wished to begin the book with that province. First of all she would write about the place where she had grown up. It was a lithe homestead, far removed from the great world, where many old-time habits and customs were retained. She thought that it would be entertaining for children to hear of the manifold duties which had succeeded one another the year around. She wanted to tell them how they celebrated Christmas and New Year and Easter and Midsummer Day in her home, what kind of house furnishings they had, what the kitchen and larder were like, and how the cow shed, stable, lodge, and bath house had looked. But when she was to write about it the pen would not move. Why this was she could not in the least understand, nevertheless it was so.

True, she remembered it all just as distinctly as if she were still living in the midst of it. She argued with herself that since she was going into the country anyway, perhaps she ought to make a little trip to the old homestead that she might see it again before writing about it. She had not been there in many years and did not think it half bad to have a reason for the journey. In fact she had always longed to be there, no matter in what part of the world she happened to be. She had seen many places that were more pretentious and prettier. But nowhere could she find such comfort and protection as in the home of her childhood.

It was not such an easy matter for her to go home as one might think, for the estate had been sold to people she did not know. She felt, to be sure, that they would receive her well, but she did not care to go to the old place to sit and talk with strangers, for she wanted to recall how it had been in times gone by. That was why she planned it so as to arrive there late in the evening, when the day's work was done and the people were indoors.

She had never imagined that it would be so wonderful to come home! As she sat in the cart and drove toward the old homestead she fancied that she was growing younger and younger every minute, and that soon she would no longer be an oldish person with hair that was turning gray, but a little girl in short skirts with a long flaxen braid. As she recognized each farm along the road, she could not picture anything else than that everything at home would be as in bygone days. Her father and mother and brothers and sisters would be standing on the porch to welcome her; the old housekeeper would run to the kitchen window to see who was coming, and Nero and Freja and another dog or two would come bounding and jumping up on her.

The nearer she approached the place the happier she felt. It was autumn, which meant a busy time with a round of duties. It must have been all these varying duties which prevented home from ever being monotonous. All along the way the farmers were digging potatoes, and probably they would be doing likewise at her home. That meant that they must begin immediately to grate potatoes and make potato flour. The autumn had been a mild one; she wondered if everything in the garden had already been stored. The cabbages were still out, but perhaps the hops had been picked, and all the apples.

It would be well if they were not having house cleaning at home. Autumn fair time was drawing nigh, everywhere the cleaning and scouring had to be done before the fair opened. That was regarded as a great event—more especially by the servants. It was a pleasure to go into the kitchen on Market Eve and see the newly scoured floor strewn with juniper twigs, the whitewashed walls and the shining copper utensils which were suspended from the ceiling.

Even after the fair festivities were over there would not be much of a breathing spell, for then came the work on the flax. During dog days the flax had been spread out on a meadow to mold. Now it was laid in the old bath house, where the stove was lighted to dry it out. When it was dry enough to handle all the women in the neighborhood were called together. They sat outside the bath house and picked the flax to pieces. Then they beat it with swingles, to separate the fine white fibers from the dry stems. As they worked, the women grew gray with dust; their hair and clothing were covered with flax seed, but they did not seem to mind it. All day the swingles pounded, and the chatter went on, so that when one went near the old bath house it sounded as if a blustering storm had broken loose there.

After the work with the flax, came the big hardtack baking, the sheep shearing, and the servants' moving time. In November there were busy slaughter days, with salting of meats, sausage making, baking of blood pudding, and candle steeping. The seamstress who used to make up their homespun dresses had to come at this time, of course, and those were always two pleasant weeks—when the women folk sat together and busied themselves with sewing.

The cobbler, who made shoes for the entire household, sat working at the same time in the menservants' quarters, and one never tired of watching him as he cut the leather and soled and heeled the shoes and put eyelets in the shoestring holes.

But the greatest rush came around Christmas time. Lucia Day, when the housemaid went about dressed in white with candles in her hair, and served coffee to everybody at five in the morning—came as a sort of reminder that for the next two weeks they could not count on much sleep. For now they must brew the Christmas ale, steep the Christmas fish in lye, and do their Christmas baking and Christmas scouring.

She was in the middle of the baking, with pans of Christmas buns and cookie platters all around her, when the driver drew in the reins at the end of the lane as she had requested. She started like one suddenly awakened from a sound sleep. It was dismal for her who had just dreamed herself surrounded by all her people to be sitting alone in the late evening. As she stepped from the wagon and started to walk up the long lane that she might come unobserved to her old home, she felt so keenly the contrast between then and now that she would have preferred to turn back.

"Of what use is it to come here?" she sighed. "It can't be the same as in the old days!"

On the other hand she felt that since she had traveled such a long distance, she would see the place at all events, so continued to walk on, although she was more depressed with every step that she took. She had heard that it was very much changed, and it certainly was! But she did not observe this now in the evening. She thought, rather, that everything was quite the same. There was the pond, which in her youth had been full of carp and where no one dared fish, because it was Father's wish that the carp should be left in peace. Over there were the menservants' quarters, the larder and barn, with the farm yard bell over one gable and the weather vane over the other. The house yard was like a circular room, with no outlook in any direction, as it had been in her father's time—for he had not the heart to cut down as much as a bush.

She lingered in the shadow under the big mountain ash at the entrance to the farm, and stood looking about her. As she stood there a strange thing happened; a flock of doves came and lit beside her.

She could hardly believe that they were real birds, for doves are not in the habit of moving about after sundown. It must have been the beautiful moonlight that had awakened these. They must have thought it was dawn and flown from their dovecotes, only to become confused, hardly knowing where they were. When they saw a human being they flew over to her, as if she would set them right.

There had been many flocks of doves at the manor when her parents lived there, for the doves were among the creatures which her father had taken under his special care. If one ever mentioned the killing of a dove, it put him in a bad humor. She was pleased that the pretty birds had come to meet her in the old home. Who could tell but the doves had flown out in the night to show her they had not forgotten that once upon a time they had a good home there. Perhaps her father had sent his birds with a greeting to her, so that she would not feel so sad and lonely when she came to her former home.

As she thought of this, there welled up within her such an intense longing for the old times that her eyes filled with tears. Life had been beautiful in this place. They had had weeks of work broken by many holiday festivities. They had toiled hard all day, but at evening they had gathered around the lamp and read Tegner and Runeberg, *"Fru"* Lenngren and *"Mamsell"* Bremer. They had cultivated grain, but also roses and jasmine. They had spun flax, but had sung folk songs as they spun. They had worked hard at their history and grammar, but they had also played theater and written verses. They had stood at the kitchen stove and prepared food, but had learned, also, to play the flute and guitar, the violin and piano. They had planted cabbages and turnips, peas and beans in one garden, but they had another full of apples and pears and all kinds of berries. They had lived by themselves, and this was why so many stories and legends were stowed away in their memories. They had worn homespun clothes, but they had also been able to lead care-free and independent lives.

"Nowhere else in the world do they know how to get so much out of life as they did at one of these little homesteads in my childhood!" she thought. "There was just enough work and just enough play, and every day there was a joy. How I should love to come back here again! Now that I have seen the place, it is hard to leave it."

Then she turned to the flock of doves and said to them, laughing at herself all the while: "Won't you fly to Father and tell him that I long to come home? I have wandered long enough in strange places. Ask him if he can't arrange it so that I may soon turn back to my childhood's home."

The moment she had said this the flock of doves rose and flew away. She tried to follow them with her eyes, but they vanished instantly. It was as if the whole white company had dissolved in the shimmering air.

The doves had only just gone when she heard a couple of piercing cries from the garden, and as she hastened thither she saw a singular sight. There stood a tiny midget, no taller than a hand's breadth, struggling with a brown owl. At first she was so astonished that she could not move. But when the midget cried more and more pitifully, she stepped up quickly and parted the fighters. The owl swung herself into a tree, but the midget stood on the gravel path, without attempting either to hide or to run away.

"Thanks for your help," he said. "But it was very stupid of you to let the owl escape. I can't get away from here, because she is sitting up in the tree watching me."

"It was thoughtless of me to let her go. But to make amends, can't I accompany you to your home?" asked she who wrote stories, somewhat surprised to think that in this unexpected fashion she had got into conversation with one of the tiny folk. Still she was not so much surprised after all. It was as if all the while she had been awaiting some extraordinary experience, while she walked in the moonlight outside her old home.

"The fact is, I had thought of stopping here over night," said the midget. "If you will only show me a safe sleeping place, I shall not be obliged to return to the forest before daybreak."

"Must I show you a place to sleep? Are you not at home here?"

"I understand that you take me for one of the tiny folk," said the midget, "but I'm a human being, like yourself, although I have been transformed by an elf."

"That is the most remarkable thing I have ever heard! Wouldn't you like to tell me how you happened to get into such a plight?"

The boy did not mind telling her of his adventures, and, as the narrative proceeded, she who listened to him grew more and more astonished and happy.

"What luck to run across one who has traveled all over Sweden on the back of a goose!" thought she. "Just this which he is relating I shall write down in my book. Now I need worry no more over that matter. It was well that I came home. To think that I should find such help as soon as I came to the old place!"

Instantly another thought flashed into her mind. She had sent word to her father by the doves that she longed for home, and almost immediately she had received help in the matter she had pondered so long. Might not this be the father's answer to her prayer?

XIX

THE TREASURE
ON THE ISLAND

ON THEIR WAY TO THE SEA

Friday, October seventh

*F*rom the very start of the autumn trip the wild geese had flown straight south, but when they left Fryksdalen they veered in another direction, traveling over western Vermland and Dalsland, toward Bohuslän.

That was a jolly trip! The goslings were now so used to flying that they complained no more of fatigue, and the boy was recovering his good humor. He was glad that he had talked with a human being. He felt encouraged when she said that if he were to continue doing good to all whom he met, it could not end badly for him. She was not able to tell him how to get back his natural form, but she had given him a little hope and assurance, which inspired the boy to think out a way to prevent the big white gander from going home.

"Do you know, Morten Goosey-Gander, that it will be rather monotonous for us to stay at home all winter after having been on a trip like this," he said, as they were flying far up in the air. "I'm sitting here thinking that we ought to go abroad with the geese."

"Surely you are not in earnest!" said the goosey-gander. Since he had proved to the wild geese his ability to travel with them all the way to Lapland, he was perfectly satisfied to get back to the goose pen in Holger Nilsson's cow shed.

The boy sat silently a while and gazed down on Vermland, where the birch woods, leafy groves, and gardens were clad in red and yellow autumn colors. "I don't think I've ever seen the earth beneath us as lovely!" he finally remarked. "The lakes are like blue satin bands."

"Don't you think it would be a pity to settle down in West Vemmenhög and never see any more of the world?"

"I thought you wanted to go home to your mother and father and show them what a splendid boy you had become?" said the goosey-gander.

All summer he had been dreaming of what a proud moment it would be for him when he should alight in the house yard before Holger Nilsson's cabin and show Dunfin and the six goslings to the geese and chickens, the cows and the cat, and to Mother Holger Nilsson herself, so that he was not very happy over the boy's proposal.

"Now, Morten Goosey-Gander, don't you think that it would be hard never to see anything more that is beautiful!" said the boy.

"I would rather see the fat grain fields of Söderslätt than these lean hills," answered the goosey-gander. "But you must know very well that if you really wish to continue the trip, I can't be parted from you!"

"That is just the answer I had expected from you," said the boy, and his voice betrayed that he was relieved of a great anxiety.

Later, when they traveled over Bohuslän, the boy observed that the mountain stretches were more continuous, the valleys were more like little ravines blasted in the rock foundation, while the long lakes at their base were as black as if they had come from the underworld. This, too, was a glorious country and as the boy saw it, with now a strip of sun, now a shadow, he thought that there was something strange and wild about it. He knew not why, but the idea came to him that once upon a time there were many strong and brave heroes in these mystical regions who had passed through many dangerous and daring adventures. The old passion of wanting to share in all sorts of wonderful adventures awoke in him.

"I might possibly miss not being in danger of my life at least once every day or two," he thought. "Anyhow it's best to be content with things as they are."

He did not speak of this idea to the big white gander, because the geese were now flying over Bohuslän with all the speed they could muster, and the goosey-gander was puffing so hard that he would not have had the strength to reply.

The sun was far down on the horizon, and disappeared every now and then behind a hill; still the geese kept forging ahead.

Finally, in the west, they saw a shining strip of light, which grew broader and broader with every wing stroke. Soon the sea spread before them, milk white with a shimmer of rose red and sky blue, and when they had circled past the coast cliffs they saw the sun again, as it hung over the sea, big and red and ready to plunge into the waves.

As the boy gazed at the broad, endless sea and the red evening sun, which had such a kindly glow that he dared to look straight at it, he felt a sense of peace and calm penetrate his soul.

"It's not worth while to be sad, Nils Holgersson," said the Sun. "This is a beautiful world to live in, both for big and little. It is also good to be free and happy, and to have a great dome of open sky above you."

THE GIFT OF THE WILD GEESE

*T*he geese stood sleeping on a little rock islet just beyond Fjällbacka. When it drew on toward midnight, and the moon hung high in the heavens, old Akka shook the sleepiness out of her eyes. After that she awakened Yksi and Kaksi, Kolme and Neljä, Viisi and Kuusi, and, last of all, she gave Thumbietot a nudge with her bill that startled him. "What is it, Mother Akka?" he asked, springing up in alarm.

"Nothing serious," assured the leader goose. "It's just this: we seven who have been long together want to fly a short distance out to sea tonight, and we wondered if you would care to come with us."

The boy knew that Akka would not have proposed this move had there not been something important, so he promptly seated himself on her back. The flight was straight west. The wild geese first flew over a belt of large and small islands near the coast, then over a broad expanse of open sea, till they reached the large cluster known as the Väder Islands. All of them were low and rocky, and in the moonlight one could see that they were rather large. Akka looked at one of the smallest islands and alighted there. It consisted of a round, gray stone hill, with a wide cleft across it, into which the sea had cast fine, white sea sand and shells.

As the boy slid from the goose's back he noticed something quite close to him that looked like a jagged stone. But almost at once he saw that it was a big vulture which had chosen the rock island for a night harbor. Before the boy had time to wonder at the geese recklessly alighting so near a dangerous enemy, the bird flew up to them and the boy recognized Gorgo, the eagle. Evidently Akka and Gorgo had arranged the meeting, for neither of them was taken by surprise.

"This was good of you, Gorgo," said Akka. "I didn't expect that you would be at the meeting place ahead of us. Have you been here long?"

"I came early in the evening," replied Gorgo. "But I fear that the only praise I deserve is for keeping my appointment with you. I've not been very successful in carrying out the orders you gave me."

"I'm sure, Gorgo, that you have done more than you care to admit," assured Akka. "But before you relate your experiences on the trip, I shall ask Thumbietot to help me find something which is supposed to be buried on this island."

The boy stood gazing admiringly at two beautiful shells, but when Akka spoke his name, he glanced up. "You must have wondered, Thumbietot, why we turned course to fly to the West Sea," said Akka.

"To be frank, I did think it strange," answered the boy. "But I knew, of course, that you always have some good reason for whatever you do."

"You have a good opinion of me," returned Akka, "but I almost fear you will lose it now, for it's very probable that we have made this journey in vain. Many years ago it happened that two of the other old geese and myself encountered frightful storms during a spring flight and were wind-driven to this island. When we discovered that there was only open sea before us, we feared we should be swept so far out that we should never find our way back to land, so we lay down on the waves between these bare cliffs, where the storm compelled us to remain for several days.

"We suffered terribly from hunger; once we ventured up to the cleft on this island in search of food. We couldn't find a green blade, but we saw a number of securely tied bags half buried in the sand. We hoped to find grain in the bags and pulled and tugged at them till we tore the cloth. However, no grain poured out, but shining gold pieces. For such things we wild geese had no use, so we left them where they were. We haven't thought of the find in all these years, but this autumn something has come up to make us wish for gold. We do not know that the treasure is still here, but we have traveled all this way to ask you to look into the matter."

With a shell in either hand the boy jumped down into the cleft and began to scoop up the sand. He found no bags, but when he had made a deep hole he heard the clink of metal and saw that he had come upon a gold piece. Then he dug with his fingers and felt many coins in the sand. So he hurried back to Akka. "The bags have rotted and fallen apart," he exclaimed. "The money lies scattered all through the sand."

"That's well!" said Akka. "Now fill in the hole and smooth it over so no one will notice the sand has been disturbed."

The boy did as he was told, but when he came up from the cleft he was astonished to see that the wild geese were lined up, with Akka in the lead, and were marching toward him with great solemnity. The geese paused in front of him, and all bowed their heads many times, looking so grave that he had to doff his cap and make an obeisance to them.

"The fact is," said Akka, "we old geese have been thinking that if Thumbietot had been in the service of human beings and had done as much for them as he has for us they would not let him go without rewarding him well."

"I haven't helped you; it is you who have taken good care of me," returned the boy.

"We think also," continued Akka, "that when a human being has attended us on a whole journey he shouldn't be allowed to leave us as poor as when he came."

"I know that what I have learned this year with you is worth more to me than gold or lands," said the boy.

"Since these gold coins have been lying unclaimed in the cleft all these years, I think that you ought to have them," declared the goose.

"I thought you said something about needing this money yourselves," reminded the boy.

"We do need it, so as to be able to give you such recompense as will make your mother and father think you have been working as a goose boy with worthy people."

The boy turned half round and cast a glance toward the sea, then faced about and looked straight into Akka's bright eyes. "I think it strange, Mother Akka, that you turn me away from your service like this and pay me off before I have given you notice," he said.

"As long as we wild geese remain in Sweden, I trust that you will stay with us," said Akka. "I only wanted to show you where the treasure was while we could get to it without going too far out of our course."

"All the same it looks as if you wished to be rid of me before I want to go," argued Thumbietot. "After all the good times we have had together, I think you ought to let me go abroad with you." When the boy said this, Akka and the other wild geese stretched their long necks straight up and stood a moment, with bills half open, drinking in air.

"That is something I haven't thought about," said Akka, when she recovered herself. "Before you decide to come with us, we had better hear what Gorgo has to say. You may as well know that when we left Lapland the agreement between Gorgo and myself was that he should travel to your home down in Skåne to try to make better terms for you with the elf."

"That is true," affirmed Gorgo, "but as I have already told you, luck was against me. I soon hunted up Holger Nilsson's farm and after circling up and down over the place a couple of hours, I caught sight of the elf, skulking along between the sheds. Immediately I swooped down upon him and flew off with him to a meadow where we could talk together without interruption. "I told him that I had been sent by Akka from Kebnekaise to ask if he couldn't give Nils Holgersson easier terms. 'I only wish I could!' he answered, 'for I have heard that he has conducted himself well on the trip, but it is not in my power to do so.' Then I was furious and said that I would bore out his eyes unless he gave in.

"'You may do as you like,' he retorted, 'but as to Nils Holgersson, it will turn out exactly as I have said. You can tell him from me that he would do well to return soon with his goose, for matters on the farm are in a bad shape. His father has had to forfeit a bond for his brother, whom he trusted. He has bought a horse with borrowed money, and the beast went lame the first time he drove it. Since then it has been of no earthly use to him. Tell Nils Holgersson that his parents have had to sell two of the cows and that they must give up the farm unless they receive help from somewhere.'"

When the boy heard this he frowned and clenched his fists so hard that the nails dug into his flesh. "It is cruel of the elf to make the conditions so hard for me that I can not go home and relieve my parents, but he shan't turn me into a traitor to a friend! My father and mother are square and upright folk. I know they would rather forfeit my help than have me come back to them with a guilty conscience."

XX

THE JOURNEY TO VEMMENHÖG

Thursday, November third

One day in the beginning of November the wild geese flew over
Halland Ridge and into Skåne. For several weeks they had been
resting on the wide plains around Falköping. As many other wild goose
flocks also stopped there, the grown geese had had a pleasant time visit-
ing with old friends, and there had been all kinds of games and races
between the younger birds. Nils Holgersson had not been happy over
the delay in Westergötland. He had tried to keep a stout heart, but it
was hard for him to reconcile himself to his fate. "If I were only well out
of Skåne in some foreign land," he had thought, "I should know for certain that I had nothing to hope for, and would feel easier in my mind."

Finally, one morning the geese flew toward Halland. In the beginning the boy took very little interest in that province, thinking there was
nothing new to be seen there. But when the wild geese continued farther south, along the narrow coastal lands, he leaned over the goose's
neck and did not take his glance from the ground. He saw the hills gradually disappear and the plain spread under him, at the same time he
noticed that the coast became less ragged, while the group of islands
beyond thinned and finally vanished and the broad, open sea came clear
up to firm land. Here there were no more forests: here the plain was
supreme. It spread all the way to the horizon. A land that lay so exposed,
with field upon field, reminded the boy of Skåne. He felt both happy
and sad as he looked at it. "I can't be very far from home," he thought.

Many times during the trip the goslings had asked the old geese:
"How does it look in foreign lands?"

"Wait, wait! You shall soon see," the old geese had answered.

When the wild geese had passed Halland Ridge and gone a distance into Skåne, Akka called out: "Now look down! Look all around! It is like this in foreign lands."

Just then they flew over Söder Ridge. The whole long range of hills was clad in beach woods, and beautiful, turreted castles peeped out here and there. Among the trees grazed roebuck, and on the forest meadow romped the hares. Hunters' horns sounded from the forests; the loud baying of dogs could be heard all the way up to the wild geese. Broad avenues wound through the trees and on these ladies and gentlemen were driving in polished carriages or riding fine horses. At the foot of the ridge lay Ring Lake with the ancient Bosjö Cloister on a narrow peninsula. "Does it look like this in foreign lands?" asked the goslings.

"It looks exactly like this wherever there are forest-clad ridges," replied Akka, "only one doesn't see many of them. Wait! You shall see how it looks in general."

Akka led the geese farther south to the great Skåne plain. There it spread, with grain fields, with acres and acres of sugar beets, where the beet pickers were at work, with low whitewashed farm and outhouses, with numberless little white churches, with ugly, gray sugar refineries and small villages near the railway stations. Little beach-encircled meadow lakes, each of them adorned by its own stately manor, shimmered here and there. "Now look down! Look carefully!" called the leader goose. "Thus it is in foreign lands, from the Baltic coast all the way down to the high Alps. Farther than that I have never traveled."

When the goslings had seen the plain, the leader goose flew down the Öresund coast. Swampy meadows sloped gradually toward the sea. In some places were high, steep banks, in others drift-sand fields, where the sand lay heaped in banks and hills. Fishing hamlets stood all along the coast, with long rows of low, uniform brick houses, with a light-house at the edge of the breakwater, and brown fishing nets hanging in the drying yard. "Now look down! Look well! This is how it looks along the coasts in foreign lands."

After Akka had been flying about in this manner a long time she alighted suddenly on a marsh in Vemmenhög township and the boy could not help thinking that she had traveled over Skåne just to let him see that his was a country which could compare favorably with any in the world. This was unnecessary, for the boy was not thinking of whether the country was rich or poor. From the moment that he had seen the first willow grove his heart ached with homesickness.

XXI

HOME AT LAST

Tuesday, November eighth

*T*he atmosphere was dull and hazy. The wild geese had been feeding on the big meadow around Skerup church and were having their noonday rest when Akka came up to the boy. "It looks as if we should have calm weather for a while," she remarked, "and I think we'll cross the Baltic tomorrow."

"Indeed!" said the boy abruptly, for his throat contracted so that he could hardly speak. All along he had cherished the hope that he would be released from the enchantment while he was still in Skåne.

"We are quite near West Vemmenhög now," said Akka, "and I thought that perhaps you might like to go home for a while. It may be some time before you have another opportunity to see your people."

"Perhaps I had better not," said the boy hesitatingly, but something in his voice betrayed that he was glad of Akka's proposal.

"If the goosey-gander remains with us, no harm can come to him," Akka assured. "I think you had better find out how your parents are getting along. You might be of some help to them, even if you're not a normal boy."

"You are right, Mother Akka. I should have thought of that long ago," said the boy impulsively. The next second he and the leader goose were on their way to his home. It was not long before Akka alighted behind the stone hedge encircling the little farm.

"Strange how natural everything looks around here!" the boy remarked. "It seems to me only yesterday that I first saw you come flying through the air.'"

"I wonder if your father has a gun," said Akka suddenly.

"You may be sure he has," returned the boy. "It was the gun that kept me at home that Sunday morning when I should have been at church."

"Then I don't dare to stand here and wait for you," said Akka. "You had better meet us at Smygahök early tomorrow morning, so that you may stay at home over night."

"Oh, don't go yet, Mother Akka!" begged the boy, jumping from the hedge. He could not tell just why it was, but he felt as if something would happen, either to the wild goose or to himself, to prevent their future meeting. "No doubt you see that I'm distressed because I cannot get back my right form, but I want to say to you that I don't regret having gone with you last spring," he added. "I would rather forfeit the chance of ever being human again than to have missed that trip."

Akka breathed quickly before she answered. "There's a little matter I should have mentioned to you before this, but since you are not going back to your home for good, I thought there was no hurry about it. Still it may as well be said now."

"You know very well that I am always glad to do your bidding," said the boy.

"If you have learned anything at all from us, Thumbietot, you no longer think that the humans should have the whole earth to themselves," said the wild goose, solemnly. "Remember you have a large country and you can easily afford to leave a few bare rocks, a few shallow lakes and swamps, a few desolate cliffs and remote forests to us poor, dumb creatures, where we can be allowed to live in peace. All my days I have been hounded and hunted. It would be a comfort to know that there is a refuge somewhere for one like me."

"Indeed, I should be glad to help if I could," said the boy, "but it's not likely that I shall ever again have influence among human beings."

"Well, we're standing here talking as if we were never to meet again," said Akka, "but we shall see each other tomorrow, of course. Now I'll return to my flock." She spread her wings and started to fly, but came back and stroked Thumbietot with her bill before she flew away.

It was broad daylight, but no human being moved on the farm and the boy could go where he pleased. He hastened to the cow shed, because he knew that he could get the best information from the cows. It looked rather barren in their shed. In the spring there had been three fine cows there, but now there was only one—Mayrose. It was quite apparent that she yearned for her comrades. Her head drooped sadly, and she had hardly touched the feed in her crib. "Good day, Mayrose!" said the boy, running fearlessly into her stall. "How are Mother and Father? How are the cat and the chickens? What has become of Star and Gold-Lily?"

When Mayrose heard the boy's voice she started, and appeared as if she were going to gore him, but she took time to look well at Nils Holgersson. He was just as little now as when he went away, and wore the same clothes, yet he was completely changed. The Nils Holgersson that went away in the spring had a heavy, slow gait, a drawling speech, and sleepy eyes. The one that had come back was lithe and alert, ready of speech, and had eyes that sparkled and danced. He had a confident bearing that commanded respect, little as he was. Although he himself did not look happy, he inspired happiness in others.

"Moo!" bellowed Mayrose. "They told me that he was changed, but I couldn't believe it. Welcome home, Nils Holgersson! Welcome home! This is the first glad moment I have known for ever so long!"

"Thank you, Mayrose!" said the boy, who was very happy to be so well received. "Now tell me all about Father and Mother."

"They have had nothing but hardship ever since you went away," said Mayrose. "The horse has been a costly care all summer, for he has stood in the stable the whole time and not earned his feed. Your father is too softhearted to shoot him and he can't sell him. It was on account of the horse that both Star and Gold-Lily had to be sold."

There was something else the boy wanted badly to know, but he was diffident about asking the question point blank. Therefore he said: "Mother must have felt very sorry when she discovered that Morten Goosey-Gander had flown?"

"She wouldn't have worried much about Morten Goosey-Gander had she known the way he came to leave. She grieves most at the thought of her son having run away from home with a goosey-gander."

"Does she really think that I stole the goosey-gander?" said the boy.

"What else could she think?"

"Father and Mother must fancy that I've been roaming about the country, like a common tramp?"

"They think that you've gone to the dogs," said Mayrose. "They have mourned you as one mourns the loss of the dearest thing on earth."

As soon as the boy heard this, he rushed from the cow shed and down to the stable. It was small, but clean and tidy. In the stall stood a strong, fine animal that looked well fed and well cared for. "Good day to you!" said the boy. "I have heard that there's a sick horse in here. Surely it can't be you, who look so healthy and strong."

The horse turned his head and stared fixedly at the boy. "Are you the son?" he queried. "I have heard many bad reports of him. But you have such a good face, I couldn't believe that you were he, did I not know that he was transformed into an elf."

"I know that I left a bad name behind me when I went away from the farm," admitted Nils Holgersson. "My own mother thinks I am a thief. But what does it matter—I shan't tarry here long. Meanwhile, I want to know what ails you."

"Pity you're not going to stay," said the horse, "for I have the feeling that you and I might become good friends. I've got something in my foot; the point of a knife, or something sharp—that's all that ails me. It has gone so far in that the doctor can't find it, but it cuts so that I can't walk. If you would only tell your father what's wrong with me, I'm sure that he could help me. I should like to be of some use. I really feel ashamed to stand here and feed without doing any work."

"It's well that you have no real illness," remarked Nils Holgersson. "I must attend to this, so that you will be all right again. You don't mind if I do a little scratching on your hoof with my knife, do you?"

Nils Holgersson had just finished, when he heard the sound of voices. He opened the stable door a little and peeped out. It was easy to see that they were broken by many sorrows. His mother had many lines on her face and his father's hair had turned gray. She was talking with him about getting a loan from her brother-in-law.

"No, I don't want to borrow any more money," his father said, as they were passing the stable. "There's nothing quite so hard as being in debt. It would be better to sell the cabin."

"If it were not for the boy, I shouldn't mind selling it," his mother demurred. "But what will become of him, if he returns someday, wretched and poor—as he's likely to be—and we not here?"

"You're right about that," the father agreed. "But we shall have to ask the folks who take the place to receive him kindly and to let him know that he's welcome back to us. We shan't say a harsh word to him, no matter what he may be, shall we Mother?"

"No, indeed! If I only had him again, so that I could be certain he is not starving and freezing on the highways, I'd ask nothing more!"

Then his father and mother went in, and the boy heard no more of their conversation. He was happy and deeply moved when he knew that they loved him so dearly, although they believed he had gone astray. He longed to rush into their arms. His father and mother were coming down the lane.

"But perhaps it would be an even greater sorrow were they to see me as I now am."

While he stood there, hesitating, a cart drove up to the gate. The boy smothered a cry of surprise, for who should step from the cart and go into the house yard but Osa, the goose girl, and her father! They walked hand in hand toward the cabin. When they were about half way there, Osa stopped her father and said: "Now remember, Father, you are not to mention the wooden shoe or the geese or the little brownie who was so like Nils Holgersson that if it was not himself it must have had some connection with him."

"Certainly not!" said Jon Esserson. "I shall only say that their son has been of great help to you on several occasions—when you were trying to find me—and that therefore we have come to ask if we can't do them a service in return, since I'm a rich man now and have more than I need, thanks to the mine I discovered up in Lapland."

"I know, Father, that you can say the right thing in the right way," Osa commended. "It is only that, one particular thing that I don't wish you to mention."

They went into the cabin, and the boy would have liked to hear what they talked about in there, but he dared not venture near the house. It was not long before they came out again, and his father and mother accompanied them as far as the gate. His parents were strangely happy. They appeared to have gained a new hold on life.

When the visitors were gone, Father and Mother lingered at the gate gazing after them. "I don't feel unhappy any longer, since I've heard so much that is good of our Nils," said his mother.

"Perhaps he got more praise than he really deserved," put in his father thoughtfully.

"Wasn't it enough for you that they came here specially to say they wanted to help us because our Nils had served them in many ways? I think, Father, that you should have accepted their offer."

"No, Mother, I don't wish to accept money from anyone, either as a gift or a loan. In the first place I want to free myself from all debt, then we will work our way up again. We're not so very old, are we Mother?" The father laughed heartily as he said this.

"I believe you think it will be fun to sell this place, upon which we have expended much time and hard work," protested the mother.

"Oh, you know why I'm laughing," the father retorted. "It was the thought of the boy's having gone to the bad that weighed me down until I had no strength or courage left in me. Now that I know he still lives and has turned out well, you'll see that Holger Nilsson has some grit left."

The mother went in alone, and the boy made haste to hide in a corner, for his father walked into the stable. He went over to the horse and examined its hoof, as usual, to try to discover what was wrong with it. "What's this!" he cried, discovering some letters scratched on the hoof.

"Remove the sharp piece of iron from the foot," he read and glanced around inquiringly. However, he ran his fingers along the under side of the hoof and looked at it carefully. "I verily believe there is something sharp here!" he muttered.

While his father was busy with the horse and the boy sat huddled in a corner, it happened that other callers came to the farm. The fact was that when Morten Goosey-Gander found himself so near his old home he simply could not resist the temptation of showing his wife and children to his old companions on the farm. So he took Dunfin and the goslings along, and made for home.

There was not a soul in the barn yard when the goosey-gander came along. He alighted, confidently walked all around the place, and showed Dunfin how luxuriously he had lived when he was a tame goose. When they had viewed the entire farm, he noticed that the door of the cow shed was open.

"Look in here a moment," he said, "then you will see how I lived in former days. It was very different from camping in swamps and morasses, as we do now."

The goosey-gander stood in the doorway and looked into the cow shed. "There's not a soul in here," he said. "Come along, Dunfin, and you shall see the goose pen. Don't be afraid; there's no danger."

Forthwith the goosey-gander, Dunfin, and all six goslings waddled into the goose pen, to have a look at the elegance and comfort in which the big white gander had lived before he joined the wild geese.

"This is the way it used to be: here was my place and over there was the trough, which was always filled with oats and water," explained the goosey-gander.

"Wait! there's some fodder in it now." With that he rushed to the trough and began to gobble up the oats. But Dunfin was nervous. "Let's go out again!" she said.

"Only two more grains," insisted the goosey-gander. The next second he let out a shriek and ran for the door, but it was too late! The door slammed, the mistress stood without and bolted it. They were locked in!

The father had removed a sharp piece of iron from the horse's hoof and stood contentedly stroking the animal when the mother came running into the stable.

"Come, Father, and see the capture I've made!"

"No, wait a minute!" said the father. "Look here, first. I have discovered what ailed the horse."

"I believe our luck has turned," said the mother. "Only fancy! the big white goosey-gander that disappeared last spring must have gone off with the wild geese. He has come back to us in company with seven wild geese. They walked straight into the goose pen, and I've shut them all in."

"That's extraordinary," remarked the father. "But best of all is that we don't have to think any more that our boy stole the goosey-gander when he went away."

"You're quite right, Father," she said. "But I'm afraid we'll have to kill them tonight. In two days is Morten Goose Day, and we must make haste if we expect to get them to market in time."

"I think it would be outrageous to butcher the goosey-gander, now that he has returned to us with such a large family," protested Holger Nilsson.

"If times were easier we'd let him live, but since we're going to move from here, we can't keep geese. Come along now and help me carry them into the kitchen," urged the mother.

They went out together and in a few moments the boy saw his father coming along with Morten Goosey-Gander and Dunfin one under each arm. He and his wife went into the cabin.

The goosey-gander cried: "Thumbietot, come and help me!"—as he always did when in peril—although he was not aware that the boy was at hand. Nils Holgersson heard him, yet he lingered at the door of the cow shed. He did not hesitate because he knew that it would be well for him if the goosey-gander were beheaded—at that moment he did not remember this—but because he shrank from being seen by his parents.

"They have a hard enough time of it already," he thought. "Must I bring them a new sorrow?"

But when the door closed on the goosey-gander, the boy was aroused. He dashed across the house yard, sprang up on the board walk leading to the entrance door and ran into the hallway, where he kicked off his wooden shoes in the old accustomed way, and walked toward the door. All the while it went so much against the grain to appear before his father and mother that he could not raise his hand to knock.

"But this concerns the life of the goosey-gander," he said to himself, "he who has been my best friend ever since I last stood here."

In a twinkling the boy remembered all that he and the goosey-gander had suffered on icebound lakes and stormy seas and among wild beasts of prey. His heart swelled with gratitude; he conquered himself and knocked on the door.

"Is there some one who wishes to come in?" asked his father, opening the door.

"Mother, you shan't touch the goosey-gander!" cried the boy.

Instantly both the goosey-gander and Dunfin, who lay on a bench with their feet tied, gave a cry of joy, so that he was sure they were alive. Some someone else gave a cry of joy—his mother!

"My, but you have grown tall and handsome!" she exclaimed.

The boy had not entered the cabin, but was standing on the doorstep, like one who is not quite certain how he will be received.

"The Lord be praised that I have you back again!" said his mother, laughing and crying. "Come in, my boy! Come in!"

"Welcome!" added his father, and not another word could he utter.

But the boy still lingered at the threshold. He could not comprehend why they were so glad to see him such as he was. Then his mother came and put her arms around him and drew him into the room, and he knew that he was all right.

"Mother and Father!" he cried. "I'm a big boy. I am a human being again!"

XXII

THE PARTING WITH
THE WILD GEESE

Wednesday, November ninth

The boy arose before dawn and wandered down to the coast. He was standing alone on the strand east of Smyge fishing hamlet before sunrise. He had already been in the pen with Morten Goosey-Gander to try to rouse him, but the big white gander had no desire to leave home. He did not say a word, but only stuck his bill under his wing and went to sleep again.

To all appearances the weather promised to be almost as perfect as it had been that spring day when the wild geese came to Skåne. There was hardly a ripple on the water; the air was still and the boy thought of the good passage the geese would have. He himself was as yet in a kind of daze—sometimes thinking he was an elf, sometimes a human being. When he saw a stone hedge alongside the road, he was afraid to go farther until he had made sure that no wild animal or vulture lurked behind it. Very soon he laughed to himself and rejoiced because he was big and strong and did not have to be afraid of anything.

When he reached the coast he stationed himself, big as he was, at the very edge of the strand, so that the wild geese could see him.

It was a busy day for the birds of passage. Bird calls sounded on the air continuously. The boy smiled as he thought that no one but himself understood what the birds were saying to one another. Presently wild geese came flying, one big flock following another.

"Just so it's not my geese that are going away without bidding me farewell," he thought. He wanted so much to tell them how everything had turned out, and to show them that he was no longer an elf but a human being.

There came a flock that flew faster and cackled louder than the others, and something told him that this must be the flock, but now he was not quite so sure about it as he would have been the day before.

The flock slackened its flight and circled up and down along the coast.

The boy knew it was the right one, but he could not understand why the geese did not come straight down to him. They could not avoid seeing him where he stood. He tried to give a call that would bring them down to him, but only now his tongue would not obey him. He could not make the right sound! He heard Akka's calls, but did not understand what she said.

"What can this mean? Have the wild geese changed their language?" he wondered.

He waved his cap to them and ran along the shore calling:

"Here am I, where are you?"

But this seemed only to frighten the geese. They rose and flew farther out to sea. At last he understood. They did not know that he was human, they had not recognized him. He could not call them to him because human beings can not speak the language of birds. He could not speak their language, nor could he understand it.

Although the boy was very glad to be released from the enchantment, still he thought it hard that because of this he should be parted from his old comrades.

He sat down on the sands and buried his face in his hands. What was the use of his gazing after them any more?

Presently he heard the rustle of wings. Old Mother Akka had found it hard to fly away from Thumbietot, and turned back, and now that the boy sat quite still she ventured to fly nearer to him. Suddenly something must have told her who he was, for she lit close beside him.

Nils gave a cry of joy and took old Akka in his arms. The other wild geese crowded round him and stroked him with their bills. They cackled and chattered and wished him all kinds of good luck, and he, too, talked to them and thanked them for the wonderful journey which he had been privileged to make in their company.

All at once the wild geese became strangely quiet and withdrew from him, as if to say:

"Alas! he is a man. He does not understand us: we do not understand him!"

Then the boy rose and went over to Akka; he stroked her and patted her. He did the same to Yksi and Kaksi, Kolme and Neljä, Viisi and Kuusi—the old birds who had been his companions from the very start.

After that he walked farther up the strand. He knew perfectly well that the sorrows of the birds do not last long, and he wanted to part with them while they were still sad at losing him.

As he crossed the shore meadows he turned and watched the many flocks of birds that were flying over the sea. All were shrieking their coaxing calls—only one goose flock flew silently on as long as he could follow it with his eyes. The wedge was perfect, the speed good, and the wing strokes strong and certain.

The boy felt such a yearning for his departing comrades that he almost wished he were Thumbietot again and could travel over land and sea with a flock of wild geese.

XXIII

ABOUT SELMA LAGERLÖF

Selma Lagerlöf was born on November 20, 1858, in the province of Värmland, Sweden. She was born at home on the family estate called, Märbacka. As a child, Selma spent countless hours writing poetry. A childhood illness left her unable to walk for a period of about two years so she spent many hours reading books and being educated by governesses. Besides the illness, her childhood was otherwise noted as a happy one.

At the age of twenty-two, she took college preparatory classes. She stayed on the family estate until she was twenty-three years old, at which time she enrolled in a teachers' college located in Stockholm. Four years later, she became a teacher for an all-girls secondary school based in Landskrona.

After five years of teaching, she had finally finished her first novel and had submitted part of it to a literary contest posted in a Swedish publication. They awarded her first place. The following year in 1891, *Gösta Berling's Saga* was published. Once the book was translated into Danish, it received notariety that propelled her success in her home country and abroad.

In 1895, Selma received financial support from the royal family and a scholarship from the Swedish Academy, which encouraged her to give up teaching and to concentrate on her writing.

Selma met, befriended, and later fell in love with Sophie Elkan, another author. They traveled to Italy together. Selma continued to write several books in Sweden and abroad including (titles listed in English): *Invisible Links* (1894), *The Miracles of the Antichrist* (1897), *Jerusalem* (1901), *Christ Legends and Other Stories* (1904), *Gösta Berling's Saga* (1891), *The Wonderful Adventures of Nils Holgersson* (1907), *Märbacka* (1922), *Memories of My Childhood* (1930), *The Diary of Selma Lagerlöf* (1932), and a trilogy called, *The Löwensköld Ring* (1931) which was later republished in 1928 as, *The*

Ring of the Löwenskölds. It should also be noted that she wrote several other short stories that were not translated into English or other languages. She wrote approximately forty titles and several articles during her career.

In her writing, she concentrated on medieval supernatural and religious themes. She had the most success with her first book, *Gösta Berling's Saga.* In 1909, she became the first woman to win the Nobel Prize for Literature. Later, in Selma and Sophie's relationship, Sophie became jealous of Lagerlöf's success in the writing field which strained their relationship.

In 1897, Selma moved to Falun. It was there that she met a lady named Valborg Olander, also a teacher, who later became a friend and worked for her. This new relationship spawned more jealousy from Elkan. Selma and Valborg were active in the women's suffrage movement and Selma was a speaker for many women's suffrage events being held in 1911. In May of 1919, women's suffrage was granted in Sweden. A victory party was held.

In 1904, the Swedish Academy, the organization that awards Noble Prizes in literature, awarded Selma Lagerlöf with a gold medal. A decade later, she became a member of the organization. She was the first woman to be bestowed these honors. In 1907, she received a law degree from Uppsala University and in 1928, the University of Greifswald's Faculty of Arts granted her an honorary doctorate degree. When World War II began, Selma was so distraught that she offered to donate her Nobel Prize and gold medal to Finland's government to help fight the Soviet Union. However, the government of Finland was so honored that they raised money by other means, just so they could return her award back to her.

Other honors for Selma include being put on a 1959 postage stamp and having her portrait displayed on a 20 kronor-bill since 1992.

Selma died at the same place where she was born, at the family estate, Märbacka. She died on March 16, 1940.

"If you have learned anything at all from us, Thumbietot, you no longer think that humans should have the whole earth to themselves," said the wild goose, solemnly. This is a quote from one of Selma Lagerlöf's books, *The Wonderful Adventures of Nils*. The flight path on the map was taken by Nils and the wild geese. The arrow on the map of Sweden shows the province of Värmland where Selma Lagerlöf was born.

THE PROVINCE OF VÄRMLAND

Värmland is a province on the western side of the southern third of Sweden. It is bordered by Norway on the west. Nobel Prize winner Selma Lagerlöf, was born in the province.

Gösta Berling's Saga, Selma Lagerlöf's debut novel from 1891, takes place on the shores of Lake Fryken in Värmland during the 1820s and 1830s. This area is known for picturesque mountains, rocks, birch trees, evergreens, ponds, streams, and small lakes, similar to the northern Minnesota landscape, which has inspired artists and authors since the 19th century. *Gösta Berling's Saga* was made into a movie starring Greta Garbo.

In the western part of the province, there are many mountainous plateaus. In the eastern part, the landscape is hilly with a few high-altitude hills. Iron ore exists in large quantities there. As part of Sweden's central mining district, the prosperous local iron trade fostered education, the theatre arts, literature, folklore, and wealthy lifestyles.

Värmland is often referred to as a Swedish version of Florence, Italy. Many have been in awe of the beauty of the landscape.

410

PHOTOS OF VÄRMLAND

*L*ängbansände consists of a few scattered houses and old industrial buildings, some of which have been turned into museums, in the province of Värmland. It is located half way between Stockholm and Oslo. This picture shows the beauty that abounds in the forests, lakes, and rolling hills.

Photo by Judit Martin

Above:
This photo was taken at Långbansände which means the tip or end of the lake at Långban. This is a rich mining area where over 300 minerals have been found.

Following page:
The photographer John Ridell lives in Älvsjöhyttan, Värmland, Sweden.
Top right: *This photo was taken in Lisin, southern Värmland.*
Bottom right: *This photo was taken in Rämmen, Värmland province. Rämmen is well known for its car rallies.*

Photos by John Ridell

ABOUT SWEDEN

Sweden's population in 2012 was approximately 9,555,893. In the 1990s, the population rate went up by approximately 100,000 people per year. However, in the 2000s, the population declined because of unrest in the Middle East and lower immigration rates.

Sweden's life expectancy rate at birth is estimated at 78.86 years for a man and 83.63 years for a woman. This is about 3 years longer than the life expectancy rate in the United States as of 2012.

The official main language of Sweden is Swedish. It was only on July 1, 2009, that this went into effect. The new law also protects Sweden's five national minority languages which includes: Finnish, All Sami dialects, Torne Valley Finnish, Romani, and Yiddish.

The Swedish language is a northern Germanic language. Norwegian, Danish, and Swedish people can usually understand each other but the Finnish language is harder to understand with its roots in the Uralic language. The Swedish alphabet consists of twenty-nine letters. Twenty-six of the letters are from the basic Roman alphabet and the three addtional letters are Å, å, Ä, ä, and Ö, ö.

The capital of Sweden is Stockholm. Sweden's land mass covers 173,860 square miles with almost 2,000 miles of coastline. The third largest country in Western Europe, it is bordered by Finland on the east and Norway on the west. Between Finland and the northern half of Sweden is the Gulf of Bothnia. The southern half on the east side is bordered by the Baltic Sea with Latvia, Lithuania, and Russia across the sea. The southwest corner is bordered by Denmark.

In 1523, Sweden gained its independence from Denmark due to cultural tensions.

SWEDEN'S CURRENCY

Sweden's currency has been called the krona since 1873. Krona means crown in Swedish. As of April, 2010, the krona was the 9th most traded currency worldwide. Bank notes are available in the denominations of 1 krona, 5, 10, 50, 100, and 1000 kronor (plural).

The 20 kronor is mainly purple in color. On one side appears an image of Selma Lagerlöf later in life with a large brimmed hat and a fur coat. The other side of the 20 kronor is an image of Nils Holgersson flying over Scania.

The 50 kronor, mostly green, has an image of a Swedish soprano singer, Jenny Lind, aka Johanna Maria Lind. She was born October 6, 1820 and died November 2, 1887. A member of the Royal Swedish Academy of Music since 1840, Jenny toured Sweden, Europe, and America with her concerts.

The back side of the 50 kronor displays the key harp with its tonal range. The nyckelharpa (key harp) is a traditional Swedish musical instrument.

The 100 kronor, mainly blue, shows an image of Carl von Linné, a Swedish botanist, physician, and zoologist. He was born May 23, 1707 and died January 10, 1778. As a professor of botany, he classified plants and animals and published several volumes of his work.

The back side of the 100 kronor, shows a bumble bee pollinating a plant. Pollination is important in agriculture because many plants are dependant on a bee to pollinate its flowers to produce fruit.

The 500 kronor, mostly red, depicts an image of King Charles the XI. He was the king of Sweden from 1660 until his death on April 5, 1697. He went on military expeditions to fight against Danish troops. Later, he went on to correct the country's political, financial, and economic situation.

The back side of the 500 kronor shows an image of Christopher Polhem. He was a Swedish scientist, inventor, and industrialist who lived from December 18, 1661 to August 30, 1751. He was noted for his economic and industrial contributions in the field of mining.

Finally, the 1000 kronor, grey, has a picture of Gustav Vasa, born on May 12, 1496 into a member of the Vasa noble family. He was king of Sweden from 1523 until his death on September 29, 1560. Gustav was compared to Moses from the Bible because he liberated his people from Danish supremacy and established a sovereign state. The day he was elected as King, June 6, 1523, became a National holiday of Sweden.

The back side of the 1000 kronor shows a harvest picture of Olaus Magnus. A Swedish patriot and writer, he is best known for his writing of the *History of the Northern Peoples* in 1555. His writing was geared towards the interest of the Nordic people.

The Scandinavian countries of Sweden, Denmark, and Norway all have their separate currencies.

SWEDEN'S GOVERNMENT

Sweden's government consists of a Swedish Parliament. Approximately seven million people are eligible to vote and will determine which political party will represent them in the Swedish Parliament, county councils, and city governments.

The Riksdag is a 349-member parliament that represents the people. Members are elected by Swedish citizens aged 18 or older. Elections are held every four years in September. The Riksdag appoints a Prime Minister who is given the job of forming a Government and personally choosing the ministers for the Cabinet. Together, the Prime Minister and the Cabinet form the Government.

At the domestic level of government, there are three areas: national, regional, and local. Sweden is comprised of twenty counties at the regional level. This level oversees health care and levys income taxes to cover the expense of health care. The local level consists of 290 municipalities which oversee housing, roads, water, waste-water, education, welfare, elderly care, and childcare. This governmental entity has the power to levy taxes to cover these costs.

In 1995, Sweden joined the European Union (EU) adding another level of government. Legal acts, common rule drafting and approval, and court decisions comprise the European Union law. Previously, some of the Riksdag issues are now covered at the EU level.

61000768R00250

Made in the USA
Charleston, SC
10 September 2016